"What if you get in trouble?" She stared into his face, wishing he'd reconsider and take her along. **"What if you're hurt?"**

He smiled, his hand cupping her cheek. "Worried about me?"

Jacie stiffened and had a retort ready on her lips, but stopped short of delivering it when she realized she was worried about him. "I haven't known you long, but damn it, I am worried about you. I kinda got used to having you around." Her hand covered the one he'd used to cup her cheek and she pulled it lower, pressing a kiss into his palm.

"Stay safe for me, will you?" His eyes dark in the dim lighting from the overhead bulbs, he leaned close and captured her lips in a soul-stealing kiss.

TAKING AIM

BY
ELLE JAMES

First published in Great Britain 2013
by Mills & Boon, an imprint of Harlequin (UK) Limited,
Eton House, 18-24 Paradise Road, Richmond, Surrey TW9 1SR

© Mary Jernigan 2013

ISBN: 978 0 263 90370 6
ebook ISBN: 978 1 472 00738 4

46-0813

Harlequin (UK) policy is to use papers that are natural, renewable and recyclable products and made from wood grown in sustainable forests. The logging and manufacturing processes conform to the legal environmental regulations of the country of origin.

Printed and bound in Spain
by Blackprint CPI, Barcelona

A Golden Heart Award winner for Best Paranormal Romance in 2004, **Elle James** started writing when her sister issued a Y2K challenge to write a romance novel. She has managed a full-time job and raised three wonderful children, and she and her husband even tried their hands at ranching exotic birds (ostriches, emus and rheas) in the Texas Hill Country. Ask her, and she'll tell you what it's like to go toe-to-toe with an angry three-hundred-and-fifty-pound bird! After leaving her successful career in information technology management, Elle is now pursuing her writing full-time. Elle loves to hear from fans. You can contact her at ellejames@earthlink.net or visit her website at www.ellejames.com.

This book is dedicated to the brave men and women
who risk their lives daily fighting
for truth and justice.

Chapter One

Zachary Adams sat with his boots tapping the floor, his attention barely focused on the man at the center of the group of cowboys. This meeting had gone past his fifteen-minute limit, pushing twenty now.

The wiry, muscular man before them stood tall, his shoulders held back and proud. He was probably a little older than most of the men in the room, his dark hair combed back, graying slightly at the temples.

"I'm here to offer you a position in a start-up corporation." Hank Derringer smiled at the men gathered in the spacious living room of his home on the Raging Bull Ranch in south Texas.

"Doing what? Sweeping floors? Who wants a bunch of rejects?" Zach continued tapping his foot, itching for a fight, his hands shaking. Not that there had been any provocation. He didn't need any. Ever since the catastrophe of the Diego Operation, he hadn't been able to sit still for long, unless he was nursing a really strong bottle of tequila.

"*I* need you. Because you aren't rejects, you're just the type of men I'm looking for. Men who will fight for what you believe in, who were born or raised on a ranch, with the ethics and strength of character of a good cowboy. I'm inviting you to become a part of CCI, known only to those on the inside as Covert Cowboys Incorporated, a specialized team of citizen soldiers, bodyguards, agents and ranch hands who will do whatever it takes for justice."

Zach almost laughed out loud. Hank had flipped if he thought this crew of washed-up cowboys could help him start up a league of justice or whatever it was he had in mind.

"Whoa, back up a step there. Covert Cowboys Incorporated?" The man Hank had introduced as Chuck Bolton slapped his hat against his thigh. "Sounds kind of corny to me. What's the punch line?"

"No punch line." Hank squared his shoulders, his mouth firming into a straight line. "Let's just say that I'm tired of justice being swept under the rug."

Ex-cop Ben Harding shook his head. "I'm not into circumventing the law."

"I'm not asking you to. The purpose of Covert Cowboys Incorporated is to provide covert protection and investigation services where hired guns and the law aren't enough." Hank's gaze swept over the men in the room. "I handpicked each of you because you are all highly skilled soldiers, cops and agents who know how to work hard and fire a gun and are familiar with living on the edge of danger. My plan is to inject you into situations where your own lives could be on the line to protect, rescue or ferret out the truth."

One by one, the cowboys agreed to sign on with CCI until Hank came to Zach.

"I'm not much into joining," Zach said.

Hank nodded. "To be understood. You might not want to get back into a job that puts you in the line of fire after what you went through."

Zach's chest tightened. "I'm not afraid of bullets."

"I understand you lost your female partner on your last mission with the FBI. That had to be tough." Hank laid a hand on Zach's shoulder. "You're welcome to stay the night and think about it. You don't have to give me an answer until morning."

Zach could have given his answer now. He didn't want the job. He didn't want any job. What he wanted was revenge, served cold and painful.

With the other cowboys falling in line, Zach just nodded, grabbed his duffel bag and found the room he had been assigned for the night. The other men left, one of them already on assignment, and the other two had places to stay in Wild Oak Canyon, the small town closest to the Raging Bull Ranch.

Zach hadn't been in the bedroom more than three minutes when the walls started closing in around him. He had to get outside or go crazy.

The room had French doors opening out onto the wide veranda that wrapped around the entire house.

He sat on the steps leading down off the porch at the side of the rambling homestead and stared up at a sky full of the kind of stars you only got out in the wide-open spaces far away from city lights.

Zach wondered if the stars had been out that night Toni had died. No matter how often he replayed that nightmare, he couldn't recall whether or not the stars had been shining. Everything seemed to play out in black, white and red. From the moment they'd been surrounded by the cartel sentinels to the moment Toni had died.

Zach's eyes squeezed shut, but no matter how hard he tried to erase the vision from his mind, he couldn't shake it. He opened his eyes again and looked up at the stars in an attempt to superimpose their beauty and brilliance over the ugly images indelibly etched in his memory.

Boots tapped against the planks of the decking and

Hank Derringer leaned against a wooden column. "Wanna talk about it?"

"No." Zach had suffered through days of talking about it with the FBI psychologist following his escape and return to civilization. Talking hadn't brought his partner back, and it had done nothing to bring justice to those responsible for her senseless rape, torture and murder.

"Do you have work lined up when you leave here?" Hank asked.

"No." Oh, he had work, all right. He had spent the last year following his recovery searching for the cartel gang who'd captured him and Toni Gutierrez on the wrong side of the border during the cartel eradication push, Operation Diego.

The operation had been a failure from the get-go, leading Zach to believe they had a mole inside the FBI. No matter who he asked or where he dug, he couldn't get to the answer. His obsession with the truth had ultimately cost him his job. When his supervisor had given him an ultimatum to pull his head out of his search and get on with his duties as a special agent or look for alternative employment, Zach had walked.

Out of leads, his bank account dwindling and at the mercy of this crackpot vigilante, Hank Derringer, Zach was running out of options.

Zach sighed and stared down the shadowy road leading through a stand of scrub trees toward the highway a mile away. What choice did he have? Crawl into a bottle and forget everything? Even that required money.

"If I take this job—not saying that I've agreed—what did you have in mind for my first assignment?"

JACIE KOSART AND her twin, Tracie, rode toward the ridge-line overlooking Wild Horse Canyon. The landmark delineated the southern edge of the three-hundred-and-fifty-thousand-acre Big Elk Ranch, where Jacie worked as a trail guide for big-game hunting expeditions.

Tracie, on leave from her job with the FBI, had insisted on coming along as one of the guides, even though she wasn't officially working for Big Elk Ranch. "Don't let on that I'm an agent. I just want to blend in and be like you, one of the guides, for today."

Jacie had cleared it with Richard Giddings, her boss. Then Tracie had insisted on taking on these two guys with short haircuts and poker faces instead of the rednecks from Houston.

Happy to have her sister with her for the day, Jacie didn't argue, just went with the flow. Her job was to lead the hunting party to the best hunting location where they stood a chance of bagging trophy elk.

Instead of following behind, the two men rode ahead with Jacie and Tracie trailing a couple of horse lengths to their rear.

"I was surprised to see you," Jacie stated. Her sister rarely visited, and her sudden appearance had Jacie wondering if something was wrong.

"I needed some downtime from stress," Tracie responded, her words clipped. She flicked the strands of her long, straight brown hair that had come loose from her ponytail back behind her ears.

Not to be deterred by Tracie's cryptic reply, Jacie dug deeper. "What did Bruce have to say about you coming out here without him?" Jacie had to admit to a little envy that Tracie had a boyfriend and she did not. Living on the Big Elk, surrounded by men, she'd have thought she'd have a bit of a love life. But she didn't.

"I told him I needed time with my only sibling." Tracie gave her a tight smile that didn't quite reach her eyes.

Jacie gave an unladylike snort. "As thick as you two have become, I'm surprised he didn't come with you."

Tracie glanced ahead to the two men. "I wanted to come alone."

Tracie might be telling the truth about wanting to come alone, but her answer wasn't satisfying Jacie. Her twin connection refused to believe it was just a case of missing family. "Everything okay?"

"Sure." She glanced at Jacie. "So, how many guides are there on the Big Elk Ranch?"

The change in direction of the conversation wasn't lost on Jacie, but she let it slide. "There are six, plus Richard. Some of them are part-time. Richard, Humberto and I are the full-timers. Why?"

"Just wondered. What kind of process does Richard use to screen his guides?"

Jacie shot a look at her sister. "What do you mean?"

Tracie looked away. "I was just curious if you and the other guides had to go through a background check."

"I don't know about any background check. Richard offered me the job during my one and only interview. I can't vouch for the rest." Jacie frowned at Tracie. "Thinking about giving up the FBI to come guide on the Big Elk?" She laughed, the sound trailing off.

Her sister shrugged. "Maybe."

"No way. You love the FBI. You've wanted to join since you were eight."

"Sometimes you get tired of all the games." Tracie's lips tightened. "We should catch up with them." She nudged her horse, ending the conversation and leaving Jacie even more convinced her sister wasn't telling her everything.

Tracie rode up alongside the men.

Jacie caught up and put on her trail-guide smile as they pulled to a halt at the rim of the canyon. "This is the southern edge of the ranch. The other hunting party is to the west, the Big Elk Ranch house and barn is to the north where we came from, and to the east is the Raging Bull Ranch." Jacie smiled at the two men who'd paid a hefty sum to go hunting that day on the ranch. Richard, her boss, had taken the guys from Houston west; these two had insisted on going south, stating they preferred a lot of distance between them and the other hunting parties.

Jacie and Tracie knew the trophy bucks preferred the western and northern edge of the spread, but the two men would not be deterred.

Supposedly they'd come to hunt, based on the hardware they'd packed in their scabbards. Each carried a rifle equipped with a high-powered scope and a handgun in case they were surprised by javelinas, the vicious wild hogs running wild in the bush.

Jacie cleared her throat, breaking the silence. "Now that you've seen quite a bit of the layout, where would you like to set up? It's getting late and we won't have much time to hunt before sunset."

Jim Smith glanced across at his buddy Mike Jones.

Mr. Jones slipped a GPS device from his pocket and studied the map on it for a long moment. Then he glanced at Jacie. "Where does that canyon lead?"

"Off the Big Elk Ranch into the Big Bend National Park. There's no hunting allowed in the park. The rangers are pretty strict about it. Not to mention, the border patrol has reported recent drug trafficking activity in this canyon. It's not safe to go in there." And Jacie discouraged their clientele from crossing over the boundaries with firearms, even if their clients were licensed to carry firearms as these two were. All the hunters had been briefed on the rules should they stray into the park.

Jacie's gelding, D'Artagnan, shifted to the left, pawing at the dirt, ready to move on.

"We'll ride farther into the canyon." Mr. Jones nudged his horse's flanks, sending him over the edge of the ridge and down the steep slope toward the canyon.

"Mr. Jones," Tracie called after him. "The horses are property of the Big Elk Ranch. We aren't allowed to take them off the ranch without permission from the boss. Given the dangers that could be encountered, I can't allow you—"

Mr. Smith's horse brushed past Jacie's, following Mr. Jones down the slope. Not a word from either gentleman.

Jacie glanced across at her twin. "What the heck?" She pulled the two-way radio from her belt and hit the talk switch. "Richard, do you copy?"

The crackle of static had D'Artagnan dancing in place, his head tossing in the air. He liked being in the lead. The two horses descending the slope in front of him made him anxious. He whinnied, calling out to the other horses as the distance between them increased.

The answering whinny from one of the mares below sent the gelding over the edge.

Tracie's mare pranced along the ridge above, her nostrils flared, also disturbed by the departure of the other two horses.

"I'll follow and keep an eye on the two," Tracie suggested.

"Richard, do you copy?" Jacie called into the radio. Apparently they'd moved out of range of radio reception with the other hunting party. Jacie switched frequencies for the base station at the ranch. "Base, this is Jacie, can you read me?"

Again static.

They were on their own and responsible for the two horses and clients headed down into the canyon.

"You feeling weird about this?" Tracie asked.

"You bet."

"Why don't you head back and let Giddings know the clients have left the property? I'll follow along and make sure they don't get lost."

"Not a good idea. You aren't as familiar with the land as I am." Jacie glanced down the trail at the two men on Big Elk Ranch horses. "If they want to get themselves lost or shot, I don't care, but those are Big Elk Ranch horses."

Tracie nodded. "Ginger and Rocky. And you know they like being part of a group, not off on their own." She shook her head. "What are those guys thinking?"

"I don't know, but I don't want to abandon the horses." Jacie sighed. "I guess there's nothing to it but for us to follow and see if we can talk some sense into those dirtbags."

"I'm not liking it," Tracie said. "You should head back and notify Giddings."

"I don't feel right abandoning the horses and I sure as hell won't let you go after them by yourself. We don't know what kind of kooks these guys are." Jacie nodded toward the saddlebags they carried on their horses, filled with first aid supplies, emergency rations and a can of mace. "Look, we're prepared for anything on two or four legs. As long as we keep our heads, we should be okay."

Each woman carried a rifle in her scabbard, for hunting or warding off dangerous animals. They also carried enough ammo for a decent round of target practice in case they didn't actually see any game on the trail, which they hadn't up to this point. Tracie had the added protection of a nine-millimeter Glock she'd carried with her since she left training at Quantico.

"Whatever you say." Tracie grimaced at her. "My rifle's

loaded and on safe." She patted the Glock in the holster she'd worn on her hip. "Ready?"

"I don't like it, but let's follow. Maybe we can talk them into returning with us." Jacie squeezed her horse's sides. That's all it took for D'Artagnan to leap forward and start down the winding trail to the base of the canyon.

"Hey, guys! To make it back to camp for supper, we need to head back in the next hour," Jacie called out to the men ahead.

Either they didn't hear her or they chose to ignore her words. The men didn't even look back, just kept going.

D'Artagnan set his own pace on the slippery slope. Jacie didn't urge him to go faster. He wanted to catch up, but he knew his own limits on the descent.

The two men riding ahead worked their way downward at a pace a little faster than Jacie's and Tracie's mounts. At the rate they were moving, they'd have a substantial lead.

Jacie wasn't worried so much about catching up. She knew D'Artagnan and Tracie's gelding, Aramis, were faster than the mare and gelding ahead. But there were many twists and turns in the canyon below. If they didn't catch them soon, they stood a chance of falling even farther behind. It would take them longer to track the two men, and dusk would settle in. Not to mention, it would get dark sooner at the base of the canyon where sunlight disappeared thirty minutes earlier than up top.

As Jacie neared the bottom of the canyon, the two men disappeared past a large outcropping of rock.

D'Artagnan stepped up the pace, stretching into a gallop, eager to catch the two horses ahead. The pounding of hooves reverberated off the walls of the canyons. Tracie and Aramis kept pace behind her. If the two clients had continued at a sedate rate, they would have caught them by now.

The deeper the women traveled into the canyon, the angrier Jacie became at the men. They'd disregarded her warning about drug traffickers and about entering the national park with firearms, and they'd disrespected the fact that the horses didn't belong to them. They were Big Elk Ranch property and belonged on the ranch.

At the first junction, the ground was rocky and disturbed in both directions as if the men had started up one route, turned back and taken the other. In order to determine which route they ended up on, Jacie, the better tracker of the twins, had to dismount and follow their tracks up the dead end and back before she realized it was the other corridor they'd taken.

Tracie stood guard at the fork in case the men returned.

Jacie climbed into the saddle muttering, "We really need to perform a more thorough background check on our clients before we let them onto the ranch."

Her sister smiled. "Not all of them are as disagreeable as these two."

"Yeah, but not only are they putting themselves and the horses in danger, they're putting the two of us at risk, as well." Jacie hesitated. "Come to think of it, maybe we should head back while there's still enough light to climb the trail out of the canyon."

Tracie sighed. "I was hoping you'd say that. I don't want you to get hurt out here."

"Me? I was more concerned about you. You haven't been in the saddle much since you joined the FBI."

"You're right, of course." She smiled at Jacie. "Let's get out of here."

"Agreed. Let them be stupid. We don't have to be." Jacie turned her horse back the way they'd come and had taken the lead when the sharp report of gunfire echoed off the canyon walls.

"What the hell?" Jacie's horse spun beneath her and it was all she could do to keep her balance.

Aramis reared. Tracie planted her feet hard in the stirrups and leaned forward, holding on until the gelding dropped to all four hooves.

More gunfire ensued, followed by the pounding of hooves, the sound growing louder as it neared them.

Tracie yelled, "Go, Jacie. Get out of the canyon!"

Jacie didn't hesitate, nor did her horse. She dug her heals into D'Artagnan's flanks, sending him flying along the trail. She headed back the way they'd come, her horse skimming over the rocky ground, his head stretched forward, nostrils flared.

Before they'd gone a hundred yards, Rocky, the gelding Mr. Jones had been riding, raced past them, eyes wide, sweat lathered on both sides, sporting an empty saddle, no Mr. Jones. Rocky hit the trailhead leading out of the canyon, scrambling up the slope.

Jacie dared to glance over her shoulder.

Mr. Smith emerged from the fork in the canyon trail, yelling at Ginger, kicking her hard. Both leaned forward, racing for their lives.

The distinct sound of revving motors chased the horse and rider through the narrow passage. An ATV roared into the open, followed by another, then another until four ATVs spread out, chasing Mr. Smith, Tracie and Jacie.

Jacie reached the trail climbing out of the canyon first, urging D'Artagnan faster. He stumbled, regained his footing and charged on.

Tracie wasn't far behind, her horse equally determined to make it out of the canyon alive and ahead of the ATVs.

Mr. Smith brought up the rear on Ginger.

As Jacie reached the top of the slope, she turned back, praying for Tracie to hurry.

Her sister had dropped behind, Aramis slipping in the loose rocks and gravel, distressed by the noise behind him. Just when Jacie thought the two were going to make it, shots rang out from the base of the canyon.

One of the ATVs had stopped, its rider aiming what appeared to be a high-powered rifle with a scope up at the riders on the trail.

Another shot rang out and Mr. Smith jerked in his saddle and fell off backward, sliding down the hill on his back.

His mount screamed and surged up the narrow trail past Tracie and Aramis.

Three of the ATVs raced up the path, bumping and slipping over the loose rocks.

From her vantage point at the top of the ridge, Jacie stood helpless as the horror unfolded.

Aramis reared, dumping Tracie off his back. She hit the ground and rolled, sliding down the slope back toward the base of the canyon.

Jacie yanked her rifle from its scabbard, slid out of her saddle and dropped to a kneeling position, aiming at the man at the base of the canyon.

The man was aiming at her.

Jacie held her breath, lined up the sights and pulled the trigger a second before he fired his gun.

His bullet hit the ground at her feet, kicking up dirt into her eyes.

For a second she couldn't see, but when her vision cleared, she saw the man she'd aimed for lay on the ground beside his ATV, struggling to get up.

One down, three to go.

Ginger topped the rise, followed by Aramis, spooking D'Artagnan. He pulled against the reins Jacie held on to tightly. She didn't let go, but she couldn't get another round off while he jerked her around.

When he settled, she aimed at the closest rider to her. He was halfway up the hill, headed straight for her.

She popped off a round, nicked him in the shoulder, sending him flying off the vehicle. The ATV slipped over the edge of the trail and tumbled to the bottom.

The other two riders were on their way up the hill. One split off and headed back down the side, straight for where Tracie lay sprawled against the slope, low crawling for her Glock that had slipped loose of its holster. The other rider raced toward Jacie.

Jacie aimed at the man headed for Tracie.

D'Artagnan pulled against the reins, sending Jacie's bullet flying wide of its target.

She didn't have time to adjust her aim for the rider nearing the top of the hill. He was too close and coming too fast.

Jacie let go of D'Artagnan's reins, flipped her rifle around and swung just as the rider topped the hill. She caught him in the chest with all the force of her swing and his upward movement. Jacie reeled backward landing hard on her butt, the wind knocked out of her.

The rider flew off the back of the vehicle and tumbled over the ridge.

Jacie scrambled to the edge and watched as the rider cartwheeled down the steep slope, over and over until he came to a crumpled stop, midway down.

The last rider standing had reached Tracie before she could get to her gun. He gathered her in his arms and stuck a pistol to her head. *"Pare o dispararé a mujer!"*

Even if she couldn't understand his demand, Jacie got the message. If she didn't stop, he'd shoot her sister.

Two more ATVs arrived on the canyon floor.

Jacie had no choice. She didn't want to leave her sister

in the hands of the thugs below, but she couldn't fight them when they held the trump card—her sister.

She eased away from the edge of the ridge and scoped her options.

D'Artagnan and the other horses were long gone, headed back to the safety of the Big Elk Ranch barn.

The ATV she'd knocked the rider off stood near the edge of the ridge. If she hoped to escape, she had to make a run for it.

Jacie ducked low and ran for the ATV, jumped onto the seat, pulled the crank cord and held her breath.

The two new ATV riders were on their way up the hill. The man holding Tracie fired off a shot, but his pistol's range wasn't good enough to be accurate at that distance.

The ATV engine turned over and died.

Jacie pulled the cord again and the engine roared to life. She gave the vehicle gas and leaped forward, speeding toward the closest help she could find. The Raging Bull Ranch.

She had a good head start on the other two, but they didn't have to know where they were going; they only had to follow.

Jacie ripped the throttle wide open, bouncing hard over obstacles she could barely see in the failing light.

The sun had completely dipped below the horizon, the gray of dusk slipping over the land like a shroud. Until all the stars twinkled to life, Jacie could only hope she was headed in the right direction.

After thirty minutes of full-out racing across cactus, dodging clumps of saw palmetto, lights appeared ahead. Her heartbeat fluttered and tears threatened to blind her as she skidded up to a gate. She flung herself off the bike and fell to the ground, her legs shaking too badly to hold her up.

Dragging herself to her feet, she unlatched the gate and ran toward the house. "Help! Help! Please, dear God, help!"

As she neared the huge house, a shadow detached itself from the porch and ran toward her.

On her last leg, her strength giving out, Jacie flung herself into the man's arms. "Please help me."

Chapter Two

Zach staggered back, the force with which the woman with the long brown ponytail hit him knocking him back several steps before he could get his balance. He wrapped his arm around her automatically, steadying her as her knees buckled and she slipped toward the floor.

"Please help me," she sobbed.

"What's wrong?" He scooped her into his arms and carried her through the open French doors into his bedroom and laid her on the bed.

Boots clattered on the wooden slats of the porch and more came running down the hallway. Two of Hank's security guards burst into Zach's room through the French doors at the same time Hank entered from the hallway.

The security guards stood with guns drawn, their black-clad bodies looking more like ninjas than billionaire bodyguards.

"It's okay, I have everything under control," Zach said. Though he doubted seriously he had anything under control. He had no idea who this woman was or what she'd meant by *help me*.

Hank burst through the bedroom door, his face drawn in tense lines. "What's going on? I heard the sound of an engine outside and shouting coming from this side of the house." He glanced at Zach's bed and the woman stirring against the comforter. "What do we have here?"

She pushed to a sitting position and blinked up at Zach. "Where am I?"

"You're on the Raging Bull Ranch."

"Oh, dear God." She pushed to the edge of the bed and tried to stand. "I have to get back. They have her. Oh, sweet Jesus, they have Tracie."

Zach slipped an arm around her waist and pulled her to him to keep her from falling flat on her face again. "Where do you have to get back to? And who's Tracie?"

"Tracie's my twin. We were leading a hunting party on the Big Elk. They shot, she fell, now they have her." The woman grabbed Zach's shirt with both fists. "You have to help her."

"You're not making sense. Slow down, take a deep breath and start over."

"We don't have time!" The woman pushed away from Zach and raced for the French doors. "We have to get back before they kill her." She stumbled over a throw rug and hit the hardwood floor on her knees. "I shouldn't have left her." She buried her face in her hands and sobbed.

Zach stared at the woman, a flash of memory anchoring his feet to the floor. He remembered his partner, Antoinette Gutierrez—Toni—in a similar position, her face battered, her hair matted with her own blood, begging for her life.

The room spun around him, the air growing thick, hard to breathe.

Not until Hank ran forward and helped the woman to her feet did Zach snap out of it.

"We'll help," Hank promised. "Where is your sister?"

The woman looked up and blinked the tears from her eyes, her shoulders straightening. "Wild Horse Canyon."

"Joe." Hank addressed one of his bodyguards. "Wake

the foreman and tell him we need all the four-wheelers gassed up and ready to go immediately."

Joe jammed his weapon into his shoulder holster and ran out the open French doors.

Hank turned to the other bodyguard. "Max, grab the first aid supplies from the pantry, along with one of the blankets kept in the hall closet. Meet us at the barn in two minutes."

"A woman needs our help." Hank turned to Zach. "Are you coming or not?"

The woman in question's eyes narrowed as she stared from Hank to Zach. "I don't care who comes, but we need to get there fast. If they take her hostage, the longer we wait, the harder it will be to find them."

"Understood."

Zach stared at the woman, his pulse pounding against his eardrums, his palms damp and clammy. "I'll come." The words echoed in the room, bouncing off the walls to hit him square in the gut. He'd committed to helping an unknown woman when he'd failed to help the partner he'd been with for three years.

Hank steered the woman toward Zach. "Find out what you can while I call the sheriff and let him know what's going on."

When Hank left the room, the woman glanced at Zach. "Are you coming or not?"

Having committed to the task at hand, Zach hooked the woman's arm, ready to get the job over with as quickly as possible. "It would help if we knew who you are."

"Jacie Kosart. I work on the Big Elk Ranch. It's a three-hundred-fifty-thousand-acre spread bordering the Raging Bull and the Big Bend National Park."

"Jacie." He rolled the name on his tongue for a second, then dove in. "What were you doing out this late?"

"My sister and I were leading a big-game hunting party for my boss, Richard Giddings. The two men who'd commissioned us didn't want to hunt on the normal trails the deer like to travel." Jacie explained how they'd come to the canyon, the subsequent shootings and her escape. "We have to get back. I think they killed the two hunters. If not, they need medical help." She gulped, tears welling again. "Tracie has to be all right. She just has to."

"We'll do the best we can to find her and bring her home." Zach tried to sound confident when he felt nothing like it. If the men in the canyon had anything to do with the drug cartels, Jacie's sister was as good as dead.

The sound of engines revving outside signaled the end of their conversation and the need to move.

Zach cupped Jacie's elbow and led her through the French doors and out to the barn where five ATVs idled in neutral. The man Zach assumed was Hank's foreman sat astride one of them giving the engine gas.

Hank, dressed in jeans, a denim jacket and cowboy boots, jogged down from the house flanked by his two bodyguards, each carrying an automatic assault weapon. Hank carried two, one of which he tossed to Zach. "In case we run into some trouble."

Zach dropped his hold on the woman's arm and caught the high-powered weapon, slipping it into the scabbard on one of the four-wheelers.

"You all right?" he asked Jacie.

She nodded. "Yeah. I just want to find my sister."

The two bodyguards mounted a four-wheeler each and Hank took another, leaving only one left.

"The girl can ride with you. I don't want her falling off and injuring herself. This way you can keep an eye on her and lead the way."

Zach frowned but mounted the ATV and scooted forward for Jacie to climb on the back.

She balked, staring at Zach and the space allotted to her. "I can take the one I rode in on."

"We don't know how much gas it has in it, and given that you've passed out once, you're better off riding with one of us."

Zach sucked in a deep breath and let it out. "Get on."

Jacie flung her leg over the back and slid in behind Zach, her thighs resting against his, her chest pressing into his back.

He revved the engine and shot out of the barnyard headed south.

With Jacie looking over his shoulder, directing him, he raced across the dark earth, dodging clumps of prickly pear cactus and saw palmettos.

The woman held on lightly at first, her grip tightening as Zach swerved in and out of the vegetation with nothing but the stars shining down on him from a moonless sky.

As they neared the edge of the canyon, Jacie pointed and yelled over the roar of the engine. "There!"

Zach pulled up short of the edge of the canyon. On the slim chance the assailants were hanging around at the bottom of the canyon, he didn't want to provide them with a target at the top. He cut the engine.

Before he could dismount, Jacie was off the back and scrambling toward the edge.

He caught her as she lunged for the trail, yanking her back from the edge and out of line of sight from the bottom. "Are you trying to get yourself killed?"

"My sister was down there. We have to save her." She struggled against his hold.

"For all we know they could still be down there."

She fought to free her arm. "Then let's go."

The other riders had pulled to a halt and dismounted.

Zach dragged Jacie over to Hank. "Hold on to her while I check it out."

"Take Joe with you in case you run into trouble."

"I do better on my own." Zach crouched low and dropped over the rim of the canyon, slipping down the trail as quietly as possible. In the light from the night sky, he could make out where the trail was disturbed, one edge knocked free. Probably where a horse, a motorcycle or a four-wheeler had run off the side.

The bottom of the trail was bathed in shadows, making it hard to distinguish the boulders from crouching thugs waiting to pounce.

Careful not to fall off the edge himself, Zach moved swiftly down the trail, reaching the bottom. The shadows proved to be boulders and one wrecked ATV, crumpled among them. Nothing moved. Zach explored among the boulders to the other side of the ATV and found the body of a man laying at an awkward angle, facedown, his leg bent, probably shattered in the fall. The ground beside him sported an inky-black stain.

Zach didn't have to guess that the stain was a drying pool of this man's blood. This guy hadn't died from the fall, based on the dark bullet-sized circle in the middle of his back. If Zach turned him over, he'd likely be a mess on the other side where the bullet exited his body.

Zach searched the area around the base of the cliff and shouted up, "Clear!"

Five four-wheelers inched down the narrow trail, lights picking out the way.

Joe led the pack followed by Hank, Max, the foreman and Jacie.

Zach frowned and met her as she cleared the trail. "You should have stayed at the top."

"Did you find her?" Jacie glanced around, her eyes wide, hopeful. Then her shoulders sagged and she slumped on the seat of the ATV. "That's Mr. Smith, one of the two hunters we were escorting." She sucked in a deep breath and let it out slowly. "Tracie's not here, is she?"

"Believe it or not, that's a good thing." Hank left his four-wheeler and crossed to Jacie. "If she's not here, it's a good chance that she's still alive."

Jacie's jaw tightened. "Then come on, let's find her."

Zach shook his head. "It would be suicide to continue searching in the dark. If the attackers are in the canyon still, they would have the advantage and pick us off from above."

"We can't leave her out there."

"Zach's right. We have to wait until daylight." Hank stood beside Zach. "Going in at night wouldn't be doing your sister any favors."

"Then I'll go on alone." As she pressed the gas lever, Zach grabbed her around the waist and yanked her off the bike.

"You're not going anywhere." Zach slammed her against his chest, his arms wrapping around her waist. "One captive is enough. We don't want to risk another. Besides, your sister most likely wouldn't want you to risk it."

Jacie struggled against him. "Let go of me. My sister is my responsibility."

"Then take your responsibility seriously and do what's smart. We need to wait until daylight before we risk going into that canyon."

The woman stopped. "I guess you're right."

When she quit struggling and seemed to settle down, Zach released her. In the next second, she shot across to the four-wheeler she'd left running, hopped on and took off on the trail leading into the canyon.

"Damn, woman." Zach ran after her, catching up as she entered the narrow trail flanked by high cliffs.

As she slowed to negotiate around a boulder, Zach jogged alongside her and jumped on the back. "Stop, damn it!"

"Not until I find my sister." She goosed the accelerator lever on the handle and nearly unseated him.

Zach grabbed around her middle and held on.

They slid around a corner, the starlight barely reaching them at this point.

About the time Zach steadied himself, Jacie hit the brakes and jerked the handles, sending the machine sliding sideways, and the tail end with Zach slipping around to the right.

JACIE COULDN'T LET the search end. Not when her sister's life hung in the balance.

When she saw the cowboy boot, she slammed on her brakes. In a random patch of starlight, a jean-clad leg peeked out from behind a large boulder.

Her heart skipped several beats and then hammered against the wall of her chest. Jacie threw herself off the four-wheeler and scrambled up from her hands and knees to run toward the leg, sobs rising from her throat, echoing off the canyon walls.

Footsteps crunched behind her. Probably Zach, but she didn't care. If this was Tracie... *Oh, dear God, please be okay.*

The other four-wheelers entered the canyon at a more moderate pace, coming to a halt behind Jacie's.

She dropped to her knees beside a body, relief washing over her as soon as she saw it was a man.

"It's Mr. Jones." She felt for a pulse, her hand still for a long time before she glanced back at Zach, a glimmer of hope daring to make an appearance. "I have a pulse. It's weak, but I have a pulse." She leaned into the man's face. "Mr. Jones, can you hear me?"

Nothing. Her hopes dying, she tried again, patting the man's cheek gently. "Mr. Jones, please. Can you hear me?"

A muscle twitched in the man's leg.

Encouraged, Jacie spoke louder. "Mr. Jones, we're going to get you some help, but can you help us?"

The man's eyes fluttered open. "Set…up." He closed his eyes again.

"Mr. Jones!" Jacie wanted to shake the man but was afraid to add to his injuries. "Please, did you see where they went? Where did they take my sister?"

His eyes never opened, but his lips moved.

Jacie leaned in closer, tilting her head to hear what he whispered.

"Not Jones."

Jacie leaned back. "What do you mean?"

The man whispered again.

Leaning close, Jacie caught what sounded like letters.

"D…E…A." As if it had taken everything he had left, the last letter ended on a raspy exhale.

Mr. Jones, or whoever he was, didn't draw another breath.

Jacie felt for a pulse. Not even a weak one thumped against her fingertips. "No pulse. He's not breathing." She clamped his nose with her fingers and breathed for him.

Zach dropped to his knees on the other side of him and leaned the heel of his palms into the man's chest five times. "Now breathe," he instructed.

Jacie blew into the man's mouth. His lungs expanded, pushing his chest up.

Zach resumed his compressions. For every five, Jacie breathed one breath.

Hank and the bodyguards scoured the vicinity while Zach and Jacie worked over Mr. Jones.

When they returned, Jacie glanced up at Hank. "Any sign of my sister?" She knew the answer, but she had to ask.

"None."

Rather than let the news cripple her, Jacie renewed her efforts to save Mr. Jones.

After fifteen minutes, Zach quit pumping the man's chest and he touched Jacie's arm before she could breathe into the man's mouth.

"He's gone."

"No." Jacie sat back on her haunches. "He might have told us where they went."

"I doubt it. From what you said, he was hit before they grabbed Tracie." Zach rose to his feet and held out a hand to Jacie. "Come on, let's get you back to the ranch. We'll start the search in the morning."

"She has to be okay." Jacie let him pull her to her feet, where she leaned against him, pressing her forehead against the solid wall of his chest. "She's all I have."

Hank patted her back. "We'll find her. Don't you worry."

Zach stood beside her. "I saw his lips moving, but I couldn't hear him. What did Jones say to you before he died?"

"I'm not sure." Jacie shook her head. She'd never had someone die on her. Hell, she'd never seen someone get shot in all the years she'd been working on the Big Elk Ranch. She'd never seen someone die of a gunshot wound. She pushed the image of the dead men from her mind and concentrated on the only clue she might have to find her sister. "At first he said what sounded like 'set…up.' Then he said 'Not Jones…D…E…A.'"

Zach stiffened against her, his hands gripping her arm. "Are you sure?"

She glanced up into his face. "As sure as I can be. The man was barely able to whisper. I could have gotten it wrong. Why?"

"Damn. These men most likely were agents with the DEA."

Hank ran a hand through his shocking-white hair and looked around the canyon walls. "Think they were set up?"

"Sounds like it."

Jacie froze. "Oh, dear God." She didn't, she couldn't have... "My sister is an FBI agent here on vacation to visit me."

Zach still held her.

Jacie was sure, if he weren't still gripping her arms, she'd have fallen to her knees. "Do you think she was working undercover, as well?"

"If so, and it was a setup..." Zach's jaw tightened. "Apparently, there's some bad blood in both agencies."

Hank sighed. "Holy hell. I was too late, then."

Zach dropped his hold on Jacie. "What do you mean?"

"I'm sorry, Jacie. I've failed your sister." Hank reached out for one of Jacie's hands. "You see, Tracie came to me yesterday asking for my help."

"I don't understand." Jacie's head spun. Had she been walking around in the clouds since her sister arrived? "My sister only got here two days ago. Why would she come to you?"

"She wanted help finding out who was the leak in her agency and she didn't want to go through official channels." Hank's gaze shifted back to Zach. "Since you are former FBI, this was to be your first assignment."

Chapter Three

Zach rode back to the Raging Bull Ranch, a knot the size of Texas twisting his gut.

Hank couldn't be serious. To ask him to take on the FBI as his first assignment? The organization that had left him and Toni to die in the godforsaken hell of the Los Lobos cartel in the Mexican state of Chihuahua?

Captured in Juarez on assignment, drugged and transported to a squalid compound in Mexico, Zach and Toni had been tortured and starved in the cartel's attempt to attain information from them about who in the FBI was supplying military weapons to their archrivals, La Familia Diablos.

He'd been forced to watch as they raped, mutilated and finally killed Toni. Bound and gagged, he'd been helpless, unable to do anything to save her.

When another gang stormed the compound, they'd crashed into the concrete building where Zach had been held, giving him the opportunity to escape under cover of the night. But it had been too late for Toni.

Wounded, dehydrated and barely able to see through swollen eyes, he dragged himself out of the compound and hid in the mountains, stealing food from a farmer until he could make his way back to the States.

Two years, surgery, rehab and psychiatric treatment

had healed the external scars, but the internal ones festered like a disease.

Jacie rode on the back of the four-wheeler, her arms circled around Zach's waist.

Hank wanted him to help her and her sister, who was certain to be experiencing exactly what Toni had been subjected to, if not worse. If she wasn't dead, likely she would be wishing she was soon.

No. Zach couldn't do this. He couldn't commit to finding Tracie, not when he knew the outcome wouldn't be good. Her twin would expect him to come back with a woman intact, healthy and cared for.

The arms around him tightened, reminding him that the woman on the back of the vehicle was already counting on him to help her.

As he pulled into the barnyard of the Raging Bull Ranch, he mentally prepared his exit speech. "Hank, I'd like to talk with you privately."

No use bringing the woman in on his cowardly departure. She wouldn't understand, and seeing the desperation in her eyes would only drive another stake through his heart.

Red and blue flashing lights shone from the road leading into the Raging Bull Ranch.

"Zach, we'll talk as soon as I've had a chance to bring the local law enforcement up to date on the situation. Meet me in my office in five minutes." Hank and his two bodyguards left. The foreman rode one of the four-wheelers to the back of the barn, leaving Zach alone with Jacie.

He glanced away from her, the look of worry and sadness in her eyes more than he could handle.

A hand on his arm precluded ignoring the woman. "Zach, what are we going to do now? How are we going to find my sister?"

"There is no *we*." His words came out sharper than he'd intended.

Jacie snatched her hand away from his arm as if she'd been bitten. "What do you mean? I thought Hank said you were the one assigned to help Tracie."

"If I chose to accept the assignment and go to work for Hank in his insane business." Zach snorted. "Truth and justice. There is no truth and justice when a gun's held to your head or a whip's lashed across your naked skin. I won't be a part of Hank's fantasy."

"You mean you're going to turn your back on my sister and leave her to die?"

Her words struck him where it hurt most. Square in his gut where guilt ate away at his insides. "I can't do anything for your sister." He turned his back to her. "She's as good as dead."

"No! She's alive. She's my twin. I can feel her presence." Jacie grabbed his arm and jerked him around. "You can't just walk away. My sister needs you. I need you. I can't do this on my own. I will if I have to. But I wouldn't know where to start."

"Don't worry, Hank will find some other cowboy to ride to your rescue. It just won't be me. I'm not the right man for this job."

"You're not a man at all," Jacie spat out. "What kind of man would run away rather than help save a woman's life?"

Zach rounded on her and grabbed her arms in a vicious grip. His heart slammed against his ribs, and rage rose up his neck to explode in his head. "That's right! I *can't* help your sister. I *can't* save a woman from the cartel. I couldn't save Toni and I refuse to watch it happen all over again. I. Can't. Help. *Got that?*" He shook her hard.

Tears welled in Jacie's gray-blue eyes, her long, rich brown hair falling down over her face. "I get it. You have your own issues. Fine. I'll do this without you." She struggled against his hold. "Let go of me. I don't want or need you or any of Hank's hired guns. I'll get my sister back. Alive! Mark my words." She shook free of him. "In the meantime go find a bottle to crawl into or see a shrink. Whatever. I don't give a damn." She spun on her booted heels and marched away from him.

The farther away she moved, the more Zach's chest tightened. If Jacie went tearing off after her sister, she'd end up captured and tortured, as well. What kind of fool would throw herself at the cartel and expect to survive?

The rage subsided, leaving Zach cold and empty.

Jacie was a fool. But she was a fool who loved her sister enough to sacrifice her life to save her twin.

Zach had begged his captors to torture him and leave his partner alone. Instead they'd tortured her in their efforts to drag information out of *him.* Sadly he didn't have the information they'd wanted and Toni had paid the price for his ignorance. His captors had wanted the name of the agent feeding their rivals information about upcoming sting operations. While the Los Lobos cartel took hits, losing some of their best contacts, La Familia Diablos got away with all their people and goods intact.

Heartsick by his own agency's betrayal, Zach had returned to the States, healed his wounds and quit the FBI. Tired of the politics, the graft and corruption.

If Tracie had been after the same person…the one disloyal to his country and fellow agents…she was crazy. The traitor kept his hand so close to his chest. No one knew who he was.

As Jacie disappeared around the corner of the ranch house, Zach started after her. Jacie, unskilled in the art of spying and tactics, wouldn't last two minutes going up against a drug cartel.

His footsteps sped up until he was jogging. Since he was on the outside looking in, he might discover who the mole was in the FBI, the man who'd sacrificed his own people to line his pockets with blood money.

Jacie had almost reached Hank when Zach caught up with her. "Wait."

The woman kept walking. "Why should I? I told you, I don't need you or anyone else to help me find my sister."

He snagged her arm and spun her toward him. "Look. Despite what you're saying, you won't last two minutes out there. The cartel employs trained killers. What kind of training have you had in shooting and dodging bullets?"

Her shoulders were thrown back, her chin held high. "I'm a damned good shot."

"At game. Ever shot a person?"

Her eyes narrowed. "Not before tonight."

"You have to be willing to shoot before you're shot."

"I'll do whatever it takes to find my sister and bring her back alive." She swallowed hard, her chin rising even higher. "Even if it means killing a man to do it. And I might just start with you if you don't let go of me."

He dropped his hold. "You were also right that I have issues. I won't go into it, but they involved the cartel. I've been on both sides of the border. I know what to expect."

"So? You just said you wouldn't help me."

He sucked in a breath and let it out slowly before capturing her gaze with a steady one of his own. "Though I think the effort is futile, I'll help you find your sister."

Jacie snorted. "No, thanks." She turned away and would have walked off.

Zach grabbed her hand and steeled himself to reveal a piece of his soul he hadn't revealed to anyone. "I watched someone I cared for tortured and killed by the Los Lobos Cartel. It's not something I want to do again. I promise to do my best to find your sister before she meets the same fate."

Jacie's eyes flared wide, then narrowed again. "How do I know you won't flip out on me again?"

"I'm a good agent." He paused. "I *was* a good agent. I know when to focus and I'm driven to get the job done."

"Then why did you quit the FBI?"

"For the same reason your sister asked for help from Hank. I was betrayed by someone on the inside. My partner paid with blood. If I can find your sister and, in the process, find the mole, my partner will not have died in vain."

Jacie's eyes narrowed even more and she chewed on her bottom lip. Finally she stuck out her hand. "Okay, then. Let's go find my sister."

JACIE SHOOK ZACH'S hand, her fingers tingling where they touched his. She wasn't completely convinced Zach was her man, and she didn't like the way her pulse quickened when he was near, but she didn't have a whole lot of choices. Going searching for the people responsible for her sister's abduction would be hard enough on her own.... Hell, it would be impossible. Having a former FBI agent on her side would be a step in the right direction. He might still have connections and contacts.

Hank led the county sheriff over to join them. "Zach, this is Sheriff Fulmer from Wild Oak Canyon. He'll be working with the FBI and DEA on this case."

Zach shook the sheriff's hand.

Jacie refused to, knowing the man's track record since he'd taken office a year ago. He tended to look the other way rather than stop the flow of drugs through his county. "When will the DEA and FBI be sending someone out to assist?" And hopefully take over the operation.

"I spoke to the regional director of the FBI a few minutes ago. They're as concerned as you are to get your sister back. As for the DEA agents, the county coroner and the state crime lab are on their way out as we speak. If you could show me where the bodies are, I'll cordon off the crime scene until they arrive."

"My foreman will take you out there," Hank said. "If I need to sign any statements, let me know."

"From what Mr. Derringer says, I'll need a full statement from you, Ms. Kosart, as you're the only eyewitness."

"I'll provide one in the morning. Right now I need to get back to the Big Elk Ranch and notify my employer of the situation and check on the horses." She hadn't even thought once about the horses since Tracie had been taken. Now she focused on them to keep from going crazy with inaction.

"I'm going with you." Zach glanced at Hank. "I'm in."

Hank nodded, ignoring the raised eyebrows of the sheriff. "Keep me informed, will ya?" was all he said; then he turned his attention to the sheriff. "Scott, my foreman, and I will show you where we found the two agents." He led the officer away.

"Give me a minute while I get my keys." Zach pointed toward a black four-wheel-drive pickup standing in the circular drive. "You can wait by my truck."

"Okay, but hurry. I'm worried about the horses." Jacie was worried about a lot more than just the horses, but she trudged toward the vehicle, taking her time, while Zach ducked into the ranch house.

Jacie recognized the truck as a model produced a couple of years before. It wasn't new, but it shone like a new truck with only a thin layer of dust coating the shiny wax finish. The man had some issues, but taking care of what was his wasn't one of them.

He returned in two minutes, carrying a small duffel

bag in one hand, wearing a black cowboy hat and a light leather jacket. When it flapped open, the black leather of a shoulder holster was revealed with a pistol nestled inside.

Jacie had spent her life around men and guns, working for the Big Elk Ranch. Leading hunting parties required a thorough knowledge of how to shoot, clean and unjam weapons of all shapes and sizes. Knowing Zach carried a pistol and was former FBI gave her a small sense of comfort that she wasn't the only one who could handle a gun going forward in the search for her sister.

Before he reached her he clicked the door lock release.

Jacie climbed into the truck and buckled herself into the passenger seat.

Zach stashed the bag in the backseat and settled behind the steering wheel. "You'll have to tell me where to go. I'm new around here."

She gave him the directions and sat back, staring ahead where the headlights illuminated the road, keeping an eye out for the wildlife that skirted the shoulders looking for something to eat. Too many times she'd had near misses with the local deer.

In her peripheral vision, she watched the way Zach handled the truck with ease, his fingers gripping the steering wheel a little tighter than necessary, his face set in grim lines. She wanted to know more about him; what made his eyes so dark and caused the shadows beneath? Had his experience with the cartel left such an indelible mark he couldn't separate that chapter of his life with a possible future?

"Toni was your partner?" she asked.

The fingers on the steering wheel tightened until the knuckles turned white. For a long moment Zach didn't answer.

About the time Jacie gave up on getting a response, he spoke.

"Yes, Toni was my partner."

"I'm sorry. You two must have been close." Jacie dragged her gaze from the pain reflected from his eyes. "Did he leave behind a family?"

"*She* wasn't married. Her father was her only relative."

Interesting. So his partner had been female. Which would explain his reluctance to go after another female when he'd failed the first. Jacie chewed on that bit of information. "Were you in love with her?"

As soon as the question left her lips, Jacie could have smacked herself. The man was torn up enough about losing his partner. Bringing it up had to be killing him. Her curiosity didn't warrant grilling him about his past. "I'm sorry, this must be painful. I'll shut up."

"Yes."

"Yes that you want me to shut up or yes that you loved her?"

His lips twitched, the movement softening his features to almost human. "Both."

Jacie sat back, her gaze back on the road, her chest tightening. "Turn left at the next road."

Zach nodded.

"Did she know you loved her?" Jacie closed her eyes. "That was too personal. You don't have to answer. I'm sorry. While Tracie went into the FBI, I knew I couldn't because I can't keep my mouth shut unless I'm out hunting."

"Pretend you're hunting." Zach turned where she'd indicated. "And no. She didn't know." He pulled up to a closed gate attached to six-foot-high fencing. "Game ranch?"

"That's what I do. I didn't go to Quantico or study to be a doctor. I got my marketing degree from the University of Texas and came back here to work as a hunting party coordinator, a fancy title for trail guide. It allows me to be where I love to be, outside, and working with horses and people." She couldn't help the defensive tone in her voice.

"I'm not judging."

"I love my sister and I'm so proud of her, but part of me feels as though I didn't push hard enough, that I'm not living up to my potential. I went on trail rides while my sister ran off to be an FBI agent working for the good of her country."

"And look what it got her." Zach's lips thinned. "Betrayal by that country she's fighting for."

"I don't believe that. One bad apple, and all that, doesn't mean everyone will turn traitor. I still believe in the FBI and the other branches of service dedicated to protecting our freedom. And I'm sure Tracie feels the same. If she knew there was a mole in the organization, she didn't run from it, she went looking for it. Especially since she asked Hank for help."

Zach nodded toward the gate. "I take it the gate doesn't open without a remote."

Jacie's face heated. She slipped from the truck and ran to the gate, punching in a code, triggering the automatic gate opener arm to swing out.

Jacie climbed back into the truck and sat quietly as Zach drove the winding road that led to the lodge at the Big Elk Ranch.

The lights shone bright, unusual for the earliest hours of the morning.

Before the vehicle came to a halt, Richard Giddings leaped off the porch and opened the passenger door to the pickup. "Oh, thank God." The tall man with the slightly graying temples reached out. His hands circled her waist and he lifted Jacie to the ground. "I'd been so worried about you. When your hunting party never returned, I had everyone out looking until midnight. When Derringer called to say you were on your way, I was relieved and sick all at once." He wrapped an arm around her shoulder and led her toward the house. He'd taken a couple of steps before he stopped and stared down into her eyes. "I'm so sorry about your sister."

Despite the exhaustion threatening to overwhelm her, Jacie planted her feet in the ground and threw back her shoulders. "Tracie will be all right. We'll get her back."

Richard smiled down at her with his warm green eyes. "She's a fighter, just like her sister."

"Damn right." Jacie backed away from her boss. "Richard, I'd like you to meet Zach." She stopped, realizing for the first time she didn't know Zach's full name. She tilted her head and raised her eyebrows, hoping he'd take the hint.

Zach stepped forward and held out his hand. "Zach Adams."

Richard's eyebrows V'd over his nose. "Should I know you?"

"Not at all." He glanced at Jacie and smiled. "Jacie and I go way back to college, don't we?"

"Y-yes. We do."

"We dated for a while, lost touch, but I just couldn't forget her. And since I was in the neighborhood, I planned on reconnecting in the morning, once I got my bearings." He shook his head. "Imagine my surprise when she found me first at Hank's place."

Richard held out a hand and shook Zach's. "You picked a really bad time."

"No, actually." Jacie crossed to Zach's side. "I'm glad he's here. With Tracie being gone and all, it's nice to have the support of…friends." She hooked her arm through his. "Do you mind if he stays in the Javelina Cabin? I know it's empty." And it was the closest one to the tiny cabin she'd called home since she came to work full-time at the Big Elk Ranch.

"Sure." Richard nodded. "You can show him the way. I'll have Tia Fuentez make up a plate of food since you missed dinner. How about you, Mr. Adams? Hungry?"

"Call me Zach. And no, thank you. I had my supper." He pulled Jacie close. "But I'll use that time to get a shower and hit the rack."

"Make yourself at home. The ranch is big, but the people are friendly."

"I've noticed that." He smiled again at Jacie. "I'm looking forward to catching up with Jacie, and maybe we'll hear something about her sister soon."

Jacie steered Zach toward the line of cabins leading away from the lodge. As soon as they were out of listening range, she whispered, "Why did you lie to my boss?"

"I'd just as soon everyone in this part of Texas think that I'm here as an old college buddy or boyfriend, rather than an agent searching for your sister. In this case, we don't know who are the good guys and who are the bad guys. So we play it neutral and I blend in. The best undercover agents are those who blend in."

"Okay, then. When do we start looking for my sister?"

"Was that a helicopter I saw out by the barn?"

Jacie frowned, taken off guard by the change in subject. "Yes, Richard has a helicopter he uses occasionally for the big game hunts or flight-seeing tours over Big Bend."

"Think he'll take us up so that we can fly over the canyon?"

Her heart fluttered with excitement. "I'm sure he will. I'll ask." Maybe they'd spot the people holding Tracie.

"Good. It would be better coming from you, since it's

your sister and you work here. Remember, I'm just a boyfriend."

Her cheeks warmed at the thought of Zach as her boyfriend, even if it was pretend. "I'll get right on it."

"I'm gonna hit the sack for a few hours of sleep. We have a busy day ahead of us. I suggest you do the same."

She nodded, staring out at the night sky, wondering what her sister was going through and if she was okay. "We're going to find her."

When he didn't respond, Jacie's fists tightened. "We *will* find my sister."

"I promise you this." He faced her, capturing her cheeks in his hands, his gaze severe, his lips pressed into a firm line. "I'll do the best I can."

A shiver rippled across Jacie's skin as she gazed into his brown-black eyes. The intensity of his stare and the tightness of his grip on her face gave her a sense of comfort and commitment. This man had lost someone he loved to terrorist cartel members. He wouldn't let it happen again if he could help it. They would get her sister back or die trying.

Chapter Four

Jacie showed Zach to the cabin and left him to get a shower.

After retrieving his duffel bag, he checked his cell phone, surprised that he had reception. Out in the boonies of south Texas, he hadn't seen much in the way of reception outside the small town of Wild Oak Canyon. The Big Elk Ranch must have a cell tower of its own.

Glad for the ability to use his own phone, Zach didn't lose time in contacting an old buddy from his Quantico days back on the East Coast.

"Hello?" a gravelly voice answered on the fifth ring.

"Jim, Zach Adams."

"Zach?" James Coslowski paused. The sound of something falling in the background, followed by a curse, crossed the airwaves. "Do you realize it's only three in the morning?"

"Sorry for the late call, but I need a favor."

"And it couldn't have waited until morning?"

"No. I need to know everything about Special Agent Tracie Kosart that you can find, and as soon as possible."

"I repeat…this couldn't wait until I've had a gallon of coffee, say after a more reasonable hour like seven?"

"She was abducted tonight by what appears to be a Mexican drug cartel."

"Damn." The gravel had been scraped from Jim's voice. "You know I'm not supposed to release any information—"

"I know. I'm asking as a huge favor. I'm working this case as a private investigator, but I need to know why they would have abducted her. Anything you can find out and share would help."

"Still, you're no longer with the agency."

Zach snorted. "Since when are you a rule follower?"

"Since I got married and have a wife, and a baby on the way."

Zach's chest tightened. "Sorry, man. I didn't know. Congratulations."

"There's a lot you don't know, having dropped off the face of the earth for the past two years." Jim sighed. "I'll do the best I can. Just don't go all vigilante and get yourself into trouble."

Zach's fist tightened around the cell phone. "What difference would it make? I didn't get any help from my employer last time. I certainly don't expect any better this time."

"Just stay safe. Some of us care what happens to you."

His heart pounding against his ribs, Zach ended the call, grabbed a towel from the bathroom closet and hit the shower.

So much time had passed since he'd been gone from the FBI. Jim had been a good friend and Zach hadn't even acknowledged his wedding. The invitation had likely been tossed with all the mail he'd ignored for so long.

About time he rejoined the human race and pulled his head out of the dark fog he'd sunk into.

JACIE HURRIED TO the main lodge and entered through the back door. Richard had only left them a few moments before; surely he hadn't gone straight to bed. Not with members of his guest list dead and Jacie's sister missing.

As she'd expected, she found him in the resort's office, surrounded by rich wood paneling and bookshelves filling two walls from floor to ceiling.

Richard sat behind his desk, scrubbing a hand over his face.

Jacie cleared her throat.

Her boss glanced up, his eyes bloodshot, the lines beside his eyes and denting his forehead deeper than she'd remembered. "Come in, Jacie." He rose from his chair and rounded his desk, opening his arms to her.

She fell into them, pressing her face against his broad chest. This man had been like a father to her since she'd come to work full-time for him. "Will we get her back?"

"Damn right we will," he said, his voice gruff, his arms tightening around her for a moment. He then pushed her to arm's length. "I've been thinking. Tomorrow at sunup, we'll take the chopper up and do our own search for her. To hell with waiting for the government to get out there. I figure the more people looking, the better."

Jacie stared up at her boss, blinking the tears from her eyes. Richard wasn't good around emotional women, and Jacie made certain she didn't put him in a position to deal with female emotions. She forced a smile, though her lips quivered. "Thank God. I was just coming to ask you if we could use the helicopter."

"I'll do everything in my power to find your sister, Jacie. This should never have happened. I should have done a better background search on those DEA agents."

"You can't blame yourself."

His hands squeezed her arms. "That could be you out there."

She hadn't thought of it that way, and she couldn't now. "But it wasn't."

"Still. I might have lost my best PR woman and trail guide. Do you know how hard it is to find someone like you?" He dropped his hands from her arms and stepped back, running his fingers through his graying hair. "We'll find her. Mark my words." His voice was thick and he appeared to be on the edge of a rare emotional display.

"Thanks." Jacie touched her boss's shoulder. "You and I better get some sleep. We have a long day ahead of us."

He nodded without speaking.

Her chest tight, emotions running high, Jacie left the lodge and returned to her cabin with her first glimmer of hope.

Once inside, with the door closed behind her, she felt the walls press in around her. She paced the inside of her tiny cabin, her heart alternating between settled and crazed. Her sister was out there with terrorists and she could do nothing about it until daylight. The canyons were dangerous enough without the cloak of darkness hiding the animals and drop-offs. It would be suicide to ride back out there. Yet every fiber of her being urged her to do just that.

A woman of action, she felt the inaction eating at her like cancer. Jacie entered the little bedroom, determined to shower and try to rest. Tomorrow would be a long day spent in the canyon. Hopefully they'd find something that would lead them to Tracie.

And to think Tracie had come here to get away from the stress of her job. Some stress relief. Or had she come for an entirely different reason?

Jacie glanced at the phone on the nightstand. Hank had promised to contact the FBI and DEA, but what about Tracie's boyfriend, Bruce Masterson? Granted, he was an FBI agent himself, but large federal agencies like the FBI didn't always communicate to all persons involved.

She hesitated.

Her sister hadn't admitted to any trouble between the two of them, but she hadn't been as excited as she'd been about Bruce the last time Jacie spoke with her on the phone. Still, the man had been Tracie's boyfriend for the past year and had moved in with her six weeks ago. He deserved to know his girlfriend was missing.

Jacie pushed aside her misgivings and reached for the phone, dialing the number Tracie had given when she'd moved in with Bruce.

On the fourth ring, a male, groggy voice answered, "Masterson."

"Bruce?" Jacie asked.

"Tracie?" The grogginess disappeared. "Where are you?"

Bruce's response told Jacie a lot. Tracie hadn't informed him of her destination. "No, Bruce, this isn't Tracie. It's Jacie, her twin."

"Oh." He paused. "Is Tracie with you?"

"No."

"She's not here, if that's what you wanted to know."

"I know." Jacie dragged in a deep breath. "That's why I'm calling."

"What's wrong?" Bruce demanded. "Is it Tracie? Is she okay?"

A sob rose in her throat and threatened to cut off Jacie's air. "I don't know," she managed, her voice shaking.

"What happened, damn it?" Bruce's voice rose.

"She came to visit the night before last and insisted on coming with me on a hunt." Jacie told Bruce what had happened, her voice ragged, emotion choking her vocal cords. "She's gone, Bruce. Captured by what appears to be members of a Mexican cartel."

For a long moment, Bruce didn't say anything. When he finally spoke, his voice was deadly calm. "I'm coming out there."

"I'm not sure who will be involved. The local law enforcement plans on a search party as soon as it's daylight. We notified the DEA and the FBI and—"

"You notified the FBI already?" Bruce asked. "Why the hell didn't I get word?"

Jacie shrugged, then remembered Bruce couldn't see her. "I don't know. Maybe they're still trying to organize a recovery team. All I know is that my sister is missing and I want her back. Alive."

"Don't worry. I'll be there by morning." The phone clicked in Jacie's ear.

She set it back on the charger, and let out a long steadying breath. The more people she had looking for her sister, the better.

If Jacie planned to be one of the search team, she had to be at her best. A shower and sleep would help her maintain her strength through what looked like a long day ahead.

After thoroughly scrubbing her hair and body, she toweled dry, slipped into a tank top and soft jersey shorts she liked to sleep in and blew her hair dry.

All her movements were rote behavior, her mind on her sister, not the tasks at hand. By the time she stepped out of the small bathroom and into the bedroom, she knew she wouldn't sleep. Her imagination had taken hold and spun all kinds of horrible scenarios Tracie could be enduring. She'd gone over and over all the events of the day, hoping to find one grain of information that might help her locate her sister. And nothing.

The walls closed in around her, and her heart beat hard

in her chest, forcing her toward the door and outside, where she felt closer to her sister than anywhere else. She didn't have any other family. Her father and mother had died in a car wreck five years ago, shortly after Jacie finished college. She had no one to turn to, to hold her and tell her it would be all right.

Jacie stared up at the stars, their shine blurred by the rush of tears. Overcome by the events, she sank down on the porch steps and buried her face in her hands, letting the tears flow.

A COOL SHOWER went a long way to waking Zach and clearing his mind, as well as dousing the craving for a strong drink to dull his wits. He lay on the bed, settling on top of a quaint, old-fashioned quilt, not ready to sleep, but hoping he'd find comfort in the reclining position.

The air conditioner struggled to reduce the heat inside the cabin after being off during the hottest part of the day. After fifteen minutes of trying, Zach gave up and rose from the bed. He checked his phone, knowing it hadn't rung and probably wouldn't until the following day.

He wished it was morning already so that he could get started on the search for Jacie's sister. Inaction drove him nuts.

Zach stepped out on the front porch in nothing but his jeans.

The cabin beside his had a soft light glowing through the window. But it wasn't the window that drew his attention.

A shadowy figure hunkered low on the steps leading up to the porch. Soft sobs reached him across the still of the night.

Careless of his bare feet, Zach left his porch and crossed the short distance to the cabin where Jacie lived.

She didn't hear his approach and Zach took a moment to study her.

Jacie's long, deep-brown hair lay loose about her shoulders, free from the band that had secured it in a ponytail for the hunt. Starlight caught the dark strands, giving her a heavenly blue halo.

Unable to stand still any longer, he climbed the steps.

Her head jerked up and she gasped, her eyes wide, the irises reflecting the quarter moon. "Oh, it's you." She sat up straighter, her hands swiping at the tears. "Shouldn't you be getting some rest?"

"I wanted to know if your boss agreed to using his helicopter."

Jacie sniffed and glanced away. "I didn't have to ask. He volunteered its use. We will leave at sunup." She glanced back at him as she rose. "If that's all, I'll be calling it a night."

Zach should have let her go, but he couldn't, knowing she'd go on to her bed and probably continue her tears into the early morning hours. He reached out and grabbed her arm before she made it to the door. "Your sister is tough. If she's still alive, we'll find her."

Jacie whirled. "Not *if*. My sister is alive. I know it. Either you believe it, or leave." Her chin tipped up and she glared through tear-filled eyes.

A smile tugged at the corners of his mouth. "You two are twins in more ways than one. I wouldn't be going after her if I didn't believe there was a chance of bringing her back alive." He brushed his thumb across her cheek, scraping away an errant tear.

"She has to be." Jacie's lips trembled. "I've gone over and over everything I saw and heard since Tracie got here. There has to be something. Some indication as to what happened. I feel like she came here for a reason."

Zach gripped her arms. "What do you mean?"

"She's never shown up unannounced until last night. Tracie has been all about the bureau since she trained at Quantico. I thought she really missed me, but the more I think about it, the more I realize she wouldn't have come without telling me ahead of time."

"Did she say anything about anyone? Was she working undercover?"

"I asked her why she'd come. She only said to get a break from work and stress." Jacie's eyes narrowed. "What worries me is that when I called her boyfriend, the man she lives with, he didn't know where she'd gone." She glanced up at Zach. "She didn't even tell him where she'd gone."

Zach didn't like it. Something wasn't right about what Jacie was telling him. "Did she say anything about the men you were guiding? Did she give you any indication that she knew them?"

"No and no." Jacie dragged in a deep breath and stared up at the sky. "I wish I'd been more persistent. But she wasn't being very forthcoming with her answers. I didn't want to butt in if she wasn't ready to talk." A single tear slipped free and trailed across her skin. She swiped at it, a frown marring her brow. "Damn it, I never cry."

"It's not a crime." Zach pulled her into his arms and held her, stroking his hand across her hair, the silken strands sifting through his fingers, the scent of honeysuckle wafting around him. She fit perfectly against him, molding to his body, her soft curves belying the strength it took to lead a hunting party into the dry, dusty terrain of Big Bend country.

She wasn't wearing a bra and her breasts pressed into his chest, the material of her shirt providing little barrier between her naked skin and his.

His gut tightened, and without realizing it, his hands slid lower, pulling her hips against his.

After a while, she looked up, her lips full and far too luscious for a tough hunting guide, her blue-gray eyes limpid pools of ink tinged with the reflection of the stars.

Zach fought the urge to bend closer and capture her lush mouth, his hands tightening around her waist.

Finally he gave in and cupped her cheek. "I'm going to hell for this…but I can't resist." He claimed her lips—gently at first.

When her hands slipped around his neck and drew him closer, he accepted her invitation and crushed her mouth, his tongue pushing past her teeth to slide the length of hers. He wove his fingers through her hair and down her back. Capturing the soft curve of her buttocks, he held her hard against his growing erection.

Her mouth moved over his like a woman starved and hungry for more.

When breathing became necessary, he dragged his lips away and sucked in a deep lungful of air. He dropped her arms and stepped back. "I don't know what the hell just happened, but that was totally unprofessional on my part."

Jacie raised a finger and pressed it to his lips. "Don't. It takes two." She backed a few steps, inching toward the cabin's front door. "I'd better get to bed. Morning will come soon and I want to be awake and alert." She touched a hand to her swollen lips. "Thanks for being here."

Zach pushed his hand through his hair. "Right, I'd better go." He turned, paused and faced Jacie again. "You gonna be all right?"

"Do I have a choice?" Jacie squared her shoulders. "Good night." Then she entered the cabin and closed the door behind her with a soft click.

For a long moment, Zach stood on the porch, his lips

tingling from the unexpected kiss and the desire urging him to repeat it.

What the hell had he gotten himself into?

Chapter Five

The alarm clock blasted through the nightmare Jacie had been having, saving her from falling over a cliff in the canyon. She sat straight up and blinked. No sunlight shone through the windows, and a glance at the clock proved it was early.

After lying awake for hours, she must have fallen asleep...for what it was worth. Her dreams had been horrifying, leaving her drained and fatigued more than ever. Used to getting up and going before dawn, she hauled herself out of bed and, in less than five minutes, pulled her hair back into a ponytail, washed her face and ran a toothbrush over her teeth.

Pausing for a brief moment, she stared at her reflection, wondering why a guy as gorgeous as Zach would kiss a woman who didn't wear makeup or fix her hair. She touched a finger to her lips, the memory of Zach's kiss sending shivers across her skin.

"Get a grip," she muttered, and dressed quickly in jeans, a T-shirt and her well-worn cowboy boots. Ready for the day, she grabbed her cowboy hat and stepped outside onto the porch. The eastern horizon showed signs of the pre-dawn gray inching up the sky. It wouldn't be long before the sun rose and they could take the helicopter over Wild Horse Canyon and hopefully find her sister.

"Sleep much?" A deep, warm voice spoke to her from the corner of her porch.

Jacie gasped and stepped backward, her face heating as the object of her musings chuckled nearby.

Zach's amusement had the opposite effect of setting her heartbeat back to normal.

After their kiss, just being around him took her breath away and made her pulse hammer through her body. What was wrong with her? She hadn't been this aware of a man…ever.

"Did you spend the night on my porch?" she asked, her voice a bit more snappy than she'd have preferred, but then he'd startled and…unnerved her.

He leaned against a thick cedar beam, his arms crossed over his chest, his boots crossed at the ankle, cowboy hat tipped down over his forehead, shadowing his eyes. He appeared relaxed, yet poised to move in a flash. "No. I slept." He tipped his hat back and studied her. "You don't look like you slept at all."

"I take that to mean I look like hell. Gee, thanks." She stepped down one step and stared out at the road leading into the ranch compound. A plume of dust rose in the distance, moving closer at a fast rate. Jacie stepped down one step. "Wonder if that's the FBI or DEA. I thought they'd be basing out of Hank's ranch headquarters since it's closer to the canyon than here."

Zach faced the oncoming vehicle. "I spoke to Hank a few minutes ago. He said both agencies called and are on their way from El Paso but not expected until around noon."

As the vehicle neared, Jacie noted it was a dark pewter pickup with no noticeable markings, and it was coming fast. She dropped down the last two steps and made her way toward the lodge.

Zach followed, his boots crunching in the gravel.

As Jacie rounded the side of the lodge to the front, she noted Richard, Trey, the helicopter pilot, and Richard's other full-time guide, Humberto, standing on the front porch. She and Zach joined them as the truck skidded to a halt in the gravel.

"Expecting someone?" Richard asked.

"No." Jacie's eyes narrowed as a tall man with short-cropped brown hair dropped down from the driver's seat. "Wait, that might be Tracie's boyfriend, Bruce Masterson. He said he'd get here as soon as possible." She glanced at her watch. "He must have broken every speed record between here and San Antonio to make it so quickly. It's okay, he's another FBI agent. Can't hurt having more help finding her."

Zach stood beside Jacie, his bearing stiff, his face unreadable.

The man approached Jacie, frowning. "Jacie?"

"Yes, I'm Jacie." She held out her hand. "And you are?"

"You look so much like your sister, it's uncanny." He climbed the steps and took her hand, staring down into her face. "Bruce Masterson. Tracie's fiancé."

Jacie's eyes widened. "Fiancé? She failed to mention that part. I thought you two were just living together to save on rent."

He gave her a lopsided grin. "Her words. I asked her to marry me before she moved in. She wanted to wait on the engagement, claiming she wasn't ready to settle down. Something about proving herself in the bureau." The smile faded. "Heard anything yet?"

Jacie shook her head. "Nothing."

As if finally aware he and Jacie weren't alone, Bruce glanced at the men gathered. "I assume you're the posse."

Jacie introduced Richard, Humberto and Trey, leaving

Zach for last. "And this is my…boyfriend, Zach Adams."
For now, it was easier for Bruce to assume Zach was her
boyfriend versus her bodyguard. She didn't want any of
the focus to shift to herself when her sister was the one
who needed to be found.

Bruce tipped his head. "I don't recall Tracie mentioning that you have a boyfriend."

Her skin heated at Bruce's intense stare. "Apparently
Tracie needs to work on her communication skills."

Zach shook Bruce's hand. "Don't worry, it's almost as
new to you as it is to us. I just showed up recently in the
hope of rekindling our college romance." Zach hooked an
arm around Jacie's body, pulling her against him. "Seems
the feelings are mutual." He pressed a kiss to the top of
her head.

Tracie's fiancé's eyes narrowed. "Zach Adams. The
name sounds familiar."

Jacie's heart clambered against her ribs. The FBI community was big, but agents ran into each other often. Would
Bruce recognize Zach? Did it matter if he knew? Zach
hadn't mentioned it to Bruce, so Jacie kept her mouth shut.

"My name's pretty common." Zach's arm dropped from
around Jacie. "Our main concern right now is getting Tracie back, safe and sound."

"Right." Richard clapped his hands together. "The chopper has seating for four."

"Chopper?" Bruce's glance shifted to Richard. "The
FBI requisitioned a helicopter for the search already?"

"I don't know about that, but we're not waiting." Richard nodded toward Trey. "We have a helicopter we use for
scouting out game. Trey is our pilot."

"I'd like to get on board if possible." Bruce glanced
from Jacie to Richard.

Jacie shook her head. "Sorry. I'm going."

"Which leaves one seat," Bruce pointed out.

"No, it doesn't." Zach claimed Jacie again by draping an arm over her shoulder. "I go where she goes."

Bruce frowned. "Wouldn't you rather a trained operative help in the search?"

"I've explored canyons before," Zach said. "I know my way around."

"With a weapon?" Bruce argued.

Zach's jaw tightened. "I know how to shoot."

Richard turned to Humberto. "Humberto, you'll take the truck and trailer loaded with two four-wheelers over to Hank's and take off from there." He faced Bruce. "If you're set on going, you can ride with Humberto." Richard pointed his finger at Trey, Zach and Jacie. "You three ready?"

Jacie nodded. "The sooner the better." She pushed aside the horror she'd envisioned of what Tracie was enduring and focused on finding her. "Let's go."

Zach cupped her elbow and led her to the back of the house to the landing pad beside the barn.

"Do you recognize Bruce from your days at the FBI?" Jacie whispered.

"No. But that doesn't mean he didn't recognize me."

"Will it be a problem if he does?"

"We don't know until he comes forward."

Jacie nodded. "In the meantime, you're just my boyfriend from college. By the way, I went to Texas A and M."

He grinned. "Good to know. Have to have our stories straight in case someone asks."

"By the way, where did *you* go to school?"

His mouth twisted into a mischievous hint of a smile. "Now, that would blow my cover if I told you, wouldn't it?"

Richard turned toward Jacie. "I'll take the front with Trey. You two can look out the side windows. We'll head for the ridge overlooking Wild Horse Canyon and go from there."

Jacie nodded. Any effort toward finding her sister was a step in the right direction. She had to focus on that and not on the evasive answer Zach had given her.

She didn't know much about him, other than that he was former FBI and now worked as a cowboy for hire with Hank.

Jacie bit her lip to keep from pressing for more answers and climbed into the helicopter.

Trey handed her a headset and one to Zach.

They tested the communication devices as Trey started the helicopter engine, the noise of the rotors drowning out any attempts at conversation without the headset.

With her seat restraints fastened securely around her, Jacie curled her fingers around the straps and closed her eyes. As she sent up a silent prayer for a safe takeoff and landing and finding her sister, a hand nudged hers.

She opened her eyes.

Zach pulled her fingers free of the belt and wrapped it in his big, warm hand. He didn't say a word but squeezed gently as the helicopter left the ground.

The man didn't even flinch or exhibit any measure of anxiety, as if he'd been up in helicopters on many occasions. Which Jacie wouldn't know, given that he hadn't shared much of his background with her. He was a stranger, yet their kiss made her feel closer to him than the other two men in the helicopter. Jacie had worked with Richard and Trey over the years; Richard was more of a father figure and Trey, an acquaintance with a wife and family waiting for his return in the little town of Wild Oak Canyon.

The helicopter skimmed past the barn and house, rising into a bright blue sky with big fluffy clouds dotting the heavens. It was like any other day, except two men were dead and Jacie's twin was missing.

She concentrated on the ground below, practicing her ability to recognize features before they reached the canyon when it would count.

The truck with the trailer loaded with two four-wheelers flew down the highway below toward the Raging Bull Ranch, making good time.

As they passed to the southeast of Hank Derringer's spread, Jacie made out a gathering of vehicles in the barnyard. True to his word, Hank was on it, organizing locals into a search party. The FBI and DEA would arrive soon and add to the number.

God, she hoped they found Tracie and that she was alive.

ZACH HELD JACIE'S hand throughout the flight.

In less than fifteen minutes, he could make out the ragged edges of a canyon, spreading out below him.

"That's Wild Horse Canyon ahead," Richard's voice crackled over the headset. "Where exactly did you enter the canyon?"

"Farther to the east." Jacie's hand tightened around Zach's fingers as she leaned toward the window, staring at the ground. "There. Right below us. A trail leads down the side of that slope into the canyon. You can see the four-wheeler at the bottom, flipped upside down. The attackers came in from the southwest."

Trey eased the controls to the right and down. The helicopter dipped to the side, swinging toward the narrower fissures in the canyon walls.

"There are so many places to look," Jacie said, her voice staticky in Zach's ear. He recognized the tone of despair the vastness of the canyon must be infusing in her.

"Just look out your window. I'll look out mine. With four people in the air and more following on the ground, we'll cover a lot of territory."

Her fingers squeezed his and she shot him a grateful look.

Zach would rather continue to stare at the fresh-faced woman than at the ground, but he pulled his attention back to the task at hand. Getting involved with the client went against his training as an agent. He knew the risks. He'd learned his lesson when he'd fallen in love with Toni. Don't get involved. It led to heartache. In his line of work, he was better off remaining aloof, impartial and alone.

He glanced at the hand he held and almost let go.

At that exact moment, Jacie's fingers tightened. "What's that?"

"Where?"

"Down there," she said, her voice tight, strained. "In that J-shaped curve. I thought I saw a reflection of light off something metal." Her gaze didn't waver as Trey circled around and brought the chopper closer.

Zach peered out his side of the aircraft as the chopper banked back to the left. "I see it. We won't get any closer in this. We'll have to find a clearing to land."

Trey rose again, his head turning back and forth. "I can't land here. I'll have to take it back the way we came a bit."

Jacie rocked in her seat. "It might be her. Oh, dear Lord, let it be Tracie."

In the middle of making a wide circle, a loud bang caused the helicopter to lurch to the side.

"Holy crap! Our rudder's been hit." Trey's urgent announcement riffled through Zach's headset. "I'm losing directional control. I have to land now, before I lose it all. Brace yourself."

As the chopper started a slow spin, Jacie stared at Trey struggling with the controls. Then she looked at Zach.

He turned toward her and cupped her face. "Hold on. I gotcha." He let his fingers slide down her arm and he clutched her hand again, bending forward, and urging her to do the same.

The helicopter rotors turned, easing the aircraft down between the tight walls of the canyon.

If they tipped even slightly to either side, the blades would hit the rocks and that would be the end of their search and possibly the end of their lives.

Zach wanted to pull Jacie into his arms and protect her from the rough landing, but they were better off trusting the seat belts. He'd save the embrace for when they landed safely.

The ground seemed to spin up to meet them faster than Zach liked. At the last moment before the skids hit the uneven surface, he prayed the first prayer he'd made since Toni's death.

The chopper hit the ground, jolting Zach so hard his teeth rattled. The scent of aviation fuel filled the air. He waited several seconds for any shifting before he flung off his belt and reached for Jacie's.

"I can't get it to unbuckle." Her hands shook as she fought with the release clamp.

Zach brushed aside her fingers and flicked it open, then dragged her across the seat and out into the open, away from the damaged craft.

Trey shut down the engine and scrambled out of the pilot's seat. Richard joined him beside Zach and Jacie.

Everyone tugged their headsets off and stared at the downed helicopter.

"What happened?" Richard asked.

"I'd get closer to investigate, but with fuel leaking, it's

best to stay back until we're sure it won't create a fire."
Trey sucked in a deep breath and let it out, visibly shaken
by the experience. "I've never had that happen here."

"Why did the helicopter shake so hard before it lost the
rudder?" Jacie asked.

"We were hit by something, hard in the tail."

"What? A bird?"

"No, more like a rocket."

"Who in the hell has rockets out here?" Richard demanded.

Zach's body grew rigid. "Maybe we shouldn't stand so
close to the helicopter and seek some cover. The cartels
have this kind of ammunition. Either provided illegally
by the black market or stolen from the Mexican Army.
Whatever, we're in hostile territory and should treat it as
such." He grabbed Jacie's hand and dragged her toward
an outcropping.

The woman dug her heels into the rocky soil. "No. We
can't give up the search now. What about the metal reflection? It could be a vehicle. They could be holding Tracie
nearby." She jerked her hand free and headed back the
way they'd come in the chopper. "We have to check it out."

Zach sighed. She was right. Though he didn't like the
idea of being trapped in a canyon with the possibility of
being shot at, he had to either catch up with Jacie or risk
her being taken as easily as her sister, or killed like the
DEA Agents.

"Will you at least wait over there in the shadows until
I get some more firepower?"

She frowned. "You can't go back to the chopper. It
might explode."

He smiled. "I'd rather risk an explosion than walk off
into a desert canyon underarmed."

She bit her bottom lip for a moment. "Okay, but hurry."

Zach nodded to Richard. "Get her over there, will ya?"

The Big Elk Ranch owner's brows furrowed. "Let me get the guns. No use you losing it on my chopper."

"Please, just make sure she's under cover."

"I'm coming with you," Trey insisted.

Zach rushed back to the chopper, grabbed four weapons hooked over the backs of the seat. He tossed two rifles to Trey and checked the other two. Each was fully loaded, safeties on. With the weapons slung over his shoulder, he and Trey ran back to where Richard and Jacie stood in the shadows of the overhanging cliffs.

Zach handed Jacie a rifle. "Know how to use one?"

She snorted. "You have to ask?"

"She's a better shot than I am," Richard admitted, taking the rifle Trey handed him. "Let's go."

On the alert for any movement, high or low, Zach took point. If they'd been shot down by a rocket, no telling what other armament the cartel had in their arsenal. He didn't like being at the bottom of the canyon, basically sitting ducks for anyone standing guard on the rim. They didn't have much choice if they wanted to get to the point where Jacie had spotted the metal reflection.

"Up ahead," Jacie called out in a husky whisper. "That's the lower end of the J-shaped crevice. What I spotted was just on the other side of that curve." She hurried to catch up with Zach.

His arm shot out and clotheslined her at the chest. He pressed a finger to his lips and waited until she made eye contact with him. "I'll take lead. No use all of us charging in and getting shot. Let me scout ahead and see what's up there. I'll whistle if all's clear."

"But—"

Zach held up his hand. "One person can move silently. Four have less of a chance."

Richard's hands descended on Jacie's shoulders. "He's right. In fact, maybe we should wait and let the FBI or DEA go in. They are better trained and equipped to handle a situation like this."

"I can do this," Zach reassured him.

Jacie nodded. "Let him. He knows what he's doing. I'll stay until you whistle."

Zach took off, the rifle slung over his shoulder, his handgun in his right hand, safety off, ready for whatever lay ahead.

He eased through the shadows, careful not to disturb the loose rocks and gravel as he rounded the corner of the rocky escarpment. On the ground beside him, he noted tire tracks. Whoever had come this way had come on what looked like an ATV. One larger than the four-wheeler back at the canyon rim.

Zach stopped several times to listen. Not a single noise reached him or echoed off the walls of the canyon. He moved forward and finally rounded the curve leading back the other way. An all-terrain vehicle with seating for four stood smashed against a rock. Two bodies lay motionless, one slumped over the steering wheel, the other crumpled down in the passenger seat.

Without making a sound. Zach stood so still he could have blended in with the rocks themselves, his gaze panning the immediate vicinity and the rocky ledges above. Nothing moved; nothing made a sound. Several vultures circled high above.

Zach stepped out into the open, crouched low, ready to duck and run if shots rang out. He eased over to the vehicle and checked for a pulse. Both men were dead, their bodies stiff, skin purple and eyes sunken. Rigor mortis had set in. These men had been dead for at least four hours.

Zach climbed halfway up a slope and stared around. As far as he could tell, he was alone.

As he puckered to whistle, a movement caught his eye at the base near the corner he'd just come around.

He reached for the rifle and stopped when he realized it was Jacie, doing as he'd done, easing around the base of the canyon walls, sticking to the shadows.

Zach's jaw tightened and he slipped quietly down the slope coming up behind Jacie as she worked her way toward the vehicle, her attention on the bodies within, not the world around her.

Zach waited between two rocks until she came within range.

"Bang. You're dead," he said.

Chapter Six

Jacie gasped and swung her rifle around.

Before she could point it and pull the trigger, the man hiding in the crevice knocked the weapon from her hands, spun her back around, twisting her arm up between her shoulder blades. He cinched his arm around her neck, limiting her air.

"Let me go." She bucked against his hold, her body stiff, her feet kicking outward to throw him off balance. "Or I'll—"

He held her steady, as if she were nothing but a child. "Or you'll what?" he whispered against her ear. "You're in no position to threaten or bargain."

"Zach?" She froze, all the fight left her and she sagged against him. "Damn it, Zach, you scared the crap out of me."

He turned her in his arms, refusing to release her yet. And frankly Jacie was glad. She hadn't liked it when he'd walked away and stayed gone for so long she thought he'd fallen over a cliff or had been captured. His strong arms around her brought back that feeling of safety at the same time it spelled danger of a completely different kind.

"I could have been one of the drug runners." He brushed his thumb over her cheek, pushing a strand of her hair that had escaped her ponytail behind her ear. "You could have been shot and killed or worse—taken in by the same terrorists who have your sister."

Her breath hitched in her throat, and her blood rushed through her veins like the Rio Grande in flood stages. His body pressed to hers, warm, sexy and overwhelming. "You've made your point. I should have stayed put."

"Yes, you should have."

"I couldn't stand waiting, not knowing whether you were all right, or if you'd found Tracie." She stared up into his eyes.

He kissed her, a brief brush of his lips, and set her at arm's length. "She's not here."

JACIE'S LIPS TINGLED and she fought back the urge to cry. Instead she squared her shoulders. "So, what's all this?" She waved her hand toward the abandoned vehicle and the dead men. "What can we learn from what we found? There has to be a clue as to who took her." She moved toward the four-by-four, bracing herself for what she'd see. The two dead men last night had been partially cloaked in darkness and still looked fairly normal. These two had been dead longer and were a waxy zombielike purple. "How long do you suppose they've been here?" Her gag reflex threatened to choke her.

"At least four hours. Maybe longer."

"Not long after they took Tracie," Jacie noted. A shiver shook her from head to toe. She had to remind herself that Tracie might not be here, but at least she wasn't one of the bodies left behind.

"Holy hell, Jacie, don't ever do that again." Richard burst into the open, huffing and puffing, followed by Trey. Behind them Humberto and Bruce emerged.

"We brought reinforcements," Trey offered.

Bruce stepped forward and studied the two bodies without touching them. "Looks like members of La Familia Diablos."

Zach stiffened, his face going pale beneath his tan.

Had Jacie not looked at him at that exact moment, she'd have missed his reaction to Bruce's words.

"How do you know?" Jacie asked.

Bruce pointed to the tattoo on the driver's right shoulder, the tail of a dragon dipping below his T-shirt sleeve. "The Diablos all have a dragon tattoo on their right arms. If you push the other man's sleeve up, you'll likely find one similar to this one."

"I'll take your word for it." Jacie had no intention of touching either of the two dead men. Instead she inched toward Zach, taking comfort in his presence. "Why would they kill their own people?"

"Who said they did?" Bruce glanced across the dead man at Jacie. "There are two crime families in this area—Los Lobos and La Familia Diablos. Any chance they get to kill each other off, they'll take it. My bet is the Diablos took Tracie and the Los Lobos ambushed them. Since Tracie isn't here among the dead, thank God, they must have her in the Los Lobos camp."

Humberto stood to the side, his eyes narrowed, his face grim. "The Diablos will avenge their *compadres'* deaths."

"Will they attack Los Lobos?" Jacie's hand reached for Zach's.

"Probably," Bruce responded. "It'll be a bloodbath."

Her fingers tightened around Zach's. "Then we have to get to Tracie before the Diablos do."

"It's not that easy," Zach said quietly. "I've heard they have tightly guarded compounds on the other side of the border. No one gets in or out without running a gauntlet of killer guards."

"But we can't give up now." Jacie stared toward the

south as if she could see the camp from where they stood in the canyon. "Tracie's still alive. I just know it. But for how long…" She turned back to Zach.

His face was set in grim lines and his lips remained tightly shut.

"There's nothing you can do but let the FBI and DEA handle this." Bruce touched Jacie's shoulder. "I'll get with them and explain my assessment. They'll decide whether or not to launch an attack and when. But as far as you and the members of the Big Elk Ranch are concerned, you should step back and let the pros handle it from here."

Zach's fingers tightened painfully around Jacie's.

"But—" Jacie couldn't let it go. She just couldn't stand back and do nothing.

"Jacie." Zach tugged her hand and forced her to face him. "He's right."

Bruce took charge. "You guys can double up on the four-wheelers to get back to the truck. Humberto and I can stay until two of you can come back to get us."

Zach raised a hand. "Jacie and I will stay back."

"I'd rather get her out of the canyon. If there was even a chance either of the gangs is still here, she'd be in danger. It's bad enough one of the Kosart women is already a captive." Bruce turned to Humberto. "You're okay with staying, aren't you?"

"No," Richard said. "The men killed last night and Tracie were my responsibility. I should be the one to stay with Mr. Masterson. Besides, Humberto needs to lead the way out of the canyon."

"I'd rather keep Humberto. No offense, Mr. Giddings. He's probably faster on his feet."

Richard's eyes narrowed. "You might be right about that. I'm not getting any younger." He turned to Zach and Jacie. "Come on, the sooner we get the two of you out of here, the sooner I can get back down here and retrieve these two gentlemen."

Jacie wanted to argue, but she didn't know what else they could do without horses or additional four-wheelers to track the men responsible for kidnapping Tracie. She climbed on one of the ATVs and pressed the start button.

Zach slung his leg over the back and sat behind her, his arms circling her waist, holding on tight.

Without a word, she twisted the throttle and the cycle shot forward.

Zach's arms tightened, his hard, muscled chest pressing against Jacie's back. It wasn't long before they climbed the narrow trail out of the canyon and came to a stop beside the truck and trailer.

Jacie waited for Zach to dismount before she got off.

Richard and Trey topped the rise and pulled up beside them. Trey climbed off.

"I'm going back for Humberto," Richard said.

"I'm going with you." Jacie turned the four-wheeler in a tight circle.

When she came to a halt, Zach grabbed her handlebar. "Let Trey." His stare was intense.

She'd hoped to check out the murder scene one last time before she gave up and called their search a failure. "No, I want to go."

"Jacie." Richard pulled up beside her. "Trey can handle this. You stay here." It wasn't a request. Her boss meant business.

She got off the bike.

Trey mounted and the two men rode back down into the canyon.

As they disappeared over the ridgeline, Jacie's vision blurred, and she fought back tears of anger and frustration. "I thought you were supposed to help me."

"I am." Zach gripped her arms and turned her to face him. "There's more to this than either of us can handle on our own."

"But she's my sister!" Jacie pounded her fists against his chest. "I can't just stand by and do nothing."

"We won't. We can do some work behind the scenes. There has to be people on the ranch or in the town who know what's going on and can help us find your sister."

"You think we can learn anything back there?" Jacie waved at the canyon. "Tracie disappeared there."

"But she knew enough to follow those men into the canyon. She knew something, and we need to find out what it was. It might be the key to who took her and where they might be holding her." Zach pulled her into his arms. "Hank hired me because he had faith in my abilities as an agent. He trusted me to do the job." Zach tipped her chin up and stared into her eyes. "I need you to trust me too."

This man hadn't shown her much of anything yet. How could she trust him? She knew nothing about him. For a long moment Jacie stared up into Zach's dark gaze. Something about the way he held her and the sorrow buried deep in his liquid brown eyes made her say, "I trust you."

For several long seconds, he held her, his gaze unwavering. Then he bent his head and kissed her.

Jacie should have pushed him away, but that rational idea didn't even enter her head. Instead she wrapped her arms around his neck and dragged him closer, needing the comfort of his arms, the pressure of his mouth on hers, if only to chase away the fear of losing her only sister.

But it was more than that. This man had known suffering. His heart still bore the scars, and despite his apparent effort to hide them, he wore them on his sleeve.

All thoughts melted away as the kiss deepened. Jacie's

tongue pushed past Zach's teeth and slid along his, thrusting and tasting the hint of coffee and mint.

His fingers dug into her buttocks, smashing her against him, the evidence of her effect on him pressing into her belly.

Jacie didn't know how long they stood, locked in the embrace. The world around them faded away, leaving them alone, until the sound of a hawk crying out overhead dragged her back to the real world.

She forced her hands between them and pushed against his chest. "What are we doing?"

Zach ran a hand through his hair and sighed. "I'm sorry. That shouldn't have happened...."

"Again," she concluded. "Why can't I keep my hands off you?" She stared down at the offending digits. "This effort isn't about you and me. It's about bringing my sister back alive."

"And the sooner we get back to civilization, we can work on that."

A hole the size of Texas opened in Jacie's heart and she looked across at Zach. "We will get her back, won't we?"

"We will." Zach's gaze bore into hers, his dark brown eyes so intense they appeared black. If anyone would fight to free her sister, Zach would. But he'd do it his way. Not ride off without a plan.

ZACH SAT IN the backseat of the king cab pickup with Jacie beside him. Richard drove, Humberto rode shotgun and Bruce and Trey sat in the truck bed. Since the others had returned, Zach hadn't spoken a word, his mind churning over what he'd learned and the information he still required to determine the whereabouts of Tracie Kosart.

As Bruce had said, the dead men in the four-by-four had been members of the Diablos. As soon as Zach had seen

the tattoos, he'd known. He'd studied the gangs prior to
taking the assignment to infiltrate the Diablos gang area in
the border town of El Paso. He and Toni had crossed into
Juarez as honeymooning tourists. Only someone in the bureau must have leaked the fact that they were undercover
agents. Within twenty-four hours, they'd been captured
and the rest was the awful history he would never forget.

His hands clenched into fists. If Los Lobos knew Tracie was FBI, she'd be in for the same treatment as Toni.

Zach's gut knotted. He vowed to himself to find her before they went too far. He glanced at Jacie. She was better
off not knowing what her sister faced. It would only make
her more reckless and determined to go to her sister's rescue. One lone woman against an army of thugs.

She sat quietly staring out the window as if she might
see her sister walk out across the dry Texas land. Her forehead was creased with worry lines.

As soon as they got back to the ranch, Zach would start
asking questions. If there were cartel members crossing
the border nearby, there were cartel members on the U.S.
side aiding them.

As soon as the truck pulled up to the Big Elk Lodge,
Zach jumped down and rounded the truck to assist Jacie.
She'd already slipped from her seat and stood beside the
truck. "What next?"

Zach cupped her elbow and turned toward the other
men. "If you need us, we'll be in town." He gave half a
smile. "Seems I left home in such a hurry I forgot a few
things I hope to pick up at the local stores."

"We have shaving cream, razors and toothbrushes in
the lodge, if that's what you're missing," Richard offered.

"Thanks, but I'd rather go to town." Zach winked at the
owner of the Big Elk. "Getting away will help keep Jacie
occupied while the FBI and DEA do their thing."

Richard nodded at Jacie. "Don't worry, darlin'. They'll get her back."

Jacie's lips formed a tight smile. "I know." Her entire countenance read *failure is not an option*. Zach could have kissed her again. She was strong and tough. The few tears she'd shed had been more out of frustration and real fear for her sister's life.

"Come on, honeycakes." He led her away from the group toward the tiny cabin where she lived. "We'll take my truck. It's not as well known around town."

"Where are we going?"

"To Wild Oak Canyon."

She let him open her door as she turned to face him. "Why are we really going to town?"

"Your sister came to visit, and from what it looks and sounds like, she had an idea that something was going to go down last night, or she wouldn't have insisted on riding out with you and the two DEA agents."

"So what does that have to do with going to town?"

"How did she find out about who and what might be happening?"

"Through her contacts at the FBI?"

"It might have started there, but she wasn't the only one around here who knew something was going to happen. Those DEA agents wouldn't have gone down into that canyon without backup if they'd thought they were in danger."

"You think they were expecting to meet someone who wasn't going to be shooting at them?"

"Yes." Zach rounded the truck and climbed up into the driver's seat. "There have to be other people nearby who knew what was going to happen. Cartel members like to brag about their kills and ambushes." He paused with his fingers on the key in the ignition. "If we find the right people, we might discover who knows something, like who's responsible and where they're holding your sister."

Jacie's eyes lit. "Then what are we waiting for? Go!"

Zach twisted the key and set the truck in motion, heading down the long, dusty gravel driveway. "Now, don't get your hopes up. Cartel members tend to be pretty close-lipped around strangers."

Jacie slammed a fist into her palm. "Then we'll beat the information out of them."

Zach chuckled. "That's my girl. Tough as nails and soft as silk."

Her cheeks flamed. "I'm not your girl," she muttered. "And I'm not soft." She stared at her work-roughened fingers. "And 'honeycakes'? Really, was that all you could come up with?"

Zach chuckled, betting she was soft in all the right places, and "honeycakes" was perfect.

He shook himself and forced his attention back to the road, headed into Wild Oak Canyon.

"Where does everyone go at one point or another to talk or share a cup of coffee?"

"That would be Cara Jo's Diner," Jacie said. "She's a friend of mine. Everyone has dinner there at least once a week to catch up on everyone else's business."

"Good. We'll start there."

Chapter Seven

Jacie entered the diner first, her nostrils filling with the comforting smells of meat loaf, roasted chicken and fried okra. Once Zach passed through the door and it closed behind him, Jacie paused, closed her eyes and inhaled deeply, letting the aromas calm her.

"Smells like home."

Jacie opened her eyes and tipped her head toward Zach. A smile tugged at the corners of his lips.

This was perhaps the first clue he'd given her about his life outside his work. "Did your mother make her kitchen smell that good?"

"Always. She loved to cook and we always had great food." His smile faded. "I miss her."

"What happened?"

"She and my father had me late in life. And all that good cooking clogged their arteries." He sighed. "They died within months of each other. Mom couldn't imagine life without Dad." Something about the grim set of his lips spoke more than his words.

"Where were you during all this?" Jacie asked.

"I wasn't there when Dad had his heart attack."

"Were you working for the FBI then?"

He nodded.

"Undercover?"

Again he nodded. "I didn't know until it was almost too late to see my mother before she passed too."

Jacie's chest tightened. She and Tracie had lost both their parents to an automobile accident. "At least you got to say goodbye to your mother," she said quietly. Then she squared her shoulders. "How about that booth in the corner?"

"I'd prefer to sit at the bar. We might learn more there."

"Right."

As she strode across the floor, Cara Jo, the diner's owner, pushed open the swinging door to the kitchen with her hip and carried a large tray full of steaming entrees to a table of cowboys. "I'll be with you in a minute. Seat yourself," she called out.

Cara Jo's shoulder-length, light brown hair swung as she spun around in her cute little waitress outfit. The retro-styled dress that hadn't fazed Jacie in the least in the past suddenly made her more aware of her dusty jeans and even dirtier shirt. Her face probably had the same layer of grime and her hair... "We'll take a seat at the bar," Jacie said.

"Suit yourself." Cara Jo laid out one full plate at a time in front of the cowboys. No sooner had she set a plate on the colorful gingham tablecloth than a cowboy practically stabbed her with a fork, diving into the vittles.

Jacie chuckled. "Cara Jo has the best food in the county."

"Isn't this the only diner in the county?"

"Only one that's stayed in business. People come back when the food's this good." She stopped at the bar. "I'm going to wash up. I'll be right back."

"Me, too. I can still smell aviation fuel and dead men." Zach wrinkled his nose. "Back in two shakes."

While Zach headed for the men's room, Jacie pushed through the door of the ladies' room.

What she saw in the mirror was worse than she'd imagined. Brown hair stuck out of the loosened ponytail, in complete disarray, windblown, not in a good way, and tinged gray with dust. Her face had a layer of fine Texas sand over it, giving her a sun-dried, tanned look that wasn't any more appealing than it sounded. When she patted her shirt, a cloud rose from her and she coughed.

Holy hell, you'd think she had more pride than to show up in town looking like…well, like one of the cowboys. People expected the men to look wind worn and filthy. But a woman was supposed to have more pride.

She squared her shoulders and stared into the mirror. "Why do I care? My sister is missing and no one really cares about how I look." Except herself. She yanked the ponytail out of her hair, bent over, her long brown hair hanging down, and ran her fingers through the thick tresses, shaking out the dust. When she flipped it back, it was better. Not great, but better.

She patted her shirt, flapped it to get the dust to fly loose, then slapped at her jeans. The light in the room grew hazy.

"This is crazy. It's not like the man sees me as anything more than the job." She sighed. "Oy, but that kiss…"

Jacie splashed her face with water from the sink, wishing she had a little lip gloss to coat her dry lips. Who was she kidding?

Semisatisfied that she didn't look like a complete loser, she stepped out of the bathroom and ran into a hard wall of muscle.

Zach caught her in his arms and steadied her. "Do you always talk to yourself in the bathroom?"

Her cheeks burned and she grimaced up at him. "Are the walls that thin?"

He nodded.

Mortified, she couldn't bring herself to ask how much

he'd overheard. "Well, then, we should start our investigation." She hurried past him, hoping he'd only heard her mumbling.

"Just so you know, you're not just the job," he called out softly behind her.

Jacie was sure her face couldn't get any hotter. She plopped into a bar stool and gave Cara Jo all her attention. "Could I get a glass of ice water?"

"You bet. Guess it's getting pretty hot out there already." Cara Jo snagged a full, frosty pitcher, poured two glasses of ice water and set them in front of Jacie and Zach. "Jacie, sweetie, who's your handsome friend?"

Jacie stiffened at Cara Jo's flirty query. "Zach Adams."

"Her boyfriend from college," Zach interjected.

Cara Jo's eyebrows furrowed, a smile playing at her lips. "You never told me you had a boyfriend from college." Still holding the pitcher of water, she planted her fist on one hip and looked down her nose. "Come on, tell all."

"Not much to tell." Jacie hated lying to her only friend outside the Big Elk Ranch. "We met in college."

"Well, it must have been more than a chance meeting for him to show up here after all these years."

"I missed her." Zach slid an arm around Jacie's waist, his breath stirring the hairs around her neck, making gooseflesh rise on her arms.

Jacie couldn't continue the lie and she had more important things on her mind. She sucked in a long, steadying breath. "Cara Jo, Tracie's missing."

Cara Jo plunked the pitcher on the counter. "Oh, my God. How? When?" She reached across the counter and gathered Jacie's hands in hers. "Oh, baby, you must be beside yourself. And to think, she was just in here the day before yesterday."

"That's when she got in town." Jacie gave her the bare-bones details of what had occurred since.

"Holy hell, Jacie, you were almost killed." She rounded the counter and hugged her friend. "What about Tracie? Do you have any idea where they might have taken her? Have the FBI and DEA arrived? Have they mounted a search and rescue?"

Jacie gave a wry chuckle. "Slow down, will ya? We have no idea where they took her and yes, the FBI and DEA are on it. But I can't just sit around and wait for them to find her. I have to do something."

"Honey, what *can* you do? You're not trained to fight the Mexican cartel. Hell, even the soldiers and agencies who *are* can't seem to slow them down." Cara Jo stopped talking when she looked Jacie in the face. "Sorry. I'm not helping, am I?" She squeezed Jacie's shoulders and stepped back around the counter. "What can I do? Want me to join the search party? I will."

"No." Jacie shook her head. "They want me to stay out of it. What I need is to find out anything I can about when my sister came to town. Did she talk to anyone? Meet anyone here in the diner? Say anything?"

Cara Jo pinched the bridge of her nose. "She asked for directions to the Big Elk Ranch…. Think, Cara." For a long moment she said nothing. Finally she looked up. "I seem to recall her talking to a man outside the diner."

"Did you see him? Who was it?"

"I don't know. He was dark haired, maybe Hispanic. Not very tall." Cara Jo's eyes widened. "Wait a minute. If I remember correctly, someone was sitting at the window booth staring out at the same time Tracie was talking to the man." Cara Jo's lips twisted into a grimace. "Oh, yeah. It was Bull Sarly. Maybe you can get that cantankerous old man to tell you who it was."

Jacie bit her lip. "All we can do is try. Maybe if he knows how important it is to find her quickly..."

"Yeah." Cara Jo snorted. "Good luck with that." She raised a finger. "If you're planning on going out there, I have something you'll need." She hurried into the kitchen and emerged a minute later with a wad of white butcher paper. "You'll need this."

Jacie smiled. "Thanks."

"Cara Jo, can you remember anything else?" Zach asked. "A conversation, maybe not between Tracie and anyone else, but one that might have to do with a meeting in Wild Horse Canyon?"

Cara Jo shook her head. "Nothing like that. I'll tell you what, though, the whole time your sister was here, she kept fiddling with her cell phone. She'd press a button, put it to her ear and then take it down and end the call before it even had time to ring. I thought it was weird at the time but figured the line was busy or something."

"Cara Jo." A pretty blonde with a miniature version of herself sitting beside her in a booth waved her hand. "Can I get a cup of milk for Lily?"

Jacie's friend smiled at the woman and called out, "Got it." Then she focused on Jacie again. "Hey, would you like to meet Kate and Lily? They just moved into the old Kendrick place."

"Maybe next time I'm in town." Jacie liked meeting people, but her sister took priority over socializing.

"I understand." Cara Jo pulled a carton of milk out of a refrigerator under the counter and poured a plastic cup full, snapped a lid on it and stuck in a straw. "It was good to meet you, Zach. I'd hang around and chat, but I have to work. My waitress called in sick. Let me know if I can do anything to help. I can shut down the diner in a heartbeat and be ready."

"Thanks, Cara Jo. I'd appreciate it if you'd keep your ears open." Jacie reached across the bar and squeezed Cara Jo's hand. "If anything comes up in a conversation that might relate to Tracie's disappearance, call me."

"You bet I will."

While Cara Jo waited on the tables, Jacie swallowed some of the ice water and stood. "Let's go find Bull Sarly."

"I take it you know the man." Zach cupped her elbow and escorted her from the diner as if she were dressed in a fine dress at a cocktail party instead of wearing jeans and a dusty T-shirt.

Jacie hated to admit it, but she liked it. After working at the ranch for the past few years, she'd almost forgotten what it was like to be treated like a lady. She'd made it a point to be one of the guys. The men trusted her as a guide more if she looked like one of them. For a long time, it had seemed like an asset, her ability to blend in with the menfolk. Since she'd met Zach, the ability seemed more a liability.

ZACH PULLED OUT onto Main Street. "Where does Mr. Sarly live?"

Jacie blew out a breath. "On a small plot of land west of town. Out by the dump." She glanced at Zach. "Let me warn you, he's a cranky old geezer. Never has anything good to say about anyone. We'll be lucky if he tells us anything. Hell, we'll be lucky to get past his rottweiler, Mo."

"We'll manage." Zach had been shot at, beat up and tortured in his line of work. What kind of grief could one cranky old man give him that he hadn't already overcome?

Five miles west of the town of Wild Oak Canyon, Jacie motioned for him to pull off the road onto a rutted track that looked more like a shallow ravine than a road. It wound through clumps of saw palmetto and prickly pear cactus, the vegetation like so much concertina wire strung along a perimeter.

"I take it Mr. Sarly doesn't get many visitors," Zach remarked, bracing himself for a meeting with the man.

"He doesn't want any. He's said as much."

"Sometimes a man might push others away to keep from being hurt. Perhaps Mr. Sarly was hurt by a woman or lost someone he loved and hasn't gotten over it."

"Uh-huh. Or he's just plain cranky and doesn't like people at all. I always give him the benefit of the doubt. But he always gives it right back in my face." Jacie shook her head. "You can't please all of the people."

"True." As they rounded a patch of scrawny mesquite trees, a tired, gray-weathered wooden house came into view. Sitting on the porch with a shotgun in his lap was a big man wearing only a faded pair of blue jeans and old brogan boots. His gut hung over his waistband and his long gray, shaggy hair blended into an equally long and shaggy beard, neither of which had been combed or cut in at least a decade. A husky red-and-black rottweiler lounged on the porch beside the man's chair, seemingly unconcerned by the approach of a strange vehicle.

Zach pulled to a halt out of range of the shotgun's blast.

When Jacie moved to open her door, Zach held out a hand. "I'll handle this."

"But—"

"Please."

Jacie shrugged. "Here, you might want this." She handed him the package wrapped in white butcher paper he'd all but forgotten.

With a frown, Zach held up the package. "What's this for?"

She grinned. "The dog."

As soon as Zach's boots touched the ground, the dog leaped off the deck and raced toward him.

"Throw the package," Jacie yelled.

Without thinking, Zach did as Jacie said and threw the package at the dog.

The rottweiler ground to a halt, sniffed at the offering and then clamped his teeth around it. He then trotted off into the brush.

"Damned good-fer-nothin' hound," Bull Sarly grumbled from the porch.

After the dog left, Zach headed for the porch. "Mr. Sarly."

"Ain't no mister up here."

"Bull Sarly?" Zach continued toward the man with the shotgun.

"That'd be me. Ya got twenty seconds to state yer piece. Take that numbskull that long to rip into whatever you brought for him. And I'll be shootin' whatever's left after the dog's finished with ya."

"Then I'll speak fast." Zach never let his gaze drift from the old man's. He studied the way the gnarled fingers tightened around the worn wooden stalk of the gun in his lap, anticipating any aggressive move on the other man's part.

"Tracie Kosart was kidnapped yesterday by Mexican cartel."

"So? I ain't no Mexican cartel. Get off my property."

"You were at the diner day before yesterday when she came in."

"Man's got a right to eat." He held up a hand. "You can stop right there."

Zach halted at the base of the steps, directly in front of the old man, his jaw tight, his knees bent slightly, ready to spring. "Before she came into the diner, she spoke with a short Hispanic man. You sat in the booth staring out at them. Can you identify the man?"

"I could…" The old man stuck a straw in his mouth and sneered. "If I gave a rat's behind."

Zach's blood boiled. While this man lorded himself over them, Tracie Kosart could be suffering horrible torture. Frustrations of the past day, no, the past two years exploded in one flying leap.

Zach climbed the steps, grabbed the shotgun, jerked it out of the curmudgeon's hands and flung it across the yard. Then he lifted the man to his feet and slammed him up against the wall of the house. "How about right now?"

The man's eyes bulged, his face and body breaking out in a sweat. "You ain't got no right to push me around on my own property. I'll have your job for this. Let me go," he gasped, scratching at the fingers pressing into his windpipe.

"You're assuming I care about my job." Zach pushed the man higher up the wall until his feet dangled. "I don't. However, I do care about finding a woman who could very well be raped, tortured and killed. Preferably before all three of those things happen." He shook the man. "Now, are you going to tell me something that will help me find her, or do I make you sorry you didn't?"

"Zach. Don't." Jacie's voice called out behind him.

"Listen to the girl," Sarly whined. "Won't do you no good if you knock me out or kill me."

"Please." Jacie's hand touched Zach's arm.

A blast of calm washed over Zach's raging nerves. Still, he wanted to beat someone's head in, and Bull Sarly was just enough of a pain in the butt to deserve it.

The hand on his arm tightened. "He's not worth going to jail over," she whispered.

"And your sister's not worth saving?" Zach rasped.

"Yes, she is, but this isn't going to help."

"Sister?" Bull stared from Zach to Jacie. "You didn't say nothin' 'bout that woman being yer sister. Let me down. Maybe I know somethin'."

Zach held him there a second longer, then let go so fast the man slid down the wall before his legs engaged and held up his bulk.

"Talk fast. A woman's life depends on us finding her sooner than later."

Jacie stepped up to the man and touched his arm. "Mr. Sarly, the cartel took my sister. We think she might have spoken to someone the day she came to town who might know where they would have taken her. Please." Her eyes filled with tears. "She's my only living relative. I'd do anything to save her."

A growl sounded behind Zach.

As Sarly had indicated, once the dog had finished the treat, he was back and ready to take up where he'd left off.

Zach pulled the pistol from his shoulder holster and aimed it at the dog. "Call him off or I'll shoot him."

"Don't." Sarly raised a hand. "Like your sister, Mo is the only family I have." He gave the rottweiler a stern look. "Sit."

A long moment passed as the dog growled low in its throat, knowing a threat when he saw it and ready to launch an attack to the death.

Zach's weapon remained trained on the dog.

"Sit, damn you." Sarly pushed to his feet and took a step toward the dog.

Mo squatted on his haunches, his lip still pulled back in a menacing snarl.

"Good boy." The older man patted his leg. "Come."

The dog trotted up the steps to his master and sat at his feet.

Zach let out the breath he'd been holding. He liked dogs and hadn't wanted to shoot the creature. But he would have, if it was Jacie's or his life over the dog's.

"Look, I don't want nothin' to happen to yer sister, any more than you do." Bull scratched his beard. "I seem to recall her lookin' just like you and I really thought it was you until she asked for directions to the Big Elk." He snorted. "Didn't even know you had a twin."

Jacie gave him the hint of a smile. "Not many people do."

"Did you recognize the man she spoke to outside the diner?" Zach pushed. The clock was ticking and they hadn't gotten any closer to finding Tracie.

"I thought it strange that you—" he nodded toward Jacie "—would be talking to a man from the wrong side of town. What with you working out at the Big Elk with yer hotshot clients."

Zach stepped toward Sarly. "Get to the point."

Sarly glared at Zach. "Back off and I will." He faced Jacie, his features softening. "I had a sister once." He sighed. "The guy she was talkin' to was Juan Alvarez. I know that 'cause he used to work at the feed store with Henry Franks. Franks fired him when he didn't show up for two days. What with all the traffickin' goin' on round here, he figured Juan was involved, and Henry didn't want no part of that."

"Juan Alvarez." Jacie glanced across at Zach. "I know who that is."

"Then let's go." Zach was already off the porch and halfway to the truck when he realized Jacie wasn't right behind him.

She stood on the porch with Mr. Sarly, shaking his hand and smiling. "Thank you, Mr. Sarly. You don't know how much I appreciate your help. If ever there's anything I can do for you, let me know."

His ruddy older face reddened even more. "Well, now. Next time you come bring ol' Mo some of whatever you brought this time. He seemed to like it right plenty."

Jacie patted Bull's hand and hurried toward the truck, climbing in without a word.

As they pulled away, Zach glanced in his mirror at the man retrieving his shotgun.

Zach's first instinct was to slam his foot to the accelerator. But the man just held it in one hand, patted the dog with the other and watched as they pulled out of sight.

The truck bumped along the rutted track to the highway, where Zach stopped and turned toward Jacie. "Where to?"

"The south side of Wild Oak Canyon. From what I know, Juan lives in a not-so-safe neighborhood on the edge of town. You'll want to make sure your gun is loaded and you're ready to fire."

Chapter Eight

Jacie's heart raced as they sped toward town. "Is this what FBI agents do? Follow clues, one step at a time to find a missing person or apprehend a suspect?"

"Yes."

Her hands twisted in her lap as she studied Zach, hoping to catch a glimpse of the former agent in him. Perhaps that would help her to understand what drew her sister to join the FBI. "Doesn't it get tedious and frustrating?"

"Yes." The word was short, with no telltale expression or anything a person could read in to.

Jacie frowned. "Anyone ever tell you that you don't talk much?"

His lips twitched. "Yes."

Jacie's stomach flipped. When he wasn't looking all fierce and deadly, the man was downright handsome.

"Are you always so forceful when you question people?" she pressed.

The hint of a smile disappeared. "Only when I'm out of time and patience."

A heavy weight pressed down on Jacie's shoulders. "Do you think we'll be too late?"

His foot lifted from the accelerator and he stared across at Jacie, his lips thin, his eyes narrowed. "No." Then he jammed his boot on the gas and the truck shot forward, faster than before. "At this point, we go all or nothing. Doubt can't be a factor. Got that?" He shot a stern frown at her, his nostrils flaring.

"You're right. My mother used to tell us not to borrow trouble." She sat back, the intensity of his stare making her glad he was on her side.

They blew into town, exceeding the speed limits, but Jacie didn't care.

"Turn left at the next street," she said.

Zach took the corner a little too fast. The bed of the truck skidded around behind them, leaving a trail of rubber in the hot pavement.

They passed houses along the road, the exteriors diminishing in care and upkeep the closer they got to the edge of town, until all that was left was a smattering of crumbling shacks and even seedier mobile homes.

"Next right." Jacie pulled her cowboy hat low on her forehead and tucked her hair beneath.

Zach nodded his approval. "You're learning."

Men sat on porches or lounged in old lawn chairs; some stood around the shade trees. A small child played in the dirt, his hair shaggy, his clothes unkempt.

As Zach passed, narrowed gazes followed the shiny pickup's progress.

Jacie squirmed at the attention, not at all comfortable. "Is it safe to stop here?"

"If Juan is here, we need to find him. Safe or not. Maybe I should take you back to the Big Elk before I conduct business."

"No." Jacie sat up straighter. "I'm not afraid for myself."

Zach's lips twisted. "Don't tell me you're afraid for me?"

She shrugged. "Maybe." She was, but she wouldn't admit it. The man had a death wish, based on the way he walked up to Mr. Sarly, an angry bully holding a gun, as if he had nine lives to spare.

A young, dark-haired, dark-skinned man stepped out on the metal stairs leading into a ramshackle mobile home.

Jacie's heart fluttered. "That's him." She nodded toward the trailer. "That's Juan." She recognized him from one of her trips to Cara Jo's Diner.

"Let me do the talking and stay in the truck with the doors locked."

"No way." Jacie reached for the door handle. "You can't go out there alone. You need backup."

He snorted. "Like you're my backup? Please."

Anger bubbled up in Jacie's veins. "Some backup is better than none."

Zach grasped her hand in a tight clamplike hold. "Just do it. If I'm worrying about you, I might not see what's coming, like a fist or a bullet."

Jacie let go of the door handle and bit her bottom lip, torn between wanting to help and hurting the situation. "What are you going to do?"

"I'm going to ad-lib and get some information."

ZACH PULLED IN front of the trailer, shot the truck into park and climbed down. "Alvarez," he called out.

Alvarez leaned against the door of his trailer. "Lost, *gringo?*"

"You owe me and I'm here to collect." Zach marched toward the Hispanic.

Juan's eyes narrowed. "I don't owe you nothin'. Never saw you before."

A couple of the men who'd been lounging against beat-up cars pushed away and ambled toward Alvarez and the ruckus Zach was stirring.

"I asked for good stuff and you gave me shit." Zach

marched up to the steps. "I want what I paid for, and I want it now."

Alvarez leaped to the ground and flipped out a switch-blade. "I don't know who the hell you are, but I don't owe you nothin'."

Before the other two men could get close enough, Zach whispered low and without moving his lips, "You spoke to a woman two days ago in front of the diner."

Alvarez froze.

Zach went on. "I need to know what you said. Come with me and you won't be hurt." Louder he said, "Do I have to beat my stuff out of you?"

Juan lunged, his knife aimed at Zach's heart.

Zach ducked, grabbed Juan's knife hand and twisted it up and behind the man, pushing it high between his shoulder blades.

"Dios!" The knife fell from Juan's grip. "It's not here. I'll take you there, just don't break my arm."

"That's more like it." Without loosening his grip, Zach scooped up the knife and held it to Alvarez's throat. "Now tell your *compadres* to back off or I use this on you. And I warn you, *entiendo español." I understand Spanish.*

Juan spoke to the men in rapid-fire Spanish.

Zach understood enough of the language to gather that Juan told his buddies he'd be okay, not to interfere, he'd take care of this.

With Juan as his shield, Zach moved toward the pickup.

Inside, Jacie unlocked the door and slid to the center.

Zach pulled his pistol from his shoulder holster and handed it to her. "Point this at him and shoot if he so much as breathes wrong."

"Will do." She aimed the gun at Juan.

"In the truck," Zach ordered.

When Juan glanced into the truck, Jacie raised her head and stared straight into his eyes.

For a moment, Juan's eyes widened and he blinked. Then he ducked his head and climbed in without further argument.

Zach slammed the door shut, then rounded the truck and climbed into the driver's seat. "Just so you know, she's actually a better shot than I am, so do yourself a favor and behave."

Juan sat silent, staring at the pistol Jacie held in both hands, her finger caressing the trigger grip.

Back through town, Zach drove, his attention alternating between the road ahead, the rearview mirror and the woman holding the gun on the man beside her.

She held it steady, her face a mask of intensity.

Once he was certain he hadn't been followed, Zach shot out into the country, far enough away from town he could be certain no one was behind him.

Juan nodded toward the pistol in Jacie's hand. "She can put that down. I won't try to run or hurt you."

"If it's all the same to you, I'll keep it right here," she said.

Zach's chest swelled at her calm, clear and determined tones. She wasn't shaking, she hadn't hesitated to take the weapon and she probably was a better shot than he was, given that she hunted for a living.

Zach pulled off onto a side road and traveled another quarter of a mile before he parked beside a large clump of prickly pear cactus.

"How do you know my sister?" Jacie started.

"I don't know you and I don't know your sister," Juan muttered. "And I don't have your stuff, because I never sold you none."

Zach nodded to Jacie. "Keep the gun on him." Then he got out of the truck and rounded the front.

"You better answer our questions. My friend gets really cranky when he has to use force," Jacie warned, loud enough Zach could hear her.

He almost smiled, but that wouldn't be effective in what he planned next for Juan Alvarez.

Zach yanked open the passenger door.

"I don't know nothin'," Juan insisted.

"Maybe I can jog your memory a little." Zach grabbed Juan by the collar of his shirt and yanked him out onto the ground, then slammed him against the truck. "The woman you spoke to the day before yesterday was kidnapped last night. Which I suspect you already knew."

Juan shook his head but didn't voice a denial.

"Think real hard before you deny it. Next I will use that pretty little gun my assistant is holding to blow each one of your fingers off, one at a time."

Jacie slid down out of the truck, her eyebrows raised. "He's not kidding. But if you want to play Russian roulette with your hands, we can oblige." She lifted the nine-millimeter pistol. "I want my sister back and I'll do anything to get her."

Juan's eyes bulged. "La Familia Diablos *es muy loco*. They'll kill me if they know I said anything."

"So, were you the one to set my sister up to take the fall in Wild Horse Canyon?" Jacie stepped closer. "Maybe I'll start with the trigger finger. Hold it out."

Zach's chest swelled even more at Jacie's ability to follow his lead. He knew without a doubt that she would never shoot another living being without deadly provocation, but Juan didn't know that.

Jacie was so convincing at her roll, Zach could almost believe she would start shooting. Zach shoved Juan to the ground and stepped on his hand, splaying the fingers wide. "What did you tell the woman?"

"I'll tell you whatever you want to know," Juan squealed. "Just don't shoot."

"Start talking." Jacie squatted next to the man.

"She got my name from my cousin in San Antonio. She came to me asking when a shipment was going down with the men from the DEA. She paid me five hundred dollars and promised not to tell La Familia who told her. That's all. Now are you going to let me up?"

Zach snorted. "I'll think about it."

"I didn't do anything," Juan insisted.

"Did you inform La Familia Diablos that my sister was coming?"

"No. I hate La Familia. They killed my brother, Roberto. I owe them no allegiance."

"Let him up," Jacie demanded.

Zach removed his foot from the man's hand, grabbed his shoulder and hauled him to his feet. "Don't try anything," he warned Juan.

Jacie's eyebrows furrowed. "You knew the woman you'd spoken to was captured?"

"*Sí.*"

Her gaze narrowed. "How?"

He shrugged, rubbing at the hand Zach had stood on. "News travels fast in the barrio."

"Then you also know Los Lobos killed the men who captured her and took her."

Juan's lips clamped shut and he stared from Zach to Jacie.

"Maybe you even know where Los Lobos are keeping her?" Jacie prompted.

"No." Juan looked away.

"Liar." Zach's lips thinned and he stepped toward Juan,

fists clenched. "Either you know or you know someone who does." He held out his hand for the gun Jacie still held. She slapped it into his open palm.

Zach's fingers curled around the handle, warm from Jacie's touch. "Save us the crap and tell us what you do know."

Juan stared from Jacie back to Zach. "You aren't going to shoot me." He straightened his shoulders. "You don't have it in you."

"Try me," Zach said, his tone, low and dangerous. His hand rose with the gun pointed at Juan's forehead.

Juan stared down the barrel. At first Zach thought he would succeed at calling his bluff. To hell with that.

Zach pointed the nine-millimeter at Juan's foot and fired off a round.

"Madre de Dios!" Juan grabbed his foot and hopped in place before he fell to the ground and pulled off his shoe. Blood oozed from the side of his foot. "You shot me!"

Jacie stood with her mouth hanging open. Then she swallowed hard, her throat working in spasms. She shook back her hair and stared down her nose at the wounded man. "A flesh wound. The next one will count." She held out her hand. "My turn."

Zach passed the weapon back to her, his eyebrows rising.

"Did I mention I'll do just about anything to get my sister back alive?" She aimed the gun at Juan's kneecap. "I want answers now, not after she's dead."

Juan held his hands over the knee, as if they would have any effect stopping a bullet. "They'll kill me."

Jacie shrugged. "Us or them? You choose."

"Okay, okay." Juan stood. "Los Lobos might have taken her into one of the caves they use to stage drug runs. In Wild Horse Canyon."

"Guess who's taking us on a little trip into the canyon?" Zach's mouth quirked upward.

Juan's eyes rounded into saucers. "No. I told you what you wanted to know. Let me go."

"Sorry. That's not an option." Zach nodded to Jacie. "Let's go. We're burning daylight." The quicker they got to the canyon, the better for Tracie. Even a trained agent didn't hold up well under torture.

Zach shoved Juan into the truck.

Jacie got in beside their captive and took Zach's gun from him.

Without uttering another word, Zach slid into the driver's seat and spun the truck around, heading toward Hank's Raging Bull Ranch.

When he passed the turnoff to the Big Elk, Jacie looked at him with a frown. "Shouldn't we go back to the Big Elk and get horses?"

"Shouldn't you take me back to *mi casa?*" Juan whined.

"No," Zach answered. "You'll be showing us exactly where this cave is."

Juan pointed at his foot. "But I'm injured. I can't walk."

"You'll be on horseback," Zach said.

Juan didn't look any happier. "I don't know how to ride."

"Can I just shoot him now?" Jacie asked.

Juan sat in silence for a moment, glaring out the front windshield. "What if I don't remember?"

"Then we'll shoot your knees and leave you out there for the four-legged coyotes to clean up." Jacie waved the gun. "Enough excuses."

Zach fought the smile. Jacie was getting into her tough-girl role, maybe a little too much. She was tough, but Zach knew the real woman beneath the attitude. She wouldn't shoot.

Zach, on the other hand, wouldn't suffer a stubborn

fool. If the man knew something, Zach would shoot one digit at a time until he got the information out of him. He wouldn't let Tracie go through what Toni had suffered. Not if he could help it.

He drove the rest of the way to the Raging Bull without speaking another word, his mind running through the task at hand. Hopefully, the FBI and DEA would prove some kind of help storming the cave. Zach couldn't do it on his own. Not as heavily fortified as the Los Lobos had proved by shooting down the helicopter. Assuming the Los Lobos had done the shooting.

An operations tent had been set up in a field beside the barn on the Raging Bull Ranch. A phalanx of rental cars and dark SUVs lined the fence railing, where people milled about, pressing handheld radios to their ears.

Zach pulled into the front drive, weaving through the cars to find a place to park among the government vehicles.

Hank met them with a frown denting his forehead. "Glad you made it."

Jacie let herself out of her side of the truck. She handed Zach the gun. "I think he'll behave as long as he's surrounded."

Zach took the Glock. "Thanks." Then he turned to Hank. "What's the latest?"

"The FBI and DEA have joined forces in the search and rescue efforts. They have boots on the ground and birds in the air in Wild Horse Canyon, tracking from the point where you found the four-by-four and the dead members of La Familia."

Jacie stepped up to Hank. "Any sign of my sister?"

Hank shook his head. "Sorry. None."

Her shoulders sagged for a moment, then she straightened and turned to Zach. "Well, then, what are we waiting for?"

Hank stared from Zach to Jacie and then to the man standing behind them. "You two find out something?"

"Yeah." Zach jerked his head toward their informant. "This is the man who told Tracie about the op going down in the canyon."

Hank's eyebrows dipped. "What's he doing here?"

"He knows where the Los Lobos hole up in a cave in the canyon when they're making a drug run." Zach gave the informant a pointed look. "He's going to show us where that is."

Juan grumbled, "If I don't, you'll blow my knees off."

Hank laughed and pounded Zach on the back. "A man after my own heart."

"Not man." Zach jerked his head toward Jacie. "Woman. She's the one who threatened to blow his knees apart and, what was it you said?"

"Leave me for the four-legged coyotes to finish off." Juan glared at Jacie. "She's an animal."

Jacie shrugged and repeated her mantra. "I want my sister back."

Hank hooked Zach's elbow and he led him away from Juan. "Are you going to let the operations center know what you found?"

Zach sucked in a breath and let it out. "I don't know."

Jacie joined them. "Don't. We don't know who is bad in the group, possibly in both agencies, given the two DEA agents weren't on orders."

"Probably a wise decision." Hank nodded. "However, going up against Los Lobos alone is suicide."

"Not if they don't see you." Zach glanced at Jacie. "Which means I can't allow you to go."

"Like hell you can't." Jacie stuck a finger into his chest. "Look, mister, that's my sister out there. I'm going to get her back. And I know those canyons better than any of you."

"I'll have to trust our friend there to get me in and out at night. I'm sure he's had practice."

"You're waiting until dark?" Jacie asked.

"Can't go any sooner without alerting Los Lobos and the team of rescuers." Zach glanced toward the western sky, where the sun made its way toward the horizon. It would be dark before long and the air rescue units would be called in, as would the ground teams.

"Are you sure you don't want to let the FBI and DEA know what we found out?" Hank asked.

Zach raised his eyebrows. "What exactly do we know?"

"Los Lobos have a cave hideout in the canyon," Jacie offered. "Not that I'm condoning asking for FBI or DEA help on this."

"Do we know for certain they do or is Juan leading us on?" Zach shot back at her.

Jacie swallowed hard on a rising knot forming around her vocal cords. "My sister might be in that cave."

"If she is, we'll need more than just you and me to bring her out. We need to recon and see what we're up against."

"Right." Jacie's back stiffened. "You said 'we.'"

"I really meant me." Zach pointed at the Hispanic lounging against his truck. "Juan is only showing me where. I'd go it alone if I knew where. As it is, I don't trust Juan any farther than I can throw him."

"All the more reason to take me," Jacie insisted. "I can watch your back."

Hank laid a hand on Jacie's arm. "Zach's right."

"Oh, please, you can't take sides. You put him on this case to help me, not replace me."

"He's trained to do this stuff. You'll only—"

Jacie held up her hand. "Slow him down, right? And

what do you expect me to do while you go fight the terrorists? Stay home and knit?" She waved at her dusty clothes.
"I'm not the stay-at-home kinda gal, in case you haven't
noticed."

Zach grinned. "No, you're not." His smile died.

"You can stay and lurk around the operations tent with
the FBI and DEA and see what they've come up with,"
Hank suggested. "Maybe you can figure out who our mole
is in the bureau."

Jacie snorted. "Like I'd have a clue."

Zach turned to Hank. "I'll need a couple horses."

"I'll have my foreman set you up. For now, get to the
kitchen and grab a bite to eat. You might need it, if you
get lost in the canyon."

"Good point. I'll be sure to take a flare with me."

Jacie stood with a frown drawing her eyebrows close,
her arms crossed. "Glad you two can joke about this."

"Come on, you could use some food too." Zach hooked
her arm and urged her toward the house, calling over his
shoulder, "Juan."

Juan sneered at him.

"If you want food, join us."

For a moment Juan remained stubbornly leaning against
the truck. Then he pushed away and followed in a delib-
erately slow swagger.

JACIE SAT THROUGH a meal quickly prepared by Hank's
housekeeper. She could barely swallow, her throat muscles
clenching each time she thought of her sister and how long
she'd been held captive by notoriously vicious gangsters.
She tried not to think about it, but her only other thoughts
strayed to Zach and what he was about to undertake.

Riding horseback through the canyon was treacherous enough during the day. At night it was deadly. If Juan

didn't know exactly where he was going, they could end up lost and another rescue mission for the local authorities.

As dusk descended, dread threatened to weigh Jacie down.

She walked with Zach and Juan to the barn and stood back as Zach tied a saddlebag loaded with provisions onto the back of his saddle.

Juan's gloomy countenance didn't help to ease Jacie's mind.

"Well, that's it." Zach patted the horse's hindquarters and led him toward the rear entrance to the barn.

Jacie walked alongside him, her head bent. "I don't like this."

"I know." Zach faced her and tipped her chin with his finger. "We'll do our best to locate your sister and get back here as quickly as possible. Maybe even before sunup."

"What if you get in trouble?" She stared into his face, wishing he'd reconsider and take her along. "What if you're hurt?"

He smiled, his hand cupping her cheek. "Worried about me?"

Jacie stiffened and had a retort ready on her lips, but stopped short of delivering it when she realized she was worried about him. "I haven't known you long, but damn it, I am worried about you. I kinda got used to having you around." Her hand covered the one he'd used to cup her cheek and she pulled it lower, pressing a kiss into his palm.

"Stay safe for me, will you?" His eyes dark in the dim lighting from the overhead bulbs, he leaned close and captured her lips in a soul-stealing kiss.

For what felt as long as a lifetime and as short as a moment at once, the world around Jacie faded away, leaving just her and Zach.

Their tongues connected, thrusting and caressing.

When Zach broke away, he smoothed his hand over her hair. "Stay here. I trust Hank to keep you safe."

She laughed, the sound lacking any humor. "I'm not the one who needs to worry about being safe."

Zach smiled, chucked her beneath her chin and strode out of the barn, leading his horse.

The men had agreed not to mount, but to lead their horses quietly away from the barn, walking close to the animals so as not to be spotted by the agencies working the case.

The activity at the operations tent increased with the search teams reporting in.

During all the confusion of agents and law enforcement personal converging, no one seemed to notice the two horses walking across the pasture. Eventually the two faded into the distance.

Jacie remained in the shadows, every nerve ending screaming for her to follow.

Chapter Nine

Hank appeared at Jacie's side. "I asked Ben Harding to accompany you until Zach returns from the canyon."

"Thanks, but I don't need a babysitter." Jacie glanced one last time into the darkness. "What I need is a ride back to the Big Elk Ranch. Zach didn't leave me his truck keys."

Hank shook his head. "Zach wanted you to stay here where you'll be safe."

"From what?" Jacie raised her hand. "I didn't get kidnapped. I'm not the one being tortured. No one is after me. Unless you know something I don't."

Hank smiled. "You and your sister are very much alike. When she came to me for help, she didn't mince words and didn't stand for any fluff." He patted her arm. "Ben should be here in less than fifteen minutes. As soon as he arrives, I'll have him take you back to the Big Elk."

"Thank you." Guilt forced Jacie to add, "I'm sorry I bit your head off."

Hank's smile disappeared. "I understand. It's hard to lose someone you love. Even harder to know that they might still be alive."

Jacie had heard about Hank's wife and son disappearing a couple of years before. She laid a hand on his arm. "Still nothing about your family?"

"Nothing."

"Mr. Derringer, Grant Lehmann's here to speak with you," Hank's foreman called out.

"If you'll excuse me. Lehmann's an old friend and a regional director of the FBI."

"Good, maybe he can get things moving on finding my sister."

Hank left her standing in the barn's rear doorway.

Jacie wandered over to the operations tent and peeked in.

Agents and sheriff's deputies were finishing up with their reports. Everyone said the same thing. No sign of Tracie Kosart, or anyone else for that matter. The ground-tracking team had followed the trail until it disappeared. They suspected the kidnappers knew enough to drag a branch or something from the back of their vehicles to smooth away their tire tracks.

"Stopping in?"

The voice behind her made Jacie jump. She spun to face Bruce Masterson, wearing black chinos, a black polo shirt and a headset looped over his head, currently pushed back from his ears.

He held out a hand, inviting her to precede him into the portable ops center. "You look so much like your sister it takes me aback every time I see you."

Jacie stepped beneath the lights strung out between tent poles before responding, "That happens with identical twins." She halted just inside and faced him, something gnawing at her since she'd first called him. "I have a question for you."

He grinned. "Shoot."

"You sounded surprised to hear that Tracie had come to see me. Why? I thought you two were living together." Jacie tilted her head to the side. "Wouldn't you know when she'd left and where she was headed? Or have your living arrangements changed since the engagement?"

The man shrugged. "She left without telling me. I assumed she was called out on a job."

"Were you two having a fight or anything?"

Bruce shook his head. "No. At least not one I was involved in."

"She didn't leave a note?"

"No. Her suitcase was gone, so I assumed she was on assignment. It was too late to call the office and double-check." Bruce fiddled with the headset, staring over Jacie's shoulder. He waved at someone behind Jacie. "I have to admit I was a little worried, but happy to hear from you to know she was with you. Until you told me she'd been kidnapped. I had to beg to get special permission to join the search and rescue mission."

His answers sounded legit; still, Jacie couldn't imagine her organized sister taking off without informing her fiancé of her whereabouts. Jacie had opened her mouth to say just that when a voice called out her name. She turned, looking for the source.

Bruce glanced around the tent. "Where'd your boyfriend go?"

Jacie hesitated, the truth the first thing that wanted to pop out of her mouth. She bit down hard on her tongue and thought before answering. "He got called away on business."

"I thought I just saw him here. Isn't it late to be called in to work?"

"Apparently he didn't think so. He headed into…El Paso to find a business center."

"Is he coming back?"

"Um, yes. Of course." Jacie sent a silent prayer that what she'd said wasn't yet another untruth.

Zach would be back, and hopefully with news of her sister. In the meantime, she had to wait.

"What exactly does your boyfriend do?"

Irritation flared in Jacie. She didn't like lying, but Bruce's barrage of questions left her no choice. "I'm not exactly sure. I think he's into security work, something high-tech. When he talks about it, I glaze over."

She forced a fake smile. To handle the guilt, she told herself she was on an undercover mission and the lies were only to protect herself and her partner. Not that Zach considered himself her partner. Still, no one, other than herself and Hank, needed to know he was out scouting the canyon for the Los Lobos cave. Not even Tracie's fiancé, who for some reason Tracie hadn't seen fit to inform of her plans.

A man wearing a black cowboy hat ducked beneath the tent. "Jacie?" It had to be the guy Hank had promised, Ben Harding.

Jacie raised her hand, relieved she didn't have to answer any more of Bruce's questions. "I suppose that's my ride."

Bruce frowned. "Headed back to the Big Elk? And here I thought you'd stick around awhile."

"I'm of no use here."

"I wouldn't say that. It's like having Tracie here." Bruce slid a finger along Jacie's cheek. "You two are so much alike."

Jacie frowned. Zach had just touched her cheek before he'd left, and this man was wiping away that warm fuzzy feeling she'd gotten the first time.

An icky sensation crept into Jacie's gut. Was Bruce coming on to her? She shook her head. No. She was reading too much into his touch and comment. "We're only alike physically. We're completely different when it comes to tastes, likes and dislikes." She added a little emphasis to the last statement as if telling Bruce *back off, you're not my type.*

The cowboy stepped through the crowd and stopped beside Jacie. "I take it you're Jacie?"

She gave him a tight smile, relieved he'd come to take her away. "That's me. Let's go." Jacie hooked his arm and led him out of the tent. Okay, if she was honest with herself, she dragged the unsuspecting man out.

Once outside in the darkness of night, Ben laughed. "Hey, what's the rush?"

"I'm not a secret agent and my sister's boyfriend was asking questions about Zach and where he was." She slowed to a stop and gave her rescuer a smile. "Sorry, that was rude of me." Jacie stuck out a hand. "I'm Jacie Kosart."

The cowboy removed his hat and took her hand. "Ben Harding. Nice to meet you. I understand I'm here to take over for Zach while he's busy."

Jacie's hand dropped to her side and she continued toward the makeshift parking lot. "No, you're just here to take me to the Big Elk Ranch, where I live."

"Oh, that's not what I had understood from Hank."

"Apparently Hank worries about the wrong people. Which vehicle did you drive?"

Still carrying his hat, Ben scratched his head. "Hank's a pretty smart guy. The dark gray pickup on the very end." He pointed to the one.

Jacie lengthened her stride, eager to be on her way before anyone waylaid her with unwanted questions. "Maybe so, but I'm not the one who's missing. I don't need a babysitter and I told him as much."

Ben chuckled. "Okay, then. Let's get you home."

"Thank you." Jacie climbed into the passenger seat and leaned back, her mind miles away from the interior of the truck, far across the Texas landscape, near the edge of the canyon with Zach and Juan. She hoped Zach kept a close eye on his informant.

Jacie hadn't trusted the guy and worried he'd try something, injuring Zach or setting him up to take a fall with Los Lobos.

Ben drove the length of the Raging Bull Ranch driveway before speaking again. "Which way?"

Jacie gave him the directions.

"Hank tells me it's your sister lost in the canyon. I'm sorry."

"Not lost...kidnapped."

"Right." Ben nodded. "I don't know much about Zach, but from what I've learned about Hank, he's a good judge of character. If he's assigned Zach to help find your sister, I'm sure he'll get the job done."

"Thanks. I just wish he'd taken me."

"Hank says you work as a trail guide at the Big Elk. I can see where that would come in handy out in the canyon. Why didn't he take you?"

"Zach gave me some crap about stealth. I think he's crazy going in alone."

"He's trained as an FBI agent. He knows the risks. And from what I've heard, he's not afraid to take them."

"As long as he doesn't get himself killed."

"There is that." Ben glanced across at her, his eyes reflecting the light from the dash. "He knows the stakes and he signed on anyway. I guess most FBI or law enforcement types understand there's always a chance you might not make it back from a mission."

Jacie sat up straighter. "Not helping."

Ben chuckled. "Sorry. I forgot your sister was—is—FBI."

"Yeah, she is and I'm not." Jacie turned sideways, facing

Ben. "What is it that drives someone into a job like that? Are they adrenaline junkies or something?"

Ben shook his head, his gaze on the highway in front of him. "Maybe for some. For most, it's a need to fight for truth and justice."

Jacie snorted. "At the risk of your own life?"

His gaze captured hers for a moment. "Don't tell me you wouldn't give your life for your sister."

"In a heartbeat. But she's not giving her life for me, she's sacrificing it for nameless, faceless people."

"No, she's sacrificing for the good of a lot of people. What about for the next child that could be molested if she didn't fight to get the child molester off the streets? Or the families with small children or young teens that live in terror while a serial killer stalks their neighborhood? Those people have faces. They are real."

Jacie slumped in her seat. "You're right. I'm just mad she didn't tell me everything when she came out here to supposedly visit. Now she's got herself in a bind and Zach could well be walking into a trap." She flung out her hands. "I hate not knowing and not doing anything."

"Understandable. Just have faith he'll be okay and we'll find your sister."

Jacie couldn't leave it up to faith. She was a doer. By the time they arrived at the Big Elk Ranch, she'd worked herself up into a silent lather. No sooner had Ben pulled up in the parking lot of the lodge than she was out of the truck. "No need to stay, I'm just going to wait in my cabin until I hear from Zach or my sister."

Ben's brow furrowed. "If you're sure you'll be all right?"

"I will." She waved. "Thanks, Ben." Then she slammed the door and took off for her cabin. Wait in her cabin, ha!

She waited as long as it took for Ben to back up, turn

around and head back the way he'd come, before she made a sharp turn toward the barn.

"Jacie?" Richard Giddings called out from the front porch of the lodge. "Is that you?"

Jacie swallowed her irritation and answered, "Yes, sir."

"What's been happening? I haven't seen or heard from you since this morning."

"Rich, I don't have time to fill you in. I need to get back out there."

He dropped down off the porch. "Out where?"

"The canyon."

"At night?" Her boss shook his head and looked around her. "That's insane. Where's Zach?"

The secrecy of the mission Zach was on required Jacie to keep the truth from her boss, but she didn't have to lie. "He had business to attend to."

"All the more reason for you to stay put. No one in their right mind should be out in that canyon at night."

Jacie stopped herself from snorting out loud. She couldn't agree with him more, but she also wasn't at liberty to say why. Not that she didn't trust Richard with her life and that of her sister, but what if someone overheard their conversation? Someone who would inform Los Lobos they had a visitor on his way to spy on them?

"Tracie's been gone over twenty-four hours."

Richard pulled her into a big bear hug. "Then come up to the lodge and stay with me until Zach gets back."

She considered it. But she'd rather go out to the canyon and follow Zach.

"No, you're not going out to the canyon tonight. I won't allow you to make use of any of the Big Elk assets to commit suicide." Richard set her at arm's length.

She stared up at him. "How do you know what I'm thinking?"

"As long as you've been working here, I think I'd know you by now. You're a doer and it's eating you up not to be doin'." He slung one arm over her shoulders. "Now, are you coming to the lodge for a beer or going to your cabin to wait?"

"Thanks for the offer, but I think I'll sit it out in my cabin. I could use a shower."

"Have it your way, but the offer remains open. I'm here if you need a shoulder."

"Thanks." Tears lodged in Jacie's throat. This man had been more than good to her. He'd been the father she missed so badly, the friend she'd needed on more than one occasion. Jacie tamped down the urge to ride off into the canyon and did as Ben had suggested and had faith that Zach would return unharmed. And with news of her sister.

Jacie trudged toward her cottage. A quick glance behind her confirmed Richard remained where she'd left him, watching her as she made her way home.

Once inside, she went through the motions of stripping off her dirty clothes. In the corner, her sister's suitcase lay on its side, just as she'd left it over a day ago.

Jacie dropped to her haunches and unzipped the case, feeling like a sneak looking through her sister's things. Maybe buried among Tracie's pajamas and blue jeans, she'd find a clue that would help her understand why she'd left Bruce without telling him and what she thought she'd find following the DEA agents into the canyon.

The suitcase was just like Tracie, neat and organized, each T-shirt folded precisely the same, the socks rolled military-style, a habit probably learned at Quantico.

Jacie unzipped a side pouch inside the suitcase and found Tracie's wallet with her FBI identification and her cell phone.

Her heartbeat picking up, Jacie recalled Cara Jo saying something about Tracie staring at her phone the whole time she'd been in the diner. Had she tried to call Bruce and he hadn't answered? Or had she been calling another contact to verify whatever she'd found?

Jacie hit the on button and waited. The screen flickered to life; a battery with a red line blinked into view. Great. Low battery. The screen warning cleared, replaced by another screen requiring a four-digit pass code.

Stumped, Jacie stared at the little boxes and rows of numbers. What would Tracie have used? She keyed in the month and day of Tracie's birthday. That didn't open it. She keyed in the month and year. Another failed attempt. The little battery indicator in the top corner indicated eleven percent.

Her heart racing, Jacie dug through her sister's belongings, searching for her phone charger. When she didn't find one, she slipped on her shirt and jeans, grabbed Tracie's car keys and ran out to the little economy car she'd driven up from San Antonio. Surely she had a charger in the car.

Once again, she struck out and her own cell phone charger didn't work on her sister's model. When Jacie emerged from the little car, she trudged back to the house. She probably only had a few more tries before either the phone locked up or the battery died.

As she stepped up on the porch, the sound of gravel shifting brought her out of her intense concentration on her sister's phone, and Jacie glanced around.

The moon shone down on the lodge and cabins, casting long shadows at the corners and sides.

Jacie listened for the sound again. Perhaps a raccoon was on its way through to the barn to get into the feed, or one of the ranch dogs had scampered into the shadows. With a shrug, Jacie entered the cottage quickly and closed the door, locking it behind her. Never had she felt unsafe at the Big Elk Ranch. All this cloak-and-dagger stuff had her spooked and she found herself wishing Zach was there with her.

How could one man become so much a part of her life in so short a time? Jacie stared at her sister's cell phone she'd laid on the bed. Maybe she'd think of the code while shampooing the dirt out of her hair.

Once again, she slipped out of her clothes, grabbed a towel out of the linen closet of the tiny cabin and stepped into the closet-sized bathroom. At least the bathtub was a normal size. Opting for a bath instead of a shower, she filled the tub and added some of the bath salts Tracie had given her for Christmas. She realized this was the first time she'd used them and she wanted to cry.

When the tub was full, she sank into the steamy water, sliding low to immerse her hair. She came up, blinking water from her eyes, and squirted a healthy dose of shampoo into her hand. Jacie went to work washing away the dust from her nearly fatal helicopter ride of earlier that day. Had it only been that morning? So much had happened since then. And yet so little.

Jacie slipped beneath the surface again, rinsing the bubbles out of her hair. A dull thump sounded through the bathtub water.

She sat up straight, water splashing over the edge of the tub, her ears perked.

A soft scraping sound reached her ears and sent her flying out of the tub, wrapping a towel around her middle as she emerged from the bathroom. "Who's there?"

The scraping had stopped and nothing but an eerie silence surrounded Jacie. She reached for the nine-millimeter Glock she kept in her nightstand, fully loaded.

"I have a gun and I know how to use it," she called out. Normally she'd feel silly about saying that out loud. But nothing about the past two days had been normal. A shiver rippled down her spine.

She rushed through the little cabin, turning off the lights. If someone was out there, he wouldn't be able to see a shadow moving around inside, and she might possibly see his figure moving around the outside. Jacie dressed in clean work clothes instead of her pajamas.

Unable to sleep and seriously afraid, she pulled the mattress off the bed and laid it on the floor, then wrapped her mother's quilt around her body. Propping her back against the wall, she pointed her gun at the only door into and out of the house. She waited for morning and the return of Zach and her sanity.

Chapter Ten

Zach forced Juan to take the lead as they found their way through the twists and turns of the canyon. The horses picked their way carefully over stones and around boulders, sliding in some places.

By the light of a near-full moon, Zach studied the walls, rock formations and crevices, memorizing them in case he ended up finding his way out of the maze on his own.

He still wasn't sure Juan knew where he was going or if the man was leading him straight into a trap. Without much else to go on, Zach had to take his chances.

The crevices narrowed and widened, but they were always wide and cleared enough to allow a four-wheel-drive ATV access.

After they had traveled for nearly an hour, the walls loomed higher, the path narrowed and the shadows made it more difficult to see.

Zach shifted in his saddle to ease the aching muscles of his inner thighs and give his sore tailbone a break. Hopefully they'd get there soon. He didn't know how effective he would be if he was too stiff to climb off his horse.

Juan halted his gelding at a giant outcropping of boulders and dismounted.

Zach rode up beside him. "Why are you stopping?" he

asked, careful to keep his voice low. Sound bounced off the canyon walls, echoing up and down the length.

"This is as far as I go on horseback." He tugged his horse to the side, into the deepest shadows.

"How much farther ahead is it?" Zach dismounted as well.

"I will show you. But we'll go on foot. The horses will make too much noise and alert the lookouts."

Zach tied his horse to a stunted tree, wedged in the crevice between giant boulders. Juan did the same, then led Zach around the outcropping, hugging the shadows along the base of the canyon walls.

They'd gone the equivalent of four football fields when Juan stopped and pointed to a dark spot ahead and on the left. "That's the cave and this is as far as I go."

Zach studied the location, the possible areas he could use as cover and concealment. "Okay." He nodded.

"I've done what you asked. Now you can let me go, no?"

Zach shook his head. "Sorry, buddy. I want to make sure you didn't lead me on a wild-goose chase, *and* I can't risk you alerting the gang in the cave. You get to stay here and wait for me to return."

Zach pulled a wad of zip-ties from his back pocket, grabbed Juan's wrist and whipped it up and behind him. He grabbed the man's other hand and slipped the zip-tie around Juan's wrists, tugging it tight.

"What are you doing?" Juan danced around, tugging his hands against the bindings. "You can't leave me here tied up. I am not a member of Los Lobos. If they knew I led you to them, they would kill me."

"Then you better keep really quiet so they don't find you. When I get back, I'll cut the ties and we'll mosey on home." Zach crossed his arms. "Now, are you going to sit so that I can bind your legs, or do I have to knock you down?"

Juan shook his head. "I promise I won't go anywhere."

"Since I don't know you well enough to stake my life on your word, you'll have to go with the zip-ties. I figure it'll take you at least as long as it takes me to get up there and back to find a rock to break them on."

"What about coyotes and snakes? Look, amigo, don't leave me like this."

"You'll be okay for the short time I'm gone." He pointed to the ground. "Sit."

With his hands tied behind him, Juan sighed and dropped to his knees and then to his butt, kicking his feet out in front of him. "You're one tough hombre. If I had my knife…"

"But you don't, and I might have some discussions with you if this is all a waste of my time." Zach slipped the plastic strap around Juan's ankles. Then he pulled a small roll of duct tape from his other back pocket and slapped a piece over Juan's mouth.

With his guide secured from running away or running his mouth, Zach proceeded around the bend and along the base of the canyon toward the dark shadow that was the mouth of a cave. He didn't hurry, careful not to scuff gravel or trip over unseen rocks. When he came within twenty yards of the entrance, he stopped and scoped the surrounding area. So far he hadn't sighted a single guard. Nothing and no one moved in and out of the cave or anywhere else around it.

Zach held his weapon in front of him. From where he stood to the entrance, there were no shadows to hug, no boulders to dive behind. He'd have to make a mad dash in case a sniper spotted him and started taking potshots at him.

With a deep breath, Zach ran toward the entrance, zig-zagging so that he didn't provide an easy target for some-one who could halfway shoot a gun.

He climbed a rise and ducked into the cave, slipping into the shadows. Deeper inside, a single light illuminated a small area. Having met no resistance, Zach took the time to let his eyes adjust to the limited lighting before he moved closer to the glow. Voices carried to him, and by the sound of them, they were in Spanish.

Two men sat in front of a fire, one holding a stick at the end of which was some dead, skinned animal, roast-ing in the flame. The other smoked a cigarette. Both men had weapons, but they lay on the ground beside them. Ap-parently they weren't expecting company or anyone else.

Besides the men and the fire, there were small wooden crates and cardboard boxes lining the walls. Zach passed one after the other. Most of them were empty.

As he neared the fire, one of the men spoke in rapid-fire Spanish telling a raucous story about a woman and her mother. The other burst out laughing.

Zach stepped forward, his weapon drawn. In Spanish he asked, "Are you Los Lobos?"

The men reached for their weapons.

Still speaking in Spanish, Zach warned, "Reach for your guns and I'll shoot you. Hands up."

One man looked at the other and dove for his gun.

Zach shot him in the shoulder, knocking him back-ward into a wall.

The man grabbed his shoulder and slid to the ground, moaning.

"Don't shoot," the other man said in halting English. He kicked both weapons toward Zach, his hands still in the air.

"Are you Los Lobos?"

"No."

Zach pointed at the downed man's other shoulder. "No lies."

The bleeding man raised his good, bloodied hand. "*Sí, señor.* We are Los Lobos."

"Where is the woman?" Zach asked.

Both men looked at each other, their foreheads wrinkled in frowns.

The man who was still standing shook his head. "What woman?"

"The one the Los Lobos murdered two La Familia Diablos guys to get."

Again the standing man shook his head. "Los Lobos didn't take a woman. With the FBI and DEA all over the canyon, we couldn't leave our stuff here. The boss had us move it. We stayed to clean up the last of it." He blinked, glancing over Zach's shoulder.

Before Zach could spin, a hard poke in his back made him think twice.

"Drop your gun," a heavily accented voice demanded.

Zach had no intention of giving up his weapon. In a lightning-fast move, he ducked to the side and knocked the barrel of the rifle the man held downward, causing the stock to lever up and hit his attacker in the jaw.

The man pulled the trigger and a bullet ricocheted off the floor, disappearing into the shadows.

The unarmed men dropped to the ground.

Zach jerked the rifle out of the man's hands and pressed his Glock into the guy's cheek. "Are there any more of you hiding or coming?"

The man with the gun in his cheek shook his head, his eyes wide. *"No comprende."*

The other man translated and received a response in Spanish. The translator faced Zach. "There are two more on their way to help move the rest of the stuff."

"Then let's get down to business." Zach nudged the gun deeper into the man's face. "Where's the woman?"

A thin sheen of sweat broke out on the man's face and he fired off his answer in such garbled Spanish Zach couldn't make heads or tails of it.

"What did he say?" Zach demanded of the translator.

"Los Lobos didn't take the woman. La Familia Diablos did."

Zach shook his head. "Then Los Lobos killed the two Diablos who took her, and now Los Lobos has her."

The man with the gun in his cheek shook his head and rattled off more Spanish.

"That is not the truth, *señor*. La Familia still has her. Someone made it look like Los Lobos killed those men."

"How about I shoot one of you at a time until someone tells me the truth?" Zach said.

All three men held up their hands. The man who understood English best spoke. "We are telling you the truth. Ramon just returned to pick us up. News from the boss is La Familia Diablos set it up to look like Los Lobos took the woman so that the Federales would look in the wrong place for her and cause troubles for Los Lobos."

For a long moment Zach continued to hold his weapon to the man's cheek. In his gut he knew what they were saying was most likely the truth. Finally he eased away from the trio, backing toward the cave entrance. He scooped up the other two weapons and slung all three over his shoulder while still holding the Glock on them.

"I'll let you live this time. Believe me when I say, if what you've told me is all lies, I'll find you and I'll rip your limbs off one at a time and make you wish you were dead long before you are."

Without waiting for them to respond, Zach slipped out of the cave and ran back across the wide-open space, weighed down by the three extra guns. When he reached the relative safety of a large boulder, he removed the bolts from the Los Lobos rifles and tossed the weapons on the ground.

A shout sounded behind him. He leaned around the boulder. The three men emerged from the cave, headed in his direction.

Zach fired off a round, kicking up the rocks at their feet. They hurried back to the cave entrance.

With no more time to play around, Zach ran back to where he'd left Juan. With Juan's switchblade, he severed the zip-ties. "Let's go."

Juan ripped the tape off his mouth. "Did you find the woman?"

"No. If you want to live, you'll get moving." Zach didn't wait for Juan; he ran back the way they'd come, reaching the horses before Juan.

The sound of engines revving echoed off the canyon walls as Zach and Juan mounted the horses.

Now that he knew that most of Los Lobos had vacated the canyon, Zach wasn't as concerned about noise as he was about getting a bullet in his back. He urged his horse to a trot, praying the animal wouldn't break a leg on the rocky terrain. They maneuvered through the maze of canyon corridors until they emerged at the base of the ridge where Tracie had been taken.

AFTER SITTING IN the dark on the floor for what felt like an hour, Jacie glanced at the clock. Thirty minutes? It had only been thirty minutes? That's it? She refused to wait around her cabin another moment. She had to get back out to the canyon. Zach could be in trouble. Maybe he'd found Tracie and they were fighting their way out and needed an extra gun to even the odds.

Jacie dressed in clean black jeans, a black T-shirt and her black leather jacket. She knotted her long hair in a rubber band and shoved it under a black baseball cap Richard had given her. After loading her rifle and her Glock with rounds, she shoved a box of bullets in each jacket pocket and shoved the chair away from the door.

If someone was out there, she was loaded and wouldn't hesitate to shoot. She switched on the porch light and flung open the door.

The porch was empty and nothing moved as far as she could see into the shadows past the illumination. When she turned to lock the door, she noticed that the oil-rubbed bronze door lock had fresh scratches in it.

Her gut tightened. Someone had definitely been trying to get in. On instinct, she went back inside, closed the door and grabbed her sister's credentials and cell phone. She shoved them beneath a plastic bag of moldy tomatoes in the bottom of her miniature refrigerator. No one would bother them there.

Having hidden the only two things she considered of any interest to anyone, she locked the front door and slipped across the compound to the barn, weapon drawn and ready.

Once inside the barn, she fumbled in the tack room for a flashlight, switching it on and shining the light around the interior for good measure. She'd had that creepy, being-watched feeling since she'd come back to the Big Elk.

Satisfied she was alone, she led D'Artagnan, her bay gelding, from his stall and tossed a saddle over his back. Once she had the saddle cinched and the bridle settled over the horse's head, she turned to lead him out the back of the barn.

A hinge squeaked and the overhead lights blinked on.

Richard leaned in the doorway, fully dressed and ready to ride. "Wondered when you'd make a run for it."

"Oh, Richard, I'm sorry. My head tells me I should stay and wait for Zach to return, but my gut says he's in trouble and might need some help. The least I can do is cover his back."

"Thought you'd feel that way. I guess it wouldn't do me any good to tell you not to go."

She shook her head, her fingers tightening on the horse's reins. "I have to go."

"You're not going by yourself."

"I don't want to put anyone else in danger."

"Too bad. You're not going by yourself. My horse is ready and waiting out front. You have to put up with me in this crazy midnight rodeo."

"You could be shot at."

"Heck, I get shot at all the time by these darned fool weekend hunters who can't figure out the business end of a gun." Richard chuckled. "Come on. Let's you and me go for a ride in the moonlight. It's a mighty fine night for it."

Jacie choked back her response, afraid her voice would shake with her gratitude. Richard had always told her he appreciated her ability to avoid the feminine hysterics most women were prone to. It was one of the reasons he'd hired her. She was a straight shooter and not at all froufrou.

Her heart a little lighter, Jacie led her gelding out into the barnyard where, sure as he'd said, Richard had his black quarter horse saddled and ready to go.

He had a rifle in his scabbard and an old-fashioned revolver in a holster slung around his hips. The man could have been a gunslinger in a former life, he looked so natural. They left the ranch compound without speaking and nudged their horses into a gallop as soon as they cleared the last gate.

If all went well, they'd be at the ridge of the canyon in less than an hour. Then Jacie would have to decide what next. She didn't know where the Los Lobos hideout was in the maze of canyon trails. Hell, she'd cross that bridge when she came to it. Right now anywhere closer to the canyon where her sister disappeared and Zach had gone to find her was better than waiting around her cabin with someone trying to break in.

ZACH AND JUAN raced back to where the trail led up out of the canyon. As Juan started up the narrow trail, two motorcycles emerged from the shadows Zach had just left. Two more shot out close behind.

Zach turned on his horse and fired at the lead cyclist. His bullet went wide of its target and the cycle continued straight for them.

Four to one wasn't the best odds. Zach could take them, but then he'd waste time. Time was something he couldn't afford to give up. The longer Tracie remained in the clutches of the cartel, the more torture she'd have to endure. And the longer he was in the canyon, the longer he was away from Jacie.

He spun his horse, aimed at the closest pursuer and fired.

The rider jerked off the bike and landed on his back on the ground. The next rider swerved to miss him and slid sideways on the rocky surface. Two down, two more to go. Without cover and concealment, Zach would be at a disadvantage defending himself and if he tried riding up the trail to the top, he might as well paint a target on his back and Juan's. The two pursuers at the bottom only had to dismount and take aim.

Out in the open and out of options, Zach leaped off his

horse and slapped the animal's hindquarters, sending it up the hill after Juan.

Zach dropped to the ground, drew his weapon and aimed at the nearest man. When he pulled the trigger, nothing happened.

The men on the motorcycles drew steadily closer.

Zach pulled the bolt back and ejected the bullet inside, then slid it home, aimed and pulled the trigger again.

Nothing.

On the ground, his gun jammed, Zach lay still, hoping to surprise the two men with the only other weapon he had on him. Juan's switchblade.

Chapter Eleven

Jacie and Richard neared the ridge at a trot, glad for the full moon and the near-daylight conditions in which to maneuver the Texas landscape.

The closer she got to the canyon, the faster Jacie's heart beat. She sensed trouble. A nudge to her gelding's flanks urged the animal into a gallop.

Almost at the edge, her horse ground to a halt and reared, his whinny filling the sky. Up over the top of the ridge sprang another horse and rider, charging straight for them.

The horse and rider skirted Jacie but didn't make it past her boss. Richard headed him off, leaned over and snatched the reins out of his hands, jerking the horse to a stop.

A string of Spanish curse words rolled out of the rider's mouth, and Jacie recognized him as Juan, the man who'd been with Zach when they'd taken off on their reconnaissance mission.

Jacie calmed her gelding and joined Richard and Juan. "Where's Zach?" she demanded.

"I don't know. He was behind me."

The sound of engines carried up to her from the canyon below.

A feeling of déjà vu washed over Jacie and she whirled her mount, heading for the canyon. Before she reached the edge, another horse topped the trail and headed her way. This one was riderless.

Damn. Damn. Damn. Jacie sank her heels into the gelding's flanks, sending him hurtling over the edge and down the trail. Below on the floor of the canyon, two motorcycles were nearly at the base of the path leading upward.

Zach was nowhere to be seen.

Then a shadow sprang up from the ground beside the first motorcycle and the rider was yanked off his seat, landing flat on his back.

The trailing bike veered straight for the two figures grappling on the ground.

Jacie pulled her rifle from the scabbard and, one-handed, fired off a round above the head of the attacker. It didn't deter him a bit. Either he couldn't hear over the roar of the motorcycle engine or he wasn't fazed by gunfire.

Now that the second motorcycle was practically on top of the tangled shadows of the men on the ground, Jacie didn't dare shoot at him for fear of missing and hitting Zach instead.

The rider leaped off his bike and joined the fight.

Jacie let her horse pick his way down the treacherous trail, while her heart hammered against her ribs. She prayed she wouldn't be too late to help.

A shot rang out from below.

Jacie's gelding sidestepped, nearly taking them both over the edge.

One of the shadows fell, lying motionless on the ground. The other two continued the struggle. One of them had to be Zach.

Jacie reached the bottom and charged toward the dueling pair, leaping out of the saddle before the horse came to a complete stop. Still holding her rifle, she pointed it at the pair.

Zach knocked the man to the ground and staggered back, bleeding from a gash on his cheek. The man on the ground rolled to the side, grabbed his fallen weapon and rolled to his back, aiming at Zach.

Jacie fired off a round, hitting the man square in the chest before he had a chance to pull the trigger. His gun fell to the side, and he lay still, his eyes open, staring up at the full moon.

Zach dropped to his knees, breathing hard. "I thought I told you not to come," he grumbled.

"And if I hadn't, you might be dead." Jacie laid her rifle on the ground and knelt beside him. "Are you okay?" She studied the gash on his cheek and searched him for other signs of injury, wishing she had a flashlight to work with.

"I'm okay." His lips twisted, then straightened into a smile and he shook his head. "Thanks."

"Now, was that so hard?" She pulled his arm over her shoulder and helped him to his feet.

"I'm really okay, just winded."

"Shut up and let me help." She led him to her horse. "Take the saddle. I'll ride behind."

Zach dragged himself up into the saddle.

Jacie assisted with a firm hand on his rear, shoving him upward. She couldn't help thinking that he had a nice behind. Some kind of thought to have when she'd just killed a man.

Holy crap. She'd just killed a man.

Her knees wobbled. The finality of her actions hit her, and her heart nearly stopped.

Zach moved his foot out of the stirrup and reached down for her hand. "Come on. We have to get to Hank's place."

Jacie didn't have time to go soft on him. So she'd killed a man. A man who would have killed Zach if she hadn't. And her sister was still missing.

She straightened her shoulders, dragged in a steadying breath and put her hand in Zach's, her foot in the stirrup.

As he pulled her up, she swung her leg over the horse's hindquarters and landed neatly behind the saddle and Zach, wrapping her arms around his waist.

Zach reined the gelding around and sent it up the trail at a slow, steady pace, letting the horse choose his steps, given that it was carrying double the burden.

Jacie leaned into Zach's back and inhaled the heady scent of dust, denim and cowboy, letting his strength and courage seep into her. She didn't look down, just closed her eyes and let the horse and the man get her out of the hell she'd just experienced.

Richard waited at the top of the hill with the reins of Juan's horse tied to his saddle horn. "I would have come down, but you had it all under control before I could. I take it we need to report a couple of deaths?"

"We'll hit the ops tent on the Raging Bull and let them handle things." Zach glanced around. "Have you seen my horse?"

"He's halfway back to the barn by now."

Jacie couldn't be sorry about that. It meant she didn't have to drive. It gave her an excuse to hold on to Zach a little longer without revealing how needy she actually felt. What was it about this man that made her want to be strong for him at the same time he turned her knees to jelly?

Richard rode ahead with Juan.

Zach and Jacie allowed the gelding to take his time. Moonlight streamed over them and they were alone in the stark Texas landscape.

After a few minutes, Jacie swallowed her disappointment and bucked up the courage to confirm, "I take it you didn't find Tracie?"

"No." The word was terse, almost angry.

"What did you find?"

"Juan was correct in that Los Lobos had a rendezvous point in a cave in the canyon, but they were in the process of relocating because of all the activity in the canyon with the FBI and DEA looking for Tracie and the people who killed their agents."

"Did you find out where they moved Tracie?"

Zach shook his head, staring straight ahead. "Every man I questioned said the same thing. Los Lobos didn't kidnap anyone and they didn't kill the two La Familia Diablos men."

"If not Los Lobos, who?"

"They think that whoever killed the men wanted it to look like Los Lobos to throw the FBI and DEA off the trail of the real killers and to stir up trouble for Los Lobos with La Familia Diablos."

Jacie leaned her forehead into Zach's back. "Then we're back to square one. We don't have a lead and we don't know who took Tracie or where."

His hand rested over hers, warm and gentle. "We'll find her."

"Are you thinking it's someone internal to the FBI or DEA who set this all up?"

"I can't be certain, but I'd bet it is."

"Where do we go next?"

"I'm not sure. First, I need to talk to Hank and an old buddy of mine I trust from the FBI."

"No. First we need to have your wounds tended." Her arms tightened around his middle for a second before she realized he might have been hit in the ribs. She loosened her hold.

"I'm fine. I just need a shower. I can get that back at the Big Elk and you can get some rest."

They rode into the Raging Bull compound and were

immediately surrounded by the agents and local law enforcement personnel manning the night shift.

Richard and the groggy ranch foreman took their horses. Richard would borrow one of the Raging Bull trailers to get the horses and himself back to the Big Elk.

After reporting on the two dead men and filling them in on what Zach had discovered, Jacie was so tired she could barely stand.

"Out and about again?" Bruce appeared at Jacie's side. "I thought you'd given up and gone back to the Big Elk." Her sister's boyfriend stood close behind her, his breath stirring the stray hairs resting against her neck.

"Couldn't sleep." Jacie took a step away from Bruce, tucking the loose strands of hair behind her ear and praying Zach would wrap up what he was doing. She was too tired to talk with anyone, especially Bruce.

"Your sister always pushes her hair behind her ear like that."

"What has the FBI come up with so far?" Jacie changed the subject, her gaze still on Zach, willing him to look up.

Several feet away, his head tilted toward the sheriff who'd been giving him the lowdown on retrieval of the two bodies in the canyon, Zach glanced across at her and frowned.

"Not as much as I'd hoped. Whoever took Tracie didn't leave much of a trail."

"At least we can rule out Los Lobos. And if it wasn't Los Lobos, either La Familia has some inside traitors or someone else took my sister. Any guesses?" Jacie finally pinned Bruce with her gaze, her eyebrows rising up her forehead.

Bruce shook his head, his eyes shadowed. "You are a lot like your sister. Get down to the business at hand. That's what I love about her."

"Where is she, Bruce?" Anger fueled by frustration and exhaustion bubbled up inside her. "You have two federal agencies and the local law enforcement on this rescue effort and what have you found? Nothing."

An arm slipped around her waist. "You ready to go, darlin'?"

Zach's resonant baritone washed over her like a soothing warm wave. The tension that had held her upright for the past hour slowly seeped out of her and left her oddly boneless and ready to collapse. Her chin tipped upward and she gave him the hint of a smile. "Yes. I'm more than ready to go."

Zach pulled her against him and stared across at Bruce. "If you don't mind, I'm going to steal my girl away and get her home to bed."

Heat flared in Jacie's body at Zach's words, the images they generated making her tingle all over. Her nipples hardened into tight little buds rubbing against the lace of her bra.

"Take me home," she whispered, leaning into him, grateful for the added support when her knees turned to jelly.

As he drew her away from Bruce, Jacie whispered, "Did you talk to Hank about our next steps?"

"He called it a night an hour ago. I hate to wake the man when there's nothing more we can do tonight."

"Good point."

"We can do that in the morning. Right now I need that shower and some shut-eye." He glanced over at the young Hispanic seated on the ground beside a parked vehicle, his head in his hands. "Come on, Juan. We'll take you home."

Juan scrambled to his feet and followed Zach and Jacie.

Jacie was past exhaustion, and the worry about her sister weighed so heavily she wanted to burst out crying. But that wasn't the way she worked. The thought of going back to her cabin and collapsing into bed sounded wonderful.

Except her mattress was still on the floor and some-one had tried to break in while she'd been in the shower.

She glanced at Zach. No, she wouldn't put that on him, not after all he'd just been through. Jacie could handle a gun and take care of herself for what remained of the night.

Zach promised the sheriff he'd fill out a police report the next day, then he grabbed Jacie's arm and led her to his truck, Juan following.

Without uttering another word, they left the Raging Bull and headed for Wild Oak Canyon then the Big Elk Ranch.

ZACH'S RIBS HURT and the gash on his cheek stung from where one of Hank's employees had cleaned and applied antiseptic ointment to his wound. He'd passed on a ban-dage, but now was second-guessing that decision.

"Dude, you're one crazy son of a b—"

"Please." Zach cut him off. "I owe you an apology for dragging you into that. But thanks. At least it ruled out Los Lobos as the people who kidnapped Tracie."

"Can I have my knife back now?" Juan asked over the backseat.

"I might be crazy, but I'm not stupid." Zach chuckled. "I'll give you back your knife when I drop you at your home."

Juan leaned back against the upholstery. "Whoever killed the two from La Familia must have wanted this woman really bad. No one messes with La Familia without retribution. As many as there are, someone will pay soon."

Jacie turned sideways and peered over the back of the seat. "If you know anyone around here associated with La Familia, now would be the time to tell us."

"What? Or you'll shoot me?" Juan shook his head. "*No estoy loco.* If I tell you who, everyone will know it was me. I'd be a marked man."

"Give us a hint?" Jacie begged.

"No." Juan stared at Zach in the mirror. "Your woman can shoot me dead, but it would be better than what La Familia would do to me."

Zach nodded. La Familia was known for its brutality with public beheadings and hangings. Los Lobos was no better, a fact Zach knew from experience. "Leave him alone. He's done enough."

Jacie settled back in her seat, her lips tight. "What about Tracie?"

"I have a contact that might be able to help. And I'll get Hank on it, as well."

Zach dropped Juan at his trailer and handed him his knife. "We're square now?"

Juan peered through the truck's open window at Jacie. "For what it's worth, I didn't know your sister would be a target. She asked when the next shipment would be handed off. All I did was tell her. She gave me five hundred dollars for that information." He snorted. "I should have asked for a lot more."

Jacie's mouth twisted. "And I shouldn't have let her go on the trail that day."

Zach drove out of the little town of Wild Oak Canyon in silence.

The back of Jacie's head rested against the seat, her profile one of natural, wholesome beauty. Unfettered, unblemished beauty that went deeper than skin. "Do you think Juan really knows someone in La Familia?"

Zach drew his attention away from Jacie's profile and back to the road before answering, "Yes."

"Then why didn't you make him tell us who it was?"

"I've seen what these cartels do to the people they deem traitors or informers. Juan did what we asked of him today. We put him in enough danger just associating with us. Besides, I don't think he's involved in what's going on with your sister."

"If he knows who we can ask…"

"He'd be dead by morning if we moved on his information."

"What about Los Lobos? Won't they be after Juan?"

"Maybe, but they didn't see me with him in the canyon. Not where they would recognize him."

Deep in thought, Zach didn't see the other vehicle until it broadsided his truck, metal slamming into metal, forcing him to swerve and bump through the gravel on the roadside. "Hold on!" He gripped the steering wheel with both hands and fought to get it back up on the road.

Jacie grabbed for the handle beside the door and held on, the seat belt tightening, bracing her against the rough terrain.

Zach veered back up onto the road, only to be hit again. This time the truck careened off the road and down the embankment into the ditch and back up on the other side.

The vehicle on the road slowed and the window slid downward.

"Duck!" Zach cried, hitting the accelerator, sending the truck back down into the ditch and up onto the road.

At the same time, the dark older-model SUV shot forward, catching Zach's truck bed.

The back end swung around, but Zach corrected and hit the gas again, propelling the truck forward.

The vehicle behind him raced to catch up.

In the rearview mirror, all Zach could see was the dark silhouette of the vehicle whose headlights were blacked out.

Something rose above the top of the vehicle behind him, and dread filled his gut. Zach jerked the steering wheel with one hand as he shoved Jacie's head down with the other.

The back windshield exploded inward with a spray of bullets. One zipped all the way through and smashed into the front glass, sending out a spider web of fissures, making it difficult to see.

Zach couldn't outrun the SUV, and the turnoff to the Big Elk Ranch was still several miles away. "Jacie, you're going to have to return fire."

"Are you kidding?"

"It's that or one of us isn't going to make it to tomorrow, maybe both. Use my rifle."

"I'd rather use mine."

She grabbed her rifle from where it rested on the floorboard, removed her safety belt and turned in the seat, steadying the gun's barrel on the back of the headrest.

"What do you want me to aim at?"

"Start with the shooter on top. Hell, just shoot at the whole damn vehicle. It'll be hard enough to hit anything on these bumpy roads."

She fired once.

The vehicle behind them swerved, then straightened.

The next round caused the man on top to duck inside.

Her third round forced the driver to drop back.

"That's my girl." Zach grinned. "You're pretty good riding shotgun."

Still sitting backward in her seat, Jacie smiled. "Knowing how to handle a weapon comes in handy sometimes, besides on the hunt."

The vehicle behind them dropped back farther until it spun around and headed in the opposite direction.

"Thank God." Jacie turned and settled back down in her seat and took stock of the truck. "I'm sorry your truck took the worst of that. And you kept it so nice and shiny."

Zach could have laughed. "To hell with the truck. You could have been hurt."

She glanced his way, one hand clasping her left shoulder. "Uh, actually..." Jacie moved her hand.

Because Jacie had been wearing a dark shirt, Zach hadn't noticed the blood until the light from the dash glanced off the liquid.

"Damn. We're going straight to the doctor." He slowed, ready to do a U-turn in the middle of the highway.

"It's only a flesh wound and I have no desire to enter into another game of chicken with the SUV that attacked us back there." She pointed to the road ahead. "I have a first aid kit in my cabin. A little disinfectant and a bandage ought to fix me right up."

Zach's foot hovered over the accelerator. "Are you sure?"

"I've lived on a ranch long enough to know a serious wound from a not-so-serious wound. I just want to go home. Please."

Still not fully convinced, Zach gave in and hit the gas, sending the truck shooting forward. He pulled onto the dusty road into the Big Elk Ranch, anxious to get there and assess the damage himself.

The trailer from the Raging Bull was parked beside the barn, empty. Apparently Richard had arrived earlier, taken care of the horses and called it a night.

If need be, he'd take Jacie to the lodge and call an ambulance if her wound was more than just torn flesh.

After parking in front of Jacie's cabin, Zach leaped down and rounded the truck in a jog.

Jacie had the door open and was stepping down.

He grabbed her around the middle and eased her the rest of the way down to the ground.

For a moment he stared down at her, appreciating that

she wasn't crying. She hadn't burst into hysterics at the sight of her own blood, and she was staring back up at him, the moon reflected in her eyes.

"Anyone ever tell you that you're an amazing woman?" Zach said.

"No, but you can say it again. It sounds nice." She smiled, and then grimaced. "I'd better get this cleaned up. And you need a bandage on your face."

"We're a pair. We look like we lost the fight."

"The hell we did. We've only just begun." She led the way up the steps to her cabin and fumbled in her pocket for the key.

Before she could find it, Zach pushed the door and it swung open. "Did you lock this door?"

Jacie frowned. "Yes, I did."

When he moved to enter, Jacie held out a hand to stop him.

"Wait," she whispered. "What if someone's inside?"

Zach pulled her to the side and lifted the rifle to his shoulder. "Stay here." He gave her a steady, stern look.

She nodded.

Zach stood to one side of the door, edged it open wider with the barrel of the rifle and peered inside.

Furniture had been upended and papers and clothes scattered across the floor. "I think whoever did this is gone," he said, his voice so low only Jacie would be able to hear him.

Ducking low, he entered the cabin, keeping out of the moonlight streaming through the windows. He worked his way around the cramped interior, checking in the bathroom and closet before he was satisfied that it was no longer occupied.

"It's clear," he called out.

Jacie came inside, closed the door behind her and

flipped on the light. The tears welling in her eyes, which she'd refuse to let fall, were Zach's undoing.

He crossed the room and opened his arms. Jacie fell into them, wrapping hers around his waist. "I'm just too tired to deal with this."

"Then don't. All we need is that first aid kit, and we're out of here."

"It was in the bathroom." She leaned away from him and he slipped into the bathroom. "And we don't have to leave. I'm okay."

He stayed in the bathroom longer than necessary to retrieve the kit under normal circumstances.

"Find it?" Jacie asked.

"Most of it." Zach emerged with the kit, stuffing bandages and tubes of ointment into the plastic container. "I have enough to work with." He glanced around the bedroom. "Was your sister staying with you?"

"Yes."

"Did she leave anything here that might explain why she came? Maybe something that would be worth ransacking this place for?"

"I went through her suitcase and discovered her cell phone and FBI credentials. I hid them before I left to find you."

Zach frowned. "Why did you hide them?"

Jacie looked away. "Someone tried to get into the cabin while I was in the bath."

Zach blew out a long breath. "Not good news."

"You're telling me." She stared at the mattress, recalling the cold chill of dread she'd had as she sat on the floor, her gun trained on the door.

"Where did you hide the cell phone and credentials?"

Jacie's lips quirked upward. "In the fridge beneath the rotting bag of tomatoes."

Zach's mouth quirked. "Smart move. Let's hope the intruder didn't figure it out." He picked his way across the floor to the refrigerator, pulled it open and rummaged around inside. He came out with the cell phone, credentials and a tight smile. "You could have been an agent, Jacie Kosart."

She shrugged and grimaced. "Not my calling."

"Come on, we're going to my cabin. Hopefully it's still intact. We can figure out the rest of this mess in the morning." Zach shoved Tracie's phone and wallet inside his back pocket.

"Come closer to the door. I'm going to turn out the lights."

Jacie stood against the wall beside the door, aware of Zach's warmth next to her.

Zach switched the overhead light off, plunging them into darkness. "I'm going out first," he whispered against her cheek.

The warm draft of his breath made gooseflesh rise on her arms. He was close enough to kiss.

"Wait until I tell you to come." He touched her hand and then slipped out the door into the night.

Jacie's heart fluttered and she held her breath for what felt like a very long time. Then the door nudged open.

"It's okay, my cabin's untouched." Zach was there again. He captured her hand in his and led her across to his cabin.

Once inside, Zach closed the shades and pulled the curtains over the windows. Then he switched on the light. "Now let's take care of that wound."

"Earlier…" Jacie stiffened when Zach's fingers reached for the buttons on her blouse. "I can do it." Jacie wasn't sure she could resist him at such close quarters. He drew her like a fly to honey and she was too tired to resist.

He shook his head, his lips firm. "Let me do this. I'm trained in first aid and buddy care."

"My mother taught me enough that I haven't died yet," she argued halfheartedly. Her arm stung and she didn't have the strength to argue. Jacie sighed. "Fine."

He sat on the edge of the bed.

Jacie drew in a deep breath. This was not a good idea. Not when her defenses were down.

Zach stood in front of her and reached for the top button on her shirt. He pushed the button through the hole, then the others, all the way down to where the shirt disappeared into the waistband of her jeans. He tugged the tails free and slid the blouse over her shoulders, easing the fabric over her injured arm.

A quiver of awareness rippled across her skin, and her breasts tightened. Jacie closed her eyes and sucked in a long, steadying breath.

Footsteps sounded, leading into the bathroom. Water ran in the sink and the footsteps returned.

Every one of her senses lit up. With her eyes still closed, she inhaled the scent of Zach, letting it wash away the fear of seeing him fighting two men at once, not being able to help for fear of shooting the wrong man. The way he'd held her the night before, the way she hoped he'd hold her again.

"I'll try to be gentle."

"Just do it," she whispered, praying he would.

Chapter Twelve

Zach was in over his head on this one, with no way to swim to the top.

Jacie sat with her eyes closed, her hair spilling down her back, the light shining down over her face, neck and breasts, giving her a golden glow.

God, she was beautiful.

His hand shook as he smoothed the damp cloth over her wound.

He would never have suspected her skin would be so soft and silky beneath her tough-gal exterior. She smelled like the Texas wind and herbal shampoo as she sat with her eyes closed, her head tilted back slightly, her breathing shallow, the rise of her chest captivating.

Tempted to steal a kiss from those full, luscious lips, he dragged his focus back to the task at hand, shifting uncomfortably as his groin tightened.

After cleaning the wound, he opened the tube of antiseptic, hoping it would bring him back to his senses with its acrid scent. It didn't.

He applied the cream, his gaze slipping to the swells of her breasts, peeking out from the top of a lacy black bra. Who'd have thought the hunting guide would have such a sexy piece of lingerie in her wardrobe? His thoughts shifted farther south. Did she wear matching panties?

Zach fought the urge to slip the strap over her shoulder and bare one of those delicious orbs. He peeled the backing off a large adhesive bandage and taped it to her skin over the injury. "There—" He cleared his throat. "All done."

She turned to him, her eyes opening, the hunger in them hard to miss. "Now your turn," she said, her voice husky and so sexy Zach thought he might lose control.

Holy cow, how was he supposed to sit while she administered first aid to him? He could barely move, he was so hard.

She rose from the bed and walked toward the bathroom, wearing her bra and her jeans, her hips swaying with every step. Perhaps she'd be appalled at how sexy she looked.

Not Zach. He couldn't tear his gaze away from her rounded bottom. A groan rose up his throat.

Jacie was the job. Making love to her wasn't part of the contract. But when she emerged from the bathroom with a damp cloth, all good intentions flew out the window.

She came to a stop in front of him, hesitated a moment, then straddled his legs and bent down to apply the cloth to the wound on his cheek. Jacie leaned close enough Zach could easily have reached out and touched one of those lace-clad breasts with his lips.

After cleaning the wound, she applied the antiseptic and the bandage, then sighed, straightening. "Am I that homely?" she whispered, then started to step away from him, a frown wrinkling her forehead.

Zach grasped her hips. "What did you say?"

Her cheeks suffused with a pretty pink and she glanced away from him. "Nothing."

"Wrong." He tugged her hips, forcing her to sit on his legs. "Do you know how hard it is to be a gentleman when you're wearing only a bra?" His hands slipped up to the catch at the middle of her back. "When all I want to do is this...." He flicked the hooks open and slipped the straps over her shoulders—gently around her wound. "I just didn't want to cross the line."

She laughed softly, letting the bra fall to the floor. "Don't tell me you're a rule follower. I can't picture you as one."

"Never." He looked up at her, his gaze capturing hers. "You've been through a lot today. Are you sure this is what you want?"

Jacie smoothed a hand over his hair. "I not only want this, I need it." She tugged his ears, dragging him within range of one full, rosy-tipped breast. "Please, don't make me beg."

He couldn't resist the temptation. He sucked her nipple into his mouth, his other hand rising to capture the other breast. His tongue swirled around the tip until it puckered into a tight little bud. He nibbled it and then switched to the other, giving it equal attention.

Jacie's back arched, her bottom squirming against his thighs. They still wore jeans and Zach wanted nothing more than to lie naked beside her and feel all of her against him.

He stood her on her feet and rose from the bed.

She frowned. "Is that it?"

"Not unless you want it to be." He shrugged out of his shirt and slung it to the corner.

"No. I want it all." She grasped the top button of his jeans and forced it through the opening. Then she worked the zipper down until his engorged member sprang free.

Zach let out the breath he'd been holding, the relief only temporary. He pulled his wallet from his back pocket, tossed it onto a pillow, then shucked his jeans.

Her gaze followed the path of the descending denim, her tongue sliding across her lips when he stood naked before her. Fire burned through his veins at the hunger in her expression. Past rational thought, he reached for her waistband, ripped the button open and shoved her jeans down her legs until she could kick free of them.

He scooped her up in his arms and laid her across the comforter and then crawled into the bed over her. "We should be sleeping," he said, pressing a kiss to her lips— sleep the furthest thing from his mind.

Her hands laced around his neck, her mouth turning up in a smile. "Sleep is overrated." She pulled him close, capturing his lips, her tongue slipping between his teeth. For every thrust of that magic tongue, an answering tug hit him low in the groin. If he didn't concentrate, it would be over before he had a chance to pleasure her.

He slid his mouth over her chin and down the long line of her throat to the base, where her pulse beat a ragged staccato against her skin. He tapped his tongue to the tip of one breast and captured the other, pulling it fully into his mouth, where he suckled until her back arched off the mattress.

Jacie's fingers wove through his hair and she tugged, urging him lower still. Her thighs parted, allowing him to lie between them on his journey down to her nether regions.

His fingers led the way, parting her folds buried beneath a light smattering of fluffy dark curls. He slid his tongue across the special bundle of nerves packed into a simple nubbin of flesh.

Jacie bucked beneath him, "Oh, Zach!" She dug her heels into the bed and rose to meet his tongue's every stroke, her fingers digging into his scalp. Her body grew rigid, her thighs tight, her face pinched as she catapulted over the edge.

Zach climbed up her body, rolled to the side and

grabbed his wallet from the other pillow, tearing through the contents until his fingers closed around a foil packet. He ripped it open with his teeth.

Jacie pulled the condom free and rolled it down over his swollen member. "Now. Please."

He leveraged himself between her legs and slipped into her warm, wet channel, sliding all the way in. Her muscles contracted around him and he fought for control.

Soon he was thrusting in and out of her, his pace increasing with the intensity of sensations filling his body. The tingling ripped through him from his toes to the tip of his shaft. He rammed home one last time and collapsed on top of her, buried deep inside Jacie's warmth.

Her legs wrapped around his middle, her arms around his neck.

For a long time, he pulsed inside her, the troubles of the world so far away they could have been on an entirely different planet for all he knew.

When his senses finally calmed and he returned to the present, he rolled to his side, taking her with him, their connection unbroken.

She lay with her head pillowed on his arm, her eyelids drifting to half-mast. "Are you always this intense?" She touched a finger to his lip.

He kissed the tip, giving her the hint of a smile. "Only when it counts."

"Um. I'd say it counted." She draped a leg over his, sliding her calf across his thigh.

"To answer your earlier question, no, you're not homely. You're beautiful." He brushed a kiss across her lips and pulled her closer, resting his chin on the top of her head.

Within seconds, Jacie's breathing slowed and her body relaxed against his as she fell asleep.

Zach lay awake for a long time, sanity crowding in on him with each passing minute.

He'd done exactly what he'd sworn he'd never do again. He'd slept with a woman whom he could very easily fall for. Hell, he was already halfway there.

Jacie was everything he could possibly want in a woman. Tall, gorgeous, open, honest and tough enough to set him in his place. She was loyal and loving and deserved a man who could give her all of himself.

Zach just wasn't that man. After what had happened to his partner, he vowed never to become so emotionally committed to any woman. It hurt too badly when you lost her and he knew his heart wouldn't survive another blow that deep.

An hour later, Zach slid his arm from beneath Jacie's neck and climbed out of the bed. He pulled on a pair of jeans, grabbed his cell phone and let himself out of the cabin.

Clouds had moved in to block the moon. Except for the porch lights on the tiny cabins and the security lights on the lodge, everything was shrouded in inky, black darkness.

Zach sat on the porch steps and checked his phone. He'd been so wrapped up in everything that had happened since he'd gone into the canyon to find Los Lobos hideout, then Jacie…he hadn't checked his calls and messages. Only one call had come in. It was from his friend James Coslowski, and he'd left a message.

Zach's heartbeat picked up as he hit the play button.

"Dude, what the hell have you gotten into? Apparently this Kosart woman was working without authority on a case that wasn't assigned to her. The whole bureau is in an uproar and the big bosses are threatening to roll a few heads. Call me when you get this message and I'll fill you in."

Zach dialed James.

"Do you know any other time of the day than middle of the night?" James answered in a whisper. "Let me get somewhere that I won't wake my pregnant wife so I can talk."

A moment later, he spoke in a normal tone. "So you got my message."

"I did. Why is the bureau all up in arms?"

"Classic case of the right hand not knowing what the left hand was doing. DEA supposedly was working the Big Bend area when your Tracie Kosart wandered in and got herself kidnapped and the agents killed. Any luck finding her?"

"None so far."

"It's a shame. I didn't find anything on Tracie. She checks out as a good agent, follows the rules—until now—and keeps her nose clean. Have it on file that she and Agent Bruce Masterson are in a relationship. I'm guessing you already know that since he's been assigned to the team responsible for finding Agent Kosart."

"He's here."

"One of the FBI big dogs, Grant Lehmann, has also assigned himself as overseer of the operation to retrieve the Kosart woman."

"I guess with the two agencies involved, they felt it necessary to have adult supervision?"

"Probably. I found it interesting that one of Bruce Masterson's past assignments was to infiltrate a drug ring in the San Antonio area. He pulled in a pretty major leader on that case and got all kinds of kudos and awards for his work."

"Seems like he needed to be a little farther west."

"Yeah, but the ringleader has connections to people in your area."

Zach sat up straighter. "Names?"

"Let me find my notes." The sound of papers being turned crackled in Zach's ear before James said, "Here it is. The file only listed one, Enrique Sanchez. Lives in a trailer six miles south of Wild Oak Canyon. The notes in the file indicate he makes frequent trips to Mexico and has been seen with members of La Familia Diablos on the Mexican side of the border."

"Anything else?"

"That's all so far. I'll let you know as soon as I dig up anything else."

"Thanks, cos."

"Keep your head down, buddy. It's likely to blow up even bigger than you think. What with two agencies fighting over jurisdiction and blaming each other for everything that's gone wrong."

"Trust me, I'm here. I know." Zach clicked off his cell phone, his heart pumping, sleep so far from his mind he couldn't stay still.

He had to get to Enrique Sanchez. If he was a member of La Familia, he might know what happened to Tracie. Trouble was that he couldn't leave Jacie alone. Not after her cabin had been ransacked. Since whoever had tossed her home had tried to break in while she was there, they weren't concerned about being seen by her. Meaning they would have either taken her or killed her.

Zach would have to wait until Jacie awoke. He'd get the cell phone to Hank's team and let them hack into it for any information they might find. For safekeeping, he'd leave Jacie with Hank and check out Sanchez.

From that point on, Zach spent time cleaning and checking his weapons. He couldn't afford to have one jam on him when he needed it most. And if Sanchez proved to be a member of La Familia, it wouldn't be an easy task to convince him to talk.

SOMETHING BRUSHED JACIE's lips, tickling her awake in the predawn of morning. She rolled onto her back and blinked open her eyes.

Zach leaned over her, dressed only in jeans and looking so handsome he hurt her eyes.

"Go away," she grumbled, slinging an arm over her face. She probably looked like hell.

"We have work to do. I got a lead."

Jacie sat up straight, forgetting for a moment that she was completely naked. Her face heated and she grabbed the sheet, dragging it up to her chin. "What lead?"

Zach's lips quirked upward, his gaze traveling over her. "The name of a man who could be connected to La Familia."

Jacie flung the sheet back and leaped out of the bed, all sleepiness forgotten. "Where are my jeans? I need a shirt. Why didn't you wake me earlier? Why are you just standing there?"

He shook his head, unable to hide his smile. "You're beautiful." Zach stepped up to her and finger-combed her hair back off her forehead, his brown eyes darkening to near black.

Jacie's body responded to his light touch. "Not fair. You have all your clothes on."

"I can fix that."

"What about the man from La Familia?"

"It's still dark outside. It can wait until light." Zach wrapped his hands around her waist and pulled her against him, the hardness of his erection pressing into her belly, telling the truth. He wanted her as much as she wanted him.

She circled her arms around his neck and pressed her naked breasts into his chest. "Then what are you waiting for?" Jacie slid her calf up the back of his leg.

Zach kissed her as he cupped her bottom and lifted her, wrapping her legs around his waist and backing her against the wall.

He reached beneath her to unfasten his jeans. His member sprang free and nudged her opening.

"Are you always this hard in the morning?" she asked.

"Always."

She sucked in a deep breath, so ready for him to come inside her, but not too far gone to be stupid about it. "What about protection?" She kissed his cheek, then his eyelid, trailing her lips across to the other eye.

Zach carried her across to the bed and dumped her on the mattress.

"Hey. That's not very romantic," she protested.

"Shut up and hand me my wallet," he said through gritted teeth.

She found the leather billfold and pulled out a package similar to the one they'd used the night before. "Last one." She waved it at him. "Better make this count."

"Oh, I will." He dove for it.

Jacie dodged him and held it out of his reach. "Not yet."

"What do you mean, not yet?"

"As you eloquently put it, shut up, and let me show you." Her lips curled in a wicked smile. She pressed her palms to his chest, forcing him onto his back. "I hope you're not one of those men who thinks foreplay is overrated."

"I am."

"Then prepare to be proved wrong." She straddled his jean-clad hips, lowering herself enough to touch his hard shaft, but not enough for him to enter her. At the same time, she kissed him full on the mouth, taking his tongue with hers in long, sexy strokes.

Oh, yeah, she liked touching him and could see herself doing it a lot more. If he'd let her.

"Hell, Jacie, I'm about to explode. Could you hurry it up?"

Her lips slid across his chin and down to his chest, where she nibbled on the tight little brown nipples. Jacie wasn't a virgin, but she'd never played with a man before Zach. She liked it a lot. Her trail led her lower, bumping over the taut ripples of the muscles of his abdomen to the thatch of curls at the base of his shaft.

She wrapped her fingers around his hard, thick member. "Is this fast enough?"

"Hell, no." He leaned up on his elbows, his eyes widening as Jacie touched her lips to the tip and swirled her tongue around the circumference.

Zach dropped to his back and sucked in a deep gulp of air. "Wow."

"Like that?" She did it again, this time followed by slipping his shaft into her mouth and applying a little suction.

He groaned, his hands lacing through her hair. "I can't take much more."

She gave it to him anyway, going down on him until he filled her mouth.

Her blood sang, the fire burning low in her belly flaring, crying out for her to get on with it and take him inside her. Now.

Unable to hold out any longer, Jacie sat up, rolled the condom down over him and mounted, easing down over him.

Zach wrapped his hands around her hips and guided

her up and down. "That's nice." Then he flipped her onto her back and thrust into her. "But this is better."

Jacie had to agree as he rocked in and out, the friction sending her to the edge and over.

At the same time as her body exploded in a tingling burst of sensations, Zach hit home one more time and remained buried deep inside.

Minutes later, they both drifted back to earth and the reality of the sunshine edging around the side of the curtains.

Zach rolled to the side, slapped her bottom and smiled. "Get up. We have work to do."

"How can you move after that?" Her body still vibrating with her release, she lay for a moment longer, basking in the afterglow. She moaned and sat up. Today they had to find her sister. "I'll be ready in five minutes." And she dashed for the bathroom.

Inside she stared at the stranger in the mirror. Her face was flushed, her lips bruised, her hair all over the place. Jacie had never felt more alive and desirable than she did at that moment.

She found a plastic-wrapped toothbrush beneath the sink, scrubbed her teeth and finger combed her hair. With nothing to tie it back with, she was forced to leave it down. Then she splashed her face with water and was finally ready to dress. That's when she remembered all her clothes were in the other room and she'd have to parade once more in her birthday suit in front of Zach.

So much for modesty. But then they'd made love twice. Why should it matter? With a deep breath, she threw back her shoulders and marched out.

Zach held her jeans and one of his T-shirts. "Yours was torn and bloody."

When she held out her hand for them, he raised them

out of reach, his gaze panning her body from top to toe. "If only we had more time."

His heated gaze made her body burn. "If only my sister wasn't still missing." She wiggled her fingers, wishing she had the luxury of lying around in bed with Zach all day. "Your T-shirt will fit me like a dress."

"It'll look better on you than it does on me." Zach handed over the clothes, his fingers dropping to tweak her naked breast before he sighed and stepped away. "I called Hank. He's expecting us in thirty minutes."

"Then we'd better get going." She slipped her arms into his T-shirt and pulled it over her body.

Zach's gaze followed the fabric all the way down.

"Eyes up here, cowboy." Jacie pointed to her own eyes and laughed.

"Can't help it. You have a great body."

Her cheeks heated again. "Let's find my sister and you can tell me more about it." Jacie pulled her jeans up over her legs and zipped them, deciding going commando wasn't so bad after all. Once she had her boots on, she glanced around the room. "You have my sister's phone?"

Zach patted his pocket. "I do."

"Then let's go."

At the door Zach pulled her back and into his arms. "You know I leave after this job is over."

Jacie swallowed hard, pasting a smile on her face. "I know. I'm just in this for the sex," she shot back at him as flippant as she could make it sound.

Then she pushed through the door, her chin held high, her heart sitting like a lead weight in her belly. Hell, she'd known from the start that Zach was on assignment from Hank's talent pool. He'd move on to the next job once they found Tracie. Jacie had known the ending of their story from the start, and she'd chosen to have sex with Zach anyway.

Still, the thought of Zach leaving made her day duller and darker than the rain-laden skies. Finding her sister would be bittersweet, but it had to happen.

Chapter Thirteen

Zach dropped the cell phone on Hank's desk. "Can you have someone hack into this and see if there are any numbers or information Tracie might have been using to go after the DEA agents?"

"Will do. My tech guy, Brandon Pendley, just got in and I had him working on hacking into the FBI database." Hank stood with the phone in his hand. "I'm sure this will be a piece of cake for him."

"While you're with Pendley, I need information on Enrique Sanchez. Anything you can find out. His address, family, friends. Anything. As soon as you can get it."

Hank's gaze moved from Zach to Jacie. "Someone we should be aware of?"

"I got word that he's connected with La Familia. Jacie and I will hit the diner and see if we can find out anything else about him. Then I'm going to pay him a little visit."

"I'll get Pendley right on it." Hank frowned. "If you think you need backup, I can have three other CCI men in less than an hour—including me."

Zach nodded. "I'll let you know. Have Pendley call or text the information as soon as he has anything."

"Will do." Hank nodded toward the window. "The joint operations team is expanding their search, supposedly sending feelers out to the other side of the border to see if they can locate Tracie. The FBI regional director is an old friend of mine, Grant Lehmann. He said he was giving the search top priority."

Jacie inhaled and closed her eyes for a moment. "It just seems so pointless. Is anyone actually going to find her?"

Zach slipped an arm around her and hugged her close. "Yes. And we're going to start by following the leads to Enrique."

"Let me get Brandon on this phone and the information you need to find Enrique. Then before you go, let me arm you with a few things you might need in your efforts. I should have given them to you before, but I wasn't sure if you'd actually employ them." Hank waved them to the back of the house and down the steps to a reinforced basement.

The first room they entered had computer screens lining the desks and larger screens affixed to the walls.

A young man wearing blue jeans, his hair hanging down to his collar and a single earring on one ear, glanced up. "Hey, Hank, who've you got with you?"

"Brandon, meet Zach Adams and Jacie Kosart."

Brandon stood and held out his hand to Jacie. "You're the twin?"

Jacie shook his hand. "That's right. I'm Tracie Kosart's sibling."

"Sorry about your sister."

"Don't be, just help me find her."

"On it." Brandon shook hands with Zach. "Nice to finally meet you in person."

"Actually," Hank added, "it was Brandon that found you and recommended I hire you."

Zach grinned. "Thanks. I think."

"Hank's a good man. You'll like working with him."

Zach made note of the fact that Brandon had said working with Hank, not for him. That indicated a level of teamwork and trust, reinforcing Zach's decision to go to work for Hank.

Hank handed the cell phone to Brandon. "Tracie Kosart's cell. Hack it for any information you can get out of it. But before you start, locate Enrique Sanchez for us."

Brandon gave a mock salute. "On it." He dropped back into his chair, and his fingers flew over the keyboard, his concentration fully on the screen in front of him.

"Brandon will have information about Enrique before you leave the ranch." Hank swept his hand to the back of the room. "Now, if you'll follow me."

Zach wondered how large the basement actually was as he followed Hank deeper into the maze.

Hank stopped at a steel, reinforced door and clicked numbers into a keypad. The door slid open and he stepped aside and gestured for them to follow. "Please."

Inside, the walls were painted a stark white and lined with racks filled with every kind of weapon imaginable.

Jacie spun in a circle, her eyes wide. "Holy crap, Hank, where'd you get all these?"

"Some of them I bought, others I had manufactured in one of my plants." He pulled a canvas bag off a hanger and handed it to Zach. One by one, he plucked armament off the shelves. "You might be able to use these incendiary grenades if you need to create a diversion." He tucked the grenade into the canvas bag and moved to the next shelf labeled CS Gas. "If you need to get the enemy out of a reinforced location, these come in handy. Here, you might need these, as well." Hank handed him a pair of night-vision goggles.

"Hank." Zach shook his head. "I'd be scared if I wasn't convinced you were one of the good guys."

"I wanted my operatives to be prepared for any event."

Zach held up his hand as Hank prepared to shove more

into the canvas bag. "I'd never get past the gauntlet of the joint ops team outside with much more than I have in here now. I could use nine-millimeter ammo and a couple tracking devices."

"Got it." Hank handed Zach several clips and boxes of rounds and a web belt with straps that would hold clips and grenades. "And take this." He handed him a shiny SIG Sauer Pro. "In case you need a backup."

Zach stuffed it all into the canvas bag. "That should about cover a small war."

"You're in cartel territory," Hank reminded him. "They have far more firepower than that." The older man handed him three small disks. "Keep one somewhere on your person at all times. Tuck it in your underwear or shoes, just don't let it out of your reach. If you get into trouble, I'll be able to locate you."

"Sounds like you expect big trouble." Jacie shivered.

Zach wished he could shield her from all this, but she was smack dab in the middle and might as well be mentally as well as physically prepared with major hardware. "When we locate your sister, she's likely being held in a guarded compound. Getting in might not be a problem. Getting out with your sister will prove more challenging."

Jacie's chin tipped upward, though her face had paled several shades. "I'm not afraid."

Hank stared hard at her. "You should be. The cartels are ruthless."

Zach nodded. "He's right. I've seen what they can do to a captured woman. It's not pretty." He closed his eyes as memories of Toni's torture washed over him. "On second thought, Jacie, you should stay here with Hank. You'd be better off here monitoring efforts than getting caught up with the cartel."

"You know how well I stay put. Take me with you now or I'll follow you anyway."

Hank chuckled. "I might have to hire you onto my team. I hear you're a good shot."

Jacie nodded. "I am. But I'm not interested. I like my job. Getting shot at by a negligent hunter isn't nearly as scary as getting shot at by an angry cartel member."

Hank shrugged. "The offer's there if you change your mind."

Zach hooked Jacie's arm. "If you're done negotiating, let's get out and find your sister."

Jacie shook her arm loose as she exited Hank's armory. "What? You don't like the idea of me playing undercover cowboy?" Her eyes narrowed. "Why?"

"It's too dangerous."

"And it's not as dangerous for you?" She flipped her ponytail over her shoulder. "Sounds a bit chauvinistic to me."

At that moment, they passed Brandon's desk. "Give it up, dude. You'll never win."

Zach growled, his gut in a knot at the thought of Jacie being in harm's way every day. She made a good point about double standards, but he couldn't help it. His instinct to protect her was strong and he was struggling to get past it. If he could tie her up at Hank's and be assured she wouldn't find a way loose, he'd have left her rather than take her with him to interrogate Enrique.

Brandon gave Zach a sticky note. "That's Enrique's home address. It's just outside town. Be careful, the man has a police record of assault and battery. He's a mean dude."

"Thanks." Zach tucked the note in his pocket and placed his hand on the small of Jacie's back, guiding her toward the stairs.

"For the record, take the job if you like. It's your life."

Jacie paused with one foot on the step. "That's right. It is my life. And you're not staying around anyway, so why should it bother you?"

His gut clenched. He'd told her that he'd be out of there as soon as the case was over. Why it hurt hearing this from her, he didn't know, but it did. Zach had to remind himself not to get attached, although he feared it was too late. "Now that we're agreed, keep moving or we'll be here all day." He slapped her bottom as she climbed the steps out of the basement.

"My, my, we're grumpy, aren't we?" She threw a twisted smile over her shoulder at him. "Didn't get enough sleep?"

Her teasing wink only made him want to spank her again, or kiss her. Either would have been just as satisfying at that point, but not nearly enough. He wanted to take her back to bed and make love to her.

Unfortunately now was not the time or place.

"Here, hold this, it will look less conspicuous than if I walked out carrying it." He handed the canvas bag to Jacie before they left the ranch house and crossed to where he'd parked his truck. He glanced up at the steely gray skies, glad for the added darkness, yet hoping the rain would hold off until he had a chat with Enrique.

Bruce Masterson emerged from the operations tent and waved at them. "Jacie!"

"Just keep going," Zach urged.

Jacie placed a hand on Zach's arm and brought him to a stop. "What if he has information about Tracie?"

Zach smiled down at her and spoke between clenched teeth. "You're carrying weapons that aren't necessarily legal for civilians to own."

"Oh." Jacie hiked the bag higher on her shoulder. "Now's a good time to tell me."

"Just make it short." Zach turned to face the FBI agent

and nodded, his arm slipping around Jacie, pressing her and the bag against his side. "Masterson."

"Adams." Bruce nodded curtly toward Zach and turned his attention to Jacie. "We got a possible lead on your sister's location."

Jacie's eyes widened and she started to take a step forward.

Zach held her firmly in place, schooling his face to give away nothing. If the FBI truly had a lead, good. In the meantime, they had their own information to follow up on. But he'd hear the agent out.

"Where is she?" Jacie asked. "Is she okay?"

Bruce raised his hand and snorted. "Not so fast. It's a lead, not yet confirmed. I sent agents across the border to check it out. I'll let you know as soon as I find out anything."

"Oh, thank you." She touched Masterson's arm.

"Where will you be? Do you have a number I can reach you at?"

Jacie hesitated.

"You can leave word at the Big Elk Lodge," Zach offered. "Giddings will pass the message on."

"Right." Jacie gave the man a stiff smile. "I'll be busy working outside, away from my phone and out of decent reception."

"Okay, then." Bruce clapped his hands together. "I feel good about this, so don't go too far out of touch in case we bring her back. I'm sure Tracie will want to see you."

Jacie sighed. "Just bring her back alive."

"We will." Bruce spun on his heel and returned to the tent.

Zach turned Jacie toward his truck.

"Why did you tell him to call the lodge?" Jacie asked. "I'll have my phone on me."

"I'd just as soon not give him the number. You don't know who in that operations tent is on our side. Remember there's a mole inside either the FBI or the DEA. We're not sure which, but I'm not willing to take chances."

"Right." Jacie nodded. "And phones can be traced through the global positioning system."

Zach handed her up into the truck and closed the door before climbing into the driver's seat.

They accomplished the drive to town in silence. As soon as they headed back out of town on the other end, Zach's fingers tightened on the wheel. "I'm not going to drive right up into Enrique's yard."

Jacie turned toward him. "I'm listening."

"I'll park the truck back about half a mile from his place, hide it in the brush and hike in on foot. I'm going to pretend I broke down. That way they don't start shooting right away."

"Sounds good so far."

He breathed in and let it out, then continued, knowing exactly what her reaction would be to his next words. "I want you to stay with the truck and watch for other vehicles that might enter or leave."

"In other words, you're not taking me in." She crossed her arms. "You know how I feel about that."

"I need live backup. By staying back, if you hear gunfire, get the hell back to town, where you'll have cell phone reception and can get Hank's help."

She shook her head. "Not getting any better. Why can't I come with you and we pretend we're the happy, lost couple?"

"Because Enrique might know you or recognize your face if he had anything to do with Tracie's disappearance. It would be like waving a red flag in the bull's face."

Jacie sat back against her seat, her gaze riveted on his.

Finally she sighed, her shoulders sagging. "I hate it when you make sense. Okay, I'll stay put, but I'm not going to like it."

"Thanks." He pulled off the highway and onto the side of the road, bumping across the uneven terrain, fitting the truck in the middle of a clump of scrubby juniper trees.

Cedar scent filled the interior of the truck.

Zach switched the engine off and faced Jacie. "I also didn't want to worry about you." He leaned across the seat, cupped the back of her neck and kissed her soundly on the lips. "Damn it, you're growing on me and it scares the crap out of me."

A lump formed in Jacie's throat. "Goes the same for me."

Zach climbed out of the truck and struck out across the scrubby terrain without a backward glance.

The sky rumbled in the distance, and a single raindrop hit the windshield. Jacie hoped the rain would hold off a little longer until Zach came back.

ZACH RAN PARALLEL to the highway until he reached the dirt track leading into Enrique's place. Old cars littered the front yard, some with the hoods lifted, others jacked up, the tires long gone.

Though he knew he'd be a big target, Zach stepped out in the open, pretending to be a motorist whose car had broken down on the highway.

"Hello. Anyone home?" Zach called out. No one answered.

The flutter of a curtain in a window of the house caught his attention. A woman's face appeared, then disappeared.

A child cried inside and was quickly hushed.

"Hello." Zach walked closer. "My truck broke down. I need to use a telephone."

The front door opened and a short, round, Hispanic woman peered out. She waved her hands as if to shoo him away, speaking in rapid-fire Spanish, almost too fast for Zach to understand.

He caught the gist of what she was saying, something about leaving before her husband returned.

"I'm sorry." Zach held his hands palms up. "I don't speak Spanish. Do you speak English?"

"No," the woman said.

"She doesn't, but I do." A man appeared around the side of the house, carrying an semiautomatic rifle. "What do you want?"

"My truck broke down on the road and I need to use a telephone."

"We don't have a telephone." He tipped the rifle. "Leave."

"You don't happen to have a tire iron, do you?" Zach moved closer, pretending to be unaffected by the presence of the rifle. "My tire went flat and I can't get the lug nuts loose."

"You can't stay here. Leave now." The man pointed the rifle at him.

"Hey, it's okay." Zach raised his hands. "I just need a tire iron with a lug wrench on it and I'll be out of your hair." He walked around the side of the house.

The man Zach suspected was Enrique followed. "You can't stay."

Once he'd rounded to the back, Zach noted a truck standing with doors wide open. Boxes and furniture had been thrown into the bed as if in a hurry. "Going somewhere, Enrique?"

Zach spun and lunged for the rifle before the man had a chance to fire. He grabbed the barrel, jammed the nose down and the butt up, hitting the guy in the face, causing his hands to loosen enough that Zach ripped the weapon out of his hands and flung it to the side. He yanked the man's arm around to his back and drove it up between his shoulder blades. "Enrique Sanchez, I understand you're a member of La Familia."

"I don't know what you're talking about." He stood on his toes, his face creased in pain.

"Really?" Zach twisted the arm tighter until the man cried out. "Wanna rethink that response?"

"Sí, sí," Enrique squeaked. "I am. So? What do you want?"

"Answers." The clock was ticking on Tracie's life, and Zach had let it go on for too long.

"I don't know anything," Enrique insisted.

"Were you there when the DEA agents were murdered in Wild Horse Canyon?" Zach bore upward on the arm.

"Sí, sí. Madre de Dios!"

"Who murdered the DEA agents?"

Enrique didn't answer.

Zach hated doing it, but he ratcheted the man's arm tighter. "Who killed the DEA agents?"

"Aya! Go ahead, break it! Nothing you can do to me will be as bad as what La Familia will do if they get to me first. So go ahead. Kill me. I am a dead man already."

"Why?"

"I was supposed to meet *mi compadres,* but when I got there, they were dead. La Familia will blame me."

"Did you see who killed them?" Zach loosened his hold, finally letting go.

"No." Enrique dropped to his knees. "I don't know."

"Did you see who took the woman?"

"No." Enrique struggled to his feet. "I have to leave. I have to get my family out before—"

"Zach, look out!"

A shot rang out and Enrique jerked forward, slamming into Zach, his eyes wide, blood oozing from the wound in his gut.

Zach staggered backward as Enrique slid to the ground, his eyes wide and vacant. The man was dead.

Chapter Fourteen

Jacie sat for as long as she could stand before she flung the door open and dropped down out of the truck. Zach had been gone too long, as far as she was concerned. He could be in trouble.

She grabbed her rifle and tucked her nine-millimeter in her waistband, then set off in the same direction as Zach had minutes earlier. Staying low, she used the available vegetation for concealment as she'd seen Zach do, moving parallel with the highway. When she came to the dirt track leading into Enrique's place, she stopped and listened, then turned and worked her way slowly toward the house.

Nothing stirred out front, so she circled wide, around the back of the house and the workshop behind it.

Voices carried to her, urgent and angry.

One belonged to Zach.

Her heartbeat fluttered and her palms sweat as she eased around the back of the workshop to get a better view, her rifle in front of her, in the ready position.

Zach stood with his back to her.

A man, who Jacie assumed was Enrique, was on his knees in front of Zach, struggling to stand. With only the one man in sight, Jacie gathered that Zach had everything under control. She had started to back away when she saw a movement from the corner of the house.

The barrel of a military-style rifle poked out.

"Zach, look out!" she yelled.

A shot rang out. Enrique, who'd managed to stand, dropped to the ground.

As a man stepped away from the side of the house, Jacie crouched to a kneeling position, aimed for the man's chest and pulled the trigger.

The shooter dropped to the ground before he could fire off another round.

Jacie's pulse pounded so hard the blood thrummed against her eardrums. She didn't hear the footsteps behind her until too late. A rock skittered by her, her first indication she was not alone.

Jacie rolled to her back, holding her rifle to her chest. Before she could aim and fire, a boot punted the rifle out of her hands.

A bulky, dark-haired, barrel-chested man grabbed the front of her shirt and yanked her to her feet.

Jacie kicked and fought to get free.

The bulk of a man spun her around like a rag doll, pinned her arms behind her and pulled the pistol from her waistband, tossing it to the side. He shoved her forward into the clearing.

Zach crouched, holding his weapon in front of him. When he spotted Jacie, his eyes widened. "Jacie."

"I'm sorry," Jacie said. "I thought you were in trouble."

"Drop the gun," the man holding Jacie demanded in a heavy accent.

"Don't hurt her." Zach tossed his pistol to the ground and raised his hands.

Another man came running around the side of the house, cursing as he leaped over the body of his dead *compadre*. He ran straight up to Zach and hit him hard with the butt of his high-powered rifle.

Zach dropped to the ground and didn't move.

Jacie cried out and lunged forward.

Meaty hands squeezed her arms so hard that pain shot up into her shoulders.

The two men spoke Spanish so fast Jacie couldn't begin to translate with her own rudimentary skills in the language. By their urgent tone and the way they kept looking over their shoulders, they were anxious to leave.

One of the men ran for the workshop.

Jacie stared at Zach, willing him to get up.

He lay so still, a gash on his forehead where the thug had hit him with the rifle.

Jacie struggled again, fighting past the pain of having her arms pulled back so hard.

Her captor loosened his hold long enough to punch her in the side of the head.

Pain rattled around her head, and fog tinged the edges of her vision.

The other guy emerged from the workshop carrying a roll of duct tape.

Pushing past her fuzzy-headedness, Jacie kicked and bucked, trying to twist loose of the hands holding her like steel clamps. If they got the duct tape around her wrists and ankles, she wouldn't have a chance.

She dug her booted heel into the man's instep and backed into him, ramming her elbow into his gut.

He yelled and hit her again.

Jacie fought the pain, struggling to stay upright and losing. This time, the gray fog won, shutting out the sunshine and dragging Jacie into darkness.

LIGHT EDGED BENEATH Zach's eyelids, and the soft keening wail of a woman crying stirred him to wake. He opened his eyes and winced at the harsh light shining straight into his face from the setting sun. His head ached as he fought to regain his senses.

The crying continued and a baby's whimpers added to the sadness.

Zach turned his head in the direction of the sound, and a bolt of pain shot through his temple, clouding his vision.

A woman knelt in the dirt beside a man's body, a baby clutched to her chest. She rocked back and forth, tears coursing down her cheeks.

Enrique. The cloud over his brain lifted and Zach jerked to a sitting position. He swayed and braced his hands against the earth to keep from falling over.

The woman cried out and scooted away, holding the baby tightly.

Zach raised his hands, then pressed one to his temple where a knot had formed. He winced. "I'm not going to hurt you." He closed his eyes and fought a bout of nausea, then pushed to his feet, his mind coming alive. His first thought was Jacie.

Everything came back to him in a rush. He dug in his pocket for his cell phone and hit the speed dial for Hank. No service.

"Do you have a phone?" he asked the woman on the ground, holding up his cell phone at the same time.

She shook her head, her tears flowing faster.

"Sorry, I can't stick around to help. I'll send someone out." He didn't know if the woman understood what he'd said, but he didn't have time to translate.

He jogged around the house and workshop, his first instinct relief that he hadn't found Jacie's body. His second, dread at what she would be subjected to. He had to get to her before the cartel carried her back across the border and did what they'd done to Toni.

A lead weight settled hard in his gut. He pushed aside

the negative thoughts and sprinted back down the road and out to the highway. Once he found his truck, he raced back to town.

As soon as he came close, he checked his service and dialed Hank.

"Zach, where have you been? I've been trying to get in touch with you for the past hour."

"La Familia has Jacie."

"Any idea where they took her?"

"None." That lead weight flipped over in his belly. With no leads, no inkling of where they'd have taken her, he had nothing. Jacie would suffer. "I need you to get Pendley to bring up the tracking devices. If she still has hers on her, we have a chance."

"Pendley hacked into Tracie's phone. Other than Juan Alvarez's number and Bruce Masterson's, there weren't any others leading anywhere."

"And how is that helping me?" Zach drove through town faster than the posted speed limits.

"Pendley checked Bruce Masterson out and found several calls to a Humberto Hernandez at the Big Elk Ranch."

"Isn't he the other guide that works with Jacie?"

"He's the one."

"Did you question Bruce?"

"Haven't seen him in the past three hours. The other agents manning the ops tent said he took off saying he was checking on a lead. I called Richard Giddings and asked him to keep an eye on Humberto until you got there. He called me just a moment ago to say Humberto is saddling a horse and that he'd try to stall him, but he didn't know how without letting on that he's now a person of interest."

"I'll be at the Big Elk in ten minutes. In the meantime, find Jacie's tracker." Zach pressed his foot down hard on the accelerator as his truck headed out of town on the highway leading to the Big Elk Ranch. With Humberto being his only lead, he had to get to him before the guide took off.

The ten minutes might as well have been ten hours. Topping speeds of over one hundred miles an hour, he reached the ranch gate in eight minutes. His truck bed spun around as he turned onto the gravel road to the lodge. Zach straightened the wheels and kicked up a cloud of dust all the way to the lodge. Without stopping, he drove around the big cedar and rock building, skidding to a halt in front of the barn.

Zach grabbed his Glock, dove out of the truck and raced for the barn.

Richard Giddings stood to the side of the door and pointed toward the interior.

With his Glock leading the way, Zach ducked around the door and into the shadows. He paused for a moment to allow his sight to adjust to the limited lighting in the barn's interior.

"I know you're there." Humberto cinched the girth around the gelding he had saddled and dropped the stirrup into place. "Don't try to stop me. I have to make things right."

Zach stepped out of the shadows into the beam of light from an overhead bulb. He pointed his pistol at Humberto's chest. "If you want to make things right, start by telling me where you're going."

"After Masterson."

"Why?"

The man bowed his head for a moment, then raised it and stared at Zach. "I made a mistake."

Zach drew in a frustrated breath. "Could you be a little clearer?"

"I trusted Masterson. He told me I was helping with

an undercover operation." Humberto slid a bridle over the horse's nose. "We had a routine. He'd call and let me know when an agent was coming through the Big Elk to pass information on to their undercover operative in La Familia. I got them to the canyon, they passed the information and I made sure they got out of the canyon. Until two days ago."

"What happened two days ago?" Zach stepped closer, his heartbeat kicking up a notch.

"You know what happened. Those DEA agents were murdered and Jacie's sister was taken."

"Why is that your responsibility?"

"Masterson told me to guide different hunters, but they canceled at the last minute. I was supposed to guide the guests going south, but Jacie insisted on taking them. If I'd known they were agents, I would have been prepared for the attack. Instead Jacie and her sister took the hit and the men were killed." Humberto's lips thinned. "I tried to tell myself Masterson had been mistaken. But the more I thought about it, the more I realized Masterson had been using me.

"The men he'd set up to make the drop backed out when they discovered DEA agents were onto them. Afterward I found out Jacie's sister was an FBI agent. That's when I knew something wasn't right." The man's hands shook as he adjusted the straps on the bridle.

Zach's gut told him Humberto was telling the truth. "Where are you going?"

"I asked one of my cousins to snoop around and find out where La Familia would hole up when things got hot. I know where to start. There's an abandoned ranch house south of here, close to the border. They could be holding Tracie there." He gathered the reins and stepped toward Zach. "I have to make this right."

Zach grabbed the man's arm. "You can't do it alone."

"I feel as responsible for those DEA agents' deaths as if I'd pulled the trigger myself. And if I had been there instead of Jacie and her sister, her sister wouldn't be missing. I have to do this."

"Not without me," Zach said. "I'm going with you."

"I'm going too." Richard Giddings entered the barn.

"No." Humberto raised a hand. "You both need to stay with Jacie and make sure nothing happens to her."

Zach's chest tightened. "It already has."

Humberto closed his eyes and muttered a curse in Spanish.

Richard closed the distance between them. "What's happened to Jacie? Where is she?"

Zach told them what had occurred at Enrique's place and that as far as he could tell, Jacie had been gone nearly three hours. Plenty of time to get far away.

"They wouldn't try to cross the border during the daylight." Humberto glanced at the barn door where sunlight streamed in, casting long shadows. "It will be dark soon."

Zach's cell phone vibrated in his pocket. He dug it out and noted Hank's number. "Did you find her?"

"Yes, south of here, near the border. I'm not sure what's out there, but we have a GPS coordinate on her. Based on the county map, it's an abandoned ranch house. Do you want me to let the joint operations folks know?"

Zach's fingers tightened around the phone. "Not yet. They might try to fly in with a chopper. There's little enough vegetation to hide a chopper, and they'd hear it long before it got close. Wait two hours and then send them in. That should give us enough time to get down there on horseback and scope out the situation. I don't want La Familia to get spooked and shoot their witnesses." His heart pinched at the thought of what might happen if the cartel got wind that they'd been discovered.

"Us?" Hank asked. "How many of you are headed out?"

"Three." Zach stared at the men beside him, realizing he was going into a tight situation with two men untrained in special operations. But he had to take what he had and get down there. If nothing else, they could shoot and provide cover for him.

"I can have myself and three other men available in the next hour," Hank offered.

"We can't wait. Send the others in only if they can get there before you notify Joint Operations. You'll need to stay and make sure the FBI and DEA launch on time." Zach checked his watch. "It should be dark in one hour. That gives us another hour to get close and locate Tracie and Jacie."

"Godspeed, Zach." Hank ended the call.

"You should take Thunder. He's one of my fastest horses and he's surefooted in the dark." Richard Giddings headed for a stall and lead a black stallion out. "Are you a good rider? This horse can be a bit high-spirited."

"I can handle him." Zach ducked into the tack room and retrieved a saddle and blanket, his pulse hammering, urging him to hurry. The longer it took them to get down there, the more time the cartel had to harm Jacie and her sister.

Richard tied the horse to the stall door and headed for another stall. He led a sorrel gelding out and threw a saddle over his back.

Zach saddled the stallion and slung a bridle over his head. "We'll need saddlebags and scabbards."

Richard nodded to Humberto. "Handle that. I need to duck up to the lodge for a moment."

Humberto retrieved the necessary items, securing the scabbards and saddlebags to the back of Richard's and Zach's horses.

Zach ran out to his truck, gathered the canvas bag, web

belt, his rifle and the SIG Sauer Hank had loaned him. He met Richard on the way back to the barn.

The man carried an M110 sniper rifle and had another slung over his shoulder. "Thought we could use some more firepower." His pockets were loaded with boxes of shells and he had two ammo belts looped over his other shoulder. He shrugged. "Our guests like to fire different types of weapons."

Zach smiled grimly. "Glad you cater to them. These will come in handy."

They loaded the magazines, fit the extras into the web belts and tested the weapons. All their preparations took less than fifteen minutes. Fifteen minutes Zach felt they couldn't spare but had to in order to go into cartel-held territory. As the sun sank toward the horizon, the three men mounted and aimed their horses south, setting off at a trot to spare the horses.

Zach prayed they were headed in the right direction and that they wouldn't be too late.

Chapter Fifteen

"Wake up," a man's voice yelled in Jacie's ear.

She wavered in and out of consciousness.

A hard slap to the face jerked Jacie out of the black abyss. She blinked open her eyes. The room around her was dark with one light shining overhead and dust moats floating in and out of its beam.

"Wake up," the deep, intense voice repeated.

Jacie turned to face her nemesis. "What do you want from me?"

"Nothing. It's what I want from her." He pointed to the woman sitting in the shadows, her wrists and feet bound to a chair, her hair drooping in her face.

As the dust moats cleared and Jacie's gaze came into focus, she gasped. "Tracie?"

"Oh, Jacie, I'm so sorry." Her sister's voice cracked. Her face was bruised, her lips split and one eye was swollen shut.

Jacie lunged toward her sister, realizing too late that her own hands and feet were bound with duct tape to the chair in which she sat. The seat toppled and she landed on her side, her head bouncing off a dirty, splintered wooden floor. It was then she noted the windows had been painted black. Even then, no light shone through or around. It could be dark outside for all she knew. How long had she been out? And what had happened to Zach?

Her heart clenched. God, she prayed the men who'd taken her hadn't shot Zach and left him to die as they had Enrique.

"Don't hurt her," Tracie cried. "She doesn't know anything."

"With her here, maybe you'll start talking." He spoke perfect English with no hint of an accent.

Jacie stared at the man with the voice. He wore a black mask over his eyes, and a black bandana covered his hair like an evil Zorro. "Why are we here? What do you want with us?"

"I want your sister to tell me why she came to Wild Horse Canyon. Who sent her?"

"I told you." Tracie shook her head, wincing as if the effort was painful. "No one sent me. I came on my own."

"Why?"

"To visit my sister."

"Lies!" The man pulled Jacie back up, chair and all, and slapped her face hard.

The blow was hard enough that her teeth rattled and her head swam.

"No, don't!" Tracie cried. "She's just a trail guide. Nothing more."

The man stepped away from Jacie and ran a finger along Tracie's face, brushing across her swollen eyes and lips. "But then you aren't, are you? Who in the FBI sent you down here?"

"No one." She heaved a tired sigh. "It's the truth."

"Then why did you come here?" He moved back to stand beside Jacie, his hand rising. "Tell me now or your sister suffers for you."

"Don't!" Tracie strained against her bonds.

"Your memory returns?" the man asked.

"I came because I read a text on my boyfriend's cell phone. One that asked a man to assist the Big Elk transfer."

"You didn't get orders from your supervisor?"

"No. I was concerned because it was the Big Elk. I wanted to know what it was about since my sister works at the Big Elk Ranch."

"Who did you notify of your search?" he demanded.

"No one."

The hand descended, lashing across Jacie's face with sufficient force to create a resounding echo in the empty room.

Jacie rocked sideways in her chair, her head reeling. "Leave her alone. She came to see me."

"No, Jacie, I came to find out what Bruce was up to." She stared across at Jacie and sighed. "I had a friend trace the text and it went to Humberto Hernandez."

"The Big Elk's guide?" Jacie closed her eyes and opened them, hoping to regain focus. "How does he know Bruce?"

"I don't know. But I couldn't let it go. I had to know what was going on and what danger you might be in on the Big Elk."

"All very touching. Who else knows of Masterson's contact?"

"No one but you, Bruce and Humberto, as far as I know," Tracie answered.

The man raised his hand to hit Jacie again.

She couldn't help it. Jacie flinched back in her chair.

"Then why did you contact Hank Derringer for assistance?" the man demanded, his hand poised to strike.

Tracie leaned forward, constrained by the bindings. "I wasn't sure what I was up against and when it would go down, so I asked him to help me. Only he didn't have anyone available right away. I didn't tell him why I'd come, just that I might need his help."

"So you came to prove your boyfriend was a traitor?"

"I didn't want to believe it, but I had to know." She slumped in her chair, tears trickling down her cheeks.

Jacie's heart bled for her sister. She looked so tired, dirty and defeated. "Let her go. She's telling you the truth."

"Shut up."

Jacie's anger simmered along with her frustration. If only she could get loose.

Then what? The man had the advantage. He was stronger and probably had weapons at his disposal. Jacie might get free, but she wouldn't leave without her sister.

The man waved a finger toward the shadows. "Bring him in."

Jacie's breath lodged in her throat and she braced herself. Who was the masked man referring to? Had they captured Zach? Was he still alive?

Two hulking Hispanics with dragon tattoos on their arms dragged a man into the light.

He slumped between the two men, moaning, his dark hair hanging over his forehead, the shadows cast by the overhead light blocking his features.

Then the henchmen let go.

Their captive slumped to the floor and rolled onto his back. Both eyes were swollen and a large bruise had formed on his jaw. His clothes were torn as if he'd been whipped.

Tracie's eyes widened. "Bruce?"

The figure on the floor moaned, "Tracie."

"Your boyfriend was more forthcoming. It seems he's been busy cutting deals with both the Los Lobos and La Familia." The masked man waved a hand at the men standing nearby. "This makes *mi familia* angry."

The man closest to Bruce kicked him in the side.

Bruce groaned and tried to crawl away from him.

"What are you going to do with us?" Jacie asked, dreading the answer.

"La Familia suffers no traitors." The man stood and walked toward the door. "They're yours. Dispose of them."

IT TOOK THEM longer to get to the abandoned house than they'd anticipated because of the ominous overcast sky stealing the light of the stars and moon. Riding through the night without light proved to be more difficult than originally expected. Thunder rumbled, teasing them with the possibility of a raging storm at any moment. But the rain didn't come, which let them progress through the darkness.

They would have missed the perimeter guard altogether had Zach not slipped on the night-vision goggles when he did. Thankfully the wind had picked up. That and the thunder covered the sound of their horses and the creaking of saddle leather as they dismounted.

"You two stay here until I take care of the outlying guards."

"We can help." Richard pulled a knife from his belt. "I was in the infantry back in the day."

"I appreciate that, but I'm the only one with night-vision goggles and we can't afford to alert the rest of the camp. Once I take this man out, Richard, you move forward to where he was. I'll be circling to the right. Give me five minutes and then Humberto can take up a position a hundred yards to Richard's right. Make sure you have clearance to fire into the compound."

"But we can't see anything," Humberto pointed out.

"Once I have the guards taken care of, I'll start the fireworks. You'll be able to see into the compound and they won't be able to see out. Only fire if you're certain of what you're shooting at. My first order of business is to find the women. When I do, I'm going to create a diversion. Be ready." Zack filled a clip with rounds.

"What kind of diversion?" Richard asked.

"Something with a lot of fire and noise." Zach pressed a hand to the incendiary grenade.

When he found the women, he'd have to distract the guards long enough to free Tracie and Jacie and hopefully get them out.

"Hank's sending out his men and will be notifying the FBI and DEA about now. If they send out their helicopter, we'll have additional firepower should we run into trouble. The main thing is to get the women to safety first."

Richard nodded. "We'll cover you."

Humberto's head hung low. "I'm sorry I got Jacie involved in this."

Zach held up his hand. "Now's not the time for regrets. It's time for action."

"Sí." Humberto squared his shoulders, his lips firming into a straight line. "We're behind you."

Zach checked his web belt one last time, memorizing the location of each item of equipment. With his rifle in hand, he slipped into the night, his night-vision goggles in place.

He made straight for the man on the northern edge of the compound perimeter. As he grew close, he slipped the goggles up on his head and circled around behind the man, dispatching him with a swift, clean stroke with his knife.

One down, still more to go before he could enter the grounds and check for the women.

Zach circled the compound, moving as quickly as he could without making noise. At the western edge of the perimeter, he found one of the compound's sentries fast asleep. The man never knew what happened. He died where he lay.

Another man on the south side was easily taken care of. At least one other remained on the eastern perimeter. The green glow of his body heat registered in Zach's night-vision goggles.

As he eased toward the man, his gaze fixed on his target, Zach didn't see the rock until he kicked it with his toe.

The sound of the stone skittering across the dry soil might as well have been the blaring of a horn.

"Que hay de nuevo?" The man lifted his weapon, aiming toward Zach.

"Es mi," Zach replied with his best Spanish accent; then he slipped around to the side of the man holding the weapon aimed at the spot where Zach had kicked the rock.

"El que?" The man's voice rose.

When Zach was behind the man, he rushed forward and grabbed him from behind.

The guard struggled, his hands still on his rifle. A shot rang out.

Damn. The entire camp would be on alert now.

Zach used his knife to dispatch the man and ran back to the south side of the compound, away from where he'd dropped the last guard and where the others would be headed to discover the source and reason for the gunfire.

With the first shot having been fired, Zach's plan would have to move a little quicker than anticipated.

With only three buildings on the old ranch, Zach snuck up to the back of an old, dilapidated barn that leaned precariously, slats missing from the walls. No light streamed from inside, and a quick scan with the night-vision goggles concluded it was empty. He pushed the goggles up on his forehead. This was the spot, and it was now or never.

Footsteps pounded against the dirt, and a shout rose,

followed by more and the clinking of metal against metal as men grabbed weapons and headed toward the perimeter to investigate the shots fired.

Zach pulled the incendiary grenade from the loop holding it on his web harness and yanked the pin. Then he tossed it into the old barn and slipped away in the shadows toward the next building. He threw himself to the ground, covering his ears.

Let's get this party started.

THE GOONS LEFT to "dispose" of Bruce, Tracie and Jacie chuckled as they hiked their rifles up and prepared to follow orders. They spoke to each other in Spanish, pointing first at Tracie, then Jacie and finally Bruce.

Jacie held her breath. With her hands duct-taped behind her, she was helpless to stop what was about to happen. She twisted her wrists, hoping to stretch the tape and allow enough room to pull her hands free. But they'd bound her so tightly, her hands had gone numb. She stared across the room at her sister, praying for a miracle.

The La Familia gang members raised their rifles, aimed and—

Jacie braced herself for the carnage, her gaze inexplicably drawn to one man's trigger finger as his finger tightened.

An explosion ripped through the air, shaking the ground beneath Jacie's feet.

The gunman jerked as he pulled the trigger, hitting the other gang member in the knee. The wounded man dropped to the floor, clutching his knee and screaming Spanish obscenities.

The man who'd shot him bent to him, speaking fast, then he ran to the front door and flung it open.

With her back to the door, Jacie craned her neck to see

what was happening. A glow filled the night sky, reflected off the low-slung clouds.

The man on the floor struggled to his feet, using his rifle as a makeshift crutch. He hobbled to the door and out onto the porch with the other man.

"Jacie," Tracie called out. "Can you make your way over here?"

"I don't know." Jacie gathered her strength and performed a kind of sitting hop, moving herself a mere inch toward her sister.

"Again." Tracie did the same. With their legs bound to the chair legs, they couldn't get much traction, but with both of them moving forward, the distance shortened.

Her heart pounding in her ears, Jacie hurried until they were almost knee-to-knee. "Pass me on your right."

Tracie hopped past Jacie.

Once behind her, Jacie scooted her chair to the side. "Can you move your fingers at all? They used duct tape on me."

"You might have a better shot at untying me than I would at tearing the tape."

Jacie strained to reach her sister's bindings, leaning forward to tip her chair backward enough to raise her hands.

The men left to kill them were shouting at people running by.

"Wh-what's happening?" Bruce lifted his head and peered through swollen eyes at the room around him.

"We don't know, but help us," Jacie whispered, loud enough for Bruce to hear.

Bruce pushed up to his hands and knees, then collapsed again, facedown on the floor.

The men in the doorway stopped yelling and turned back to the house, guns raised.

"Jacie." Tracie spoke quietly. "We've got trouble."

THE EXPLOSION ROCKED the ground beneath Zach.

Shots rang out in the distance.

Zach prayed the guards hadn't found Richard and Humberto. For a moment, he second-guessed his decision to bring them along. They weren't trained in these kinds of operations.

Pushing aside his concern for the two men, Zach inched around the side of the small building. He stayed in the deep shadows cast by the fire growing in the barn. The grenade did its job and set the building ablaze. It wouldn't take long to burn to the ground. The ancient timbers would be easily consumed.

A man raced by, sporting an M110 similar to the one Zach carried. Where had the man gotten the American weapon?

As soon as he passed, Zach ran to the next building.

A motorcycle revved and took off out of the melee, a man wearing a black bandana and a black mask heading north, lights extinguished.

Above, thunder boomed in the night and the first drops of moisture splattered the earth.

More shots were muffled by the descending clouds.

Behind Zach, the fire grew, undaunted by a few drops of rain and building in heat and intensity. Chaos reigned.

Banking on the confusion, Zach pushed through the door of the small outbuilding. Light shone through the windows from the barn's fire. The building contained boxes and burlap sacks, but no people. With only the ranch house remaining, Zach steeled himself. He quit the smaller outbuilding and raced across the grounds.

As he neared the house, a man leaned out over the deck, his weapon pointed toward Zach. *"Que hay de nuevo?"*

Zach didn't bother answering; he shot the man and dove

for the shadows, rolled to his feet and rounded the corner to the back entrance.

Another guard leaped off the back porch, heading straight for Zach.

Zach didn't give him the opportunity to ask who was there. A single bullet pierced the man's chest, downing him where he stood, leaving the back door unprotected. Zach sucked in a deep breath and nudged the door open with the nose of his rifle.

As soon as he pushed through, he dodged to the left, out of the backlight from the burning barn. He'd entered through the kitchen. If they had the women in this house, they'd be in the living room or locked in one of the bed-rooms.

Zach moved from room to room. Above the shouts and rumbling of thunder, Zach heard low thumps and scraping sounds. He headed toward the sound, stopping at a corner. There it was again. The bumping, scraping sound.

Crouching low and staying as much in the shadows as he could, Zach peeked around the wall.

Bound to chairs, Tracie and Jacie sat back to back. He recognized Jacie by the clothes she'd been wearing ear-lier. She faced him. A man lay sprawled across the floor. He looked vaguely like Bruce, only banged up. Standing in the front door was a large Hispanic man, wielding a semiautomatic rifle aimed at Tracie's chest. If he pulled the trigger at this close range, the bullet would cut right through Tracie and lodge in Jacie, killing both women.

His heart skipped several beats and the world whirled around him. Images of a similar style of torture flashed through him. Toni being beaten by the men of Los Lobos while he remained tied to a beam, powerless to help her.

His breathing grew shallow, his hands clammy. The

hopeless feeling washing over him made his hands shake, crippling him.

"Let her live," Jacie begged. "Kill me if you must, but let my sister live."

Jacie's words rang out, cutting through the fog of Zach's memories. She wasn't Toni. Zach wasn't helpless this time. His heartbeat settled into a smooth, deadly rhythm, his hands growing steady.

Zach refused to let Jacie die. He wanted more time with the woman who'd brought him back to life—the woman who marched bravely into battle and who wouldn't give up on her sister or on him.

He tipped the nose of his rifle around the corner and lined up the sights.

Jacie's eyes rounded when she spotted him.

Zach pulled the trigger.

Chapter Sixteen

Another shot rang out.

Bruce jerked on the floor beside Jacie and moaned. Blood pooled on the floor beside him.

A loud thump was followed by a shout from the doorway.

Jacie scooted her chair halfway around so that she could see what was happening.

Zach leaped past her to the front door.

The cartel man with the wounded leg had thrown himself off the front porch into the dirt, yelling at the top of his voice.

More La Familia gang members came running toward the house.

Zach stepped back and closed the door. He yanked a blood-encrusted knife from a scabbard on his thigh.

"Look out, Jacie!" Tracie cried. "He's got a knife."

"It's okay. He's a good guy," Jacie reassured her.

Zach sliced through Jacie's bindings and then Tracie's. "We have to get out of here before they surround us."

Jacie leaped from her chair and steadied herself on Zach's arm.

Tracie was not so fast, having been starved for the days she'd spent in captivity and beaten on multiple occasions. She stumbled to her feet and pitched forward.

Jacie and Zach grabbed for her before she fell to the floor.

Zach looped Tracie's arm over his shoulder, then tossed his pistol to Jacie.

She caught it and aimed it at the front door as Zach half dragged, half led her sister to the rear of the house.

"What about Bruce?" Tracie asked.

"Leave him. He'll slow us down," Zach said.

Jacie hated Bruce for what he'd gotten her sister into, but she knew what his fate would be if they left him with La Familia. "They'll kill him if we leave him."

Jacie followed Zach, inching backward, her gaze trained on the front of the house, torn between helping the man and getting out alive.

At any moment, La Familia Diablos could storm the house to find the people responsible for their buddy's commotion. They'd find Bruce, blame him and finish him off.

"I can't leave him. He's still alive." Jacie stopped backing up.

"He's not worth it," Zach insisted. "He's a traitor to his country."

"Yeah, but let the courts sentence him. Not La Familia." Jacie took a step back the way she'd come.

"No, Jacie! Zach's right. Saving Bruce isn't worth your getting shot." Tracie dug in her heels and stopped herself and Zach.

"Don't, Jacie. If anyone should go back, it should be me." Zach reached out and grabbed her arm. "He'll be heavy. You can't lift him on your own. Get your sister out of here."

Jacie chewed her lip. "No, I can't let you go in there."

"We don't have time to argue about it. Take my gun and get Tracie out." He looped Tracie's arm over Jacie's shoulder, pressed a kiss to Jacie's lips. "I want a real date when we get back to sanity."

Jacie's heart turned a somersault and she grinned. "You got it. Don't stand me up." Her chest squeezed hard as Zach ducked past her and back into the front room.

Jacie forced herself not to think about what he might be facing. With Tracie leaning heavily on her, she hurried through the house to the back door.

"Wait." Tracie laid her hand on the door, refusing to let Jacie go through. "There could be men outside the door. Check through the windows first."

Jacie propped Tracie against the wall and crossed to the bare window, careful not to stand behind its glass. Although it was dark in the kitchen, she couldn't take the chance of someone seeing her.

She eased her head around the window frame and peered out.

Men gathered in the yard between the barn and the house. Some faced the barn. They were talking and waving their hands at the flames leaping toward the sky, stirred by a strong crosswind.

One man faced the house. He spoke to another and pointed toward Jacie. She ducked back away from the glass, her pulse hammering. Had he seen her? Did it matter? With that many men standing out in the barnyard, they didn't have a chance of sneaking out the back door.

"We have to find another way out." Jacie helped Tracie into one of the bedrooms, eyeing the window on the far wall. It was on one of the house's sides, out of view of the barnyard and the front yard. She checked out the window for movement. That side of the house was shrouded in shadows. She watched for a full thirty seconds. Nothing moved. "Think you can make it out this window?"

"It's either that or die trying." Tracie's chin lifted. "I might need a boost from you."

"You got it." Jacie pushed and shoved the window, the old paint having congealed, sealing it shut. "I can't get it open."

Tracie slipped out of her shirt and handed it to Jacie. Her body was covered in deep purple bruises. "Wrap your arm with my shirt and break the glass."

Jacie swallowed her anger at what the cartel had done to Tracie and did as her sister directed. She kicked the glass away, praying La Familia couldn't hear the noise over the roar of the fire and the thunder of the approaching storm.

Using the shirt, Jacie cleared the glass from the windowsill. When it was safe enough, she shook out Tracie's shirt.

Her sister put it on, wincing as she raised her arms over her head. "Let's get out of here."

"Not without Zach." Jacie ran to the bedroom door, her gaze panning the empty hallway.

What was taking Zach so long? He should have Bruce and be back by now. So far no more shots had been fired close to the ranch house. Still, Jacie was worried.

Given the short amount of time she'd known Zach, she wasn't sure why she was so concerned. Other than that he made her heart beat faster and his kisses curled her toes.

She waited another minute. When he didn't appear in the doorway, Jacie returned to where her sister leaned against the wall. "We're getting you out of here." Jacie stooped to give her a boost.

"That'll be a challenge." Tracie raised her foot and stepped into Jacie's cupped hands.

Jacie sagged under her sister's weight, then pushed up with her knees and shoved Tracie through the opening.

Her sister lodged halfway through, moaning as her ribs hit the windowsill.

"Hang on, I'm going to shove you out." Jacie planted one of Tracie's feet against her own shoulder and leaned into her, pushing her over the edge.

Tracie half slid, half rolled out, dropping to the ground onto the broken glass.

Jacie leaned out the window and whispered loud enough that Tracie could hear but the cartel couldn't, "Okay out there?"

"Will be," Tracie grunted, and righted herself, "as soon as you're out here too."

She hated leaving Tracie all alone. Not when her sister was so weak and barely able to hold herself up. "Lie low for a minute. I'll be right back. I'm going to see what's keeping Zach. Stay in the shadows."

"No, Jacie!" she called out.

Jacie ran for the living room. Zach had lifted Bruce off the floor, and struggled to throw him over his shoulder in a fireman's carry.

"What are you doing in here?" Zach staggered under the other man's weight and glared at Jacie. "I told you to get your sister out."

"I did, but I thought you might need help."

"Do you ever do what you're told?"

"Quit arguing, mister. There's a man headed this way." She held her gun steady. "I've got you covered, first door on the left."

"Yes, ma'am." Zach sagged under Bruce's deadweight. The man had been beaten to within an inch of his life and had suffered a gunshot wound to his abdomen, but he still had a pulse. Much as he wanted to, Zach couldn't leave him to die at La Familia's hands.

He entered the bedroom.

Jacie entered behind him, closing the door.

Zach peered over the edge of the windowsill. "Tracie, move out of the way." With no time to spare or take it easy on the injured man, Zach shoved Bruce through the window.

Tracie did her best to cushion his fall, ending up knocked to the ground for her efforts.

Then Zach nodded to Jacie. "You next." He scooped her up and stuck her legs through the window. Jacie dropped to the ground as raindrops splattered across her cheeks.

"I think he's dead," Tracie mumbled.

Bruce lay at an awkward angle, his head cradled in her lap.

Jacie crouched beside the man and touched her fingers to his neck, searching for a pulse.

It took a moment before she felt it. But it was there and very weak.

Zach hauled himself through the window and dropped to the ground. He ran to the back corner of the house and then to the front, returning with a sigh. "We're not out of the woods yet."

"Which way?" Jacie asked.

A voice shouted from inside the house, and footsteps pounded across the wooden floors.

"Follow me and you'd better move fast." Zach grabbed Bruce's arms and yanked him up and over his shoulder. Then he ran due east, away from the house.

Jacie wrapped an arm around her sister's waist and followed Zach into the shadows. The farther they moved away from the flames of the burning barn, the less likely anyone would see them.

Unfortunately they didn't move fast enough to avoid detection.

A man called out behind them.

Zach dropped Bruce to the ground and shouted, "Get down!"

Bullets winged past them, kicking up plumes of dry Texas dust.

Jacie fell to a prone position at once, dragging Tracie down with her.

"What do we do now?" she cried. If they got up to run, whoever was shooting at them would have an easy target. But they couldn't stay glued to the ground forever. Soon others of La Familia would join the shooter. It wouldn't be long before Zach, Jacie, Tracie and Bruce were full of lead.

"Now would be a good time for the backups to show," Zach muttered.

"We have backup?" Tracie asked.

"In a perfectly timed world, we would, but given the weather, I'm not sure the FBI and DEA can get the helicopter off the ground."

As if to emphasize Zach's point, the wind whipped across Jacie's face, twisting her hair.

Bruce lay beside Jacie, his eyes blinking open. "Tracie?"

"No, I'm Jacie," Jacie corrected.

"I'm here." Tracie took his hand and held it, tears shimmering in her eyes as she stared into Bruce's face.

"I'm sorry." Bruce coughed, spitting out blood. "Please forgive me."

"For almost getting me and my sister killed?" She shook her head. "I can't."

"I never meant to hurt you."

"Yeah, well, you did." The tears were flowing in earnest by now from swollen, bruised eyes. "I trusted you and you lied to me."

"I wanted out," he whispered. "But I knew too much. You have to believe me."

"You had two DEA agents killed." Tracie's hand smoothed over Bruce's face. "Where was the mercy? I don't even know you anymore."

"I'm still the same person," he insisted.

"You're not the same man I fell in love with."

"I didn't…" Bruce's voice gurgled, as if his lungs were taking on liquid. "I didn't order those two men killed."

"Then who did?" Tracie demanded, leaning up.

The man in the house fired on them, the bullet hitting the dirt in front of Jacie's face, kicking it up into her eyes. She blinked and rubbed the sand out.

Bruce's eyes closed, his breathing growing shallower.

"Don't you die on me." Tracie shook the man, tears flowing freely down her dirt-streaked cheeks. "The least you can do is tell me who is behind all of this."

"He's powerful," Bruce whispered.

"Was he the one interrogating us?" Tracie sucked in a deep breath.

"Yes."

"What's his name?"

"Too dangerous…FBI…can make people disappear."

"What do you mean?" Zach asked.

"Hank's wife and son…" Bruce's body shuddered and he coughed up more blood, and then settled back against the earth, his face creased in a grimace of pain.

"What does he have to do with Hank's family?" Zach demanded.

Bruce inhaled, the gurgling sound more pronounced. "Still alive."

"Where?" Zach grabbed the man by the collar.

Bruce's eyes blinked open, found Tracie's and they closed. "I loved you," he said, the words released on his last breath. His body went slack.

Tracie leaned her face against his chest, her shoulders

shaking with silent sobs. "Damn you, Bruce. Damn you for everything."

Jacie's heart ached at her sister's distress.

Bruce had made some big mistakes. He'd betrayed his country and betrayed Tracie, but deep down had never stopped loving her.

Though tears welled in her eyes, Jacie refused to let them fall. She couldn't dwell on Bruce's mistakes, not when they were pinned to the ground, unable to move for fear of being hit.

Shouts rose from the barnyard. Flames climbed higher into the descending clouds.

Zach glanced over his shoulder and sighed. "I believe the cavalry has arrived."

Headlights shone in the distance from half a dozen vehicles. The advancing army had the remaining La Familia members scrambling for motorcycles and jeeps.

The man who'd pinned them apparently didn't know he was being surrounded and kept shooting random shots—some bullets hitting far too close for comfort.

Zach's cavalry pulled in to the ranch compound and skidded to a stop in the gravel. Doors flung open and men wearing flak vests and carrying guns poured out. The remaining cartel thugs were quickly killed or held up their hands in surrender.

As the last man standing, their sniper suddenly stopped shooting and spun, his weapon now aiming for whoever had entered the room behind him.

Two shots were fired. The sniper slammed against the windowsill and tipped out onto the gravel below. Another face appeared in the glassless window. A man wearing a dark cowboy hat instead of the dark gear of the FBI.

"Well, I'll be damned. Hank must have sent in his guys as well as the FBI. If I'm not mistaken, that was Ben."

After a moment Zach stood. "I think that was our cue. Come on, let's see if they brought a medic." He reached down to grab Jacie's arm, hauling her to her feet.

Jacie touched her sister's shoulder. "We have to go."

"Go without me," Tracie said, her voice catching on a sob.

"Can't." Jacie shook her head. "You're a part of me. You're my sister. I could never leave you behind."

Tracie slid Bruce's head from her lap and pushed to a kneeling position. "Why did he have to go and be an idiot and play both sides?"

"Who knows what motivates different people?" Jacie answered. "For what it's worth, it sounded like he loved you."

Tracie snorted. "Apparently he loved himself more." She stood, swaying slightly.

"What I want to know is who the hell was the man in the mask?" The beast of a man who'd been so harsh to her sister and herself would forever haunt Jacie.

"I'm done with the bureau." Tracie pushed her hair back from her face, revealing more bruising.

Jacie flinched at all the damage. "What do you mean?" She cast a glance toward the vehicles crowding the compound, hoping they brought medical personnel to treat her sister's wounds.

Tracie's dried, split lips pulled back in a sneer. "What good is it to be an agent when you can't tell the good guys from the bad?"

Zach grabbed her shoulders and forced her to stare into his eyes. "The important thing to remember is that *you* are a good agent and that you are vital to this nation, to our country, to keeping us safe."

She stared into his eyes. "Who are you?"

"I'm Zach Adams." His hands dropped to his sides. "I used to be a special agent like you."

"Why did *you* quit?" Tracie asked.

"I lost hope." Zach faced Jacie. "Someone helped me find it again." He held out his hand to Jacie.

She took it, butterflies storming her belly and gooseflesh rising on her arms. The man definitely turned her inside out.

Tracie turned her bruised and battered face toward Jacie. "I feel like I missed something." She gave the hint of a smile. "Do you two know each other?"

"We didn't. Now we do." Jacie gave a shy smile.

"We can talk later." Zach slipped Tracie's arm over his shoulder. "Right now we need to have you seen by a doctor."

Jacie looped Tracie's other arm over her shoulders and together, they closed the distance between them and the vehicles parked near the burning barn and outbuilding. Floating embers landed on the house, lighting it like a tinderbox.

As the house burned, Jacie couldn't feel regret for the old structure, not when it held memories of terror and torture. She hoped never to feel that trapped and hopeless again.

ZACH'S PULSE HAD finally returned to normal. After finding Jacie and Tracie tied up and on the verge of being executed, he thought life had come to a standstill. Thank God, he'd arrived just in time. Bringing them out of that house alive had lifted a weight heavier than the current situation from his shoulders.

It was as if now he finally knew the meaning of his life. When he'd been a captive of Los Lobos and they'd tortured Toni to death, he'd asked God why he'd spared him and took her. Seeing Jacie and her sister about to be killed had brought his life back in focus. God had a purpose for him. He'd led him to Hank and this amazing woman. Zach was meant to fight for truth and justice, the fight he thought he'd joined the FBI to accomplish.

As the three staggered into the open, Hank Derringer broke away from a group of agents and cowboys.

"Zach, Jacie!" He took over for Jacie and, with Zach's help, led Tracie to the back of a Hummer. The hatch was open and a man was applying a bandage to Richard Giddings's forehead.

Zach held out a hand. "Thanks for covering me." He glanced around. "Where's Humberto?"

"Already on his way back to the Big Elk."

"Any injuries?" Zach asked.

"Humberto got off without a scratch. I would have too, if I hadn't tripped over my two left feet and landed a faceplant in the gravel." Richard grinned at Jacie. "You don't know how happy I am to see my best field guide on her feet and alive."

"Thanks, Richard." Jacie gave the man a hug, moisture glistening in her eyes.

After a quick once-over, the medic cleaned one of Tracie's facial wounds. "Won't know what else is damaged until we get her back to the county hospital in Wild Oak Canyon and get some X-rays. Might even take her into El Paso for CAT scans."

"The county hospital," Tracie insisted. "And a hot shower, please. Then I think I could sleep for a hundred years."

Hank bundled her into another Hummer. Jacie and Zach climbed in on each side of her. As they pulled away from the ranch compound, Zach's gut clenched as the enormity of the situation hit. He'd almost lost Jacie.

The few raindrops the clouds had released did nothing

to extinguish the fire that had completely consumed the house by now. Hank called ahead on his satellite phone and had the local doctor meet them at the county hospital, machines warmed and waiting.

After what seemed an interminable amount of time and X-rays, Tracie was shown to a room where she'd spend the night monitored by a competent staff. Zach insisted that the doctor look over Jacie, as well. Though she protested that she was fine and didn't need a doctor, she went with him.

Throughout Jacie's examination, Zach paced in the waiting room, clenching his fists, frustrated and angry at what Jacie and Tracie had gone through.

When she finally emerged, she smiled. "Told you I was fine. Other than an ugly bruise on my cheekbone and a split lip, I'll survive." The doctor found no signs of concussion or brain trauma from the multiple hits she'd taken at the hands of the mystery interrogator.

"I'm glad you're okay." Zach gathered her in his arms and pressed a gentle kiss to her forehead. "And for the record, you look great."

"Liar." She leaned into him, her arms circling his waist, her forehead pressed to his chest. "I'm glad it's over."

"Me too." He smoothed her hair from her forehead and tucked it behind her ear.

Jacie tipped her cheek into his open palm and pressed a kiss there. "Thank you for coming for us."

Zach's chest tightened as he stared down into her gray-blue eyes. "Wild horses couldn't keep me away."

Her gaze broke from his, her eyelids drifting downward, hiding her emotions. "I want to see my sister."

Zach wanted to take Jacie somewhere they could be alone and hold her until his arms ached and the desperation of the past twenty-four hours abated. Instead he led her to her sister's room.

Tracie lay with her damp hair spread across her pillow, her damaged cheeks wiped clean of dirt and grime. Her eyes were closed, her face relaxed.

Jacie paused with Zach in the doorway. "I'm staying with her tonight," she whispered.

"No, you're not." Tracie's eyes blinked open.

Zach's fists clenched at all the swelling and the purple bruises.

Jacie stepped forward. "I'm not letting you out of my sight for a while."

"Yes, you are." Tracie's lips quirked upward slightly. "I know you want to help, but Hank assured me he'd have someone stand guard throughout the night. And I should be okay to leave the hospital tomorrow. You've done enough and need rest as much as I do."

"Still," Jacie sighed, "I'd feel better knowing you're okay."

"And I won't get any sleep with you hovering over me." Tracie closed her eyes. "Please, I just want to sleep."

Jacie closed the distance between them and gathered her sister's hand in hers. "Are you sure?"

Tracie sighed. "Yes, I'm sure." Her eyes edged open again. "Zach?"

Zach joined Jacie beside the hospital bed, the scents of alcohol and disinfectants making him itch to leave. "Yes."

Tracie disengaged her hand from Jacie's and held it out to Zach. "Thank you for coming to our rescue. I don't want to think about how this day could have ended." She laid his hand over Jacie's. "Now get her out of here. And you'd better be good to her, or you'll have me to contend with."

Zach laughed. "If you're anywhere near as tough as Jacie, I'll be shaking in my boots."

"Got that right." Tracie's eyelids drifted closed as

though they weighed a ton. "I'll see you two in the morning."

Zach led Jacie out of the room.

Jacie cast one last glance over her shoulder. "I don't like leaving her."

"You heard her. She wants to sleep." Zach hugged her middle. "Hank assured me that Ben Harding is one of the best ex-cops you'll find. He'll make sure Tracie is safe."

Jacie leaned into Zach. "It's been a helluva day, hasn't it?"

"You were so brave."

"And stupid. If I'd stayed put when you told me to, I wouldn't have been caught."

"And I'd be dead. You saved me." In more ways than one, and he'd spend a lifetime thanking her. "And that tracking device you had in your shoe led us to you and your sister. I'd say it worked out okay." Zach paused for a moment in the hallway of the hospital and touched a thumb to the bruising on her cheek. "I have to admit, though, it was a little too close for comfort." He kissed her cheek, careful not to apply too much pressure. His mouth moved to her lips.

"Ouch." Jacie backed away.

"Sorry." Zach straightened. "Did I tell you I'm really glad you're okay?"

"Yes, you did." She laughed up at him. "Do we have rides back to the Big Elk?"

"Hank let us have use of the Hummer. He'd like to see us tomorrow if you're up to it."

"Ask me tomorrow. Right now I just want to go home to bed." Her hand slipped into his and they walked out of the hospital.

The drive back to the Big Elk Ranch was accomplished in silence.

At first Zach thought Jacie had fallen asleep, she was so quiet. But a glance at her face proved him wrong. Jacie stared straight ahead, her eyes open, her bottom lip captured between her teeth.

When they pulled up in front of her little cottage, Zach leaped down and rounded to the passenger side of the vehicle to help her down. He walked her to her door. "You know, we never did have a chance to put your cabin back together."

Jacie's shoulders sagged. "I'll manage."

"You could stay in mine," he offered, turning her to face him.

Jacie's gaze rose to meet his. "I don't know if I can keep my distance."

"I'm counting on that."

"I don't know if I want to get any closer to you. Now that it's all over, I'm afraid you'll be gone tomorrow." Her eyes filled with moisture, the blue-gray of her irises swimming. "I almost lost you today to a bullet. I'm not strong enough to lose you again."

"You're not going to lose me." He slipped his hands beneath her legs and scooped her up into his arms. "I want that first real date and a lot more after that."

"Are you sure? I thought you didn't want a lasting relationship. And I won't settle for less."

"I was wrong, and for once, we're in agreement." He strode across the yard to his cabin and twisted the key in the doorknob while balancing her in his arms. "A little help here?"

"Not until you answer one question."

"Fire away."

"Do you think you could ever love me like you loved Toni?"

Zach stood still, his gaze captured by hers. Then he shook his head. "No."

Tears welled in Jacie's eyes. "Put me down. I can't do this."

He refused to let her go, his hands tightening around her. "Hear me out."

"I refuse to fall in love with someone who can't love a second time. It's hopeless."

"I don't think so." He laughed, the vibrations of his chest warming her. "I can't love you like I did Toni because you're a different person. Sure, I loved Toni. She was my partner. I'd give anything to have been able to save her life. We were a team."

"See? I can't compete with that. I'm just a trail guide."

"And a very beautiful and courageous one at that." He brushed a kiss across her undamaged cheek. "You never gave up. You taught me that anyone can make a difference, if they care enough."

"I didn't make a difference. *You* saved us." Her brow furrowed. "Put me down. I need to be alone."

He shook his head. "You made the difference, Jacie. You saved me, not only from that gunman at Enrique's place, but from myself." He held her tighter. "I could very well be falling in love with you, something I thought I could never do again."

Her eyes widened. "You're falling in love with me?" She squeaked and grasped his cheeks between her palms, her frown deepening. "But I thought you couldn't love me like you did Toni."

"I can't love you like Toni because you're Jacie. I'm falling in love with you, if you'll give me a chance."

Her eyes filled with tears, and a smile spread across her face. "So what's keeping you?"

He laughed and pushed the door open to the cabin. "I

don't want to make any rash decisions when we've known each other less than a week."

"Ever heard of love at first sight?" Jacie tipped her head. "Or in our case, maybe it was second or third sight."

Zach set her on her feet and pulled her into his arms. "Whatever, I want to spend time getting to know you better."

"Now you're talking." Jacie pushed the door closed behind him, shutting the world out and them in.

Epilogue

Hank leaned against the front of his desk. "Zach, thank you for helping Jacie and Tracie out of a tight situation. I knew you were the right man for the job, and you didn't disappoint."

Zach held tight to Jacie's hand. "I'm glad I could help. Thanks for the opportunity." His gaze was on Jacie, not Hank.

"Although we didn't get the man behind it all, at least we uncovered one of the moles in the FBI."

Tracie sat in a wingback leather chair, her color returning, though her eyes seemed dull and unhappy. "I wish I'd known sooner about Bruce's activities."

"What would you have done that you didn't do once you learned of them?" Jacie asked.

Tracie stared at her hands. "I wouldn't have fallen for all his lies."

"The thing to remember is that you stayed true to your country and your duty as an FBI agent. I commend you on your spirit and desire to seek justice and truth." Hank drew in a deep breath and opened his mouth to go on. "Which brings me to—"

Zach held up his hand. "Don't you think Tracie makes a perfect FBI agent?"

Hank smiled. "I guess you know I was about to offer her a position?"

Tracie shook her head. "Although I'm disappointed that some of our agents are bad, I'm not giving up on the bureau. I still believe in it and what we can do to preserve justice in this country. Between you, Zach and Jacie, you reminded me of what an honor it is to serve."

Hank waved a hand. "If you decide to retire from the bureau, please consider my team."

Tracie smiled and nodded. "You bet I will."

Hank turned to Jacie. "What about you? You're quite a good shot, brave and a seeker of truth and justice—"

Jacie held up her hand. "Though I know I could do the danger thing in a pinch, it's not for me. I like leading hunting parties and promoting the Big Elk Ranch."

Zach squeezed her hand.

Warmth flushed her neck and cheeks at the memories of all the places those hands had been throughout the night and halfway through the morning. "Thanks, but I think I'll stay where I am."

"That leaves you, Zach. I consider the job you did a trial on your part and mine. I'm convinced you will be a valuable asset to this organization. Care to continue?"

Zach nodded. "If Jacie has no objections, I'm in."

Jacie raised her hand. "No objections here, as long as I get to see you between jobs."

"Then that's settled. I have my contacts searching for the leader of the stateside La Familia gang that held you two ladies. Until then, stay on your toes in case he seeks retribution."

"One other thing, Hank," Zach interrupted. "Before Bruce died, he mentioned the man was powerful with connections in the FBI. Bruce said that he could make people disappear. He mentioned your family. He intimated that they may still be alive."

Hank's face blanched and he closed his eyes, dragging in a deep breath. "Any clue as to where he's keeping them?"

"Sorry, Bruce died before he could say more than that. He didn't know a location or in what condition they were."

Zach didn't want to think about what physical state Hank's wife and child would be in. Given the mystery man's propensity for pain, it couldn't be good.

His arm slipped around Jacie's shoulders. "I'll do anything in my power to help you find him and bring him down. After what he did to Jacie and Tracie, the man deserves to die."

Hank rose from his seat, crossed the room and held out his hand to Zach.

Zach stood and gripped the outstretched hand.

"Thank you, Zach," Hank said. "I'll be taking you up on that offer."

* * * * *

"To protect you I should step back."
He rubbed his thumb along her
bottom lip. "But the idea of some-
one else being with you, touching
you is more than I can tolerate."

Her hand played with the scruff on the tip of his chin. "I wouldn't let anyone else touch me."

"What about me?"

"You can touch me as much as you want." She whispered the response because it felt right to let the words dance softly off her tongue.

After that his mouth dipped and his lips slipped over hers. Heat beat off her body and blood rushed to her head. Sensations walloped her—dizziness, elation. She craved his touch and wrapped her arms around his neck to pull him in closer.

RUTHLESS

BY
HelenKay Dimon

First published in Great Britain 20__
by Mills & Boon, an imprint of Harlequin (UK) Limited,
Eton House, 18-24 Paradise Road, Richmond, Surrey TW9 1SR

© HelenKay Dimon 20__

ISBN: 978 0 263 90370 6

British Library Cataloguing in Publication Data are available.

10-0612

Harlequin (UK) policy is to use papers that are natural, renewable and recyclable products and made from wood grown in sustainable forests. The logging and manufacturing processes conform to the legal environmental regulations of the country of origin.

Printed and bound in Spain
by Blackprint CPI, Barcelona

MILLS & BOON

First published in Great Britain 2013
by Mills & Boon, an imprint of Harlequin (UK) Limited,
Eton House, 18-24 Paradise Road, Richmond, Surrey TW9 1SR

© HelenKay Dimon 2013

ISBN: 978 0 263 90370 6
ebook ISBN: 978 1 472 00739 1

46-0813

Harlequin (UK) policy is to use papers that are natural, renewable and recyclable products and made from wood grown in sustainable forests. The logging and manufacturing processes conform to the legal environmental regulations of the country of origin.

Printed and bound in Spain
by Blackprint CPI, Barcelona

Award-winning author **HelenKay Dimon** spent twelve years in the most unromantic career ever—divorce lawyer. After dedicating all that effort to helping people terminate relationships, she is thrilled to deal in happy endings and write romance novels for a living. Now her days are filled with gardening, writing, read- ing and spending time with her family in and around San Diego. HelenKay loves hearing from readers, so stop by her website, www.helenkaydimon.com, and say hello.

To my husband, James, for believing when
I was ready to give up hope.

Chapter One

Kelsey Moore balanced a tray of croissants and gooey pastries on one arm and counted how many she had left for the end-of-the-morning rush. Ten in the morning was too early to break out the sandwich menu, which meant she had to make the breakfast offerings last for another hour. Hard to do if another round of the fanny pack and matching T-shirt crowd descended.

Not that she was complaining. The summer season had finally hit full swing in Annapolis, Maryland, as the increased number of buses and lack of on-street parking spaces showed. Tourists poured in to visit the quaint shops, check out that Naval Academy a few blocks over and wander down to the City Dock, also known as Ego Alley thanks to the expensive yachts that pulled up there.

Her coffee shop, Decadent Brew, sat in a prime location on Main Street, midway between the waterfront and the Maryland State House. She'd love to take credit for having the foresight to buy the two-story slim town house, but that honor went to her aunt, who ran it as a coffee and knitting shop for years.

Kelsey dropped the yarn part when she inherited it because she could barely sew on a button let alone figure out how to knit or purl. She had added a lunch menu, local art to walls, bookcases and sofas. In a rough economy, the small changes allowed her to survive and build a loyal following over the coffee chains. Not thrive, but pay the bills…usually.

Using tongs, she loaded up the display case with the last two doughnuts and the rest of the chocolate croissants. About half the tables were full, many with patrons more intent on typing on their laptops than actually eating anything. Still, silverware clanked, and the low rumble of conversation mixed with the piped-in music.

The steady beat and cheerful mood suited her. She liked to be busy, liked to see the seats filled, but never lost focus. After two years in business she knew how to keep one eye on the college kid making the lattes—this year his name was Mike—and the other on Lindy, the cute new high school senior who spent more time flirting and tugging on her short skirt than cleaning off the tables.

If Kelsey had a third eye she'd keep it locked on the front door because it was time. *He* came around this time every day, or he had for the past two weeks.

He'd walk in, his gaze searching for her. The corner of his mouth would lift in that breath-stealing smile and her stomach would do the stupid bouncing thing that made her feel younger than Lindy. Certainly more like fifteen than twenty-six, which she was.

As if thinking about him could conjure him up, the bell above the door chimed. Kelsey glanced up to see him holding the door for a family heading outside. He stood a bit over six feet with the kind of broad shoulders that made women look and then turn and look again. Dirty blond hair and eyes she knew from past encounters edged the border between brown and green.

Between the faded jeans and the trim gray T-shirt, she could easily call up a mental image of his bare stomach without ever having seen it. Something she'd done a little more often than she wanted to admit.

He nodded a welcome to a table of sixty-something women, who rotated between staring at him and whispering to each other. But he saved the wave and that killer smile for Kelsey.

Her hand tightened on the tray to keep from dropping it. "Hey there."

"Good morning," he said when he stopped across the counter from her.

"So far. How are you?"

The couple off to his left ran through the exact makeup of a caramel macchiato with Mike, which gave her an extra minute with Paxton. An unusual name but she'd remember his even if it were something easily forgettable, like Bob. A long line a few days ago gave her the excuse to ask his name. Owning the place did have its benefits.

"Not to scare you, but there's one of those walking tours a few blocks away and headed in this direction."

She enjoyed the flirting, but she didn't ignore business. "Let's hope they're thirsty."

"In that case I'm happy I'm here first, before it's standing room only in here." He leaned against the counter, because that's what he always did.

The combination of the slight limp and short hair made her think military, possibly returning from an overseas tour. Living in a navy area tended to take a person's mind in that direction. Still, he had the muscular build, complete with bulging biceps and a vine tattoo peeking out from under his sleeve. Military or not, it amounted to a pretty lethal punch to her usual common-sense theory of not mixing business with pleasure.

She tried to think of something clever to say. When nothing came to her, she winced over her complete lack of smoothness and set the tray down. "You want the usual?"

He pointed at the display case. "Add in whatever you have extra of or might have trouble selling today."

As if she didn't already have a crush on the guy.

She went to the tap at the coffee-of-the-day dispenser as the bell above the door dinged again. One look around the counter and she realized she'd need a trip to the stockroom because there was only one to-go cup left after the one for Paxton.

A group of kids came in, all shouting as their gazes stayed fixed on their phones. She turned to face the front of the store again to send a quiet-down gaze and spied the two guys hovering behind the noisy kids.

Black suits, dark scowls and a laserlike focus on…well, her. She immediately thought *politicians,* but the Maryland General Assembly wasn't in session. That left lawyers or government types. Either way, something about their intensity had her squirming.

Paxton cleared his throat. "You okay?"

Her gaze went back to him. She read concern in his narrowed eyes, heard it in the sudden roughness of his deep voice, and forced a smile to her lips. She hoped it rose to the level of sunny. "Absolutely."

She snapped the lid on his coffee and snuck a few more peeks at the suited patrons while she scrambled to get Paxton a bear claw. She pretended not to notice as the suit-wearers closed in a step at a time, never saying a word to each other and not bothering to look at the menu board over her head.

She put the plate down on the counter harder than expected in front of Paxton. The smack of ceramic against glass had both Mike and Paxton staring at her. Before she could babble out some excuse, Paxton put a hand over hers. Warmth seeped into her skin.

"Maybe you should sit down."

"I'm fine." And by that she meant spooked. The two guys

hadn't done or said anything, yet their presence had her swallowing and shifting her weight around.

"We could go out front for second."

"Really. It's okay." She said the words because she wanted the men out, and the only way to have that was to wait on them. They now stood right behind Paxton's impressive shoulder, and for some reason she wanted them away from him, too.

Still, he hesitated. He balanced his coffee and his wallet. "If you're sure."

"Absolutely. And today is on me." She pushed the plate closer. Before Paxton could argue, she glanced at her unwanted guests. "What can I get the two of you?"

For a second they held on to their silence. Finally, the taller one on the left blinked. "Black coffee to go."

"Two?" When he frowned at her, she tried again. "I mean, do you each want one?"

Paxton held his position at the counter, and the men didn't try to shove around him. They didn't look at him, either, but he stared at them as if he had them under some sort of visual scan.

"One cup only," the taller man said.

Unusual but not scary. She repeated that mantra as she turned back to the coffeepot and the blank space where the last cup sat a second ago. Another look and she watched Mike top off a latte with foam in the cup she wanted.

She could send him on a restocking run, but with the way her chest tightened she suddenly needed to gulp in as much air as possible. Better to do that away from the patrons. She held up a finger. "I'll be back in one second."

Before the men could argue, she took off. She shuffled around and pushed open the door to the narrow hall behind the main dining area marked Private. She kept moving as she passed the door to her office on the right and the stock-room on the left and finally hit the back entry.

Two slams against the safety bar and she had it open. The humid air rolled in, giving her the sensation of standing in front of a low-watt hair dryer.

With her eyes closed she counted to ten and tried to calm her overreaction. This is what happened to her now. Ever since her brother stopped communicating, her mind played vivid and scary games with the benign truth around her. Last night a guy stood on the sidewalk outside her upstairs apartment too long and she immediately assumed he was casing the place. It was as if her life had become a strange action movie.

When she reached ten in her silent countdown, she let out one final dramatic breath. Time to get back to work.

Fearing the air-conditioning would never stop running and her electric bill would soar if she kept the door open, she yanked on it, hearing it creak and moan as she tried to slam it shut. The thing weighed a ton, but she wrestled it closed every single day. Not that she had a choice now. Another min-ute away from the counter and Mike might sit down with his own laptop and play on the internet instead of work.

She smiled at the idea as she glanced over her shoulder toward the front of the shop. At the end of the hall stood one of the tall unwanted visitors. Seeing him there, in the small space between her and the freedom of the front room wiped out any amusement she'd felt.

She forgot about locking the door and turned to face the unwanted stranger. She said the first thing—the only thing—that popped into her mind. "You can't be here."

He closed the distance between them in a few steps. If he reached out he could touch her, but his hands remained at his back. "We'll be leaving by the door behind you."

We? Yeah, no way. "Wrong."

"I'm not playing." His arm dropped to his side.

She blinked at the gun in his hand and a paralyzing fear streaked through her nerves. "I'll scream."

"And put everyone out front in danger? I don't think so."

She turned to race out the back door and it burst open, bouncing with a crash and pinning her against the hallway wall. Unwanted visitor number two filled the entrance. She opened her mouth to let out the scream rumbling around in her chest when the man behind her grabbed her and clamped a hand over her mouth.

She kicked and threw her elbows. Even tried bending forward in the hope of breaking the guy's hold.

He snapped her back into him, almost lifting her off the floor. "One word and we shoot everyone in the shop."

When the attacker's hot breath blew over her cheek, she choked back the bile rising in her throat. Her mind raced as she mentally flipped through her options for saving herself and everyone in her shop.

Yell, run, fight. The most important thing was to not let these guys drag her away. She knew that much from the safety class she'd taken through the police station. But she had to get somewhere other than a claustrophobic back hallway.

To stall, she nodded. Instead of easing, the attacker's arm wrapped tighter against her neck. Muscle pressed against her windpipe. She clawed against his forearm in a futile attempt to keep him from crushing out her air supply.

The taller one pointed at the back door. "Let's get her out of here before that kid realizes she's gone and tries to play hero."

Mike.

Paxton.

Her brain flashed to images of all of them. To all the innocent people on the other side of the wall. Then her attackers started moving. She dragged her feet and grabbed for a hold in the chipped wall. Fingernails scraped against old paint, but she couldn't halt his progress.

Inhaling deep and gathering all her strength, she lifted her foot and nailed her attacker in the shin. At the thud of heel on bone, they slammed to a stop. The guy swore as he threw her body against the wall and held her there with his weight against her back.

Her head hit plaster and the world around her tilted. She gasped, trying to drag enough air into her lungs and brain to keep thinking.

The crunch of her nose against the wall sent pain spiraling through her. She turned her head and blinked when the crushing ache of her cheek against the wall threatened to be too much. Her body felt as if it were being ripped apart and smashed into a small ball at the same time.

In the next second, all the pressure vanished. The sudden change had her dazed and sliding to the floor. As her body fell, she saw a flash of gray.

Limp seemingly gone, Paxton moved in a blur. His body honed and aimed like a weapon, he came in the back door fighting. He jammed an elbow into the smaller attacker's head and knocked him into the wall. The guy went down in a motionless whoosh.

Something whizzed in front of her. She glanced over and saw Paxton standing with his arm out and his furious glare aimed at the taller attacker. She followed the line of Paxton's body and watched the other attacker scramble, his shoes scuffing against the floor, before he dropped. A red blotch spread on his stomach a second later as his gun dropped and spun across the floor.

Her first look at the knife was of the way it stuck out of the attacker's body. Even with his eyes closed and his body slumped to the side, he scared the crap out of her.

It all happened so fast and with less sound than if she had been moving boxes around back there. The pulsing tension seeped out of the hallway, but she couldn't take it all in. Sounds muffled, but she thought she heard someone talking. With her head tilted back, she saw Paxton grab the abandoned gun and point it at the bleeding man before hitting him with the end of it.

Paxton was talking but not looking at her. The words refused to come together in her brain. Finally, he glanced down at her, and the scowl marking his forehead eased. He dropped down to balance on the balls of his feet and winced as he went. The move put them face-to-face.

"Are you okay?" he asked.

The calm words brushed against her and she answered with the truth. "No."

His gaze traveled all over her. "Were you hit?"

"I don't think so." She closed her eyes to keep the room from spinning, but the reality of where she was had them popping open again. She tried to sit up, hoping her legs would hold her if she somehow wrestled her fatigued body to her feet. "My employees and the people—"

He put his hand on her noninjured knee, and the light touch held her down. "Everyone is fine. They don't even know anything happened back here."

The noise. The slamming doors. The grunts and yelling. None of that fit together with his assurance. "How is that possible?"

"I need a team and possibly medical." He talked to the air.

He kept issuing orders. Something about identities and watching the front. She really focused on him then, letting her gaze wander over the firm chin and across his broad chest. Apparently he threw knives. He had the attacker's gun plus another one.

In a matter of minutes he'd morphed from cute flirty guy with an injury to scary fighter guy.

"Is the limp real?" She blurted out the question before she could stop it.

"Yes." He touched his ear. "Now, Joel."

"Joel?"

Then she saw it. A tiny piece of silver. He had a microphone and was talking to someone who wasn't actually in the hallway.

Her eyes closed as a wave of nausea rolled over her. She hadn't dreamed any of it, and all of her fears of walking into the middle of a terrifying gun battle had come true.

That left one very big question.

She opened her eyes and stared at him again. "Who are you really?"

"Same guy you served the coffee to."

She tried to scoff but she didn't have the energy or extra breath. "I don't think so."

"You should probably call me Pax." He had the nerve to smile at her as he stood up.

This time she didn't buy the full mouth or twinkle in his eyes. "You're not a normal coffee customer."

"I am, but I'm also something else."

Dread spilled into her stomach. "What?"

"Your informal bodyguard."

Chapter Two

From the huge brown eyes to the grim line of her mouth, Kelsey looked about two seconds away from striking out. Maybe screaming her head off. Both options sounded bad to Pax. He wasn't a fan of throwing up, either, and the sudden green taint to her skin suggested that was a real possibility.

He reached down to help her up, but she shrank back against the wall, her petite frame curling in on itself. In the tucked position, her long hair fell over her shoulders, shielding her face from view and hiding the ripped strap holding her shirt on her shoulder. The denim shorts showed off her lean legs and a red welt right above her knee.

Seeing her injured and scared dropped a black curtain of rage over him. Every cell inside him craved revenge. He seriously considered removing his knife and then plunging it into the bad guy a second time.

But attack mode would have to wait. They had to get out of there, which meant providing a dose of comfort and reassurance. Not two of his strengths, sure, but since joining up with the Corcoran Team he'd been polishing the skills.

These jobs weren't like the ones he'd worked at his old employer, the Defense Intelligence Agency. There, he'd tracked down military intelligence leaks. He dealt in bad guys, dangerous situations and threats to service members.

In his new life he still went after bad guys, but now his

main objective centered on rescuing kidnapping victims. Or even better, stopping kidnapping threats before they happened, something he'd basically failed to do with Kelsey.

"Kelsey, it's going to be okay." Pitching his voice low and keeping it as soothing as possible, he said the words even though he knew she was in no condition to hear them.

She glanced at the body on the floor just a few feet away from her thigh and then back to Pax. "How can you say that? Look around you."

He wasn't sure what to say or how much to share about his real reason for visiting her shop almost every day for weeks, so he tried to evade. "Admittedly, the attack was a surprise."

Her eyes narrowed as fire sparked behind them. She added to the angry-warrior-woman stance by brushing her hair off her shoulder and staring him down. "That's your response?"

So much for thinking she was scared.

She shook her head. "You pretend to be injured—"

"I actually am injured. Well, was."

"—and you storm in here."

"By that you mean walked in the front door and ordered coffee, though from your comment I would guess my limp wasn't as well hidden as I thought." And didn't that tick him off.

The cracking sound came the second after she clenched her jaw. "You flew across the hallway a second ago, so stop pretending you're hurt and tell me who you really are."

"Maybe we could agree on the term *recovering*."

She blew out a long breath as her shoulders slumped. "Are you trying to be annoying?"

In light of her response, Pax wasn't sure how he should play this. "My brother would tell you that comes naturally. I don't have to try very hard at it."

He'd hoped to take her mind off the death choking the air around them by keeping the mood light. Seeing her pressed against the wall a few minutes ago started his mind unraveling. He'd assumed he'd clean up the mess and she'd be grateful. Maybe do the terrified thing and shake and cry, possibly need some consoling.

That was a normal reaction. This was not. She came out swinging. He half expected her to fight off his attempts at calming the situation and punch him in the groin.

Tension continued to zing around the enclosed space. Guns down and his knife still in use in the unidentified man's stomach, and yet Pax couldn't let his guard ease. Not when the woman in front of him vibrated with unspent energy and seemed determined to question everything he said.

She didn't even blink. "So now you have a brother?"

"Technically I've always had one since he's older." When the mumble of conversation from the front of the shop seeped through the walls and someone banged on the door to this back area asking why it was locked, Pax talked louder to drag her attention back to him. "His name is Davis."

She waved the comment off. Came very close to knocking against him while she moved her hands around. "I don't understand who you are or what's going on. And who are these two guys and why did they try to drag me outside?"

Pax surveyed the carnage. He had to move her off the property before these guys' friends missed them and came looking for trouble. "All good questions."

"Care to answer one?"

"Once we're out of here." Pax tapped the mic in his ear. "Ben? Finish clearing the shop and close the place down. Blame a gas leak and then get a medic because we have two down. Joel, I need you back here. Now."

Her sneakers scraped against the rough floor as she bent her knees and brought her feet closer to her butt. "Really?"

Pax wasn't clear which word led to the reaction. "What?"

"You're really doing some sort of spy-act thing in the middle of all this?"

He despised that word. The way Hollywood portrayed undercover agents and people in law enforcement as if they all used shoe phones and exploding pens was ridiculous. "It's possible you watch too much television."

She sat up even straighter, her shoulders coming off the wall and her hands falling to the floor on each side of her hips. "Okay, Mr. Good Samaritan. How about calling the police…and what do you mean by medic? Call an ambulance. I have customers and employees out front and need to know they're safe."

From the clear eyes and stronger voice he guessed she'd found her emotional and physical footing. That likely spelled trouble for him.

"Then there's the mess back here. That one will wake up eventually." She pointed at the downed man closest to the back door. "And that one is losing blood thanks to your knife skills."

Pax hoped she didn't expect an apology. "Yeah."

"He's not dead, is he?"

"Unfortunately, no. Unconscious and bleeding." Pax glanced at the other man. "And that one is lucky not to be bleeding. I'm thinking about stabbing him just because."

She swallowed and made a face that suggested she didn't like whatever she'd tasted. "In a few seconds I'll have to go over there and try to help the bloody one, and the idea of touching him after…well, it makes me want to throw up and kind of furious at you."

Yeah, she'd definitely moved from scared—and that had been pretty fleeting—to ticked off. As the clear target of whatever thoughts bounced around in her head and put that scowl on her face, he dropped the lighter tone. It wasn't working anyway. Didn't take a fancy shoe phone to figure that one out.

He held up his hand in a gesture he hoped telegraphed peace and maybe a touch of surrender. "Everything will be handled, but not in the way you're suggesting."

Then it started. She slid her hands closer to her body and shifted in a move so slight he almost missed it. He guessed she intended to struggle to her feet and then make a run for it. He was ready for the bolt. He just wished they could short-cut the disbelief and go right to the part where she got in the car and let him take her to safety.

Not that he deserved that level of trust from her. They barely knew each other. Sure, they'd flirted and he'd benefitted in the form of free bear claws now and then, but dough-nuts didn't change the facts. He was there to watch over her, to see if her missing brother made contact.

It was supposed to be a simple surveillance op, since that's all anyone at the Corcoran Team thought he could handle post-shooting incident. Little did they know the supposed "easy" job would lead to a backroom shoot-out.

"Don't even think about it." When she frowned at him, he filled her in. "Whatever big exit plan is in your head? Forget it. You're not getting by me. We need to get you somewhere safe, and then we can talk all of this through."

"We?"

"I think he's referring to me." Joel stepped over the man at the back door and moved inside. He hitched his thumb over his shoulder toward the alley outside. "Car's waiting."

Pax reached down a second time to get her off the floor. "Come on, Kelsey."

Her gaze bounced from him to Joel and back again as she crowded closer to the wall. "No way."

"These guys on the floor could have partners," Joel said.

Pax welcomed Joel's verbal assist but could do without the smirk. "I can guarantee that's true."

"Why should I trust you? I don't know you." She peeked around Pax's legs at Joel. "Or him."

When she drew in a deep breath, Pax dropped to his haunches again and bit down on his lip to keep from yelling. Ignoring the shot of pain, he held a hand over her mouth, careful not to get his palm too close to those teeth.

"Don't do that." She mumbled something against his hand but he ignored it and kept lecturing. "I know you want to yell for help but screaming could bring more attackers. Do you want that?"

She took several breaths before she shook her head.

Pax inhaled long and deep, trying to see this from her perspective and keep his anger in check. With her family history it was no wonder she went with wariness over fear. He knew only the scraps in her brother's file about a deceased mother, but the background of Kelsey's criminal father wasn't a mystery. His name had seen a lot of time in the papers a few years back. The truth, whatever really went on in this family, could be much worse.

"You see me every day," Pax pointed out as he stood up again. This time it took longer and more energy. Too many more deep knee bends and he'd crash to the floor.

"As a customer only."

Joel chuckled. "And she lands a verbal blow. I bet that hurt."

"You're not helping," Pax said under his breath and included a string of profanity to make his point.

Last thing he needed was a real-time reminder of just how attracted he was to Kelsey and how it suddenly seemed to run in only one direction. Especially since she was scowling at him, looking as if she might be planning his funeral.

"Joel, is it?" She shifted her weight and slid her body up

the wall. When her knees wobbled, she reached out for Pax, grabbing on to his forearm and steadying her balance again. Her hand dropped a second later.

"Joel Kidd. Yes, ma'am." The corner of Joel's mouth kicked up in a smile when she talked to him.

"Call the police."

The smile fumbled. "I'm afraid I can't—"

"Do that. Yeah, I get it." She stepped away from the wall and inched closer to the far end of the hallway. "Paxton…or whatever his name is, said the same thing."

"My name really is Paxton. I just prefer Pax."

But she'd stopped listening. She glanced around the floor and took a wide jump over the bleeding attacker's body. "I'm going to go out front and check on Mike. I might even scream if it looks like it's clear and you're the problem instead of the solution."

Pax grabbed her arm in time. He had her spinning around and standing only a few inches in front of him. At six feet he loomed over her by a good six inches. All those years playing football and the genes from a father he never knew had gifted Pax with broad shoulders.

His size tended to intimidate people. Using the factor to get his way never bothered him before. If it meant saving her, it wouldn't bother him now, either.

"No." Enough talk. He started walking toward the back door, taking her with him. He didn't squeeze or pull, but with his elbow tucked and her body swept in close to his, he had the balance advantage and moving her didn't take much pressure against her skin.

"Excuse me?"

He kept the lock on her elbow. "I tried this the nice way."

"When?"

They blew by Joel, who had dropped to the floor to check the pockets of both fallen attackers. "Uh, Pax."

The tone signaled caution as much as if Joel had thrown up a flashing red light. Pax shortened his stride and stopped a few steps from the back door.

"We are going to walk out there and get into the SUV." He lowered his voice, forcing the tension to leave his jaw before it cracked from the pressure. "We are going to get out of here and to somewhere safe. Then we can talk all of this out. But, Kelsey—and you need to understand this—we are leaving. No discussion."

The muscles in her arm went slack. All of a sudden it was easy to glide her across the floor and direct her where he wanted her to go. Pax knew that was a very bad sign.

This lady had the moves down cold—force your body to relax, and the person holding you will ease the grasp. Pax knew because he taught self-defense classes at the YMCA and had advised more than one class of women to avoid ever getting into a car with an attacker.

As the realization hit him, her body jerked. She slammed to a halt and pivoted away from him as she whipped her arm up, shrugging out of his hold. When he reached for her again, she ducked under the arc of his swing. Doubled over and head down in determination, she sprinted.

With his messed-up leg, she could have vaulted and took off and left him sputtering, but her sneaker snagged on the foot of the guy on the ground and she tripped. Her momentum took her flying and stumbling. She crashed against the wall next to the back door and stopped.

He swooped in before she could take off again. "Whoa."

He trapped her against the wall with his body, ignoring the uneasy sensation rumbling through him from mimicking the actions of the man who had attacked her earlier. Pax slapped his palms against the uneven cement on each side of her head and rested his body against hers, careful to crowd her but not smash into her.

She clearly saw it differently because the second his body touched against hers, she whipped into a wild frenzy. "Not again."

She kicked out behind her and raked her fingernails against the back of his hand. With her head shaking and shifting, she struggled and grunted. Energy pounded off her as every limb, every muscle, moved in concert against him.

This time, he threw his weight into the hold. He pressed his chest against her back and grabbed her wrists and stretched her arms out to keep them from flailing. Their heavy breathing mixed together as air pounded in his lungs. Beneath him, he could feel the rise and fall of her upper body on rough gasps.

She turned her head to the side and stared at Joel. Until that moment, Pax had forgotten his partner was even there. So much for calling in reinforcements. He could only hope Ben was having an easier time with the crowd out front.

"You could help me," she said to Joel.

"If it's any consolation, I plan on telling everyone back at the office about how close you came to getting the jump on Pax."

Pax swore under his breath. As if the shot to the thigh wasn't enough cause for ribbing. Now he'd have to hear about this. "Kelsey, listen to me."

"Why should I?" The harsh words lost their impact under the weak thread of her voice.

"You're in danger."

She turned her head and balanced her forehead against the wall. The position cut off all potential of eye contact with Pax and Joel. "Obviously."

"Not from me."

"You're the one who threw the knife. The same guy who's holding me now." She shrugged. "You're hurting me, by the way."

He eased his stance, shifting his weight to his heels and thinking to move away. Then he stopped. In addition to the sweet face and impressive legs, she was smart and skilled. He wouldn't put it past her to use guilt to break free.

He tried logic one last time. "There are men after you."

"Why?"

Pax glanced at Joel. The slight shake of his head mirrored Pax's feelings on the subject. It was too early and they had too little information on Kelsey to dump the truth on her. They needed to press her for information on her brother. But not here. Certainly not now.

Joel cleared his throat. "That's what we're here to figure out."

"And you two just happened to show up—"

"Three," Pax said.

"What?"

He didn't see a reason to hide the team. "Ben's out front."

"How comforting." She wiggled and pushed until he let her turn around. Anger and confusion battled in her eyes. "You understand why I'm confused. You guys all conveniently show up, claiming to be the good guys."

Pax knew he'd never used those words. "I get it."

"And?"

She deserved points for good questions and intelligence. The instructor side of him would pass her without trouble. In real life, her discomfort meant danger. And facing him, she had a clear shot at using the first attack move he taught women to use against men, and he had no intention of falling to his knees in pain.

That meant the conversation was over and he would end it. Right now.

"We're done with this." Her breath hiccupped and the sharp intake echoed in his ears as he bent over and lifted her off the ground. She landed on his shoulder with her head at his back. "Let's go."

Joel shook his head. "Man, this is a bad solution."

"It's the only one I have."

Kelsey stammered and spoke in half sentences. She finally got out a string of words. "What are you doing?"

"Since you want to do this the hard way, we will."

Then he walked out the back door as she started to scream.

Chapter Three

Kelsey stopped kicking and squirming as her brain rebooted. She looked down and saw his jeans and back, an odd from-above shot of his butt and the ground racing by beneath his feet. Being upside down with his fat-free shoulder digging into her stomach, she didn't have a good angle to nail him in the back. That was okay. She needed to save her energy and come up with a plan to get off this guy and out of there.

She also had to beat back the wave of disappointment swamping her. The wounded military hero backstory she'd created in her mind and spun into interesting tales didn't fit the real man at all. She'd secretly declared him a hottie and thought about him far too often once the workday ended and she lay in her bed.

Now she knew she'd picked the wrong description. Something that summed up a bossy, manhandling secretive liar would have been more appropriate.

Paxton or Pax or whatever he wanted to call himself carried weapons and got all grumbly and demanding when he wanted something. The idea she'd once thought of him as sweet and had piled all those free doughnuts on him…she wanted every delicious calorie back. The least he could have done was gain weight because really, she needed something to slow him down.

Even with the slight limp—an injury she now totally

viewed as an act—he'd stalked down the alley with only the barest crunch of gravel beneath his shoes to give away his position. The bouncing steps continued as they rounded the car and walked within a few feet of the SUV's back door.

Once he got her in there, breaking free could be impossible. No way was she going anywhere with two men she didn't know. She'd taken the lessons and listened to the lectures. She'd already lived through an attack once in her life, years ago.

She would not be a victim again.

She'd be smart, pick the exact right moment and then run in the direction of the nearest person or telephone, screaming her head off as she went.

The door on the opposite side of the car opened. Twisting around on Pax's shoulder, she looked through the window and spied Joel sliding across the passenger side of the backseat. She could only guess he was her assigned babysitter for their ride to wherever.

Just as she saw the gun in his hand, her butt smacked against the side of the car as Pax balanced her weight. Keys jangled and the world spun around her, the clear blue sky whizzing by, as her feet finally hit the ground.

Pax kept a steady hand on her arm as he reached for the door handle. "We're done with the nonsense, right?"

Whatever that meant. She nodded, trying to look obedient and terrified, though that last one wasn't much of a stretch for her limited acting skills. If the blood pounding in her ears and wild flip-flopping of her stomach were any indication, she registered pretty high on the terror scale.

He ducked his head and stared straight into her eyes. "Kelsey?"

"Fine, yes." She just needed him to shift an inch or two to the side, move a little out of the way, and she was out of there.

With a click, the door opened. He pulled it toward him

with slow precision, coaxing her into the small space he created. Inch by inch she crept closer to being penned in and
vulnerable.

No way was this happening a second time. The first
scarred her, left her sleep tortured and her trust in tatters
for years. The seventeen-year-old version of her made a vow
never to go back to that dark place, to fight no matter what,
and she intended to honor that promise.

Angling her body, she turned to get a better position and
set her weight so she could spring off her back leg and race
down the alley to the open street beyond. She launched and
miscalculated the opening. Her hip banged off the edge of
the door.

Red lights danced in front of her eyes and her leg went
numb. Then the pain came roaring on, pulsing and knee-
buckling in its intensity. Her mouth dropped open to yelp
but no sound escaped.

He threw the door open wide and put his hands on the
sides of her waist in a gentle touch that somehow managed
to hold her upright. Concern showed in his narrowed eyes.
"Are you okay?"

"That hurt like a—"

"I bet."

He touched his fingers against the throbbing spot on the
side of her leg. The rubbing eased the burning enough for
her concentration to rev up again. She pushed out all sense
of comfort and lowered her head, getting him to look down.

With her hands on his arm, she shoved with all her strength
and bolted. She heard him swear as his body thudded against
the side of the car. But she was gone. She sprinted down the
alley, glancing around for any sign of life or a place to duck
and hide. The wind whipped around her as footsteps thudded behind her, growing louder with each step.

"Kelsey, stop!" Pax's husky voice, fueled with fury, bounced off the brick walls, magnifying the sound.

She saw the bright light at the far end of the alley and headed for it. Thirty feet away, half the distance between the SUV and freedom, a shadow moved in. She opened her mouth to scream for help as she heard the skid of stones and felt a muscled arm band around her waist. The smell she associated with Pax—a mix of citrus and pine—fell over her.

She tried to wrestle away from him until she saw the familiar black suit on the stranger at the end of the alley. And the gun he held in his hand.

"Get down." The heat of Pax's body enveloped her the second before his words sank in.

The air rushed out of her and her footing failed. Pax's legs tangled with hers as his body wrapped around hers from behind. His weight pummeled into her and they both dropped through the air. She raised her hands and closed her eyes, waiting for her face to smack against the hard pavement and hoping her fingers could somehow minimize the painful blow.

Noise thundered around her until she couldn't tell the sounds of her screaming from the other shouts filling the air. Her legs took flight behind her. One minute she saw the ground racing up and the next they twisted and she landed with a hard smack against Pax's chest. He grunted and swore as his hand curled around her head and his body absorbed most of the impact.

They'd barely landed when he rolled and tucked her under him. In a continuous move, he came up over top of her and swung out his arm. One, two bangs boomed above her. She smelled a faint scent of burning and heard people yelling at the end of the alley for someone to call 911.

Pax's hand dropped and his body grew limp, pressing deeper against her. "Got him," he whispered.

In her head the whole scene took an hour, but she guessed it was less than a minute in real time. She let her head drop against the ground as she watched a puff of white cloud shift as it skimmed the blue sky. It took another second for her breathing to return to normal and her heart to stop knocking against the inside wall of her chest.

Her head fell to the side and she glanced back at the SUV. Joel lay stretched out on the seat with his hands still fixed on the gun with the weapon aimed. That fast, she remembered the suited man, and her gaze flipped back to the opening to the street where people now gathered. A man was down with a gun visible by his hand.

When she looked up again, Pax loomed over her, staring down. "I had to."

She tried to raise her hand and put her palm against his cheek, but her arms suddenly weighed a ton each. "You shot him."

Pax winced as if she'd struck him. "He was going for you."

She didn't understand the look of pain in his eyes. Who he really was and why he'd walked into her life were still parts of a greater mystery, but this time she didn't doubt his protection.

Maybe it was intuition or adrenaline, or just the shock of so much violence on the quaint streets of Annapolis. "Right."

His eyes narrowed as he struggled to sit up and help her do the same. "This is about your brother."

"I...wait, what?" Of all the things she expected him to say, that wasn't even on the list. "What are you talking about?"

"Your brother ticked off the wrong people and now someone wants to bring you in to flush Sean out."

The words pelted her. They scrambled and unscrambled, but she couldn't put them together in any logical way in her brain.

"Talk later. We need to get out of here." A shadow fell

over them. Joel bent over with his hands on his knees. His voice wobbled a bit on each word. "Ben's handling things out front, but the police are coming and we need to be gone."

She nodded because she had no idea what to say. This, like so much in her life, was about the men in it. First her dad, now Sean. Their choices. Their actions.

Pax grimaced as he stood up and stretched his legs. When he reached down to her, this time she grabbed his hand and jumped to her feet. Standing in front of him, her fingers speared through his, an odd calm blanketed her. They weren't out of danger and none of what had happened made sense, but for the first time since Pax walked through her door this morning, a sense of safety radiated through her.

He gave her hand a squeeze. "No more running."

"I don't trust you, but I'm not stupid. You always go with the guy who saved your life."

"Smart woman."

But she wasn't ready to turn to mush and follow every order he threw out. "I want answers."

"Then get in the car."

BRYCE KINGSTON BALANCED his palms against the sill and looked out his office window. His fingers tapped against the glass as he watched the steady lines of traffic move in each direction and with amazing slowness on the highway sixteen floors below.

After a quick glance at his watch, he shook his head with a harsh laugh. Never mind the hour of the day, barely lunchtime and nowhere near rush hour. The close-in proximity of Tysons Corner, Virginia, to Washington, D.C., meant cars idled and passengers baked in the burning sun and claustrophobic humidity as they tried to go anywhere in the summer heat.

The high-rise space, with its soaring windows and plush carpet, telegraphed the business image he wanted. The granite lobby and bank of security monitors, all designed by him with a team of high-priced architects, created the desired public impression of safety and wealth. He didn't have a fancy water view or the prime location near the Kennedy Center, but he had the end of the cul-de-sac spot in a business park within a reasonable drive of the airport.

Then there was the real-estate advantage in terms of the clients, and that's all that mattered to him as the founder of Kingston Inc. One division provided high-speed communication services to the government, ensuring continuous service and functioning networks.

But the new division would be the key to the company's future. He was sure of it. The high-tech division dealt with top-secret electronic surveillance and assisted the intelligence community and military in collecting and relaying information.

Not bad for a guy who spent most of his youth getting beat up on the school bus for spending so much time in computer class.

After a few years of leaner times and financial insecurities, the business plan was back on track. Well, not all of it. Sean Moore proved to be a wild card. Bryce never expected a low-level computer programmer to sit at the heart of potential corporate-ruining disaster.

"Sir?" Bryce's assistant, Glenn Harber, stuck his head in the small space he made when he opened the door.

Bryce didn't hear the knock, but he knew Glenn didn't skip that requirement. Tall and lean and still an expert rower and member of a team of young businessmen who met on the Potomac River well before dawn twice per week, Glenn knew about structure. He was not a man who shortcut the rules or invaded privacy without a care.

Four years out of business school and loaded down with two master's degrees and a host of other useless academic information, Glenn had demonstrated his commitment to the company. He came in early and left late. He often flew on the corporate jet for meetings and visits to military bases for demonstrations. And right now he looked as if he'd eaten a heaping plate of rotten conference food.

"Come in." Bryce pushed away from the window and sat down in his overstuffed desk chair.

The wife had chosen the décor. To Bryce, the dark furniture, set off with patriotic photos and framed flags, bordered on too much. He didn't think he needed to wear his commitment to country with such obvious fervor, but Selene disagreed.

It was part of her campaign to remind him just how much of her family's Old South money she'd invested in Kingston and how significant her personal stake really was. From the boys in their private high school to the family's sprawling three-story Georgian-style home in nearby Great Falls, she played the role.

He despised the personal part. Let him stay at the office, away from the ridiculous chatter and incessant arguing over things like limits on the boys' television watching and picking the "right" school activities, and his satisfaction level remained high.

Except for Sean Moore.

Glenn stepped up to the opposite side of the oversized desk. "We were unable to reach Sean's sister in Annapolis as hoped. She wasn't at her shop."

Bryce glanced at his watch a second time, even though he was very aware of the hour. "This should be the one time of the day she's there."

The businessman in him balked at the idea of an owner walking away at the busiest part of the workday. Summer in Annapolis meant tourists and profits. She ran a small business. She'd have to be insane to leave her shop during peak hours.

Glenn nodded. "I agree."

Bryce turned his pen end over end, tapping it against the desktop with each pass. "Then tell me why her shop is closed."

"The police surrounded the place."

His pen hung there, stopped in midair, when he heard the exact comment he dreaded. "Someone called the police?"

"Yes."

The last thing he needed was outside interference. "Find out who and while you're at it, find her."

Glenn swallowed hard enough for his throat to bobble. "Right."

"We find her, we find her idiot brother."

"And then?"

Bryce knew the next step. He didn't have the benefit of growing up in an expensive neighborhood lined with trees and home to rounds of nannies, which in this case would have been a detriment anyway. The Baltimore docks had taught him a thing or two about life.

"I'll handle Sean Moore."

Chapter Four

Fifteen minutes later, Pax created a false trail. He doubled back and looped around, using skills he learned long before reaching adulthood, when he'd been trying to hide from Davis after curfew and downing more beer than his dimwitted teen brain could handle. With the road behind him clear except for the usual summer traffic, Pax eased his death grip on the steering wheel and let his shoulders slump back into the seat.

He eyed up Joel and Kelsey in the backseat of the SUV. They sat on opposite sides of the vehicle, with Kelsey pressed tight against the door, her head resting on the glass.

Pax, usually comfortable with silence, felt the need to say something. "I'm hoping this next part of the plan goes better."

Joel smiled but his attention never wavered from his scan outside the window. "We have a plan?"

"Not exactly what I wanted to hear," she mumbled.

Pax eased his foot off the gas and tapped the brakes so he could make the steep turn into the driveway behind the Corcoran Team property. The bounce under the wheels had his leg shifting and his back teeth grinding together.

The ride through slim streets, historical and perfect for the charming look of the tourist town, made the trip bumpy. The constant lookout for following cars kept his focus off the road just long enough for him to hit every stupid pothole between Kelsey's shop and the team headquarters.

She rested a hand against the window. "This looks like a house, not a workplace."

Pax understood the confusion. On top of the emotional roller coaster, he drove her deeper into the heart of the historic section of Annapolis and straight up to a house sitting amid tall trees. It was a federal-style standalone and a bit imposing the way it soared three stories into the air, except for a small portion, about a third, of the top floor that functioned as an open porch area—which they never used because the site would leave them too exposed.

"Don't worry," Joel said. "It's a home on the top and office on the bottom."

Pax was done talking and ready to find a bottle of painkillers. "Let's go."

He slammed the car into Park the second he pulled into one of the open garage bays at the back of the office property. He had the door open and jumped down, hoping to walk off the big band thumping in his thigh.

The small white stones that paved the space between the separate garage and the redbrick building crunched under his shoes and further threw off his balance. Much more of this and he'd be back on crutches, and he vowed to burn those as soon as he found out where Lara had hidden them.

Lara Bart Weeks, his brand-new sister-in-law and the absolute best thing ever to happen to his big brother, Davis. He was two years older and even now off enjoying the end of his honeymoon while Pax handled the coffeehouse mess.

Not that this job was supposed to blow.

Pax had been ordered to desk duty until his leg healed. The only reason the boss let Pax handle the assignment was he threatened to shoot out the surveillance screens in the office if he had to sit there and do paperwork for one more minute. That led to a low-risk operation, a stakeout of the coffee shop. Just sitting and eating doughnuts.

In some ways, it was an easy stakeout because no one expected Sean to seek out his sister. Nothing in their relationship suggested he would, not when he was deeply mired in trouble. And boy was he. But Sean had surprised them all.

They'd gotten halfway across the open space of the yard when Connor Bowen slipped out the back door of the house and stood on the small porch, just under the overhang. He wore black dress pants and a long-sleeve blue dress shirt, and managed to blend in despite being totally out of place in the relaxed summer environment.

But that's who he was. After years in the field doing work and traveling to places Pax could only guess about, Connor craved air-conditioning and a desk.

"So much for the idea of resting the leg," he said as he crossed his arms over his chest and stared Pax down. Being only seven years older didn't keep Connor from looking every inch the in-charge boss man.

Kelsey stopped biting her lower lip and came to a halt in the clearing. Her arm shot out and she grabbed Pax's. "You really are injured?"

Connor's eyebrow lifted. "You can't tell?"

Joel snorted as he passed them all by and went straight to the back door. "I need food and the bathroom, and not in that order."

"Knock yourself out." Connor shifted to the side to let Joel pass, but then he restaked his ground. Legs braced, arms folded and hovering by the door as if to say anyone who went in had to go through him first.

Pax got secrecy and understood the operation, but they were blown. There was no way to salvage this assignment as set up and feed Kelsey some line about being legitimate agents who just happened to stumble into her coffee shop in time to rescue her.

Pax doubted any sane woman would buy the story, and he knew Kelsey was far too smart to go there. Combine that with her survival instinct, which appeared to tick in the expert range, and their options for handling this in a quick and easy manner decreased significantly.

She put her hand above her eyes and squinted against the sun as she looked Connor over. "Who are you…or am I not allowed to know that, either?"

"I take it from that response things didn't go well this morning."

Pax hid his smile. Connor knew exactly how the mess unfolded at Decadent Brew. He was tied in to the communications link, ran the unexpected removal of Kelsey from back in his office while watching his bank of monitors, and by now had placed the right calls and talked to the right people to keep the Corcoran Team's name out of this and ensure the gas leak story led the news.

That was the job. He was the handler. The guy who made it all possible behind the scenes.

"Connor Bowen, my boss." Pax put a hand low on her back, thinking to steer her inside. There was no need to stand out in the open and invite gawking.

She didn't move. "And what exactly is your job again? All of you, any of you, any response would be welcome."

Connor opened the back door. He threw out an arm and motioned toward the house. "We'll explain inside."

She hummed. The tune was quiet, almost as if it kicked on as her brain began to spin, but Pax could hear it. As a fellow under-the-breath singer, he recognized the almost imperceptible sound. And he'd heard it from her before when she made intricate coffee drinks for other customers while he waited in line for his.

He didn't know what her humming meant or why she did it, but the idea of having some extra time with her to figure it out…well, he didn't hate the idea.

Before he could push or try another attempt at issuing an order he knew she'd ignore, neither of which he wanted to do with her in this tenuous state and Connor standing right there watching, she moved. She hesitated before stepping inside, stopping to stare at the out-of-place dark square on the wall next to the back door.

A retinal scan and a handprint reader. Admittedly not the usual office setup, but he doubted she knew what she was looking at and since Connor had clearly disabled it remotely when he stepped outside, Pax didn't have to give a demonstration now.

She pointed at the pad. "More secrets, I guess?"

The woman didn't miss much. "You'll get used to it."

"Not so far."

KELSEY TRIED TO take it all in. She'd expected a fancy high-tech room filled with gadgets. She got an open kitchen, complete with blue cabinets and a huge farm sink. No food on the counters, unless you counted the two half-empty chip bags.

The really strange thing was the overabundance of coffee-makers. Not fancy ones. Normal coffeemakers…all four of them. The sight made her wonder how many people worked here, if any were women and if they ever ate regular meals. It also made the shop owner part of her think they should pay for her to provide better beverages.

A swinging door led to a wide-open space. A double room, probably what should be a combination living and dining room, but in this case housed desks and computers in individual work spaces. Closed cabinets with locks lined the far wall, and a conference room table sat in the middle of everything.

Everywhere she looked she saw television monitors, some big and some small. One looked as if it piggybacked traffic cams, with images flickering from intersection to intersection. Another showed a front door, she guessed to this address.

On the one across the room...wait.

She headed for Joel. He sat slumped in a chair, running his hand through his dark hair, with his feet on the countertop and a mug of something she guessed was coffee in his hand. Peeking over his shoulder, she watched people scurry around out front of Decadent Brew, the place where she worked and lived and worried about losing almost every day.

A couple tested the doors and then stared at the sign with the posted hours. Being closed, knowing what the loss of income and product could cost her later, had a lump clogging Kelsey's throat. Heaviness tugged at her muscles, and she had to fight the urge to sit down.

Everything she owned, all she was, centered on that building. The dark, strangely spooky building. The lights were off and something—she leaned in closer and studied the scene, maybe drapes of some sort—covered the windows.

She spun around and met Pax's emotionless gaze. "Is this your doing?"

"Mine, actually." Connor walked in, carrying a pot of coffee. He set it in the middle of the table on a tray surrounded by unused mugs.

It was all so normal yet so wrong.

"Where is everybody?" Pax dropped into a chair and blew out a long breath. He stretched his right leg out in front of him as he massaged his thigh.

She wasn't sure what caused the injury, but she believed it existed. She was about to ask him about it when she sensed a gaze on her. A quick glance at Connor and she caught the small shake of his head.

"Davis is enjoying his final days in Hawaii, as you know. The rest of the group is cleaning up the mess in Catalina, except for Ben," Connor said as he poured her a cup of coffee. "Ben is on his way to the hospital to check on your injured attacker. I'll head out in a second. Sounds like I have a very angry investigator to calm down and a few explanations I need to give."

Pax slumped down farther in the black leather chair. "I don't ever want your job."

Without turning around, Joel saluted with his cup. "Yeah, no envy over here, either."

The information collected and piled, and Kelsey tried to mentally flip through and analyze it all. The really tall, dark and businesslike one was in charge. If this Connor guy wasn't the overall boss, he should be because he acted like it and his six-foot-three-or-four height suggested no one mess with him.

The younger, black-haired, scruffy-chinned one, Joel, seemed to be connected to the monitor. There was a brother named Davis roaming around out there somewhere, some guy named Ben and a group of people, she had no idea how many, in California.

It was a lot to take in.

She grabbed on to the back of Pax's chair while a wave of dizziness crashed over her. With everything that happened during the past hour or so and the rapid-fire confusion bombarding her brain, she was fading. Fatigue crept into her muscles, and the coffee in four pots might not be enough to keep her on her feet and functioning.

As if he read her mind, Connor poured another cup, skipped the sugar and extras, and downed it black. "I'll get this worked out and then we can figure out our next steps."

The words snapped her out of the haze that had started washing through her. The conversation replayed and she wondered if they even knew they talked in code. "And the *this* in that sentence would be what?"

She was treated to three blank stares and a sudden abundance of quiet. Even Pax did a twisty-turny thing to look up and give her eye contact, but no one said a thing. A wall clock ticked somewhere and garbled noises came from the earphones Joel now had around his neck.

If she'd known such a simple question would get their joint attention, she'd have asked one an hour ago.

Connor was the first to move. He sat across from Pax and on the other side of the table from her. "The scene at your store."

"Is everyone okay?" Pax asked.

"All the good guys are."

The men were off and running again on a topic other than the one she'd introduced. They offered a snippet of information, failed to explain anything and then moved on. She never knew how annoying that was until now.

She raised a finger, but that did nothing for the balls of anxiety bouncing around inside her stomach. "Um, excuse me?"

Connor smiled. He flashed his soft blues eyes and shot her the I'm-listening stare Pax tended to use on her. Clearly whatever group all these guys worked for taught the same facial expressions in a Pacify-the-Ladies class.

"Your customers and employees are fine," Connor said. "They think there was a gas leak as cover for a burglary at another store, and you got caught up in it but are fine."

Even though she heard that sort of thing on the news every night, it sounded ridiculous when applied to her life. Anyone who knew her would expect her store to stay open, or at least for her to be out on the street giving away the unused inventory. Not that all that many people knew her, not with her work hours.

But she didn't purposely hide in her house. Not anymore. "Who told people that story?" she asked.

"Me."

She had a feeling Connor would be the one to pipe up with an answer. "Because that's your job?"

Pax laid a hand on her closed fist and brought her around to the side of his chair. "Have you seen Sean in the past few weeks?"

She ripped her fingers out of Pax's hand. As they all continued the male staring ring, her knees went soft and the ground beneath her moved in a rolling wave. Her brain tried to shut out any reference to her brother. At twenty-three he was three years younger and had spent more time than she could count in trouble.

She swallowed and cleared her throat, but the words would not come. It took a good minute before she could force out a question. "You mentioned him before. What exactly do you know about Sean?"

Pax didn't flinch. Didn't bother to look guilty or worried. He just sat there rubbing his leg. "Everything."

"How?"

He made a noise, something dismissive and all male. "Not important."

She slapped a palm on the conference table and watched his gaze move to it before bouncing back to her face.

She wasn't trying to make noise. All she wanted was to hold her body upright. "It is to me."

"Kelsey?"

Connor said her name, but she refused to look at him. She wanted Pax to tell her, to come clean and finally let her know what was happening and who he really was. "No."

A thundering silence returned to the room. This time even the clock stayed silent.

That was fine with her. Balanced on the table, she could

stand there all day. She *would* if that's what it took to make her point.

After another moment of ticking tension, Pax exhaled in that women-are-so-tiresome way men did when pushed to talk about something they wanted to ignore. "That's a shame. Finding him sooner rather than later would be safer for you."

Yeah, he still didn't get it. "I mean, no, we're not going to play it this way."

"Excuse me?" Pax's eyebrow ticked up and the last signs of the charming guy with the love of black coffee disappeared.

"You know about me, and apparently my brother, and I don't even want to know what else. Until I understand what's happening and where you all fit in, I'm not saying another thing."

"There's a limit on what we can divulge," Joel said from the relative safety of the other side of the room.

As if she was going to accept that nonsense excuse. "Then take me to the police. I'm sure they'll want to question me about this supposed theft you made up."

Pax's cheeks rushed with color and his fingers dug deeper into the arms of his chair. "No, they don't."

"I have no idea what that means."

The finger lock on his chair didn't ease. "We were hired to watch over you."

"By whom?"

Connor was already shaking his head. "We can't tell you that, but we can say we're the good guys and we're here to keep you safe."

"Because you would tell me if you were the bad guys?"

Joel chuckled. "We should check her injuries and Pax's, maybe get her a change of clothes and some food."

"I don't need—"

"Good idea." Pax struggled to his feet.

When his body started to fall again, she put an arm around

his waist and held him up. A backache settled in a second later as she wrenched her muscles and locked her knees and arms to support him. He braced his hands against the table and leaned on her.

She looked up, thinking to ask Connor for help, and saw the strain across his face. More than that, worry. These men might work together, but their bond went deeper. She wanted to curse them all for making this situation so hard on her. They expected her blind faith and gave nothing in return.

She thought about it another second and decided that wasn't true. They gave her protection, but she still wasn't clear on why she needed it.

If Pax had just stood up without trouble or had the courtesy to stay seated, she would have kept fighting him. Thanks to the mention of her injuries, every muscle and cell inside her started to ache. Talk about the power of suggestion.

But the real problem was Pax.

Her gaze traveled over him. Over the way he kept weight off his right leg and the cut along his cheek. If the clenched jaw were any indication, he was in pain. She was confused and angry, but the guy who stormed in to save her, protected her from a crushing fall and killed for her looked unsteady on his feet and ready to drop.

It was the wake-up call she didn't want but couldn't ignore. She swallowed back the rest of her questions and fell deep into appreciation mode. She didn't know him but she owed him.

She faced Connor and skipped over the stuff she wanted to know to the stray comment that caught her attention. "You have women's clothes here?"

His white-knuckle grip on the edge of the table tightened. "My wife's."

Now, there was a bit of news she didn't see coming that

sent her gaze zipping to the thin band on Connor's finger. "Where is she?"

"Out of town."

Yet another person not there. That appeared to be the norm around this house…or office…or whatever it was. "Fine. If someone checks Pax's injuries, I'll clean up, then you can all decide that I deserve to know more and start talking."

Pax snorted. "Wrong."

Before that minute she'd forgotten she held on to him. She gave his waist a reassuring squeeze and then dropped her arm. "That's the only solution I'll accept."

Joel glanced at Connor. "Told you."

He nodded. "You're right."

They'd lost her in all the partial sentences. "What are you two talking about?"

Joel shot her a huge smile as he stood up. "Don't you worry. I'll take care of Pax."

"You're qualified?"

If possible that smile grew even wider. "Yes, ma'am."

"Well, I don't agree to the schedule." Pax practically snarled when he said the words.

Tough.

This time Connor stood. Something about the way he moved had all eyes focused on him. "I do. The lady is—"

"Kelsey," she said.

Connor gave her a nod. "Kelsey is right. Pax gets treatment, she gets changed and a once-over for injuries, and we meet back here in thirty. No arguments."

Pax pushed off the table and stood up straight. His large frame wobbled but he didn't fall this time. He didn't match his friends' smiles with one of his own, either.

When he looked at her, his mouth had fallen into a flat line. "One thing you should know."

Dread tumbled through her. "What?"

"We control all the doors and windows, so there's no way for you to escape once you're up there."

Honestly, the man was clueless. She'd turned that corner when a third attacker showed up and a bullet whizzed by her head. "Why would you think I would try?"

"Experience."

Chapter Five

Dan Breckman appeared in Bryce's office doorway shortly after three that afternoon. He carried a file and wore a scowl. Neither of those proved unusual for the man. He was sixty, retired military and a constant nuisance.

"We have a problem."

Bryce tried to mentally count the times Dan had wandered out of his corner office and said that each week. Whatever the number, Bryce didn't have time for his nonsense now. "I have a phone conference in a few minutes."

"This can't be ignored."

Bryce tapped his pen against his keyboard and cursed his decision to hire Dan as a consultant. With his knowledge and reputation, the man added a level of legitimacy to the new intelligence division as it fought its way through a corporate field loaded with big players, but he was far too used to being in charge. He turned out to be the hands-on type rather than that sit-quietly-and-collect-a-check type, as Bryce had hoped.

Dan failed the keep-your-enemies-closer test. Giving him the office turned out to be a fatal mistake. Access to programs and business plans was one thing, but Dan tried to worm his way into every aspect of the new operations, including personnel issues, which were out of his purview. Bryce said no, but people in the workplace talked. Shared information.

And when Dan started asking questions about the one subject for which Bryce did not have a satisfactory answer, telling the older man to get back to work only solved part of the problem. Bryce could push Dan off but that didn't solve the Sean issue.

Dan didn't wait for a conversation opening. He stepped up and hovered on the other side of Bryce's desk. "Sean Moore didn't show up for work again today. That's sixteen weekdays in a row."

Bryce knew exactly how long it had been. Right down to the minute, and he could feel each one tick by inside him. Hear the knocking in his head.

The click of the pen beat into one long, rapid-fire drumming line. "I had human resources use all of our contact information to find him. It would appear he left town."

"In light of his history, I can't say this is a surprise, but I continue to be confused about how he was hired and why he was put on my team."

Each accusatory word scraped against the inside of Bryce's brain, inflaming the anger already burning there. He shouldn't have to handle hiring at the lower levels, to oversee every bothersome detail. He had too much work to do running the company without sitting in on the interviews of every petty administrative assistant and mailroom clerk.

From now on Glenn would have that task. With his charts and spreadsheets, he would be in charge of ensuring that stupid mistakes like this never happened again. Either that or he'd lose his job.

But Bryce had no intention of sharing any responsibility with Dan. "You're referencing Sean's father's history. Sean's academic record and criminal history were perfect."

"He failed his recent lie detector test."

A fact Bryce had buried but Dan had clearly uncovered. While he was investigating this matter, ripping it apart and

dissecting every piece of paper, every line, Bryce would look
into Dan's role, as well. The man knew too much, too quickly,
and Bryce vowed to find out where the information leak in
his office came from.

"I am aware of young Sean's test. As the owner of this
company—" Bryce emphasized the word *owner,* letting the
syllables bounce off his tongue "—I am advised immediately of this sort of thing. When an employee's clearance is
revoked, since the clearance is a condition of employment,
the job position is pulled, as well."

"But this young man conducted preliminary computer
work on the new Signal Reconnaissance Program *before* his
security clearance had been approved."

Another piece of information Dan should not know. Each
word moved him closer to the top of Bryce's things-to-handle
list. "And if the time comes, I will contact NCIS."

Bryce had spent his youth being pushed around, but those
days were long behind him. He dropped his pen on the desk,
letting it thud against the wood, before he stood. He stretched
every vertebra as he straightened to full height. Dan may
have worn a uniform, but Bryce had the sort of shield that
came with harsh and unwanted life experience.

"You're depending on my reputation to open doors for
the company at the Pentagon." Dan dropped the file on the
desk and balanced his fists on each side of it, allowing him
to lean in close across the expanse. "That gives me some
rights, including the right to question employment choices."

Dan's point about needing an "in" at the Pentagon wasn't
wrong. Starting tomorrow, Bryce would begin the search
for another consultant to handle that. One satisfied to collect a check and confine his work to wining and dining former colleagues. Someone who would know when to shut up.

"You know, Dan, I get that you're used to a certain chain
of command and being at the top of it, but that's not where

you are now. I do not answer to you nor do I appreciate your interference."

A tense silence followed the comment. It took a few seconds for Dan to relax the grim line of his mouth. "Fine."

He pushed the file across the desk.

Bryce didn't make a move toward it. In this game, he would not be the one to blink. "What exactly is that?"

"All the intel I gathered on Sean Moore and his family." A small smile played on his mouth. Gone was the blank stare and muscle twitch in his cheek. "You're not the only one with connections."

"Which is supposed to mean what?"

"Just trying to make sure we have an understanding. An investigation into Kingston and the issue about having a non-cleared individual working prematurely on a top-secret project, even in the planning stages, could be a problem for the company's contracting status with the government. That's why I am willing, you could even say insisting, that I be allowed to help resolve this."

The threat wasn't an empty one. There were laws associated with entering into contracts with the government and lists of rules to follow. Bryce didn't flinch. Didn't even blink. "I'll consider the request."

MINUTES TURNED INTO hours before Pax made it downstairs again. He took the last few steps from the second floor without letting up on his death grip on the stair railing. His sneakered feet fell with heavy thuds, but at least he could still walk. While standing under the scalding shower spray twenty minutes ago, he doubted he'd be able to maneuver his body to get where he needed to be. Relief replaced his growing headache when he realized he'd been wrong.

He limped into the main workroom, ignoring the plates piled on the table's edge. They'd switched the afternoon

agenda and eaten first. With limited conversation except for
Joel's ongoing commentary about the movies he'd recently
seen, the food went down easy, and Pax no longer worried
Kelsey would dive out the window at the first chance. Yeah,
she'd promised previously, but watching her smile and laugh
and never once scan the room for an exit convinced him.

After the shower and rounds of unnecessary medical attention, Pax now had a rebandaged thigh from his old gunshot
wound and a constant dull ache that flared into full-blown
raging pain when he put too much weight on that side. Made
walking tough but not impossible. The treatment combined
with clean clothes, and he felt ready to go again.

But he planned to do it from a seated position for the next
hour or so. He dropped into the closest chair and leaned back
into the soft leather. A quick glance around the room started
a buzzing in his head. "Where's Kelsey?"

"Calm down." Joel walked in from the kitchen and ex-
changed a new pot of coffee for the old one. "She's upstairs."

"Good…and I'm fine. Perfectly calm." Except for the
adrenaline kick that still had his heart triple-timing. Pax
closed his eyes and tried to steady the beat.

"Uh-huh."

At the hint of amusement in Joel's voice, Pax's eyes
popped open again. He shot his friend a you're-on-the-edge
frown. "Don't do that."

"The woman has you spinning."

Spinning. Fantasizing. Forgetting his training. Losing
control. All of that. "She tried to run before, so I was just
checking."

"Which brings up another point." Joel balanced a thigh on
the conference room table. Sat right there, a few feet away
from Pax, and talked with a thread of laughter in his voice.
"Your lady skills need help. You now have them all but jumping out of cars to get away from you."

"I was watching over her."

"Oh, I noticed."

"There's nothing else between us but the job. That's it." Pax repeated the lines over and over in his head, as he'd been doing for days, and he still didn't buy them. He'd moved beyond watching for danger and started just plain watching her a week ago.

Joel closed one eye and looked at the ceiling as if pretending to count. "So many words in that denial."

"I can think of two words for you."

Joel laughed out loud that time. "Man, don't make me say 'uh-huh' again."

Letting out a long, exaggerated exhale, Pax gave in. "Clearly, you have something to say. Get to it."

"I see the way you look at her." Some of the amusement left Joel's voice this time. He spoke lower, quieter.

Pax knew he all but drooled in Kelsey's presence and hated that Joel had noticed the weakness. "I'm watching to see if she's going to bolt and whether I'm going to get injured running after her."

"Nope, that's not it."

Since hitting the subject head-on didn't appear to be working, Pax went for the obvious parry. "Where's Connor?"

Joel tapped his thumb against the rim of his mug. "Are we changing the subject?"

"Definitely."

Joel got up from the conference table and headed for his usual desk, the one lined with monitors and other assorted equipment. "Connor headed out to play cleanup, then was meeting up with Ben to see if they could identify your attackers. The one you stabbed and put in the hospital is still out but he has to wake up sometime."

"Let's hope."

"Ben is standing guard, just in case." A rhythmic clicking

filled the room as Joel tapped on the keyboard and sent the one monitor flipping through streets around the historic district. "Any chance Kelsey is involved in her brother's mess?"

Joel dropped the question without fanfare. Just put it out there and dragged that elephant right to the middle of the room.

Still… "Excuse me?"

Joel shrugged. "You said yourself you don't know her. You've just been watching her. She could be Sean's partner."

"That's not true." Pax refused to let the doubt take hold in his mind.

"My mistake. I guess you know this woman better than I thought."

But he didn't, and that was one of the problems.

Chapter Six

"Sounds like I'm interrupting something important," Kelsey said in a near whisper.

Pax almost jumped out of his chair. Forget the increased heart rate. Every cell inside him whipped into a frenzy at the surprise sound of her voice until he had to grab on to the chair to stay in it.

She'd snuck up on them. *Them.* The undercover operatives with all the training. No way that happened without her trying to make it happen, which made him wonder what information she'd hoped to overhear.

Then there was her outfit. Frayed gym shorts and a trim white tee. She smelled sweet, like fruit. He had no idea what women used in the shower to make their skin glow, but Kelsey had found some of it. Even now the ends of her long hair curled as they dried.

A man could take only so much before he had to dunk his head in a bucket of ice water, and Pax was right on the edge. "It was nothing."

She shot him that look women gave when they knew they had the upper hand. "Oh, it was something. Care to tell me what?"

"Kelsey." Joel stood up. Even cleared his throat, but that didn't hide the sudden flush to his skin. "How are you feeling?"

"Nice try at throwing me off, what with that make-the-ladies-swoon smile and all, but answer the question." She could have picked any chair. She headed straight for the one next to Pax. "One of you, both of you, I don't care."

The compliment about Joel went overboard, in Pax's view. He was about to point that out when she started walking and talking, and something about that combination left him speechless, if only for a second.

Joel started to put his earphones on. "Once Connor gets back—"

She sighed at them. "No."

Joel froze. "What?"

Pax weighed the risks. There was protocol for this type of situation, but they'd already blown through the rules by bringing her here. The hide-and-seek portion of the day was over. If she had information, he needed it and wanted her to give it up without the games. "Sean disappeared with top-secret information."

The front two legs of Joel's chair hit the hardwood floor with a crack. "Pax, what the—"

"She deserves to know, and she's not going to take 'it's nothing' or some big stall for an answer." Pax had already tried that game and failed. Kelsey was not a woman to push to the side and feed trite lines so she'd stay quiet.

"Thanks for recognizing I'm not an idiot," she mumbled under her breath.

Pax didn't bother whispering. "It would be easier if you were."

"That's charming."

Since that wasn't his goal at the moment, the comment didn't bother him at all. "Do you know about Sean's job at Kingston Inc.?"

"We are not exactly on speaking terms, but you probably know that, too."

There was no use in denying it. Pax had read the files. They all had. "I have some information about your past."

"Like how my dad wrote bogus insurance policies for people then took their money and left them with no coverage? It's a lovely family story, one Sean thinks is a mistake. He refuses to listen to reason or look at the evidence, and there's a ton of that."

"Those details were in the news." Joel kept hitting that computer key. "The fraud case was pretty famous."

"Well, living through it was not exactly a joy. Sean remembers pieces only. I had just turned seventeen. He was thirteen and his mother fed him a constant line about how the Moore family was being oppressed by jealous poor people. I was the evil stepchild from the forgettable first marriage, so I was shut out of her little us-against-the-world club."

Pax knew all these pieces, right down to how her father spent less than two years in prison thanks to later "found" evidence implicating his assistant. They traded places and her father returned to his wife and her family money, leaving Kelsey alone.

The cycle sounded familiar. The numbness and pain. His own mother had dealt him those dual blows. Different circumstances, but abandonment was abandonment regardless of the specifics. "I understand."

"No offense but I doubt it." Her eyebrow lifted and her voice dripped with disbelief.

"I know about bad parents." Knew, lived through and somehow survived them, which was all a credit to Davis. As they were passed from relative to relative, from trailer parks to shacks unfit for humans, Davis held them together.

The idea of Kelsey not having someone like Davis to protect her made Pax's stomach lurch.

"Now I'm dying to ask about your life." The hard edge left her voice and her eyes.

Understandable, but there was no way Pax was going down that emotional road. His past left him closed-off and he preferred it that way. "Finish your story."

She gnawed on her bottom lip a second before continuing. "Sean wanted to believe our father, but I knew better. He had to touch every check that came into the office. There's no way his office manager set him up. My father lied. He went to jail then got lucky. Now he's out and that's all the time I want to spend talking about him."

Fair enough. She'd shared and now so would he.

Ignoring the shake of Joel's head, Pax explained. "Sean got a low-level job at Kingston, a communications firm that's moved into government contracting. He did some computer work and now he's missing."

There it was. Out in the open. Over Joel's eye rolling and the vivid memory of Connor's training and specific warnings about confidentiality, Pax had spilled more than he should. She had to be satisfied now.

Her head tipped to the side and her damp hair fell over her shoulder. "What piece are you leaving out?"

Apparently not. "What?"

"Why do you think he is?" Joel asked.

"Because he's assuming Sean did something wrong rather than assuming he's hurt or on vacation or something…. Or is my family name the reason you're jumping to conclusions?" Her focus never left Pax. Her gaze searched his face, and her attention did not waver. "I'm wondering if you're looking at my father's crimes and condemning Sean and maybe me."

"I never said that." That wasn't who Pax was. Not how he operated.

She traced an invisible pattern over the tabletop with her finger. "You wouldn't be the first person to make that logic leap."

"Stop painting me as the bad guy here." Pax put his hand

over hers and didn't let go when she tried to pull away. "I don't think you're involved. I also don't think your brother is hurt. Not yet, but his actions, innocent or not, put him in grave danger."

"The computer logs, the same ones Sean tried to destroy and would have succeeded if he'd known about the automatic backup he'd triggered, show he downloaded proprietary corporate material before he walked out the office door," Joel said. "Problem is the military views the stolen material as theirs, which means Sean's actions have national security implications."

She started shaking her head before Joel finished his sentence. "No way. He's immature and has made mistakes—believe me when I say I get that—but Sean would never betray his country."

"I'm not accusing him of that, but I am saying the surveillance tapes show he did everything without anyone standing over him with a gun, so we need to assume he had a reason to take what he took and figure out what it was," Joel said.

Her hollow cheeks and vacant eyes mirrored her shock. "I can't imagine Sean doing this on his own or at all."

"He emptied his bank account and canceled utilities then climbed in a car and raced out of the office parking lot." Pax couldn't let her hope of a simple misunderstanding grow, so he rushed the words out. "Does that sound like a guy who got kidnapped?"

She blinked so fast she looked as if she'd been hit in the head. "You seem to have a lot of details. Exactly who are you guys?"

This time when she tried to move her hand, Pax let her go. "We conduct high-priority but under-the-radar kidnap-rescue missions. Our clients are the government and private industry."

"You're kidding."

"We try to set up training and maneuvers to ensure kidnappings don't occur in the first place, but people don't always listen to us, which leads to the rescues. You'd be amazed how many times a corporation will send an employee into a dangerous situation without any prep."

Joel made a sound between a scoff and a huff. "Pax, really. You've said more than enough."

Pax held up his hand. He kept his gaze locked on hers and blocked Joel and his protests right out. "This time the government hired us. See, someone reported Sean's behavior and missing data to the Department of Defense. No one at Kingston has filed an official report yet, but we know."

She jerked in her chair. "What are you saying?"

Pax had come this far and refused to pretty it up now. This was a serious game, a deadly one, and the men would keep coming until and unless the Corcoran Team ferreted this out. "We don't know who the bad guys are or how far they'll go to find Sean, which is why I was watching you at Decadent Brew."

"And probably why those men attacked you. You're a link to Sean, which suggests he's still on the run and, for now, safe. We plan to keep you and him that way." The flat tone of resignation in Joel's voice was tough to miss.

"And my father?"

"Our orders are to watch you and protect Sean. That's it." Pax guessed the FBI already had someone watching over the father thanks to his criminal past.

She looked between the men with her mouth opening and closing. It took a few times before any sound escaped. "You have to admit this is a pretty unbelievable story."

"Is it? Look around you." Pax had heard so much worse. Only a few months ago he watched his boat explode at the marina as someone tried to kill Davis and Lara. Terrible things happened all the time, even in a place as idyllic as

Annapolis. "I mean, with what you've lived through with your dad and how he weaseled out of the conviction, and with what you see in this room, is it really that impossible to imagine there's a group that does what we do?"

She pushed her chair back, putting a good foot between her stomach and the table. "Why didn't you tell me all this before?"

Joel gave the keyboard one last loud tap. "We're not supposed to be telling you now."

"What does that mean?"

That was a problem for another time. Pax's instincts screamed at him to take this step. He was willing to take the hit from Connor if it came to that. Pax loved this job, in part because the government red tape and paperwork he hated so much at the DIA didn't bind him here. But this was one of those times he needed loose strings.

"We weren't sure how much you knew about your brother's activities," Pax explained.

"Meaning, you thought I might be involved in whatever he did, whatever happened, at this company."

There was that smart-woman thing again. Pax sensed that would trip him up a lot when dealing with Kelsey. She would not be easy to fool. He was starting to wonder if she'd be hard to leave.

He pushed that thought out of his head. "At the time, possibly."

"And now?"

"I just told you everything about us and the case, didn't I? That should tell you everything you need to know about my trust in you."

The lip-chewing thing started again. Much more of that and she'd start bleeding. He was just about to point that out when she jumped in. "We need to go back to the shop. To my house."

Pax sighed inside, careful not to let the noise out. He got it. It had kicked at his gut to lose the boat. It exploded with all his possessions, but he'd never cared about stuff. The loss went deeper than that. The boat was a part of him. He'd scrubbed it, cleaned it, refurbished it. Being on the open water gave him a needed sense of freedom, a break from the difficult situations he dealt with every single day, and losing it was like having that freedom snatched away.

For Kelsey the loss could be even bigger. He'd lost one thing. He couldn't imagine walking away from his home and his work at the same time. She had to be stewing in her chair over the loss of control, but, for now, that had to happen. "Kelsey, listen. I know how important work is to you. I've seen you there. But it's not safe for you right now."

"I get that." Her eyes looked clear, and she was calm.

He had no idea where she was going with this. "Then you know you can't stay there. Let's hunker down here and relax."

"You don't understand. I'm not talking about staying there. We need to retrieve the package Sean sent me."

Joel jumped out of his chair and came over to stand next to Kelsey. "What?"

Pax understood the shock. It was rumbling through him from head to foot right now. "Not possible."

"Yeah, it actually is. But now I'm wondering why you would say it that way." She crossed her arms in front of her. Even made a "hmm?" sound.

Pax's response was automatic. "No reason."

She homed in on him, angling her chair to face Pax and give Joel more of a side-to-back view. "Pax?"

He could see Joel over her shoulder. His gestures mimicked his response. "Don't do it, man."

Pax shut down the internal mental battle and blocked Joel's suggestion. He'd gone this far and stopping now didn't make much sense. "We've monitored your mail from the beginning, within days of Sean not showing up for work."

Her cheeks puffed in and out. "You…did…"

"Yeah."

"That's just spectacular." She tipped her head back and stared at the ceiling.

"The word you want is *necessary*."

Joel swore under his breath as he shot Pax an open-mouthed, bewildered look. "When did you get so chatty?"

Pax refused to back down. "Do you really think we would have gotten anything done unless we told her the truth?"

"Thanks for that. I think." She dropped her head again, looking back and forth between them, as if analyzing to see the best way to get the answer she wanted. "Now that you shared, I will. The package came with an inventory delivery but didn't have a carrier tag on it. I thought it was weird at the time but figured something had gotten mixed up somewhere."

Pax tried to figure out where they had a hole in security and couldn't picture it. He'd hand that one over to Connor to ferret out. "What was in the box?"

"That's just it. I didn't open it."

"You weren't curious?" Joel asked.

"Sean and I aren't close. I made the choice long ago not to race around after him."

"I still don't get it."

Pax appreciated Joel saying what they were both feeling.

"He'd sent stuff before. Stuff to make me feel guilty, about our father and his health. Stuff from our childhood."

Pax was starting to hate her family. Thinking about her in that house, with her mother dead from cancer and her father immediately remarried to a younger woman with obvious social-climbing expectations, made everything inside Pax squeeze and tense. He wanted to hit something. "Sounds like a great guy."

"Yeah, well. He *is* in trouble now, isn't he?"

That was enough family talk. Pax needed her mind back on the box. "You think the delivery could mean something."

"Now that I put the timing together. It came a few days before you started showing up at the shop."

Joel threw his hands in the air. "There's your answer."

She ignored him and pointed at Pax. "And before you start issuing orders and throwing your weight around on that bad leg, I'm coming with you to retrieve it."

She'd clearly lost her mind.

"No."

"You dragged me out of the shop. Now you're stuck with me." She glanced at his leg. "Besides, I think I can run faster than you at the moment."

Pax didn't realize he'd been rubbing the injury until he followed her gaze and looked at his thigh. Great, he now massaged it without thinking. "Those are fighting words."

"You take me or I scream loud enough to bring the police running."

A trickle of unease sliced through him. "I thought you didn't want to escape."

"I don't, but you're not escaping me, either."

He could live with that.

SEAN RAN THROUGH the series of dark parking lots scattered under the Whitehurst Freeway. The Potomac River sat off to his left and the noise and traffic of Georgetown ran a few blocks up to his right. He'd been on the move long enough he didn't care about either.

As the humidity slammed into him and sweat soaked through his jeans and drenched his tee under his backpack, his entire focus centered on how he'd messed up. Ending up in the one part of Washington, D.C., without Metro access proved to be a huge tactical mistake. So much for the theory of using the computer lab at George Washington University and getting in and out and finding the information he needed on who was screwing him over back at Kingston. That's where he'd started but he was nowhere near there now.

He'd bypassed the security by swiping some student's access card and then lain low until the classrooms shut down one by one. He'd even used the password workaround he set up in the Kingston system for emergencies, the one that couldn't be traced back to him, but the echoing footsteps in the hall and the two guys walking around who looked more like they could lift a garbage truck than that they were part of the late-night cleaning staff ruined everything.

He'd been ducking, hiding and running ever since. And now it was getting dark, which would help hide his presence but make progress even tougher.

Instead of heading toward Dupont Circle as he should have done coming out of GW, he'd made his way to Georgetown and now he was stuck. Kelsey wasn't answering her phone, and he didn't have the cash for a bus ticket or a car to get to Annapolis.

No way could he use anything in his name. Credit cards and ATMs were out and the money he withdrew at the beginning of this mess weeks ago was running out. Getting more wouldn't work because the transaction would be tracked in a second.

They were everywhere, watching and following.

But there was one other place he could go. One person he could trust. Not the guy who dragged him into this mess with big promises. Someone else. It would take the last of his cash to get there, but he didn't have a choice.

Chapter Seven

Kelsey doubted her decision to tag along with Pax almost from the second she suggested it. More like, insisted on it. So much for his comments about her being so smart. Now, two hours later, she stumbled around at dusk as she stalked her own building.

Yeah, this was a normal evening.

They walked down the street, starting several town houses away from her storefront and scanning the area as they went. She grabbed a fistful of Pax's shirt from behind and wedged her body under his arm, hoping the move looked loving to anyone who might be watching, but really she just wanted him close. He'd proved to be the right guy to have around when the bullets started flying, though she hoped they were done with that…forever.

When he zigzagged to shift out of the shine of the overhead flickering streetlamps, he took her with him. They were far enough from the City Dock to avoid most of the tourist and late-dinner traffic, but people still passed by, some stopping to gawk in the windows of the businesses a block away.

Then there was his limp. Add that to the panic churning in her stomach, and she couldn't help but second-guess every decision she'd made today. And had it really been that morning when the thugs attacked her and Pax rushed in?

No matter the number of hours, her nerve endings wouldn't

stop jumping. She kept glancing behind them just in case. It was as if her skin suddenly shrank to a size too small, and all she wanted to do was pull and tug and get someplace where she could sit down, close her eyes and not fear being shot.

She hated the twitchy, panicked feeling rolling over her. But she had no one else to blame. By mentioning the box to Joel and Pax, she'd all but guaranteed a trip back to her house. It sounded like a great idea when it first rolled off her tongue. Now, in the growing dark with hidden corners everywhere, not so much.

Ignoring the sticky heat, she cuddled in closer to Pax's side, stretching up to whisper in his ear. "Retrieving this box was a fundamentally terrible idea. I'm sorry I even mentioned it."

"You said that already." He slipped an arm around her and rested his palm on the small of her back. "Three times, actually."

"Maybe the fourth will convince you."

He treated her to one of those warm smiles that had his eyes twinkling. Man, she loved that look. It managed to be sweet and hot at the same time, and it wiped away a good portion of her growing dread along with her common sense.

Her cheeks warmed as his gaze roamed over her face. "What is it?" she asked.

"Joel and I can do this without you." Pax stared at her lips as he said the words. "You can wait in the car or go back at the house. Connor should be there soon."

Lost in the husky sound of Pax's voice, she almost missed the comment. "Joel is already back in the office, heading up the comm."

Pax reached over and rubbed a finger along her chin. "Didn't take you long to pick up the work lingo."

"I'd like to take credit but I'm only repeating what Joel said."

As if on cue, Joel's deep voice echoed in her head. "And I'm in your ear and can hear everything, so keep it clean you two. Or not. I'm flexible and happy to listen in."

Her hand went to her ear, and she glanced around to see if anyone else could hear the voice. "That's an odd sensation."

Pax shrugged. "You get used to it."

"That's not what you normally say." Joel chuckled as he talked. "I usually hear a lot of swearing and complaining. Then you tell me I should shut the—"

Pax cleared his throat. "Correction, you get used to ignoring Joel. That's what I meant to say."

They were one town house away from her building, the same one she'd scraped clean of wallpaper and then painted and loved even as it sucked every cent out of her bank account. Pax's tempo didn't change. His shoes tapped against the sidewalk in a steady beat, a weird rhythmic clicking that eased the pounding in her temples.

When she concentrated on the sound, she picked up something else—a slight drag on every other step that matched with a tensing in his jaw.

Her hand pressed against the firm muscles of his back. "How's the leg?"

The last of his sexy smile fell. "Fine."

"The stress lines around your mouth suggest otherwise."

His fingers clenched against her. "Those come from having to answer the question every hour or so."

Before this morning she might have let the subject go, assume she was out of line and feel guilty for asking. But so much had happened within hours and so little was in her control that she grabbed on to what she could. "Is your curt response supposed to get me to drop the topic?"

"Actually, yes."

"That's not going to work."

"You're like a female version of Joel."

"For the record, I'm not sure he means that as a compliment," Joel said, his voice crisp and clear inside her head.

When they crossed the small open space between her building and the legal firm next door, her steps hesitated, but Pax's arm against her back propelled her forward. The move didn't make much sense. "I don't understand."

"Keep moving. Look forward or look at me like I'm the best-looking thing you've ever seen."

He kind of was. Not in the pretty-boy way. No, he didn't possess that scrubbed-clean, out-of-a-prep-school-manual rich-boy look. He was all man—rough around the edges, tall and lean with a swagger that overtook that limp.

He was the guy who protected all and stayed fiercely loyal to the rare few people he let into his life and loved. She barely knew him and she knew all of that was true.

They broke off the conversation until the only sound came from their shoes and a random car horn blocks away. Right as they passed the large front window of her shop, he turned his head and coughed.

They were a full building past hers before he spoke again. "Nothing obvious going on in there, though it's hard to see through the paper Connor put over the windows."

The whole scenario struck her as out of context. Her mind immediately went to one word: subterfuge. If Pax was trying to stop the conversation, it worked…temporarily. "Want to tell me how it happened? The leg, I mean."

He frowned at her. "Now? Really?"

"Yes, really." When he looked as if he was going to roll his eyes, she aimed for fat but couldn't find any, so she gave the skin on his back a little pinch.

"Fine." He winced and the word came out through clenched teeth. "I got shot."

Only Pax could boil down something so big into three little words. No way was that the whole story. "That's it?"

"It was a pretty big deal at the time."

"With a gun?"

His footsteps faltered. "How else does one get shot?"

"You're serious?"

"Very." There was no space between her building and the one on this side. He guided her past the window of the tailoring and backed her up against the bricks. His hands went to the wall on each side of her head as he leaned in.

"Well, that getting-shot thing is not comforting at all." Neither was the thing where she kept swallowing and her breath wheezed out of her as if a tight band constricted her chest.

"I generally manage not to get shot, if that helps."

This part of their act had her head spinning until she had to hold on to him for balance. Putting her hands against his chest sent a flush of warmth through her entire body. "Strangely, no."

She was about to say something when a car raced down the narrow street. A boy hung out the back window and whistled as he went past. A round of nasty catcalls followed. The engine continued to rev and the laughter floated all around them. The tires squealed as the driver took the corner too fast at the end of the block.

Even ignoring the annoying horny-boy part of what just happened, she tried to remember a time when she felt that free. She couldn't come up with an instance.

Pax put a hand under her chin and turned her face back to his. "Look, you're safe with me."

"I know that."

His head snapped back. "Then what's with the questions?"

"I was more concerned about how much pain you must be in. We probably shouldn't be out running around until you have a chance to rest."

"Oh."

"Interesting response. It probably says something about the women you hang out with."

His face fell. Every muscle shifted and his expression went blank. "Here we go."

She'd almost forgotten why they came. If that was his plan, to tie her insides up in a twisty knot and cause her brain to hiccup, then he'd succeeded. "Now?"

The warmth surrounding her dissipated as he inched his way back toward her building, with only his fingertips reaching out to still touch her. This time he hugged the wall and played only in the shadows.

"Looks clear from here," Joel said, breaking into the relative quiet.

Worse than forgetting to panic, she'd forgotten all about Joel and his front-row seat to the conversation with Pax. The heat hitting her cheeks could probably light the street.

But a stray thought found its way through the embarrassment. "Where exactly do you have cameras that you can see in my shop and house?"

"Don't worry." The click of a computer keyboard pounded over Joel's words. "Nowhere interesting."

Only a man would see that as a good answer. "Again, you guys need to work on your comfort skills."

"I'd rather work on speed." Pax's fingers laced through hers as he tugged her closer, right to the edge of the building where it turned down the narrow alley next to her building. "Let's move it."

"Hold up. Looks like you've got one moving in behind the building." A few minutes ticked by with Joel's breathing being the only noise on the open line. "He's leaning against the wall right outside her back door, the one that leads upstairs rather than the one that goes into the shop."

Pax shifted and his knee buckled but he regained his balance a beat later. "There's only one guy back there?"

"Is it Sean?" she asked. Her brother had visited that one time more than six months ago, so he knew where she lived. The position at the "right" back door suggested some level of knowledge about the layout of the building.

"Only if he aged ten years and put on about fifty pounds of muscle," Joel said.

Pax glanced over his shoulder at her. "Oh, okay. Now I see what you mean about the things we say and the lack-of-comfort thing."

"Told you." She rested her forehead in the deep groove between his shoulder blades. The sexy spot, the scent of his skin and heat rolling off his body, refueled her. Gave her strength when she didn't even know hers was running so low. "Now what?"

Pax gave her one of those shrugs that suggested he thought the answer was obvious. "I take him out."

"Assume he has a partner."

Joel's warning had barely settled in her brain when Pax took off. She held on to his shirt and used it to stop his momentum. "Wait a second."

He turned around, which snapped her hold. He found her hand and covered it with his as he pressed it against her chest. "Do not move."

Before she could get out a warning or pull him in close and hold him there, he pivoted and headed down the dark alley in a crouch. His right foot seemed to skim across the ground as he moved without making a sound.

Forget the loose gravel and few cans. He dodged it all and ended with his back flattened against the bricks at the far end, closest to the back service alley.

With the darkening sky she couldn't see everything, but she thought she spied a gun in his hand. The anxiety pinging around inside her like a pinball gone wild increased until the balls bounced hard against her rib cage.

She shifted her weight, moved forward and then stepped back again. Seeing him peek around the corner and brace his body for attack brought home how real the danger was. Because of her. No, because of Sean and her family and whatever new disaster they'd tripped and fell into now.

Pax stepped in and saved her. Yes, it was his job, but that didn't mean she didn't owe him.

He lurched and spun around the corner, out of sight. She heard shouts and grunts and what sounded like shoes scuffing against the ground. It was enough to get her moving.

She took off down the alley, skimming her hands along the close-in walls and ignoring whatever she kept stepping on. Near the end, her ankle overturned and she stumbled, her shoulder smacking against the bricks and scraping her bare skin.

The sound of Joel's voice finally penetrated her mind. "Stop, Kelsey. Now."

She ignored the warning, blocked out everything except the screaming in her brain that told her to get to Pax and help however she could. She kicked something hard and heard metal clank. Dropping down, she felt around for whatever she hit, hoping she could use it as a weapon. But the sound of male pounding male had her standing up again.

She slipped around the corner as the noise grew louder. She watched as they rolled across the concrete. The attacker wore all black and had dark hair, but she could see the sweat dripping from his forehead when he wrestled Pax's back to the ground.

They punched and kicked. The attacker landed a vicious shot to Pax's stomach that had him coughing even as he swore, The attacker was on top of Pax with hands wrapped around his throat. Pax bucked his body and swiveled his head from side to side, but the other man was choking the air out of him.

Tension swirled around her as she raced over to the trash bin, looking for something—anything—to knock the attacker out. Joel kept shouting but she could make out only the word *wait,* the one thing she knew she couldn't afford to do.

She turned back around, helpless and empty-handed, determined to crash into the attacker and at least buy Pax a few seconds of air. What happened after that she had no clue. She started the mental countdown and headed for the confusing pile of arms and legs. Through the thrashing, Pax glared at her. His eyes told her to back away, but this time he was the one who needed protection.

She would not let him down.

Right when she would have kicked out or climbed on the stranger's back, Pax's strength seemed to double. He lifted his back off the ground and slammed a fist right into the attacker's face. The man dropped like dead weight on top of Pax.

The whole thing unspooled in seconds, but she couldn't take it in. Couldn't get her feet to move or her breathing to restart. He'd been at the edge of death and now acted as if he'd been toying with the guy the whole time.... Had he?

Joel's voice broke into the silence. "Someone talk to me."

Pax pushed and shoved until the other man fell to the side. Sitting up, Pax wiped a hand across his mouth and a red smear stained the back. He shook his head. "He's down but it was too easy."

"Sure seemed quick," Joel said.

What was happening? "Are you both crazy? The guy was choking Pax."

"You were supposed to stay out front." With one hand balanced against the ground, Pax pushed up to his feet. His right leg stayed bent as he rolled his shoulders back. "The deal in bringing you along was that you would do what we say."

"I thought you were in trouble." Even to her ears she thought her voice rang hollow.

His teeth clamped together as he stepped over the downed body to get to her. "So, you came running?"

"You wanted me to leave?"

His eyes twinkled but not in a flirty way. In a way that flashed fire. "I want you to stay alive."

"Kids, we still have a problem and a job to do," Joel said.

Pax fought off a bruiser who outweighed him by more than a few pounds and yet they acted as if they'd lost this battle. She would never understand men. "I hate to ask what that means."

"We likely have a partner around here somewhere. Hard to imagine there's only one guy out here ready to cause trouble. Guys like this usually work in pairs." Pax bent over and searched the attacker's pockets and came away with a phone but nothing else. Pax whipped a white plastic tie out of his pocket.

"What are you doing?" Her real question had to do with how most people didn't carry those things around with them.

"Keeping him quiet for a few minutes." A flip and a turn and Pax had his knee in the attacker's back and the guy's hands tied. Pax dragged the guy to the opposite side of the trash Dumpster and stuffed something in the unconscious man's mouth. "I'm going up."

She was smart enough to know that qualified as a bad idea. "No, Pax. Not without Joel or someone else here to help."

"I sense a lack of trust in my abilities." The scowl had morphed into a determined stare.

She didn't like either look. Not when they led to him walking straight into danger. "We should get out of here for now."

"This isn't a vote." When Joel exhaled into the comm with enough force to make the line crackle, Pax closed his eyes. They had cleared when he opened them again and walked back to her. "This is my job, Kelsey."

"And?"

"Let me protect you."

"I am."

"Good." He winked and then got to her back door. He used the key she'd given him and disappeared up the staircase.

She stammered, choking out a few words before finally getting one out. "Does he always move that fast?"

"You should see him without the injury," Joel said.

"I'm just hoping he doesn't make the leg worse." She really wanted Pax to say something in response, but he'd gone silent on the comm. The longer his silence lasted, the more her worry festered.

She bit her lip as she stared at the closed door. More than anything she wanted to break in and run upstairs just to check on him. To hear him talk. To see him.

"He'll be okay," Joel said as if reading her mind or seeing the concern on her face.

She didn't know which one, but she wanted a guarantee of his assurance. Joel started swearing. Not just a word or two. No, this was a whole line that spelled trouble. "We have a new problem."

"I'd guessed that." The line filled with three long clicks that had Kelsey tapping the mic in her ear. "What was that?"

"A signal for Pax." Joel's breathing grew louder. "Kelsey, you have someone rounding the corner and about to head down the alley in your direction."

Her heart thundered in her ears until everything sounded stuffy and distorted. The sounds of the small city blended into the background as she fell against the wall and struggled to breathe. "It could be someone who works or lives on the street."

"I did the facial recognition scan and it turned up negative."

She shook her head, trying to block out the fear that was

slowly swamping every inch of her body. "You can do that from your desk miles away?"

"Kelsey, I want you to go inside," Joel said.

"And?"

"I'm on the way down." Pax's low voice finally rumbled into the quiet. "Kelsey, move."

Chapter Eight

Pax stopped halfway up the narrow staircase to Kelsey's apartment above the coffee shop when he heard Joel's warning about their new guest. Balancing his hands on the walls that were barely a shoulder width apart, Pax pivoted on his good leg and took the stairs two at a time back to the entry.

As he neared the bottom, the outside door opened and Kelsey slipped inside. With wide eyes and a face paled to a color that almost matched the off-white paint, she stared up at him. She tugged her bottom lip between her teeth and hugged the black T-shirt she'd slipped on before they left the team headquarters.

He would be happy to go a lifetime without seeing that fear on her face again.

Careful not to bang his feet against the steps or make any unnecessary noise, he closed the distance between them, stopping on the step right above her. She didn't say anything. Didn't have to. Her frozen facial features and the subtle tremble moving through her and shaking her shoulders said it all.

Before he could talk through all the cons and argue against the idea, he put his hands on her upper arms. The touch sent a shot of electricity through him. It wasn't until he blinked out the need clouding his brain that the coolness under his palms registered. It had to be eighty degrees outside, but her skin felt as if she'd walked through a gusting fall wind.

She moved in as he bent his head. His lips pressed against her forehead and into her soft hair. The scent of strawberry hit him a second later.

He mumbled against her skin, trying to forget they weren't alone in any sense. "It's going to be okay. I'll get you out of here."

Instead of answering, she nodded and kept doing it as she wrapped her arms around his waist and tucked her head under his chin.

At her touch, his body stiffened. Not that he didn't crave the feel of her but because he'd imagined her like this for weeks, burrowed against him, and the live version blew the fantasy away.

This was the wrong place and about as wrong a time as she could pick. But he let it happen. Closed his eyes for the briefest of moments and fell into the heat that sparked just from holding her close. His shoulders relaxed but the rest of him kicked into gear.

What he wanted with her started with closeness, but it blew way past that fast. He was a normal guy with serious needs. He'd been watching her for weeks, dreaming about her every night since, imagining her in his bed with her clothes on the floor. A minute more of this and it wouldn't matter who stood just outside the door or listened in.

Since he refused to have their first time together happen on a dark staircase with danger lurking nearby, he had to let go. She probably only wanted comfort anyway. A sure arm and a minute to gather her strength. Taking advantage of that, letting his fantasies fuel his actions, made him a complete jerk.

Gritting his teeth and forcing his thoughts away from the softness of her skin and the perfect fit of her body against his, he slipped his hands behind his back and felt for her hands. Bringing them around and trapping them against his chest as he held on, he met her gaze. He saw eyes clear yet wary, but something else lingered there. Determination.

Now there's a good woman.

"We're going to head up to your apartment and call in reinforcements."

She gave him a weak smile. "I like that plan."

That's funny because he hated it, but there was a limit to how much she could take. She wasn't an operative or trained in serious combat. He'd seen hints of a self-defense class graduate, but that didn't mean she could fight a bullet or men twice her size.

He nodded toward the top of the stairs. "Head up."

"Not without you." Her hands clenched against his stomach as she whispered.

They both kept their voices low, barely registering above a hum. "I'm going to be right behind you. I just want to double-check the door lock."

"Pax—"

"You can watch me as you go." He guided her around him. Not an easy task, since only a breath or two separated them already.

"Somebody move," Joel said, breaking through one kind of tension to remind Pax of the one that should be his focus.

Still, Joel's breathing and sarcastic tone didn't kill the mood. Kelsey's body brushed against Pax and his brain caught fire.

Beating back every stupid male thought, he mentally counted to twenty. When that didn't work, he tried it in Spanish. Finally, she stood above him, close enough for him to reach out and touch, but far enough for some of his lost air to rush back into his body.

Pax descended the last three steps and stood at the small foyer leading to the outside. He knew from Kelsey's run-down of the property back at the team house that this door locked automatically. She used the key from the outside to double lock it. From this side it was a matter of throwing the dead bolt.

With a slow, steady turn, being as quiet as he could, he set the top lock. He winced as it caught with a soft click. Later he'd talk with her about a new security system complete with blaring alarms and a direct line to his phone, but right now he wanted the extra insurance the door would hold.

He looked around for reinforcements. There was a hook on the wall and a lock on the door. Neither would keep out a guy determined to bust his way in.

He glanced over his shoulder and saw Kelsey nearing the top of the staircase. She walked with her back skimming the banister against one wall and her gaze trained on him. He nodded to let her know she was doing great.

Any other civilian he knew, except maybe Davis's wife, Lara, would be curled in a ball on the floor. Certainly crying and clinging. Not Kelsey. She fought back and didn't run.

Just when he thought she couldn't get any sexier, she did.

He reached into his back pocket and took out another security tie. He wanted to wedge something under the door, but there was nothing there to work with. That left strengthening the lock's hold.

"How's it coming?"

Pax answered Joel's question with a grunt. It was all he could manage and more than he could afford if he wanted to keep his presence just inside the door hidden.

Without turning the knob, he slipped the tie over the handle and stretched it. The mail slot on the opposite side of the door was his only choice. He worked his finger into the plaster behind one side of the metal rim until he made a small hole. Wedging the thinner end of the tie through the space he made, he shoved and pushed until it came out the other side. He finished it off by looping it around and clicking it into place.

He heard the rustle of clothing and glanced up. Kelsey hadn't moved from her position on the stairs, leaning against the wall. He had to smile at the way she lounged up there, as if being inside with him made her feel safe. She was, just not from him and the need kicking hard against his gut.

He couldn't fight off a smile as his feet fell on the steps with a practiced light touch. The muscles in his right leg had stiffened until bending his knee proved difficult, but nothing was going to stop him from getting up there to her.

They stood a few feet apart with him on the stair below hers. "Let's get in your place so we can put another lock between us and the guy outside."

"Definitely."

Pax tapped the mic to press it snug in his ear after all the up-and-down pounding on the stairs. "Joel, let Connor know we need some help here."

"Already done."

Pax put his hand on Kelsey's lower back and guided her up the remaining steps. There were two doors at the top of the landing. She went to the one with the peephole. He stood in front of the other.

"What's this?" He pointed at the unidentified door.

"Hot water heater."

Sounded small and cramped. Pax nodded and turned away. Then he turned back to it. Closed doors made him twitchy. The entrance to the outside had been locked down with no obvious signs of a break-in. Still, Joel's cameras didn't capture this area, and the in and out of this operation had run smoothly. Well, better than most operations, including the last one, which got him shot.

Kelsey stood with her hand on the doorknob. "Where's the key to my place?"

He slipped it out of his jeans pocket. "I'll open it."

But he couldn't force his body to move or his gaze to meet hers. An ache started at the base of his neck and moved right up to the back of his head. In seconds he went from a vague sense of uneasiness to a pounding in his brain.

Kelsey stepped over and put her hand on his arm. "What's wrong?"

He shook his head. He'd just opened his mouth to respond when the utility door slammed open, right into Pax's head. His neck snapped back and his vision blinked out. A wave of black threatened to swamp him, but Kelsey's sharp intake of breath stopped his downward slide.

She couldn't scream. He couldn't shoot. Not without bringing the guy outside crashing in.

Before his vision refocused, Pax kicked out. A sharp whack followed by the crack of bone. The attacker fell back into the heater. The tank shook and metal clanged against metal as the attacker's gun hit it.

Pax had just enough time to shove Kelsey into the corner and as far away from the fight as possible on the six-by-six landing before taking a punch to his side. He bent double, his free arm moving too late for the block.

"What's happening?" Joel yelled his question into the comm.

"Guest." That was as far as Pax got, all the words he could force out over panting and groaning, before the attacker hit him dead-on.

Head down and shoulder aimed, the guy made a run for Pax's already sore midsection, pounding him against the far wall. Air choked out of Pax's lungs as his right leg slipped underneath him and his gun fell to the floor. He shifted his weight, and the bottom of his shoe hit the edge of the first step. Throwing his body to the opposite side, he put a little distance between him and a serious fall.

He traced his foot over the floor in search for his weapon. He struck something hard and lifted his foot to grab it the best he could, but he hit only carpet. He tapped around and nothing. The gun was gone.

Pax resorted to punching. The attacker huffed and grunted as his stomach weathered the punishing blows. Still, he kept a hold on Pax, shoving him against the wall and screwing the leverage he needed to put his full strength behind the hits.

The attacker let up and then plowed against Pax's stomach even harder a second time. Momentum doubled the pressure and pushed him harder against the wall. Before he could catch his breath, the guy laid his forearm against Pax's throat and pressed.

Pax heard Joel's voice in the distance but couldn't make out the words. Something about being quiet and hitting square. Pax was too busy trying to stay on his feet and not get killed to analyze the words. He needed an opening and fast.

With his jaw locked, the attacker opened his mouth, baring his teeth in a snarl. "I'm done playing with you."

"I'm not stopping you from leaving."

"I'm taking the girl with me."

No way in hell was that happening.

The guy leaned in until his face hovered just inches from Pax's. "Nothing smart to say to that? No comeback?"

Pax said a silent thank-you to the idiot attacker for getting so close. Knowing it would hurt but not having a choice, Pax slammed his forehead into the attacker's nose. There was a crack and a wave of dizziness just before Pax felt something pinch in his neck.

At least he wasn't alone. The attacker reeled back, bringing his empty hand to his face as he let out a battle-cry roar that cut off when Pax punched him in the jaw. When the attacker looked up again, a seething rage filled his eyes.

Pax knew he had seconds only. He shook his head, trying

to fight off the sensation of the room spinning around him. Blinking and stumbling, he scanned the floor for his gun but didn't see it. How was that possible?

Panic clawed at him as he lifted his head, prepared to block the oncoming blow as he made a last grasp for the attacker's weapon. Pax had barely focused on the guy when he saw Kelsey, arm raised and the butt of a gun ready. He couldn't figure out where she got it or where she found the courage to leap in.

Without any hesitation or even a glance in his direction, she brought the weapon down in a slamming arc. Then did it again. The multiple shots did the trick.

The guy's eyes rolled back right before his body went limp. He dropped the gun and followed it to the floor. He hit the landing and bounced off the top step…and kept going. His body rolled, feet slamming into the wall as he picked up speed, until he landed in a heap.

Pax glanced at the lifeless body of the once-fierce attacker. The guy lay in a sprawl on the bottom landing with one leg bent back at an odd angle and his head tucked under his arm in a way that looked unnatural.

Heavy breathing echoed through the small space. It took Pax a second to realize it came from him. He crashed back into the wall and rested his palms on his knees as he inhaled big gulps.

One look at Kelsey and he saw an openmouthed stare. Her focus didn't shift from the sick scene at the bottom of the stairs.

Joel's voice cut through the odd quiet a second later. "Someone talk to me."

"We're okay." Pax slipped his gun out of Kelsey's limp fingers. She didn't try to tighten them or start when he touched her. He knew that was a very bad sign.

Taking the steps two at a time, sliding across the wall to

keep from putting any more weight on his leg, Pax got to the bottom of the stairs. A quick check told him what he already knew. "The guy's dead."

It was rough and messy, but it was over. This round anyway.

"Did she do it?" Joel asked, shock evident in his voice.

There was only one "she" around here. Pax's gaze zipped back to Kelsey. She stared at him with a face tight with stress.

"No, she knocked him out. Looks like the fall is what actually killed him."

"I did it. Oh, my God, it was me." She wrapped her arms around her waist, and her body rocked.

He made his way back up the stairs to stand in front of her. "You stopped the attack. You didn't kill him. Don't take that on."

She nodded but it wasn't convincing. Her gaze bounced off the walls and to the ceiling. Anywhere but to him and the guy at the bottom of the stairs.

He bowed his head until she looked at him again. "That guy picked the location at the top of the stairs. It's not your fault he fell the way he did."

She swallowed several times. "I just did everything he told me."

Pax still had no idea what was happening. "Who?"

"Me. Didn't you hear me calling out directions over the comm?" Joel scoffed. "Not bad for doing it blind, and it sounds like our girl did great."

Pax's mind exploded in fifty different directions. Kelsey saved him. He shook his head as he let that fact sink in.

"Kelsey?" He reached out to her but grabbed only air when she slid down to sit on the top step.

"That was more than I expected. It looks so easy on television. And back at the office? It sounded clear and simple. Go in, get the box and get out." She said the words nice and slow, putting a long pause between each one. "But in real life—"

"I know."

She held out her arm in the direction of the dead man at the bottom of the stairs. "That happens. I didn't expect how it would look or how empty I'd feel. I mean, I get that I didn't have a choice, but…"

She choked and Pax worried she'd throw up. "I'm sorry it was you."

"I'm sorry about all of this."

Pax did an internal assessment and couldn't come up with a body part that didn't ache. From his head to his leg, every muscle begged for a rest. "Makes two of us."

She pulled back her arm and held her hands out in front of her. Turning them over, she studied every inch. They shook hard enough to make the key in her hand jingle. "I…yeah, I kind of need to sit down."

"You already are." He braced his palm against the edge of the landing and sat down hard on the step below her. "You okay?"

"No."

He took her cold hands in his, rubbing them in an attempt to bring life back into her cells. "Breathe."

"I can't remember how."

"Don't talk." He put a hand on her thigh and held it there until she looked at him. "That's it. You're doing great."

She frowned. "How can you say that?"

"I'm witnessing it." Man, she had no idea how amazing she was. She held it all together when it counted. "You rushed in and saved me. You didn't worry about the danger to you, and I'll lecture you about that later when I'm not feeling as grateful, but I gotta tell you not many people have stepped up to rescue me."

It was an odd feeling. He sensed lightness and darkness

moving through him. It was as if his brain couldn't analyze it even as a part of him wanted to smile.

Davis had stepped up for him. The guys on his team and former teammates at the DIA.

But this was different. She didn't have a tie to him, and yet she didn't hesitate. It was heroic and stupid and fierce…and he didn't see how he'd ever build a shield against her now.

"I would do it again." She squeezed his hand hard enough to cut off the blood circulation. "But I have to admit I was scared to death."

"Congratulations, you're human." He'd let her hold him—even strangle the life out of him. Whatever she needed to get through the next few minutes, he'd do.

Without any warning, she switched into hyperdrive. She talked in a rush, her words tripping over each other until he had to strain to separate it all out and understand what she was saying. He leaned in to pick up the harsh whispering.

"—and despite everything, the terror the pain, the panic, all I want to do right now is kiss you, which is totally wrong, and not something I should want."

He sat back, sure he was dreaming because she was saying what he *wanted* to hear not what he ever expected to hear. "What?"

"Crazy, right?" She rubbed her thumb over his palm. "We've known each other for a day, and it's all I can think about right now."

"It's been weeks." He knew the exact number because he'd started measuring his day by the number of times she smiled at him and how she'd make time to talk with him.

Man, he had it bad for her.

She rolled her eyes the same way she did when rude people left her shop and she thought no one was watching. "I agree I knew a version of you for that long. I'm talking about this side of you. Actually, I don't know what I'm talking about since those two parts seem to be merging and my anger at you pretending to be this injured sweet guy is gone."

"Technically, I am injured." And just mentioning it made his thigh thump.

But they had a bigger issue to deal with. His heart took off in a hammering run the second after she said the word "kiss," and the sexy touching only added to his building excitement. Between the near heart-attack beat of anticipation and the pressure pushing against his zipper there was no blood left for his head. "As for the kiss—"

"Forget that."

"Admittedly, your timing on this subject sucks."

She nodded. "It's been that kind of day."

No kidding. "Except for that timing thing, I'm in."

She leaned against him with her head dipping in close. "Are you sure? Because I'm probably going insane."

The more the idea of kissing tumbled around in his head, the more desperate he became to taste her. "It's meant to be."

"My impending insanity?"

"The kiss. We've been circling each other since the first day I walked into the shop."

"How romantic."

This time her smile lit up her face. But he remembered the forced calm and the flash of fear from earlier, and the memory sucked the life right out of him. He knew he had to grab on to his control and stick to his training no matter how his body begged for the opposite result.

He lifted their joined hands and kissed the back of hers. "Can't lie, I've wanted to throw you on that counter since that first morning you handed me a coffee of the day, but that was the wrong time and so is this."

"Who are we kidding?" Her shoulders sagged. "It's adrenaline. We'll get over it."

She definitely didn't understand some very important facts

about him. But she would. "Yeah, I'm not likely to let that happen."

"You kiss all the people you protect?"

How she missed the signs and threw herself into the category of the easily forgotten or just like every other woman was a mystery to him. Time for a wake-up call. "You'll be the first, but later, when I can really concentrate on the task."

A forced cough crackled over the comm. "Do I get to listen in then, too?"

Pax wanted to curse, but he had no one to blame but himself for this one. "Joel, I swear I—"

"Okay, kids. Let's finish this job before we start celebrating."

Kelsey held a hand over her mouth. This time her wide-eyed stare had nothing to do with fear. "For a second I forgot he was there."

Joel chuckled directly into their ears. "I love hearing that. You'd be amazed what I pick up from back here."

Gathering all of his concentration and dropping her hand, Pax got back to the operation. It was either that or risk both of their lives on a simple box retrieval. "What about the company in the street?"

"Still there. He's down the alley a bit and pacing."

"What does that mean?" she asked.

The tapping of the keyboard served as background noise to Joel's side of the conversation. "No idea but even with Connor on the way, the quicker you two finish whatever it is you're doing, the better off we'll all be."

She exhaled as she stood up and held out a hand to Pax to have him join her. "You heard the man. Let's get this done."

Chapter Nine

A knock sounded at Bryce's office door. At this time of night, hours after most of the staff went home and the nightly cleaning crew moved in, his visitor could be only one person. At least it was someone he could tolerate for more than a few minutes at a time.

"Come in," he said without taking his attention away from the computer programs running on the monitors.

The door opened a fraction, and Glenn stuck his head inside. "Sir? Did you need anything before I leave for the day?"

The man was loyal to the end. He'd grabbed his briefcase two hours ago in a rush to get to a dinner date and then dropped it again when Bryce announced he was staying to look deeper into the Sean Moore situation. Glenn mumbled something about canceling and sticking around. Soon after that takeout food containers appeared on Bryce's desk and files were placed on the edge of his desk. He combed through it all, reviewing Glenn's report on Sean Moore, including a list of places to look for him.

Glenn produced good work. Some holes existed, but Bryce filled those in on his own. He went beyond the paperwork and the investigator's report. He knew where Sean wasn't at the moment and how few resources he had. That meant the young man would be feeling desperate soon.

Having gone to expensive prep schools and lived in Daddy's gated mansion for most of his life meant Sean's survival skills were likely pretty limited. He didn't have a web of friends or a stash of secret cash. Like many people he depended on a base level of intelligence and comfort to get by, and when something shook the latter the former suffered.

Sean would make a mistake. It was just a matter of time. Bryce just had to wait and find the right way in, which led him to an area in which he was an expert. Electronic surveillance. If Sean so much as burped in the D.C. metro area, Bryce should be able to hunt him down.

For extra insurance, Bryce put behind-the-scenes pressure on Sean's family, which consisted of a half sister and his infamous father. Neither had been contacted by Sean through any of the usual channels Bryce now monitored. He used strategically placed cameras to be ready if Sean found another way.

Which uncovered this evening's most interesting piece of information. Not that Bryce had figured out the connections. It would all be in the details. He needed to gather those.

He glanced at the program running on his main computer. Photos of faces raced by as the program searched for an identity match. But maybe there was an easier way. Maybe Glenn could offer some insight, see something Bryce missed since Glenn spent more time on the floor and dealing directly with employees.

Reality was Bryce made it a priority to know every face in the building. He didn't hire them all, but he had a sense of who should be here and who shouldn't. But the man he was trying to identify could be tangentially related to Kingston or someone who worked there—possibly a delivery guy or someone in the building or associated with a competitor— and Bryce might miss the connection.

He sat back in his chair and pointed at the large computer monitor on the credenza perpendicular to his desk. "Do you have any idea who this is?"

Glenn frowned as he stepped farther into the room. "What are you looking at?"

"Footage."

Glenn's hand tightened around the notepad in his hand. "Of what?"

"Private citizens walking around."

"Excuse me, sir?"

Bryce hoped Glenn didn't bring up a lecture on the web of privacy laws that added unnecessary jumps to simple searches but also made Bryce a great deal of money by defeating those barriers...for the right price, of course. "It's the camera in front of that coffee place Sean's sister runs."

"Owns."

That grabbed Bryce's attention. "What?"

Glenn waved his hand in the air as he continued to stare at the screen. "She owns it."

"I don't care whose name is on the deed." Bryce barely cared about Sean, and that disdain was quickly spreading to his family. From what Bryce could tell, none of them had managed to amount to much of anything, and Sean blew the one chance he had of making a future for himself. "This footage is from more than a half hour ago."

"We have a camera outside of her shop?"

"We have cameras everywhere." A satellite system saw to that. So did the network of police and security cameras Bryce set up throughout the entire region thanks to low job bids he instinctively knew would serve him well in the future. Where he didn't have eyes, he could usually hook into someone else's system and take a look around.

The back door he kept open for his continued use on the systems he designed paid off now. Even now he reversed and fast-forwarded to find the exact frame he needed.

Glenn dropped into the seat across the desk and studied the footage. "I had no idea."

"That's the point." Figures moved across the screen and Bryce stopped the picture on an outline of two people walking down the street, stopping and then turning back again. It was the turn that gave him their faces. He tapped a key to zoom in. "There. The woman is Kelsey Moore or someone who looks a great deal like her. Who's the man?"

"I don't know."

"Here. This will help." With a few more keystrokes Bryce clarified the photo and cropped it to highlight the man's face. "I'm running the facial recognition software but no hits yet."

"Never seen him."

"Think about it. Has he been in the building or with Sean or any other employee?"

Glenn's eyes narrowed. "Not that I know of. What are you thinking about this guy?"

"Sean answers to someone. He's not smart enough, or dumb enough, depending on how you look at it, to pull off this information dump on his own. He knows his way around computers, but we have checks and fail-safes. He bucked them all until he got to the lie detector test. I found the rest when I backtracked after that, but he would have gotten away with it, at least for a while." A fact that continued to burn through Bryce every minute of the day.

Thanks to Sean and his betrayal, Bryce got stuck dealing with people like Dan. Sean would pay for that when Bryce made him pay for everything else.

"And you think the guy on the screen is the person who helped Sean steal data?" Glenn asked.

"I think Sean is looking for a big check, and this man might be the one writing it." Someone pulled the strings. The person at the head of this thing wanted money or propriety software or highly sensitive passwords, or all of it.

"But why would someone involve Sean's sister?"

A simple question. One Bryce found beneath Glenn's skill

set, and he scowled to make his position clear. "Why not? We have."

"True." Glen straightened. "I can check into it."

"No need." This project Bryce needed to handle on his own. He'd delegated too much responsibility, and now he had a personnel disaster that could blow into something much bigger. After he cleared out the employees who failed him, he would impose stricter rules to ensure a security breach like this never happened again. "We'll let the computers do the work for a few hours. If this program doesn't work, I may need to call in some favors and access a more intricate system."

"You're talking about something like at the NSA or CIA?"

Bryce would do whatever it took to secure his company's future. He'd worked too hard for too long, balancing his father-in-law's expectations and risking his wife's wrath to gain a solid reputation and foothold in the market. He would not go backward now. "You can go home."

Glenn's gaze bounced from screen to screen. "If it's okay with you, I'd prefer to stay."

Bryce thought about Dan and his threats. He was the type of employee Bryce didn't need. But Glenn, he was starting to prove himself very capable. "Take a seat."

KELSEY HAD BEEN AWAY from her apartment for exactly one afternoon, but it dragged on as if it were months. She opened the door, expecting the dank scent of the apartment being closed up all day in the humid weather to hit her. Instead, everything looked and smelled normal.

Well, what she saw of it. Pax pushed her into the hallway and put a finger over his lips. The same lips she came within inches of kissing. Yeah, talk about a dumb idea. The man was her assigned bodyguard and even now stalked around her shadowed apartment with his gun up and his attention trained on every corner.

The only light came from a small lamp on an end table. She left it on whenever she was out. Now it shone a soft yellow glow over everything. She reached for the light switch, but his finger snapping stopped her. So did the curt nod of his head.

She'd never been a fan of overly commanding men. She generally associated the trait with the jerky-male type. Those guys who insisted everything be done as they wanted it and slipped into rage-fueled, sometimes abusive fits when things moved off plan. She wondered now if that assessment had been too harsh or at least too general.

When Pax wanted something, he sure didn't have any trouble being bossy to get his way. She should hate that, be on her guard, but from him it calmed her frayed nerves. Sure, sometimes she pushed back or wanted to roll her eyes, but she instinctively knew he'd accept either reaction.

Trust didn't come easy for her, and it should be impossible with Pax in light of how they met, but the opposite proved true.

Even when he acted in a way she didn't understand. Like now. He opened closet doors and ducked to check under furniture. The same furniture that likely served as home to dust bunny families because she sure never checked under there.

When he ducked into the bedroom, she had to fight the urge to follow him in there and check for underwear all over the floor. She wasn't exactly expecting company, after all.

A minute later he stepped back into the family room. This time his arm hung at his side and his gun didn't point at anything or anybody. "All clear."

Her heart clunked as it fell an inch. "Did you think someone would be up here?"

"Let's just say after the day we've had, I'm not taking any

chances. That includes keeping the lights off so we don't draw attention to your place."

Since she was admittedly a below-average housekeeper, it probably looked better in the dark anyway. She tried to see the place through his eyes. To her, the exposed redbrick walls and bunches of plants near the front window were charming.

The open floor plan appealed to her. Standing at the door she could see the family room with the sectional she found on sale last year and the kitchen stretching along the wall off to her right. Only the bedroom and a small bath were tucked away from immediate view.

The whole space took up less than half of the first floor of the Corcoran place. It was small and cozy and all hers... hers and the bank's. Mostly the bank's.

He glanced around. "The box?"

She dropped the keys on the small table next to the door. "The kitchen."

Pax spun around until he faced the breakfast bar on the family room side of the butcher block island. "You eat with the box? Is that some sort of woman thing I don't know about?"

"I eat with the television. When the workday is over I want mindless entertainment." She pointed at the couch and the flat-screen hooked to the wall. "And I engage in said laziness right there."

That sexy smile appeared out of nowhere. "I approve of that arrangement. Have been known to engage in the same now and then."

She couldn't imagine him ever being lazy. "Just you and your gun, huh?"

"I'd rather try your couch and skip the gun."

She chalked it up to the leftover adrenaline and the fact they stood in the middle of the most private part of her life, but all she wanted was to climb onto the couch and drag Pax there beside her. "Maybe I'll show you sometime."

"At breakfast?" He picked up the box. It was one of those Priority Mail kind you could stuff full and still pay only a set fee. "Once all of this is over and you're safe, if you invite me, I guarantee I'll be here."

"Uh, folks? I'm still listening in," Joel said in a monotone, almost bored voice.

Pax winked at her. "As if we could forget you."

"I'm not the only one you should be worried about," Joel said. "Alley guy is on the move."

Pax's smile disappeared as quickly as it came. "Unbelievable."

She didn't know why he was surprised. Luck had failed them at every turn today. "We can't catch a break here."

"If he's the partner of the one at the bottom of the staircase or the one you stuffed in the corner by the Dumpster, he's probably getting antsy and looking around," Joel said.

Pax tucked the box under his arm. "How close?"

"Right at the outside door downstairs. He keeps looking around and checking the lock. Tugging on it."

Hope flickered to life in her belly. "Good thing Pax fixed it."

"Not to scare you, but if the guy wants in, he'll get in. That's the dirty secret the security companies don't like to admit." Pax's gaze fell on her phone on top of the bar. He held it up. "Your cell?"

What, did he think she had a boyfriend on the side and he dropped it there? "Of course."

"Password-protected?"

She shook her head. It never dawned on her to lock her phone. Half the time she forgot to carry it, which explained why it was up here instead of downstairs in her office or in her back pocket, which would have been a help any one of the times she'd been attacked.

"Speaking of interesting security choices." He tapped a few buttons before his gaze flew back to meet hers. "I don't see anything on here from your brother."

The words slammed into her, pushing her back against the wall. Her mind went blank but her legs suddenly weighed a thousand pounds each. "What does that mean?"

Pax slipped the cell into his jeans pocket. He wore a frown and wasn't paying any attention to her. "I'm not sure yet. I'd just think your brother would call. I mean, how many people can he depend on?"

She wasn't convinced Sean thought of her in those terms, but still…

"Remember our conversation about comfort and how you sort of stink at it? This right here, Pax?" She moved her hands around in small circles. "This is a good example of that."

His head popped up and his eyes narrowed as he focused on her face. "I figured you'd appreciate the honesty."

"Turn off the GPS on that phone and bring it with you," Joel said.

"Got it. Did the same on the attacker's phone earlier." Pax blew out a long breath. "Okay, Joel. How much time do we have?"

"Minutes only."

She tried to think about what she needed. Clothes and some paperwork. She had some cash in her checkbook…oh, and her actual checkbook. Not that there was much in there. "I have to pack a bag."

Pax spared her another glance as he checked the lamp shades and behind a picture frame on the wall of the family room. "Not necessary."

"Maybe to you, but—"

Pax held the mic closer to his ear. "What's Connor's ETA?"

"Almost there. He's breaking away from a conversation with the coroner and should be on the line any second."

Her stomach rolled. Actually disconnected and did a full flip. "I think I'm going to be sick."

He stepped in front of her. "I made you a promise, and I plan to keep it."

"To join me for breakfast?"

"Oh, that's absolutely happening as soon as I can manage it, but I meant about your safety." His palm cupped her cheek. "You're going to be fine."

Before she could answer or even close her eyes and hope he would finally lean in and give her that kiss he'd been promising, Joel broke in on the line. "The guy's really working the lock downstairs. I'd be ready for company any second."

Pax dropped the box on the couch and then reached for his gun. "Resourceful, isn't he?"

Violence wasn't her thing. After a disgruntled employee of her father's kidnapped her all those years ago and demanded her father return a retirement account, she stayed away from scary movies and anything with a lot of bloodshed. The sight of either brought the memories rushing back.

Evan Klinger didn't follow through with the quick death he promised, but the twinges of fear never really went away. She could feel his breath brush over her ear and smell the alcohol on his breath.

And after law enforcement burst in, she could see nothing but Klinger's head as it exploded from the rounds of gunfire. The paper said he "went down in a hail of bullets." If she closed her eyes the headline screamed across her senses.

Despite everything she'd gone through that weekend long ago, or maybe because of it, she always thought she'd be the last person to pull a trigger. Now she knew differently. She'd already used one end as a weapon. She wouldn't hesitate to use the fatal end, either.

"Shoot him if you have to," she said.

"I like her style." She could hear the smile in Joel's voice as he said the words.

"You stay here." Pax talked right over her when she started to argue. "I'm not going to worry about where you're standing during a shoot-out. Understand?"

"That goes both ways." The idea of him getting hurt nearly doubled her over. She thought about his leg and a guilt-edged sadness filled her. If she were the reason for another injury, if he sacrificed his life for hers... Her mind closed down at the thought.

Pax held up his gun. "You forget I have the upper hand."

She could think of a couple of advantages he had over every man she'd ever known. "You mean Secret Weapon Joel?"

He laughed. "Thanks for the vote of confidence."

Pax pressed his finger against the door. "The peephole. I can see the bad guys coming."

"I wish I were as positive about this as you are."

"Go stand at the entrance to the bedroom. Listen to Joel and do not come out unless I tell you it's okay." When she tried to protest, he put a finger over her lips. "I need you here, safe and where I can sort of see you. Anything else will distract me and put us both in danger. Now, I'll ask again. Do you understand?"

She nodded because she didn't trust her voice to speak.

His thumb brushed across her bottom lip before his hand dropped. After one last smile he turned back to the door and she headed to the wall separating the bedroom hallway from the rest of the space. She could hear him whispering but didn't know what he was saying. For some reason the comm in her ear went deathly silent.

Pax stopped at the door. "Joel?"

A quiet buzz filled the line. Pax glanced at her and she shook her head. She couldn't pick up anything and from the way all emotion wiped clear of his face, she guessed he couldn't, either.

He pointed toward the kitchen. Since he seemed to know something she didn't, and whatever it was had his face flushing and his eyes snapping with fury, she followed his direction. She bent down and made a determined rush for the island that separated the kitchen from the rest of the apartment.

Peeking from behind it, she saw him hold out his hand and press it palm down, which she took as a signal for her to drop. She did, scraping her knee as she went. Her butt hit the floor and she shifted to her knees before glancing up again. She hugged the corner and watched.

He stood next to the door rather than right behind it. From that spot there was no way he could see out the peephole. She didn't understand how he could even turn the knob from that awkward position.

He motioned for her to bend down even lower and cover her head. She was about to do that when he reached over and flicked the knob.

The door flew open and bounced against the opposite wall. Gunfire boomed a second later. A rapid succession of five shots had plaster kicking up. The wood on the door splintered and a glass shattered somewhere off to her right. She stayed tucked but peeked up in time to see Pax shift around the corner of the open doorway. One shot and a series of thuds. Then silence.

He darted out of the room and footsteps echoed on the landing. She couldn't wait one more second to see what happened. She got up, slipping around the outside of the room and sticking to the walls. When she looked out the door, she saw Pax bending over a still body sprawled at the top of the stairs. Blood splattered against the wall and spread in a dark circle on the downed guy's forehead.

Pax slipped a gun into the back of his jeans and conducted another pat down. One more cell appeared before he pocketed it. After all the work, he looked up at her. "You okay?" He wasn't even out of breath.

"You got him."

"We were lucky he fell for the subterfuge." Pax looked at her and then down at the obviously dead body. "Don't look at him."

"That's kind of hard."

Pax tapped his ear and called for Joel, but the line stayed silent. "It was him or us, Kelsey. These guys aren't giving us options."

"I get that." If someone had told her this morning that she'd be dealing with dead bodies and a shoot-out in addition to the pastry inventory, she would have passed out. Somehow living through it, surviving and staying on her feet even though danger lurked in every hallway filled her with a strength and fearlessness she always wished she'd had.

Definitely some weird sort of adrenaline rush.

While Pax moved around with an almost scary level of detached efficiency, she put the puzzle pieces of the past few minutes together in her mind. "You wanted him to fire first."

"It gave away his exact location." Pax stood up.

She did a visual search of his body. There were no signs that one of those bullets hit him. Relieved, she sagged against the doorjamb and let her gaze linger over her apartment. It had not fared as well.

She spied a ripped sofa cushion and shards of glass from the picture frame sprayed over everything. There was a hole in her door and an odd gash in her brick wall by the television. Her perfect place of solace, the one spot she could go to relax and unwind, had been violated in a way that had her stomach dropping to her feet.

She couldn't deal with that right now. "I'm ready to leave."

Then he was there. She turned her head and his face hovered over hers. One hand balanced above her and he leaned in close. "Any chance you're also ready for that kiss?"

"I kind of feel like I could throw up."

He stepped back. "So, we'll go with later on the kiss then."

He didn't get it. How could he, because she could barely accept it enough to talk about it. Still, she had to try. "People depend on me. I have a mortgage and a business loan. I can't be closed, but I can't put people in danger, either."

"Hold up for a second and listen to me." He rested his hands on her hips and held her still. "You still need to breathe."

"Right." She nodded but the whole air thing wasn't happening.

He rubbed her arm, caressed her face. With gentle touches and a soft voice he brought her back from the brink of a full-on emotional breakdown. Her emotions whipped between fury at her brother for putting her in this position and a sick dizziness as the smell of blood and mix of sulfur hit her senses.

But when he stood there, so close, wooing her back from the edge, she grabbed on to the mental lifeline.

"We're going to fix this and you're going to reopen, and I'll buy enough coffee to make up for a day or two of being closed." His fingers trailed along the line of her chin.

Everything he said turned the thunder of terror into a soft ripple. "You're sweet."

"Not really." His thumb traveled across her lips. "My point is it's going to be okay."

She lost herself in the sensation of his touch. "How do you know?"

"Because I'm guaranteeing it."

"And you're a man of your word." It wasn't a question, because she knew the answer.

"Exactly."

"You may just get that kiss later after all." She almost didn't recognize her breathy voice, but she understood the rapid tapping of her heart.

The door at the bottom of the stairs shot open, and a man jumped into the space.

Pax shoved her behind him and aimed his gun. Tension vibrated off him and smacked against the walls of the small space. But as quickly as it came the stiffness left his shoulders. He held up his hand. "Whoa. It's us."

The fear clogging her senses eased, and she focused on the guy aiming the gun at them from below. Connor. He dropped his weapon, but the frown didn't let up. "What the hell happened in here?"

Pax shifted his weight and brought her to his side. "You didn't hear the fight?"

"My comm went cold. Couldn't pick up anything until a second ago." Connor gave the explanation, but Kelsey would have answered the same way.

Pax swore under his breath. "Nice work, Joel."

"I wasn't me." Joel bust on the comm with the usual tapping sound in the background. "Well, it was. Sort of."

"What does all of that mean?" Connor asked after a healthy string of profanity of his own.

"Someone was piggybacking my signal. I killed it to keep them from listening in, just in case the attackers were monitoring your positions."

The bad news just kept coming, and Kelsey barely understood this part. "Wait a second—"

Joel rushed over top of her comment. "But whoever it was is skilled. They blocked all other signals. I had to switch to a backup to stay on you guys."

Pax's mouth dropped. "You waited until now to tell us all of this?"

"Hey, knowing a few minutes ago only would have made you panic."

"I'm not sure how I feel about that answer." She mumbled the response but Connor nodded in agreement.

"My point is, the person who crashed our party has the kind of equipment we do."

At Joel's comment, she opened her eyes again.

Pax glanced down at Connor. "I thought we had government-grade, top-of-the-line stuff."

Connor was staring right at her. "Looks like there's a big player in this thing, and your brother is getting that person's attention."

"Didn't we already know that?" She glanced between Pax and Connor. "I mean, someone in the government hired you guys. Who was that, by the way?"

"I'm not sure how you know all that, but yes," Connor said. "Someone at the Department of Defense called us in."

Pax piped up. "And now we know why."

Maybe they did. She didn't. "We do?"

"Your brother didn't just take some information. It's very possible he's planning on selling it." Connor put his gun away. "If so, this game just got a whole lot more dangerous."

With the way her body started shutting down, every inch falling into a fatigue-hued exhaustion, she doubted she'd be on her feet much longer even if she skipped asking. So she went ahead and asked. "Why?"

"Honestly?" Joel's deep voice cut through the sudden silence. "Because Sean's playmates won't stop until they kill him."

Chapter Ten

It was almost midnight when Bryce rubbed his blurry eyes and read the last line in the stacks of compiled information about Sean Moore. For a twenty-something, there seemed to be a lot of paperwork on the kid. No wonder his security clearance took longer than expected.

Probably also had something to do with attending three colleges, getting kicked out of two and having a father who'd spent time in jail for bilking people. The same father who had two children from two different wives, and both wives were dead.

It was quite a life story.

Sean's mother died in a car accident when Sean hit nineteen and the sister, well…Bryce still couldn't figure out where she fit in. There wasn't so much as a photo with them together. She lost her mother to cancer and then her father did a family-restart and Sean was the result.

Now it looked as if he'd been the wrong kid to hire, but he'd possessed very specific math skills described as "off the charts" by more than one reference. Human resources pushed for him to be added to the team, something about him being a near-perfect candidate in terms of aptitude.

Bryce did a cursory sign-off because the idea of a loner who needed a second chance sounded like a familiar story. It appealed to him as a way to breed loyalty. His uncle had once given him a similar chance, and Bryce ran with it. Clearly, history did not repeat itself with Sean.

Lesson learned.

Bryce lifted his head and rubbed his aching neck. The stiffness had traveled over his shoulders and down to his lower back. But he couldn't let up. Sean was a loose end Bryce needed tied up.

Being in a position where someone like Dan had the upper hand made Bryce furious. His business plan centered on using Dan's history to Kingston's benefit and otherwise ignoring the man. Having it work any other way was absolutely unacceptable.

Bryce shook his head, and a single light shining in the area just outside of his office door caught his attention. The floor was dark but Glenn hadn't gone home. Since he hadn't made a noise in over thirty minutes, Bryce wondered if the younger man had dropped off.

Bryce eyed the empty coffee carafe before his gaze went to the computer screen. The photos had stopped flipping by, meaning the program had found a match.

He pulled his chair up tight against his desk, hearing the wheels creak underneath him as he read the information on the screen, limited as it was.

Paxton Weeks. That was it. A name, a photo and a black bar marked Confidential.

Bryce fell back in his plush chair. He felt nothing except the rush of air moving in and out as his breathing picked up its pace.

The notation could indicate many things, but it did suggest Sean and his sister weren't regular citizens scrambling to get by. This Paxton Weeks character was highly connected, which meant Sean knew powerful people. Potentially dangerous people.

People who could ruin Kingston without providing Bryce an opportunity to salvage anything.

The game had just changed. Dan and Sean were no longer Bryce's biggest headaches. This Paxton Weeks guy was.

PAX SAT AT the conference room table back at team headquarters. He'd showered and changed and managed to chug back two cups of coffee. Not that he needed the caffeine. Adrenaline powered him now. That and painkillers. If he took one more tablet he might kill some brain cells along with the residual thumping in his leg.

The idea turned out to be more of a temptation than Pax expected. Something about Kelsey being in danger kept him on edge. Even now he wanted to grab her up and take her far from there until all signs of trouble disappeared.

She sat across from him, tapping her fingernails on the box they'd picked up at her house and staring at it while she chomped on her bottom lip. With her damp hair pulled up in a ponytail and her face scrubbed clean, she swiveled her chair from side to side.

The outfit she'd put on was giving him fits. The V-neck shirt looked about a size too big. It kept falling off her shoulder, revealing a thin strip of a bra strap. She even managed to make oversized navy sweatpants look sexy.

The woman was killing the last hold on his control. To get his mind back on the job, he focused on Connor. The leader paced the space behind Kelsey's chair.

"Where's Ben?" Pax asked.

Kelsey edged her nail along the seam of the box. "I'm starting to think this guy doesn't exist. I hear about this Ben person but have never seen him. Call me skeptical."

The joking comment helped Pax find his first smile in hours. "He'll love knowing you think he's fictional."

"At least she thinks about him. That's something," Joel said and then turned back to the computer when Pax glared.

"Ben is at the hospital." Connor continued his trek over the carpet as he stared at his feet and drank his coffee. "He's had trouble."

Joel's head shot up again. "What does that mean?"

"Someone came after the comatose bad guy, which suggests whoever paid him to kidnap Kelsey doesn't want him waking up and talking."

Pax nodded.

"Ben figured out the situation and diffused it, but the attacker got away." Connor exhaled. "Apparently, Ben didn't want to shoot around all the sick people."

"Good call." Pax could imagine the whole thing and how Ben, the former NCIS agent and straightest arrow of them all, must have hated missing his target.

For Ben's sake, Pax hoped there was a good-looking nurse on the floor to ease Ben's pain.

Kelsey frowned. "These people after Sean, whoever they are, are now causing trouble in hospitals? What kind of person risks the lives of innocent people like that?"

She missed a pretty important piece of the puzzle. Pax didn't. "You're innocent and they came after you."

"Yeah, these are the kind of folks you don't want to meet in an alley behind your shop," Joel said.

Pax knew the real answer was so much worse than Joel's light tone suggested. People like this—hired killers, mercenaries without any loyalty—crawled out from under many rocks and worked for the highest bidder. It was a lousy way to make a living but pretty lucrative.

Even though he wanted her to feel secure and ease up on the killer clench of her fingers into fists, he needed her to be careful. "These men? They'll do anything to get what they want."

"Which is? I'm still not completely clear on that," she said.

Connor reached over her shoulder and flattened his hand against the mysterious box. "This might give us an idea."

It was time. They'd stalled long enough, trying to take fifteen minutes away from the draining case to clean up and recharge, but they couldn't put off looking. All the coffee and small talk in the world could do only so much to battle the anticipation that had them all twitching.

If Joel shifted one more time he might accidentally unplug a computer. And Connor, well, his feet fell harder and faster with each pacing pass.

As much as Pax wanted to rip into the box and get on with it, the right to open it belonged to Kelsey. He held out a hand. "Go ahead."

She glanced around the room at all of them before nodding. Without saying anything, she picked it up and put it on her lap. She picked at the tab and carefully ripped it open.

That had to be one of the differences between men and women. Pax knew he would have torn it apart with his bare hands and dumped everything out in less than five seconds. They'd already be searching through the contents for a lead.

But not Kelsey. She opened it as if it were the most precious gift.

Even with the longer route she finally got there and dumped it upside down. Papers spilled across the table and something clicked as it performed an awkward roll. A smack of her hand stopped it.

She gathered everything in her arms and read off an informal inventory. "Memory stick, a stack of papers written in some weird code and copies of some documents."

Connor reached over her shoulder again, this time to page through the papers strewn in front of her. He separated a stack and held them up. "Some of this looks like a job for Joel."

"Your temporary tech expert is happy to be at your service." Joel's chair creaked as he wheeled it closer to the table.

Connor shot Joel a one-eyed scowl. "You could get up, you know."

"I'm good here."

Her hands froze. "Temporary?"

Joel took what looked like a ream of papers from Connor. "I'm a gun guy filling in as a computer nerd while our regular nerd is with the other part of the team in Catalina."

"Whoa." Kelsey lifted out of her chair and smacked her hand against the papers before Joel could drag them away. Even ignored his "hey" of outrage. "Gentlemen, before you go running in different directions and talking in annoying half sentences, please fill in the newbie. We're not doing the confuse-the-nonoperative game anymore. From here on in, I'm one of you, only without the shooting skills."

Connor's eyebrow lifted. "Excuse me?"

She didn't roll her eyes, but she sure looked as if she wanted to. "Don't bother with the I'm-in-charge voice." She threw her arms out wide. "Tell me what all of this is."

Pax didn't bother to hide his smile. Seeing the matching stunned expressions on Joel's and Connor's faces pretty much made Pax's horrible day take a left turn into more tolerable territory.

They were friends as well as teammates. From watching them interact with Lara and seeing Connor with his wife, Jana, though that had been awhile, Pax didn't doubt his friends' appreciation of strong women.

Erica Dane had been on the team for almost a year and no one treated her as an afterthought. Probably because her sniper skills rivaled Connor's. But with Erica on consecutive out-of-country jobs, Lara on her honeymoon with Davis and Jana inexplicably away, there had been little female input lately. Having Kelsey step up and make a claim seemed to throw Connor off, and to a lesser extent Joel.

It wasn't often a potential victim wandered into the tactical end of the business. They were used to finding a clue, picking it apart and then establishing a plan.

Having Kelsey, the person they viewed as the subject of their operation, make a demand stopped their momentum. She didn't blindly accept everything happening around her and beg for help when things blew up. She asked questions.

Pax took it as a sign they needed more women on the team. He'd be fine if they started with Kelsey, so long as she never left the desk and hypersecure space patrolled by armed guards. He decided that was a totally logical requirement, since he'd reached his end on seeing her in danger.

Before the room exploded in questions or anything else, Pax reached into the not-quite-empty box and pulled out a slip of paper. The temptation to read it proved great, but he slid it in front of Kelsey. "Here."

"A note?" She turned it over in her hands and then read it. A deep exhale followed a second later. "Leave it to Sean to push up the drama with a cryptic letter. The only letter, email, card or even sticky note he's ever written to me, by the way."

"What does it say?" Connor asked.

"Not much. 'Hold these for me—I'll explain later' and that's it." She handed it to Connor. "No explanation."

That's not what ticked Pax off. "No apology."

"I didn't expect one." She smiled but the expression didn't hide the sad note in her voice.

With that, the brief window of amusement Pax had been enjoying slammed shut. He shot out of his chair and did some pacing of his own on this side of the table. "What the hell is wrong with your brother? He put you in the middle of this mess and doesn't bother to warn you or make sure you're okay."

"I doubt he cares." Kelsey divided up the contents of the box. Connor got the documents. Joel got the readouts and memory stick. She held on to the note and likely didn't realize she traced the words with her finger. "We weren't—"

"Close. Yeah, I got that the first few times you said it. It's burned in my brain at this point, not that I need the reminder. Your brother's actions speak loud enough." Pax tried to shake off the frustration bouncing through him. The idea her family would dump her into danger and then run off and leave her to handle it sent a spike of white-hot rage shooting to his brain.

He paced and swore under his breath. It took him another few minutes to realize he was the only one making any noise. He felt the attention on him and looked up to find three sets of eyes focused on him. "What?"

"Something else you want to say about my family?" she asked in a soft voice.

He knew that expression. He could spot a furious female within a hundred feet, and this one looked ready to burst into flames. And not in a good way.

He did what any smart person would do. Stayed as still and quiet as possible. "No."

She stood up, almost in slow motion, but something about the force of the move had her chair spinning behind her. She balanced her palms against the table. "I know we're not perfect. We might even be the lead example for dysfunctional."

"That's not up for debate, but I'm talking about Sean's behavior, not—"

She silenced Pax with a sudden whip of her hand through the air. "Do you and your brother share everything?"

Pax still wasn't clear where this was going or how it had spun off track, so he kept to short words. "Most of the time."

"Such as."

Connor cleared his voice and pointed toward the kitchen. "We can step out."

Joel didn't move. If anything, he leaned back farther in his chair.

"No, stay." She said it to them but stared at Pax as she walked around the table and stopped right in front of him.

Not exactly how he liked to unload his family history, but Connor knew most and Joel knew some. There weren't any big surprises here. Nothing happy or fun, either.

Pax crossed his arms over his chest. "Our story isn't all that original anyway. Dad died in a car accident, mom lost it, then lost custody of us, and we were forgotten."

"We? You're referring to this brother I haven't seen?"

Pax sensed some female grumbling but let it slide. This kind of story came out better in one telling. No need to draw it out. "Me and Davis. He's older and more responsible and made sure we were okay. I owe him for that. For a lot of things, actually, but mostly for that."

"Yeah, well, not all of us had that sort of sibling protection."

"Meaning?" But Pax knew. From the pieces he gathered from the news and the longer renditions from her father's criminal file, the readily available statistics about Kelsey's life followed a poor-little-rich-girl theme.

Not that the description and personality type fit Kelsey. There was nothing spoiled or entitled about her. Lost at times, yes, but not limited. If anything, she far surpassed what could be expected from her upbringing and all the negatives handed to her. She had become driven, smart, determined and far too tempting for his control to handle.

But even if he hadn't read the file, even if he'd never read one line about her life or known about her mother's death from cancer, he'd know a secret part of her.

There was an unspoken club for survivors of terrible parents, and her father definitely qualified as that. The offspring who stumbled around, trying to find their equilibrium as they made their way in a world that ignored them and struggled to put the past behind them so it wouldn't infect their futures.

In Kelsey, Pax saw a fellow fighter, someone who stepped up because no one was there to lift her. Someone who refused to be a victim. He recognized the symptoms because he shared them.

"My mom died and my dad's replacement wife stepped in almost immediately." The words spilled out of her slowly at first and then picked up to a tumbling pace. Her gaze darted around the room and finally landed back on Pax with eyes bleak and dark with sadness. "I was the part of the deal she *had* to take, and when Sean came along, she quickly figured out that having me around potentially decreased his share of the family fortune. She took care of that by shipping me off to boarding school and limiting my visits home."

"There's a word for women like that." And Pax was tempted to yell it.

"No arguments here." Kelsey's shoulders slumped. "In her mind, I needed to be ignored, forgotten and kept out of town."

Not a surprise but still hard to hear. The way her family treated her, as an afterthought and nuisance, explained a lot about Kelsey's fierce personality. She fought hard because she'd been taught to do so while a kid.

"I'm sorry." The words were so useless, and he knew they meant almost nothing after hearing them from social workers and well-meaning but ineffective professionals his whole life, but the emotion behind them this time was real.

"My relationship with Sean never had a chance. My already strained bond with my demanding father never recovered after he remarried."

"Not a big loss," Joel mumbled.

"I'm not in the will, which is truly a blessing because in the Moore family money equals power in a very destructive way. I'm not mentioned in any interview or during any conversation. And since I refused to testify for him, I'm not even a thought at the holidays. I can't hide behind the lie of seeing family only at Christmas, because I'm not invited."

Connor frowned. "But your stepmother died."

"I prefer to think of her as my father's wife and eliminate any reference to a real relationship between us, and yes. A car accident some said was fueled by alcohol. I don't know, but I don't doubt it. My father asked me not to come to the funeral, so I stayed away."

One more thing they had in common. Lives touched by car accident tragedies. For Pax, the loss changed everything when he lost a parent. For her, the accident highlighted how little she meant to her dad. Both instances sucked.

The driving need to touch Kelsey shocked Pax. He ached for her loss and the young girl who deserved so much better. The audience and timing stopped him.

Plus he had a bigger point to make. Something he wanted her to see and understand even though he doubted her ability to take it in after everything else she'd been through today. "You're here, helping Sean. There's a tie. Maybe a thin one, and something your father and his mother tried to destroy, but it's there."

This time she did roll her eyes. Didn't put much energy behind it, but she did it. "I'm trying not to get killed and hoping he doesn't, either. I'm not convinced that makes me Sister of the Year."

But maybe she wasn't as alone in the world as she wanted to believe, and Pax hoped she would somehow fight her way through all the confusion and pain and see that. "I think you're doing okay."

"I'm amazed with every minute that passes without me throwing up."

That certainly broke the serious mood enveloping the room. "Makes two of us."

"Look, I think we need to call it a night. It's late and even without the injuries this has been a rough one." Connor kept his death grip on the paperwork as he started issuing orders disguised as suggestions. "Kelsey, there's a room on the third floor you can use. It's a crash pad of sorts. Towels and sheets are clean, and no one will bother you up there."

Joel laughed. "You sure about that?"

Connor set down his mug on the table with a sharp whack and shot Pax a back-off look. "She needs sleep."

"Why are you looking at me?" But Pax knew.

Hands in the air, Joel shook his head. "I'm not touching that comment."

The clapping started a second later. Two quick smacks followed by a men-are-so-annoying sigh had everyone looking at Kelsey. "Before this totally disintegrates into juvenile boys locker room talk, I need to ask one question."

"Only one?" The fact she managed to follow everything going on around her and handle being in the middle of so much danger impressed Pax. He couldn't imagine her taking on one more thing.

"Why would my brother steal this information? I know all the possible answers are bad, so I'm not seeking some made-up response that makes him sound patriotic or noble. What I really want is to get a sense of how much trouble he's in here." She made a deflating sound as she blew out a long breath. "Are we talking about selling to foreign countries or other companies? Is this a treason issue? What are the possibilities here?"

Since holding up his weight on the one side became harder by the second, Pax slipped his thigh on the edge of the table. He hoped to ease the pounding of blood down his leg. "These things generally break down into a few possible motives. Political statement, revenge, sex or money."

"There's no evidence of a woman, or man for that matter,

who has Sean's interest." Joel flipped through the pages of the document as he talked. "From his history, Sean doesn't appear to be a political radical. As for revenge, Kingston gave him a lot of responsibility from the start, so I don't see bad workplace blood, but who knows?"

"So, most likely it's money." She glanced around the room. "He's been brought up to believe he's the sole heir to my father's fortune, but with the court case, claims against his company and a freeze on family funds from Sean's mother's side of the family, I don't think there's much left over for Sean."

"Combine that with the fact he hasn't exactly been taught survival skills to make it on his own, and the opportunity for stupidity and criminal behavior rises," Pax said.

But she had the skills. Pax had seen them, admired them and been a bit in awe of them. But none of that meant Sean could find his way out of a room with an open door. The stunt he pulled with the work documents showed that.

"There are people—governments—who would pay a lot of money for certain information." Connor's voice got softer and his rough demeanor lightened. It was as if he, too, feared causing her more pain. "Do you understand what I'm saying?"

She nodded. "Someone gave Sean access to stuff like that?"

"I was about to ask the same question. But I can see he definitely did by looking at the stuff he smuggled out to you." Joel shook his head as he talked, but most of his focus centered on the page he spread out across his end of the table.

"Kingston recently moved deeper into intelligence work." And from what Pax could tell it had been on the edge of trouble ever since.

He doubted the owner and board of directors at Kingston understood the level of concern by the higher-ups at the Department of Defense. Sean played a dangerous game with some big and deadly players.

"The owner, Bryce Kingston, is supposed to be a brilliant innovator, and he's been working on something called the Signal Reconnaissance Program. It's a way to break into the military communications of other militaries," Connor explained.

"And, of course, someone filled you in about all of this top-secret stuff." She said it as a statement instead of a question.

Pax answered anyway. "Someone at the Pentagon who is more than a little concerned about Kingston's internal security tipped us off. Yes."

Before Pax could launch into a detailed explanation, Connor talked right over him. "Point is, with this program from Kingston the U.S. can monitor not only the movements of foreign military assets but listen in as if they're sitting in the middle of a Russian sub. It's in the testing and development stage, but it's—"

Joel snapped his fingers without lifting his head. "A game changer."

"It will be if it turns out to be effective. The government handed Kingston a lot of R&D money to get this program off the ground. There is a big push to move it into beta testing. Word is the initial trials are positive," Pax said.

She nibbled on her bottom lip as wariness fell over her features. "If Sean got his hands on that program, or parts of it, and knew how it worked…then what?"

Joel finally looked up. "He could make a lot of money. Like, buy-an-island-and-hide-out type of money."

But Pax knew that wasn't the real issue or the one that should matter to Kelsey. He cut right to it. "Or he could end up dead."

Chapter Eleven

Sean walked down the long driveway and crept up to the gate. Trees lined the property, covering all but the smallest peak of the three-story stone house sitting back off the road. He'd grown up in the Virginia mansion, complete with gardeners and maids and a full-time staff. They'd belonged to country clubs, even a ski resort. His life once revolved around parties and private schools and a second home on the beach in Delaware.

That was before. Before the allegations. Before his parents' violent outbursts and vicious fights. Before the police came and the money dried up. Before his mother threatened to walk out but died before she could get the house packed.

Before Kelsey refused to come back and help.

Things were supposed to be different now. Sean made it through the boredom of school and earned some recognition through the math department. He'd turned his love of video games into a real-life application by combining it with his natural ability at calculations.

He had a job and a life, or he did until a few weeks ago when it all turned upside down. He'd been tasked with a top-secret project and subjected to random drug tests and other unnecessary security measures.

The lie detector was the worse. Strapped to a chair and a machine and forced to answer moronic questions. It was

all a waste of his time. He wanted to work, not get bogged
down in stupid crap.

One day he signed in, fine-tuned the program, fixed the
mistake and left without leaving a data footprint. Just as he
was supposed to do. He'd been promised easy and unseen.
Sneak the files out and act as if nothing happened.

He did everything he was told and didn't tip off any
alarms. But then men started following him and his studio
apartment got turned upside down. The few possessions he
owned and had taken with him that weren't frozen in his father's mess had been broken and destroyed.

He'd been on the run ever since. With a limited cash flow
and few places to go, he'd ended up here. Amazing that no
matter how hard he tried to break free, he ended up back here.

Bryce Kingston knew the truth and now someone wanted
Sean dead, so even this house might not protect him.

He threw his bag over the top of the fence as he'd done
hundreds of times as a kid. Back then beating the security
system had been a game. Now it was a necessity. Using the
metal rails of the gate, he grabbed on to the decorative knobs
and wedged his sneakers in between the bars.

He'd spent most of the past few years sitting at a computer,
but he wasn't out of shape. With a grunt and a concentrated
yank, he climbed. Swinging his leg over the top, he skipped
the rest of the vault and jumped down.

The night's hot air blew around him as he fell, but he mis-
judged the distance and dropped longer than expected. He
hit the soft grass with a sickening thud. His feet hit and one
ankle overturned.

One minute he stood and the next his leg buckled, dragging him down. He dropped as he called out. Rolling around
on the ground, holding his leg and swearing into the dark
night, he tried to work out the kink.

He froze when lights clicked on over his head. A whirring

sound echoed around him. One he couldn't place. He'd just struggled to a sitting position when footsteps thudded by his head and something hard nailed him in the back. His face smashed into the turf and grass filled his mouth. Shifting and struggling, he pushed up and turned to the side, breathing in a huge gulp of air despite the weight pounding against him.

He braced to flip over when he heard a distinct click. He'd never heard the exact sound before, but combined with the hard metal pushing against the back of his skull it wasn't a mystery. After all that running he'd been found.

"Do not move."

At the sound of the stern voice, Sean let out a loud exhale. His shoulders slumped in relief. "Hello, Dad."

Fingers dug into Sean's arm and then turned him over. His father loomed above, hands on his hips and wearing a golf shirt and khakis, the daily uniform he'd adopted after prison.

Gone were the expensive suits and shiny watches. He insisted those days were behind him, along with his ability to earn a "decent" living. Resting on the money still in his bank while his attorneys went unpaid qualified as roughing it to Dad.

Sanford Moore, Sandy to friends, as well as to those who believed he'd defrauded them and the journalists on the talk show circuit who enjoyed bringing him on their programs even now, stared down with fury turning his face purple. "What are you doing sneaking onto my property?"

Sean wasn't sure when he'd become a visitor in his family home. "I needed somewhere to hide."

"You come through the front door or you don't bother coming home at all. And you call first. You're a grown-up now. Act like it."

Since the family's finances no longer allowed for paid guards and a top-of-the-line security system, Sean thought going in quietly was the answer. Just in case someone followed him here. "I didn't want to put you in danger."

"Why do you think I have the gun?"

"I have no idea. When did you get that?" Sean couldn't believe anyone would sell him one.

"I still have people dropping by the gate, whining about losing money and blaming me."

Sean had heard the complaint every day for nine years and didn't have the time to argue about it now. "I know, Dad."

"Then you should know better than to be skulking around in the dark." His father glanced around. "Where's your car? I didn't see it drive up."

That answered the question of whether the security cameras still worked. Sean could imagine his father spending hours a day sitting over them, watching the screens. His paranoia had bloomed into a restless living thing, and with his professional reputation in tatters, all he had was the money from Sean's mother's estate—the part her relatives couldn't figure out how to take—plus the money for the book he'd just sold. The same money every fraud victim wanted to grab away before his father could spend it.

"I don't have my car. I hitched." Three drivers and a drop-off a mile away, but Sean got there.

The clenched jaw suggested his father was not impressed. "Have you lost your mind?"

Sean was starting to wonder. "Someone's following me."

"Because of me." His father reached down and jerked Sean to his feet. The gun stayed within sight but was no longer aimed.

Sean suspected that could change at any moment. His father's temper was well-known, and Sean tried very hard not to tweak it. "No, because of *my* work."

The older man's eyes narrowed right before he turned and

faced the house. He took three steps before looking over his shoulder and motioning Sean to join him. "What did you do?"

Despite the throbbing ankle, Sean grabbed his bag and rushed to keep up. "Nothing."

"Come on, Sean."

He brushed the overgrown branches out of the way, making a path through a group of trees that were once manicured to perfection weekly by a small staff. "I have some work documents and now I'm in some trouble."

His father eyed him. "What kind of documents?"

No way was Sean divulging every last piece of information. Kelsey had called him naive when he'd stuck up for their father years ago. She never understood that he saw Dad's flaws.

Sean could also look at the numbers and see how, if the market hadn't taken a sudden downturn, Dad could have replaced the missing money and made a fortune for his clients. It was a money game, and for years he'd landed on the winning side, until the one time he didn't and everything fell apart.

But Sean also learned from Kelsey's mistakes. She took Dad on directly. Sean preferred to play the role of loyal son and pick his battles. This wasn't one. "Important documents about government programs."

"You have these documents on you?"

His dad's visual tour suggested he was a second or two away from hunting for them in Sean's jeans and baggy shirt. "I mailed them to Kelsey."

His dad stopped then. Fury washed over his features, pushing his mouth down and pulling the skin tight over his cheeks. "What were you thinking? She's not an ally. Ever. Kelsey is out for one person and one person only—Kelsey."

Sean knew the look and recognized the building rage, and

he didn't welcome either. "I figured no one would look for me near her. It's not a secret we're estranged."

His father scoffed. "*Estranged.* Ridiculous word."

"No one would suspect I'd confide in her, and she isn't interested in anything about my life. She'll dump the package in her house and forget it."

"She could get rid of it."

Sean doubted that. Not a box. She might open it and ignore it. He couldn't see her throwing it away. After all, she'd kept the handwritten notes Father told her to throw away all those years ago. The same ones that outlined Father's deposits into accounts he claimed not to own. Instead of listening, she'd kept everything and turned it all over to the prosecution.

Their father would never forgive her for that betrayal, but it suggested to Sean he'd picked the right person to hold the documents. "She has a history of holding on to things. Important things."

They stood in silence. Neither moved as the motion sensor light over their heads flickered to life. Finally, his father nodded. "True."

"But now I need the papers and calculations. The few times I've been able to borrow a phone I haven't been able to reach her."

His father swore and then started walking again, his long legs and large frame eating up the distance to the house in minutes. "Figures."

"I thought I could try to reach her from here."

"Kelsey does owe me." A smile kicked across his father's face. "Maybe it's time Kelsey comes home and does her duty."

KELSEY CHANGED INTO the pajama shorts set Connor found for her in his wife's things and dropped back on the mattress. The soft comforter swallowed Kelsey, and a pile of pillows propped her head up. She stared at the ceiling with the intricate moldings and fancy light dropped on a chain right above the double bed and tried to imagine Pax moving around on the floor above. The footsteps had faded, so she strained to get a sense of him. No luck so far.

She expected a makeshift cot on a cramped third floor. They'd described the third floor as a crash pad, and that just did not sound appealing to her at all, but she'd sleep curled up on the floor if it meant a few hours for her to rest.

The day had been long and exhausting. Every time she closed her eyes she saw bodies piled up around her. Keeping them open didn't exactly blink the visual image totally away either, but the memory lessened.

After some grumbling and arguing between Pax and Connor, she'd been assigned to the guest room on the second floor, the same floor she now knew acted as Connor's home. And Pax wandered silently somewhere above in the so-called crash pad and managed to be quiet about it.

Because of the high mattress, her feet barely grazed the floor. She swung the one, letting her bare foot ease across the fluffy carpet. From the canopy bed to the soft blue walls, the room telegraphed comfort. It could be in a magazine, the kind she paged through and drooled over. She guessed Connor's wife deserved the credit.

But it wasn't her apartment, and Kelsey couldn't get around that. Humble and made up of mismatched secondhand furniture, that apartment belonged solely to her. Her hard work shaped it. Not being there, not being able to protect it or serve her customers daily as she'd done since she'd taken over the place made her antsy.

Her skin jumped and shifted, pulling to get free, just thinking about the ruined inventory and lost profits. The mortgage company wouldn't care that her inability to pay was somehow her brother's fault. She barely understood the connections reaching from his actions to her livelihood. She doubted anyone else would, either.

She turned her head and glanced out the window. The panes looked normal, but she guessed there was some sort of voodoo security film coating on them. Still, they were shut. The cool breeze in the room came from the air conditioner vent blowing across her body. Everything she needed to sleep was there—cool room, comfortable bed and complete safety.

Everything but Pax.

A soft tap on the door dragged her attention away from the dark sky outside. She glanced over in time to see Pax walk into the room. *Limp in* was more accurate. He wore navy sweats and a tee and he'd never looked better to her. Broad shoulders, muscled arms and a face that made her sigh a little inside when he glanced in her direction even for a second.

She sat up, balancing her upper body on her elbows. A smile inched across her face before she could catch it. On some level she'd known he would come. The house grew quiet and everyone talked about rest, but she knew in her soul he would wait and then visit. She guessed that's why he fought against her being placed right across the hall from Connor's bedroom—no privacy.

He leaned back against the door without venturing farther into the private space. "You okay?"

"I should be comatose with sleep by now."

"Sometimes it's hard to shake off the adrenaline rush and calm down. And heaven knows you've been through a lot today. Men coming at you, me shoving you around."

Funny how she'd long forgiven him. All that anger drained away until her focus shifted to wanting him around. "I got used to the last part."

"Oh, yeah?" His eyebrows lifted.

"Yeah."

He pushed off the door and came deeper into the room.

Instead of stopping a respectable distance away and keeping up the charade of bodyguard/client, he sat down on the bed next to her.

The move had her sitting the whole way up and leaning in close. She blamed his greater weight and the way the mattress dipped around him, but deep inside she knew the truth. She was right where she wanted to be…with him.

She ran a palm over his knee and waited for any sign of pain. If he even flinched, she'd wake Joel. "How's the leg?"

"Medicated to the point of being numb."

That explained the glassy look to Pax's eyes. "Did you really get shot?"

"I can show you the wound." He messed up his naughty innuendo and wiggling eyebrows by picking up her hand and holding it in his. So soft and gentle. So opposite of the guy who fired guns and threw knives. "The bullet was coming and it was either me or Lara, Davis's new wife. I picked me."

Between the words and the touch, Kelsey's heart flipped. "Sounds heroic."

"Not really."

She'd bet Lara would disagree. And if it turned out that Lara was one of those entitled types who didn't praise Pax for his bravery, Kelsey might just punch her. "Will the wound always hurt?"

He leaned in, meeting her part way, until their shoulders touched. "I get a lot of 'we'll have to see' type of responses from doctors and physical therapists. I feel as if I've been off it and taking it easy forever. I'm ready to be back to normal again."

From the serious expression and continued brushing of his thumb over the back of her hand, she guessed he actually believed what he'd just said. "You think today qualified as being off your leg?"

"Sure."

Men never ceased to fascinate her. Even the good ones said odd things, and she knew for certain from everything she'd seen and experienced that he fell into that category. "Interesting."

"Either way, it seems clear I won't get full use back."

She tried to imagine what being limited in any physical way did to a man like him. He rescued and saved. Not being able to do that could break him. Could endanger the work he appeared to love. "Does that bother you?"

"Bother?"

The repeated question sounded like a stall to her. "You're familiar with the word, right? *Upset you, anger you, tick you off.* Any of those, or do you shrug and take it all in stride?"

He lifted their joined hands and kissed the back of hers. "All injuries are bad, but the only ones you need to worry about are the ones you don't survive."

"Wow, that's…"

His mouth lifted in a half smile. "True?"

"Maudlin."

He threw back his head and laughed, deep and throaty, genuine and free. "Says the woman who's been mauled and attacked and shot at today."

The laugh still rumbled through her even after he stopped talking. She tried to think of one thing about him that turned her off and couldn't come up with anything. From his looks to the emotional depth hinted at behind those eyes and in his words, she got sucked in.

After all those months of keeping her life commitment free. All those other guys who stuck around but meant nothing. She finally found someone who challenged and excited her. She just wished the danger he walked into so willingly didn't scare her so much.

But that didn't mean they couldn't have a moment.

She rested her cheek against his shoulder and inhaled the scent of soap on his skin. "Have I thanked you?"

He shrugged. "That's not necessary."

She knew he'd say that. Her head dropped, inching closer to his collarbone and that delicious spot, the dip where bones met muscle at the base of his neck. "Oh, Pax, ignoring my compliments makes it very hard to seduce you."

He leaned back and looked down at her, the smile softer but possibly deeper, and those eyes darkened and so appealing. "Is that what's happening?"

She wanted to say yes. She could have said yes and been telling the truth. The bed, the room, the heat bounced between them. It didn't take a genius to figure out where they were headed.

"Not quite, but I am trying to get you to kiss me as you promised earlier." She lifted her head as she said it, making sure to drop her lips right below his.

"You could just ask."

His whispered words blew across her lips. "I was kind of hoping I didn't have to.

"So we're clear—" he rubbed his thumb along her bottom lip "—I want to almost every second of the day. I see you and my brain misfires. To protect you I should step back, maybe let Joel take over, but the idea of someone else being with you, touching you, is more than I can tolerate."

Her hand played with the scruff on the tip of his chin. "I wouldn't let anyone else touch me."

"What about me?"

"You can touch me as much as you want." She whispered the response because it felt right to let the words dance softly off her tongue.

After that his mouth dipped and his lips slipped over hers. Heat beat off her body and blood rushed to her head. Sensa-

tions walloped her—dizziness, elation. She craved his touch
and wrapped her arms around his neck to pull him in closer.

The light touch of a firm mouth morphed into a blinding kiss. The gentle brush of lips against lips gave way to a
devouring need. His mouth slanted and his hands roamed.
Palms pressed against her back as his lips traveled over hers.

His body surrounded her, slipped over hers. Air rushed out
of her and she couldn't draw enough in, but she didn't care.

Before she knew what was happening, her back hit the
mattress and his firm body hovered over hers. The kiss set
off explosions throughout her body. Her skin heated and her
nails dug into his shirt.

One hand speared through his hair as his mouth pressed
against hers and their tongues met. She recognized the
pounding she heard as a kick up in their breathing. If her
heart hammered any harder, she'd need an ambulance.

The kiss went on forever but didn't last nearly long
enough. When he lifted his head for air, she balked and found
his mouth again. His palm spread over her bare stomach, and
her fingers inched under the band of his tee.

She was ten seconds away from begging him to strip off
her shirt when a door banged in the hallway.

They both jumped. Pax jackknifed to a sitting position
and she bounced on the bed, shifting just outside of his grip.
The sudden separation left her skin cold and her mind reeling. She could actually feel her head spin as the wonderful,
sexy tension dissipated.

"What was that?" She nearly panted out the words.

The bed creaked as Pax shifted his weight. "If I had to
guess, I'd say Connor."

The anger in Pax's voice had her blinking even as she tried
to understand the sentence. "What?"

"I think he's warning me to use my head."

Sitting next to him, she slipped a hand over Pax's back,

loving the ripple of his muscles underneath, and then wrapped the other arm around his stomach. "He cares if we're together?"

Pax's hand brushed up and down her bare arm. "Only if it means we're not safe."

"Am I safe with you?"

He faced her then, all traces of fury gone. "Always."

"Well, then—"

"And to prove it I'm going to be a gentleman and leave." He finished the vow with a quick kiss on her mouth.

She wanted more but he'd pulled back and away. Not at all what she wanted. "We seem to be experiencing a communication issue."

He opened his mouth and closed it twice before finally getting a word out. "Not at all, but you need rest."

She was all for the chivalry thing, but this might be too much. "Really?"

"But tomorrow…"

The promise hung right there. She could see it in the soft shine of his eyes and quirk of his mouth. "Yes?"

With one final kiss—this one lingered longer and held a touch of teasing—he stood up. "Get some sleep and you'll find out."

Chapter Twelve

Pax came downstairs just after six the next morning. The sun already beamed in the window by the front door, casting shadows across the hardwood entry floor. He took a sharp turn at the bottom of the stairs and went through the sliding doors into what he always thought of as the War Room. The news played on one of the television screens and a police scanner buzzed in the background.

Joel already sat at the bank of computers, tapping on a keyboard and scanning the screens in front of him as he typed. A pile of papers from Sean's box sat next to his left hand and more were scattered at his feet.

Between his messed-up hair and rumpled clothing, Pax wondered if Joel bothered to sleep last night. It was quite possible he hadn't moved from that chair since Pax left him six hours ago.

Connor was a different story. Dress shirt and pants—check. Hair combed and watch in place—check. If the man slept Pax didn't think it was for very long. He bounced up every morning looking as if he could walk into an important meeting at the Pentagon. And sometimes he did just that.

Munching on toast and downing a cup of coffee, Connor walked around the table and grabbed the newspaper off the edge of Joel's workstation. From the pot, it looked as if he carried his second or third cup.

Caffeine fueled the man, and since he had Corcoran running with little trouble and just the right amount of oversight, Pax didn't argue with the method.

"You crash here?" he asked Joel.

"I used the couch. Made more sense than running back and forth to my place." Joel glanced away from the screen for more than his usual second. "Where did you sleep, or am I too young and impressionable to know?"

"Feel free to shut up."

"Hey, if it's easier for me to make it up in my head, say the word and I'll start."

Sometimes the limited sleep and a prolonged lack of female influence had the conversation dipping into the junior-high level. Pax was grateful Kelsey stayed upstairs and missed this part. "Third floor. I was up there alone."

Connor snorted. "Not for lack of trying."

Which brought up another complaint. "Subtle and well-timed door slam, by the way. You'll be great if you ever have teen girls."

"It's my house." Connor didn't lift his head but he smiled.

"Any reason for the angry-father routine other than the obvious explanation that you're watching over me?"

"You're a big boy and your love life only matters to the extent it creeps into the office."

A slow anger snuck up on Pax out of nowhere. "Which never happens."

"Until now," Joel mumbled without turning around.

"For the record, I'm not watching you. I'm watching over Kelsey." Connor blew on his coffee and then gulped half of it down. "Is she still sleeping?"

Thinking about her in bed, the mattress and those little shorts…yeah, that was the last place Pax wanted his mind wandering unchecked this morning. Not at work. Not now. Certainly not in front of his friends.

He reached for a clean mug on the tray in the middle of the table. "I want her to get as much rest as possible. Yesterday was a fairly rotten day for us, and we're trained. Supposedly we are accustomed to this stuff, but she isn't. She's a civilian and I don't want to lose sight of that because she happens to have a fighter streak that rivals ours."

Connor dropped the newspaper on the table and poured Pax a mug before refilling his own. "Point taken."

"You conceded that argument kind of fast." Which Pax knew from experience meant bad news would slam into him any second.

"It's early." Connor made the dry statement before taking his seat at the head of the table.

That put Joel and Connor at one end and Pax on the other. Something about the setup reminded him of being called to the principal's office as a kid. Back then pulling a fire alarm struck him as a challenge. Thank goodness he'd gotten smarter as he aged or he'd likely be in a prison cell.

"Since you're down here instead of upstairs where it's more interesting and clearly need to find something to do to keep your mind off the woman upstairs—" Connor turned the pages of the paper with an annoying slowness "—you may as well know we have a new problem."

And here we go.

Joel spun his chair around to sit next to Connor and face Pax head-on. "A big problem."

"You really need to stop saying stuff like that." Pax looked at the plate of doughnuts and muffins in front of him, wanting to ignore Joel's newest issue.

"Sorry, but it's unavoidable," Joel said, sounding the exact opposite of sorry.

The crinkling sound of the paper as Connor refolded it ripped through Pax's brain. If they wanted his attention, they had it. He dropped the doughnut and stood with his hands at his back and legs apart, braced for whatever was about to come.

"Tell Pax before the nosiness kills him." Connor put his hand over the top of the oversized mug Jana bought him one year as a joke and which he'd used ever since. A file slid down the table with a whoosh and landed exactly in front of Pax. Joel nodded, satisfaction obvious on his face that he managed to spin the papers that far and complete the landing. "Someone tapped your personnel file."

Pax's hand stopped halfway to the file. "What?"

"You're been investigated, or at the very least checked out." Joel put a second file in front of Connor, who didn't even open it.

For someone in Pax's position, the news spelled disaster. He no longer worked in black ops under false names, with limited contacts and constant moving around. Those days had ended when he'd left government service and thrown in with Connor.

But his current position required a certain level of confidentiality. People couldn't know background information on him or where he lived, which at the moment, with his boat gone, amounted to right upstairs in the crash pad.

That's why having his boat ownership uncovered in his last active job proved such a mess. A mole related to the NCIS case had uncovered the title information, tracked him down and almost blown up Davis and Lara in the process. Finding out someone new had started excavating and bumped into his file ticked Pax off.

"How exactly did that happen? This stuff is supposed to be sealed." Pax scowled at Joel. "By you."

"I'm the temporary tech guy, but I see your point."

"It's bad for all of us, Pax. Not just you." Connor opened the cover of the file and then closed it again without reading a word. "We all have confidential files. Even if someone broke into the DOD database and found your name, that's all the information the person could get."

Pax used to buy that. He knew Connor still did, but Pax had reason to be skeptical. "I have a thousand pieces of a blown-up boat and a bullet in my thigh that suggest otherwise."

The release of all private information, any information, required a top-secret clearance. Even then, the person checking had to be read into the specific program and have a need to know. Not just anyone could go tripping through. Their files were purposely hard to locate, and anyone who did wasn't just stumbling around for fun. But that didn't mean Pax trusted everything to work as planned.

Joel stuttered a bit while glancing back and forth between Pax and Connor, but he got the words out. "Tracing the breach back to its source, someone did a facial recognition search on you and landed on your government file. That means the person had access to high-level recognition software."

Connor shook his head as if he were reasoning it all out. "We're talking about someone with clearance and skills. Someone who could get in and out without raising a flag."

Before Pax could ask a million questions about his identity being compromised and what that would mean for the caseload, Joel spoke again, this time much louder until his voice carried over them all. "Before you both panic, though I think I'm a second too late, the person looking only got as far as your sealed file. The security held. Everything worked as it was supposed to."

The knot in Pax's gut didn't untie. "You're sure?"

"There was nothing to see, but DOD has a program that flashes us a warning whenever anyone comes checking up on us. Without that we wouldn't even know. It's an extra layer meant to make us feel more confident, not cause unnecessary panic."

No one had ever accused Pax of panic before. Before the anger could fester and explode, Pax tramped it back down again. He was willing to chalk the entire conversation up to Joel's lack of sleep and Pax's stupid injury that refused to heal.

The leg made the others wary. He understood the concern, but he wasn't the type to get injured and then hide in the house, and it was time for all of them to deal with that fact. "The worry feels necessary to me since it was my file."

Connor held out a hand to stop whatever had Joel leaning forward. "I think what Joel means is, we now have a warning system, though it is true we also have a problem because someone *was* checking on you and we can't ignore that."

When the bad news came, it sure seemed to come in waves. Just once Pax wanted an easy case with a simple answer. This wasn't it. He tried to imagine when "this" had happened. Never that he could recall.

"Okay, so someone tripped this warning program, right?" Pax despised this part of the job. The constant scrutiny. The checking and rechecking. The reality that he forfeited privacy when he decided to serve his country.

"Yes." Joel reached behind him and dragged his wireless keyboard onto the conference table in front of him.

It wasn't like Joel to give a quick answer, not when it came to this stuff. The sudden lack of eye contact raised a red flag for Pax. "Can we trace it back to the actual person behind the facial recognition check?"

"Not quite that far." Joel tapped on the keys as lines of code scrolled across one of the screens behind him. "The guy has cover and knows how to go undetected."

"But you did find him. You detected him."

Joel glanced up with a smile. "Because I'm better and I

will trace the file breach back to someone, though I think we all have an idea where this started."

Connor nodded. "Exactly. Ground zero is the coffee shop. You were there every day but you happened to be out on the street in front of it with Kelsey right before the file breach occurred."

With that Pax's next breath wheezed out of his lungs. "You're not saying that she—"

"He's saying the person following her spied you out in the open, likely on the sidewalk, and decided to investigate." Connor didn't say "don't be ridiculous," but the vibe was there under his words.

"By now they've seen the confidential warning on the file. It's not subtle. See for yourself." A few more taps and the monitor on the top right of the panel blinked to life.

Joel and Connor spun around to look at the screen. Pax's face, or a slightly younger version, with a black bar stamped Confidential across it filled the screen. "If the person looking has any sense or experience, he'll know he stumbled onto something big."

"DOD was notified when we were," Connor said.

"Since when?" Pax wasn't clear on when they'd added all these levels of security, but he was grateful for whatever redundancies and fail-safes were in place.

Joel raised his hand. "That was the deal. I wanted the warning as a precaution. DOD only agreed to the install after I gave them the program to use with their other files. They also threw around allegations of 'hacking' but I ignored that."

"You forgot to mention that part to me," Connor said.

Joel shrugged. "Point is our contact should be calling Connor within the next fifteen minutes to report all of this. Connor here gets to act surprised."

"Why does everyone look as if their favorite puppy died?" Kelsey asked the question from the doorway to the main

entry. She wore the same pajama shorts but hid most of them
under an oversized sweatshirt pulled over the tiny sleep top.

Pax had to fight the urge to carry her upstairs and finish
the kissing they'd started last night. "Apparently someone has
a photo of me and is doing a search through my work file."

She let her head fall back against the wood. "And you
think this is related to Sean?"

"Don't you?"

She huffed and shook her head. Did the whole men-are-so-
clueless repertoire as she walked into the room and stopped
next to Pax's chair. "Not to state the obvious, but you have
other cases. I'm guessing you have enemies."

He held a hand to his heart and pretended to be offended.
"I'm wounded that you would think that."

"Gee, what was I thinking?"

"You have to admit, Kelsey, the timing is suspicious."
Connor motioned toward the coffeepot and started pouring
when she nodded. "But to be sure, Joel will do a deeper trace
and we'll double-check."

She took the mug and grasped it in a double-fisted clench.
"But right now the evidence points toward Sean and this
case."

"Kingston is someone with the skills and resources to
break into law enforcement systems and run illegal checks."
Joel sat back in his chair. "In fact, it's possible they let him
use the programs. He designs the things and is in the intelligence business now. In theory he's not a threat. His risk
level should be low."

"Theory." That one word shifted everything in Pax's head.
So much for hanging around and letting her reboot.

The Corcoran Team had rules and protocols for this sort
of breech. Having Kelsey at his side didn't change any of
his core responsibilities. The precautions were there for all

of their safety. In this case, Kelsey's safety was paramount and that meant a change.

"Did you have more to add, or are you only repeating after Joel for some reason?" she asked.

Pax held up a finger. "The risk is low in theory. We don't know the reality."

She sighed as she dropped into the seat next to him. "And why do I think that comment means something bad for me?"

Not the word he would use. *"Bad?"*

"Annoying, then."

Pax couldn't help but smile. "Smart woman."

Chapter Thirteen

They stayed at the Corcoran Team headquarters all day, poring over the contents of the box from Sean and deciphering what the men in the room referred to as code. Kelsey thought the lines resembled gibberish. While the guys pored and deciphered, she read up on the Kingston corporation and its off-the-radar but very wealthy owner.

She asked about a billion questions about the team's past cases, only about three of which they agreed to answer. Really, that was three more than she expected. The questions mostly kept her mind off her store and the inventory rotting on the counters.

And that kiss. She dreamed about that one.

The ongoing discussions also gave her a front-row seat to their logic and problem solving. Their gun skills bordered on amazing, but their intelligence was much more impressive. In the case of Pax, it was off-the-charts attractive.

And by sitting there she could close her eyes and enjoy the men's voices and smile over their verbal jabs at each other. Something about being around the three of them soothed her. The ever-elusive Ben even called in and she met him via teleconference. He had a face and everything.

Not that she cared about any face except Pax's. Watching him work, seeing him concentrate while his expression turned serious and he poured all of his formidable focus into a project…downright sexy. At one point she'd whispered his name just to have all of that attention shift to her. His eyes, cloudy at first, cleared and a smile tugged at the corner of his mouth.

Doubly sexy.

No question that despite a flip-flopping stomach and concerns about her impending poverty, the day went well. No one tried to kill her or shoot at her. She didn't fall down the stairs. Amazing how twelve hours of straight terror could alter what you viewed as a good day. Her bar was low enough that surviving warranted a cake and coffee celebration.

But that was the afternoon. This was now.

The dark and humid night had taken a turn that started an unwelcome shiver rocketing through her. They walked on the creaky dock at a marina about a half mile from the City Dock. Metal clanged on metal as the boats' sails whipped around in the warm prestorm breeze.

With each step, water sloshed and churned. The path below her seemed to bobble and sway as they walked down the lines of slips, almost every one filled with a boat bearing a whimsical name, such as *Lady Luck* or *My Children's Inheritance.*

She'd clearly forgotten to mention the whole terror-at-the-thought-of-water thing to Pax. She lived in a water resort town and vowed never to go on another boat. She stayed away from the ocean, the nearby Chesapeake and large pools. Well, she did until Pax dragged her here tonight.

He moved along, his long legs eating up the dock several planks at a time and showing only the slightest limp. She doubted anyone who didn't know could pick up on the injury.

Every now and then his foot fell too hard and his weight shifted ever so slightly. She knew because she stared him down with practiced tunnel vision. It was either that or give in to the violent tremors rolling through her.

Her breath raced up her throat and got caught there. She swallowed it back. "One question."

"Hit me."

She slid her hand in his and felt her heart hiccup when his fingers tightened around hers. "What are we doing here?"

"Protocol says—"

"If one of you is under scrutiny then you separate from the team headquarters to assess the danger. The team is never exposed." Those words had been drummed into her brain. "Yeah, I got that part this afternoon. Connor isn't exactly subtle when he launches into the live version of your office manual. That guy can talk."

Pax's warm laughter filled the quiet night. "The type of training he provides and the relentless repetition make us good at what we do. Without it, we'd likely be shot at even more often."

"There's a scary thought."

"His lectures can be annoying, but they are effective if for no other reason than you only want to hear them once."

"I won't even ask where Connor learned all those under-cover skills, since you'd never tell me anyway." Her nerves kept zapping but the frequency lessened when she heard the mumble of conversation and a stray booming laugh in the distance.

She peeked through the bobbing boats and over the rows to a double-decker boat with lights that outlined its deck. People moved around and hung near the sides. She couldn't make out faces or even the sex of some from this distance, but she knew fun, and that crowd sounded like fun.

"Good call on the too-much-information-about-Connor issue. He's not an oversharer in general and even less so when it comes to his work past. It's part of what makes him good at his job," Pax said.

"I figured it was a need-to-know thing like everything

else about you guys." The calmer mood broke into a wild-frenzy panic inside her when she heard a splash. She jerked back and scanned the water.

"What's wrong?"

A completely irrational fear of big fish. "Nothing."

"Really?"

Something slipped up and out of the waves and then disappeared again. She kept an eye on the spot, waiting for a repeat performance. "Back to my original question. What are we doing at the marina?"

"We need to stay overnight somewhere until the facial recognition thing works itself out." He guided them to the right and steered them past an older couple walking back toward the shore.

She wanted to follow those two to dry land. To anywhere that wasn't here.

"I thought we were going to a hotel." She strained to remember the conversation.

All that talk about an alternate location. Pax had her pack a few things, most of them belonging to Connor's wife. Even now Pax carried the bag over his outside shoulder.

"We're staying on a boat. Not mine because it's gone. It wasn't moored here anyway. It was at another marina, but that cover is blown."

No matter how many words he said, her reaction was the same—*no way.*

She stopped under a light and nearly had her arm ripped off when it took him a few more steps to realize he walked alone.

He turned around, one hand already on the gun she knew he carried. He scanned the area and the smile downshifted into a serious scowl. "What's going on?"

A horn sounded in the distance. The droning matched the heaviness tugging at her. "We have a problem."

The bag fell off his shoulder and hit the deck. His gaze landed everywhere but on her as his gun swept across the landscape. "What did you see?"

The water rippled and the creature made a second appearance. It stayed up for a few beats and then slid under again. The sight had icy fingers clawing at her insides. "First, what was that?"

He lowered the gun. "Wait, what are you...did you see someone or not?"

"I'm serious. Right there." She pointed at the spot where the malformed head stuck up a second ago. It would come up again. It had to or Pax would think she lost her mind.

"It's water, Kelsey. The night makes it look more ominous, but it's nothing but the wind kicking up."

"I'm talking about the big mound that keeps popping up." She ventured a few inches closer to the side of the dock but shifted her weight to her back leg to keep from falling in. "I'm thinking monster fish, shark or a distant relative of the Loch Ness Monster."

He slid his gun back into the holster under his arm. "Okay, fill me in on what's really going on here."

As if she was going to tell some big hero dude about her small fears. Talking made it sound so much sillier, so she forced down the anxiety screaming through her and tried to step around him. "Just asking a question. Let's keep walking."

He caught her arm. "Uh, Kelsey?"

She tried to tug her arm loose but Pax held on. He didn't move, either. If the raised eyebrow was any indication, he didn't intend to.

Fine. Humiliation it would be. "The water makes me crazy."

"Crazy?"

"Like makes me want to crawl out of my skin."

"Okay." The light above them cast strange shadows around them but the stunned look on his face was very visible. "Are we talking water in general or—"

"The salty, dead-fish smell. The constant movement. The fear of drowning. Add it all together and it's taking all of my control not to double over."

"Okay."

"I think it's the wide-open space and lack of control I'd have in there, but I'm not a hundred percent sure. I haven't taken the time to explore the fear in depth. Avoiding it is easier." This wasn't the first time she'd threatened to lose a meal, but this time he handled it better. Seemed to ignore the possibility completely.

Little did he know the real threat was her bursting into tears. Unless Pax had some male gene the rest of his species missed, the weeping thing could be the one issue to bring him to his knees.

"You're really afraid of water?" he asked.

The word was so small for such a big source of paralyzing panic. But she refused to be embarrassed about this. Maybe if she carried a gun and could shoot the sharks, it would be a different story.

"I am, which makes me a very smart woman. The ocean is huge, and humans are tiny by comparison. You do the math."

"Sorry I didn't ask first." He wiped a hand through his hair. "Honestly, I didn't even think about it."

"Because you're not afraid of anything."

He blew out a breath and then picked up the bag and slung it over his shoulder again. "Wrong."

Right.

"Name one thing." She inched away from the edge and closer to him. If she fell in, she wanted him with her. That way she had a shot at going out of this world with one last kiss.

"Lara gets motion sickness, so I know boats aren't for everyone. I just assumed with the way you were raised..." He screwed up his lips and made a face. "Guess not."

Kelsey got caught on the Lara reference and the rest of the comment zinged by before she could process it. Time to back up. "Care to finish that sentence you left there in the middle?"

"Your father used to sponsor a boat racing team. He owned sailboats."

For a few seconds at a time she could forget they didn't have a normal relationship, that Pax didn't know every last detail about her messed-up past. But he did.

Still, there were some things that likely didn't make it into a list of facts in some government file. "My terror was the subject of endless enjoyment to my father."

"I see." Pax's expression stayed blank.

She tried to read him but couldn't. After a quick check of the party boat to make sure the music and laughter went on, she turned back to Pax. "What does that mean?"

"This, the water thing, it all connects to your father." Pax shrugged. "Makes sense."

She refused to let this be some sort of father-induced phobia. "It's about being afraid of dying."

He nodded. "Okay."

For some reason, his automatic-understanding reaction lit a match to her fury. Anger poured over the trembling fear, bringing heat back into her body. "Yeah, I know it's okay."

After a tense minute of rocking boats and clapping water, he pivoted and faced the shore and small store at its edge. He held out a hand to her. "Come on. We'll find another sleeping solution."

Here she was raging and hovering right on the verge of yelling, and he took it. So clear and calm, so utterly accepting of her craziness.

All the indignation rushed right back out of her, leaving her shoulders curling in on her. "That's it?"

His squinting eyes and flat lips could be described only as a look of confusion. "What, did you think I was going to throw you in the murky waves and watch you panic?"

Actually… "You wouldn't be the first one to do so."

He swore under his breath as he stared at his shoes and shifted his feet. "I want to beat almost every member of your family."

Yeah, that wasn't anger she was feeling right now. Light and relieved, drained and excited. "That's strangely sweet."

He gave her an I'll-never-understand-women frown. "I love sailing. I love the water."

He said it so matter-of-factly, as if he was reading it from a card. Not that she was surprised by the admission. He'd mentioned his destroyed boat about a thousand times in thirty-six hours. She knew all about Davis and Lara hiding on it before someone packed it with explosives.

"I picked up on your water fetish."

"But you being comfortable is more important than a boat or the water. I want you to be somewhere you feel safe, and if it's not here we'll go." No fanfare. No big scene. He just said the words and watched her as he spoke.

Her nerves jangled with a certain awareness from the minute they pulled into the marina parking lot. Before the tingling signaled disaster. Now it lit with a spark of life. His words, his support, turned the dread weighing down every step across the dock into something fresh and clear.

"Well, that's just about the most romantic thing I've ever heard." And that was not an exaggeration. It took all her self-control and a good sniff of the dank water to keep her from climbing on top of him.

He shot her a shy smile. "I have skills."

And he kept dragging more and more out to impress her. "You'd give up sailing for me?"

His head bent to the side and one eye closed as his gaze

drilled into her. "That sounds like you plan to stick around after we save Sean and get you back to work."

The words were out and she couldn't call them back. Smart or not, she'd made it clear this wasn't some sort of adrenaline-fueled temporary thing. She planned to see more of him... on dry land. "I'm finding you hard to get rid of. You seem to have staying power."

"You can count on that, sweetheart." His hand slipped through hers again. They'd taken two steps when his body froze. "Hold up."

The last words came out as a whisper and sliced through her with the force of a knife. Her gaze traveled over the scene in front of her. Boats on each side and a long dock to the few buildings sitting there just on the edge of the parking lot on the shore.

The boats moved. The docks moved. A few people in the distance moved to their cars. Nothing else seemed to move.

"What is it?" Not that she really wanted to know.

He shuffled them behind a sleek racing boat and ducked down, taking her with him. "Two men. Black suits."

The idea was so awful she pretended not to notice how close his foot was to the edge of the dock. The tip of his sneaker actually hung over.

No matter where he stood she couldn't take another gun battle. "No."

"Stay calm." He wrapped an arm around her waist and pulled her in tight to his side. "I need you to trust me."

The light swayed above them from the force of the light summer wind. She took that as a bad sign. "I do."

She balanced her palms against the dock to keep from falling forward. The header almost happened anyway when he slipped the bag off his shoulder and lifted it up and onto the front of the boat they were using as a shield. The bow bumped

against the front of the slip as the small waves pushed it forward and back again.

Some people probably liked that sort of thing, found it
soothing. She was not one of them.

"We are not getting on that boat." Her throat burned from
her effort not to scream the words.

"The men are walking down the floating dock on the other
side of this one and have been moving in closer. If they keep
going, this area is next on the search."

"Maybe they aren't looking for me."

"How many guys wear black suits and hang out at the
marina at night? It's too much of a coincidence to ignore."

Fear shook every cell in her body. "I can't do this."

Any of it. Terror froze everything inside her until she
could barely breathe.

"I won't let you fall in."

"Pax, I—"

"I promise. I will hold you and keep you safe, but we
need to hide and can use the noise from the movement of
the boats as cover."

It all sounded so logical. For some people, jumping out of
a plane probably sounded sane. Not her.

He shifted his weight, holding on to her and watching the
area around them at the same time. "Ready?"

"No." She'd never even agreed to this stupid plan. Then
there was the part where her legs refused to move.

None of that stopped Pax. Without a word, he coaxed and
guided. His hand rested on her lower back. He didn't push
or shove, but he had her stretching her upper body and one
foot leaving the ground.

The material of the boat chilled her warm hands. Shaking with teeth rattling, she lifted one leg and then the other.
Waves of fear pummeled her, but she kept her gaze forward

and down until she could see only the boat and a small sliver of sky above as she shifted and climbed on board.

Then he was there. His body covered hers as she crawled. The rough feel of the bow dug into her knees, but she didn't stop or let her mind wander to his leg injury for even a second.

Maybe it was her imagination, but she heard the footsteps, slow and steady and coming closer. The men talked but the breeze caught the tone and she couldn't make out the words.

She'd gone a few feet and slid down onto the padded seats when he pulled her with him to the floor of the front seating area and flattened his body over hers. The heat from his skin and the brush of the air had her sweating and sticking to the hard fiberglass underneath her cheek.

She closed her eyes, trying to fight off a new wave of terror, but without a focal point the rocking of the boat had her shifting from side to side. Much more of that and she wouldn't have to be in the water to hate it.

"Nothing here." The stranger's deep voice sounded so close, just above her.

She even held her breath to keep from giving away their location. With her palms against the floor and her body spread as low as possible, she tried to make out the conversation. She'd settle for anything to make all of this worthwhile. One piece could be the difference between her running and getting back to her life.

"We need to check in," another voice said.

The sounds came from all around her. The water, the wind, the men. Everything pressed in on her until she had to bite back the scream rushing up her throat.

It felt like hours before the footsteps grew softer and the quiet of the night took over again. She didn't move but Pax shifted. He slid to the side and all of a sudden the weight was gone. Only the smelly air suffocated her now.

"Wait here." Pax whispered the near-soundless command against her ear.

She stayed plastered to the floor but peeked up at him.

Instead of jumping out of the boat or standing up, he slipped up onto the front bench, seemingly boneless in his movements and not hampered by the leg. Their bag sat on the edge of the boat, and he crouched down as he looked over the area toward the shore.

With a small tap against his ear, he started talking. "Now you can listen because I need eyes here. We had company and I need to know how many more are out there."

Kelsey knew the words went back to Joel and Connor, who would somehow handle it all from a distance. She appreciated the backup plan, but it didn't change the facts in front of her. She wanted off the boat, and her skin itched to jump from it.

"Let's go." He motioned for her to stand up.

She didn't hesitate. "There has to be a hotel around here. Preferably one nowhere near the water."

Every muscle in her body shouted for her to sprint off the boat and right back to the car, but she didn't. Seeing the boats shift and bob around them, watching them bang against the slips, would not ease the fear pulsing through her and scrambling whatever was left in her stomach.

Pax felt around the front of his jeans. "My phone."

Oh, no, no, no. "We can get you a new one."

"It can't be found there. I can lock and wipe it wirelessly, but we don't want to take the risk," Joel said into the comm. "If these guys are fishing based on your love for boating, that's one thing. If they get confirmation you were there, they won't give up on your trail until they pick you up again."

She hated it when Joel got all logical.

Before her brain could signal flight, she dropped back to

the floor and he joined her. The light on the dock didn't reach into this area of the boat, which had made it such a good hiding place but also hard to find anything. They had to pat and feel their way around. Her fingers hit against ropes and hard objects she couldn't identify.

"Got it."

The words had barely left Pax's mouth before she jumped to her feet. She had one leg on the edge of the boat and a winding terror in her gut when Joel's voice cut across the comm again. "They're coming back."

Pax stared at her. "What?"

"Directly for your end of the dock," Connor said. "Move."

Pax pushed her toward the back of the boat and deeper into the darkness surrounded by water. The back of her thigh smacked into the chair by the wheel, and the shot of pain had her vision going black. Her legs got tangled up and her footing fumbled, but Pax's strong arms grabbed her before she hit the floor with a thud. He rushed her forward and had her pressed up against the back edge of the boat in a muscle-cramping crouch when the footsteps and talk closed in.

"I saw it back here," the one with the deeper voice said. "Just sitting there."

"You should have said something the first time."

She didn't know what they were talking about, but the conversation seemed to center on their area. Then she remembered the bag and her head dropped back. They were coming right in her direction.

Dizziness crashed in on her from every side. Pax stood bent over in the shadows, hiding behind the windshield with his body covering hers. But if the attackers came on the boat, the impromptu hiding place would not protect them.

As the attackers' voices grew louder, Pax pressed back

even farther. His butt hit against her stomach and threw her off balance.

She made a stumbling step and her calves hit the edge. A cry for help bounced around her head but her body kept going. She fell over, her hands flapping as she tried to grab on to anything that would break her fall before she slapped against the water. The air whipped through her hair and she held her breath, waiting for the horrible dunk.

Just when she thought she'd hit, her body jerked to a stop and her sneakers splashed in the water. Her eyes flew open and Pax's face filled her vision. He looked at her from his position, bent over the side of the boat and holding her around the waist and one thigh. He'd caught her like a net and left her hanging like dead weight off the side.

"I have you." That's it. A soft whisper that backed up his earlier promise.

In the darkness with attackers lurking and dead weight in his arms, he acted as if none of it added up to a big deal. The individual pieces would break most men, never mind the pileup of problems.

He took it in stride and held on with a death grip that had his fingers digging into her side. His jaw clenched and his forearms shook. He even choked up on his hold when the water splashed into her hair.

The potential attackers had arrived at the front of the boat and even now discussed the bag. Kelsey searched her mind to remember if there was anything in the duffel that gave away their identities. Connor had been very specific about that issue, but she'd thought the worry amounted to overkill. And it would have if they'd actually ended up at a hotel as she expected instead of hanging over the terrifying black water she had avoided for her entire grown-up life.

Her head fell back and water trickled over her cheek. She

lifted up fast enough to cramp her neck. It was like the worst stomach crunch ever.

She heard shuffling noises and looked around for any signs of light. The men grunted and argued and made enough noise to contrast with Pax's complete silence. If he was breathing, he did so without making a sound.

More footsteps and a thud. "Leave it," the deep voice said.

It was another minute before the echo of their footsteps receded. Pax held on through it all. She strained to hear the conversation, but only the ding of the lines on the boat and the shifting of the wooden deck greeted her.

She tried to raise a hand to touch Pax's face, but gravity pushed it down to her stomach again. "I think we're okay."

Pax nodded but didn't pull her up. "Joel?"

"All clear."

Pax slammed his teeth together and yanked her up, bending his arms inch by painful inch. In the last second he went for speed and yanked her harder. Her body slipped up over the lip of the boat. Momentum picked up from there. She flew through the air and crashed into Pax, taking them both down to the deck. She landed in a sprawl over top of him with her legs on each side of his slim hips.

This time she gave in to the need to run her fingers over Pax's cheek. "That weight-lift trick bordered on showing off."

"It was fun."

"Which part, where we almost got discovered, or where I almost ripped your arms out of their sockets?"

He sat up, keeping his hand pressed against her back and easing her along with him. "Both, but now it's time to find a place to sleep tonight."

She straddled his lap, facing him, and had no desire to move, but she would bolt if he answered this question wrong. "Please don't say a boat."

"I have something much better in mind. Should have

started there and skipped the marina, but I promise you'll be happy with the second choice."

If he wasn't talking about a hotel, she might just kill him. "Lead the way."

Chapter Fourteen

It was almost midnight when Bryce stumbled out of his office. He'd been working on a statement about the initial testing of the new program. He had to report to a special Senate subcommittee in private session. He didn't have a choice. This was a command performance requested by members. To be more accurate, ordered.

He stopped in front of Glenn's desk and scanned the papers thrown around in an uncharacteristic mess. Bryce's able assistant's keys sat on the corner with a suit coat resting against the back of the chair. He'd gone somewhere, but Bryce didn't know where.

He started to leave and then stopped. His gaze went back to the papers. Glenn's obsessive tidiness was well-known in the office. Bryce depended on the efficiency that came with having everything in its place. The riot of paperwork didn't fit Glenn at all.

As the boss, Bryce had the right to know about everything that happened in his workspace. That rule was explained in great detail in the employee manual. There could not be any confusion.

Rather than wait and ask for permission, he picked up the documents half tucked under the keyboard and read the name on the top sheet. Kelsey Moore. This was part of her file, which meant Glenn continued to work the sister angle.

Once again Glenn exceeded Bryce's expectations. They'd been unsuccessful so far in tracing the sister's location, but Bryce sensed she was the key and wanted her in front of him as soon as possible, and Glenn ran with the possibility.

Bryce swore under his breath. Looked as if he'd under-estimated the coffee girl. She'd gotten out of town at the right time and somehow managed to stay off the grid. Her helper likely had something to do with that. Bryce still worried using the facial recognition program had tipped this Paxton Weeks off, who was even now tracing the personnel file breach back to Kingston. The concern kept Bryce in the office late and had him turning in bed for hours last night.

The only thing that made Bryce question Weeks's role as anything more than a boyfriend was the quiet. There was a way about these things. You tripped into the wrong government file, and the FBI or some agency with a few letters would come banging on the door, asking questions.

Bryce had his excuse ready, but he hadn't had to use it yet. That delay made Bryce question all of his expectations.

The what-if game brought him right back to the file and Kelsey Moore.

Glenn walked into the area with a can of soda in his hand. The space consisted of four half-wall screens and stacks of work. Glen didn't waste his time with personal objects or ridiculous stuffed animals, which Bryce admired. No need to clog up the head with mindless chatter and silly hopes during the workday.

Glenn slid by Bryce and into his chair. "Sir?"

"You should go home. You're no good to me after consecutive nights without sleep."

Glenn tapped on his computer keys to bring up lines of code. "I've developed a matrix to determine where Kelsey might be."

Bryce could answer that question without a fancy com-outer program. "Wherever Paxton Weeks is we'll find her and, likely, Sean sniffing right behind them both. This is one big circle—Sean to Kelsey to Paxton Weeks."

"I have a list of possibilities."

Bryce took the paper and scanned down the line. "Most of these locations are out of town."

"As you said, she doesn't have a huge number of friends."

Bryce handed the sheet back. "The last line is the answer. She's in Annapolis."

"How do you know?"

This is why he was the boss. Why people like Dan would never ruin him. "I know."

SHE HATED THE WATER.

Pax flicked off the bathroom light with a click and walked down the hallway on the second floor of his brother's row house. Less than a mile from Corcoran headquarters and located in the historic section of Annapolis, the two-story fixer-upper had been Davis's refuge when Lara walked out. Now it was the place they'd build a family and life.

Pax had spent many nights in the house, having dinner and staying over when the idea of the office crash pad had him finding excuses to stay. Not that he needed one. He had a standing invitation by Davis and Lara to move in with them until he got his living situation worked out post-boat destruction. But he didn't want to interrupt. Not when they'd just found each other.

But Davis being Davis, he made sure Pax had a key and knew the security codes. Title to the place was buried under a series of fake corporate names.

Attackers had once come to the door looking for Lara, but those days were behind her. Connor zipped up the security hole so that Davis wouldn't have to move out of the home he loved so much.

Pax trusted the cover to hold. No one could trace this house to him, or to Davis for that matter. He stayed on guard but didn't hunker down by the windows holding his gun. He could relax here.

Tonight he'd showered off the slime from crawling around on the docks and checked in with Connor. But he couldn't wrap his mind around the news of her fears. Traffic and crowds choked him. Open water handed him his breath back

And she hated the water.

He rolled his sore shoulder back and repeated the idea again in the hope of accepting it better this time. No such luck.

That fear of hers was going to be a problem. It wasn't as if he could ignore that tremble in her voice or the way her moves turned jerky and frantic when she ventured too far to one side of the dock. If the plan was to finish this job and put her back in the coffeehouse and then walk away, all would have been fine. But he'd already decided the only walking he'd be doing was *to* her, not from her.

He turned the corner and came to a slamming halt in the doorway of the guest bedroom. Dresser, bed…and Kelsey. He'd set her up in the master bedroom after changing the sheets and clearing out all evidence of Davis, including his extra watch on the nightstand and pants thrown over the chair in the corner by the window.

She'd slipped down the hall and landed here.

The woman sure knew how to test a man's control.

"Everything okay?" His voice sounded thick and muffled to his ears.

She leaned back stiff-armed with her hands on the bed behind her and her feet on the floor. "Yep."

The outfit she had on slowly killed off the last of his good sense. Tiny straps on the flimsy shirt and shorts that barely reached the middle of her thighs. The pajamas had tiny purple flowers all over them. Probably meant to be sweet, but his gaze kept slipping to the deep V-neck and the shadowed valley between her breasts. The same breasts not bound by a bra.

He had no idea where she'd gotten the set, but he wanted to rip the thin pieces right off her.

The countdown to poor judgment started in his head and radiated right down to his pants. Being alone in the house with her proved tough enough. He'd spent every minute of his quick cold shower imagining her dropping her bath towel and slipping into the cool white sheets he just tucked into the king-size bed in the other room. Seeing her on the small mattress five feet away had his mind scrambling and the alphabet slipping from his mental grasp.

"I thought you were sleeping in the other room." That was the deal he made with his lower half. A short kiss and then hands off.

She smiled as she crossed one leg over the other and let her ankle swing in the air above the plush carpet. "Nope."

"No?" The seductive move sucked all the moisture out of his mouth. He almost swallowed his tongue, which was obvious from how the word slurred.

She shook her head and then patted the space next to her. "Come sit."

She. Was. Killing. Him.

"I'm not sure that's a good idea."

Her head tilted to the side and her long hair brushed over her shoulder, the strands shifting and picking up the light. "Does your leg hurt?"

That was just about the sexiest thing ever. Wait…

"What?" His leg. Everyone wanted to talk about his leg. "No."

Well, not until she mentioned it. Any talk of the wound started the intense throbbing from his knee to his foot. Seemed fair since the rest of him now was, too.

"What about your arms?" she asked.

"My what?"

"You held my dead weight for a long time over the side of that boat."

His shoulder picked that moment to freeze up. "It's fine You're not heavy."

He groaned inwardly at his lack of smoothness. Yeah, be cause every woman wanted to hear that sort of thing.

"Aren't you sweet?"

Huh, maybe they did.

She glanced around the room, her focus falling on the photograph on the dresser of Pax with his brother and Lara "You never told me whose house this is."

He was pretty sure he had, but he welcomed the idle chat ter. It gave his brain cells an opportunity to regroup and po tentially begin firing again. "Davis and Lara own it."

"And the older woman next door who waved to you from the upstairs window? Wasn't expecting that. Not at mid night."

Pax knew she would be there. She guarded Davis from a distance, believing he was some sort of superspy…and at one time he had been. "Mrs. Winston? She's a very nice and slightly nosy neighbor. Davis watches over her and vice versa."

And Pax had no idea why they were talking about the neighborhood. Not when Kelsey had pulled the drapes and turned on the light on the far bedside table, casting the en tire room in a soft glow. Not when she sat like that and he could barely stand.

"Mrs. Winston just sits in that window?"

"It's a long story, but she played a significant role in help ing Davis handle the men after Lara."

Kelsey's ankle continued to wave back and forth. "Re ally?"

Pax leaned against the door frame. No way was he going an inch farther into that room. "Don't let the white hair and petite frame fool you. She possesses a lot of strength and a loyalty streak for Davis."

But whom was he telling? Kelsey greeted customers with a smile and filled out her blue work apron in ways Pax always found interesting. Who would have guessed she'd have a stronger will than him?

Her hands slipped against the comforter and her back dipped closer to the mattress. "Are you coming to bed?"

He ignored the way she said that. The way her body moved, so sleek it made him crazy. "Kelsey, if I get on that mattress we are not going to get an hour of rest before dawn."

Her eyebrow lifted. "And?"

"You need sleep. Hell, I need sleep." His mind went to the condoms he'd thrown in the nightstand right before his shower. He chalked it up to a healthy dose of wishful thinking.

Truth was he put them in the bag back at team headquarters and hid them in this room when he'd handed the bag over to her twenty minutes ago. Didn't want her to find them and for him to come off as too sleazy or presumptuous.

Protecting a woman was mandatory for him. He viewed that as the man's job in the bedroom and out. But he grabbed the packets back when he thought the terror of the night was ebbing and they could spend a few hours winding down in the most interesting ways. Then he'd subjected her to terror-by-water, somehow got through it and decided she'd had enough for one day.

"Is that what you want?" One leg slid off the other and she curled them up under her as she lay on her side with her head resting on her hand. "For me to go into the other room and leave you alone?"

Still killing him.

But why lie? "No."

She smiled in that way women did when the men in their lives strayed into their sexy little mind traps. "Then come to bed."

He debated the pros and cons, thought about every angle and heard Connor's arguments running in his head. That took all of two seconds. Pax spent the rest of the time on his walk to the mattress, imagining how good her bare skin would feel against his.

He stopped at the edge of the bed and skimmed his fingers along her side, over her hip and onto her upper thigh. "You are so beautiful. From the first time I saw you, I wanted you."

"My hair was in a ponytail and my feet ached from waiting on the rush hour crowd." She slipped her hand over his and brought his palm back up to her waist. "Yeah, I remember the first time you came in, too. All hot and sexy with that five o'clock shadow and the faded jeans."

Now that sounded promising…and hard to resist no matter how chivalrous he intended to be. "Sexy, huh?"

"You can't be that clueless." She shifted to her back as she pressed his hand against her bare stomach. "You do own a mirror, right?"

Physical looks weren't on his radar. Hers, yes. His? No.

He sat down next to her, and she scooted over to make room for him by her hip. There were so many things he wanted to do. So many places he wanted to touch. He settled for lowering his head and pressing his mouth against hers.

Her soft lips opened under his as her hand slid up his thigh. Hot and wet, he kissed her, letting her feel the buildup of need that had been haunting him all day. Electricity shot between them and his heart smacked against his breastbone. The kiss went to his head and then spread through the rest of him. The intoxicating touch made him wonder how he'd waited until now to have her.

But he wanted more. His mouth traveled over her chin to the thin line of her neck. Every inch of her tasted sweet and smooth. His fingers brushed up her stomach to the underside of her breast. He cupped her, caressed her. He had to see her.

In one swift move he had her shirt up and off. With infinite care, he traced his finger around her bare breasts to the center. Fire raced through him a second later as her back lifted off the bed and her arms wrapped around his neck. He touched her everywhere. With his mouth and his hands. His fingertips rubbed against her nipples as he marveled at how her body reacted to his.

There wasn't a breath of air between them. He sprawled over her, careful not to crush her under his weight. Up on his elbows, he could see her expressive face and watch her skin flush as his hand slipped under the waistband of her shorts. He kept going until he felt her heat and wetness against his skin.

Never breaking contact, he reached out for the nightstand drawer. His fingers fumbled on the knob and slapped against the top. With a yank the drawer came out in a rush and hung from his hand. He grabbed for a condom and then let the wooden drawer crash to the floor.

She never stopped kissing him. Her mouth skimmed along his throat as her hands rolled his tee in a ball before wrenching it off. Skin hit skin and everything inside him tightened and coiled. He wanted to rush and get inside her, but he needed to slow down. He had to make this good for her.

He thought about kissing down her belly and tasting the very heat of her, but she had other ideas. Her fingers went to his zipper, and it ripped through the room as she lowered it.

One minute his erection was cramped in his tight jeans. The next she freed him, sliding her hand inside and closing her fist over him.

His mind spun, and all intelligent thought raced from his

brain. His concern centered on stripping her naked and roll
ing around in those sheets with her. They could sleep later
Right now he needed her.

When he lowered his mouth to hers again, he felt a tug in
his hand and a scrape against his palm. The condom slipped
out of his grasp. He wanted to lift his head and see what hap
pened, but a tearing sound ripped through the room. She had
the condom out. Then she rolled it on him.

His brain screamed for him to slow down and savor, but he
was too far gone. The combination of her tongue against his
and her hand moving up and down his erection made slam
ming the brakes on impossible. Instinct took over. His finger
met hers as he helped her fit the condom to him.

Then his fingers slipped inside her. Her thighs opened on
each side of his hip and her hips bucked against him. He slid
into her, back and forth, harder with each push.

"Faster." She whispered the word right before she bit down
on his ear.

He blocked out everything but the unsteady pulse of her
breathing and the slide of skin against skin. Blood hammered
as it rushed to his ears and drummed there.

A mix of excitement and need spun inside him. The churn
ing revved as he pressed in and out. Light exploded in his
brain just as her head rocked against her mattress. She was
sexy and vibrant, and when her fingernails dug into his back
he knew what he found with her was more than a onetime
thing.

Chapter Fifteen

The next afternoon Joel stopped clicking on his keyboard and threw his fists in the air in triumph. "He's good but I'm better."

Connor leaned over Kelsey's shoulder and dropped a plate of premade deli sandwiches on the table. "A general topic would be helpful."

"And some idea about the 'who' in that sentence would be nice." Since this was the third time Joel had declared his brilliance during the past hour, and she still didn't know why, she didn't get too excited. Instead, she picked through the tuna choices until she found turkey. Boss or not, the man sure knew how to order food.

Joel spun his chair around to face the conference room table. His gaze switched from Kelsey to Pax, who sat across from her. "I traced the check on Pax's file to its source. As we thought, a facial recognition program using a video of Pax pinged the DOD file. Took twenty hours of nonstop work, but I made the connections."

She almost hated to ask a simple question when Joel's huge smile suggested he was pretty proud of his accomplishment. She just wished she knew what that accomplishment was. "How exactly?"

Joel waved her off. "Trade secrets."

She would have bet money he'd say that. Even Pax chuckled at the obvious response. She went with an eye roll and sarcastic tone. "Well, of course it is."

"Not from your boss it isn't." Connor sat down next to her with his ever-present cup of coffee. "Spill it."

"I'll fill in the details later, but by tapping into the FBI's database on—"

Connor groaned. "Forget it. I don't want to know. If you skip this part I can maintain plausible deniability when I get called into the FBI to explain, and I'm betting I will."

Pax, who had been quiet since they came back to headquarters at Connor's request an hour ago, leaned back in his chair. "Was there a point to all the celebration?"

"Bryce Kingston. To be more specific, or less specific, depending on how you look at it, Kingston's office. The security breach about Pax's identity was initiated there. We thought so and now we have proof."

Joel didn't say "busted," but for some reason she thought it was implied.

"So he did see me with Pax outside my shop." She'd expected this answer, but knowing someone watched her every move made her want to shower for a decade.

"Can you pinpoint which desk or computer? I want to tag Bryce with this but it could be someone under him. Someone he will throw under the bus when the time comes." Connor scooped up a sandwich and put it on the napkin in front of him. He didn't eat it. Just let it sit there.

"No one is that good," Joel said.

She glanced at Pax and spied him looking at her. The smile spread across her lips before she could stop it. The rush of heat to her cheeks was harder to hide. She settled for holding a coffee mug to her mouth, forgetting that it was empty. She hoped Connor didn't pick up on that fact.

But sitting there trying to act cool and together after spending hours last night rolling across the guest room bed with Pax proved difficult. Being with him topped all her expectations and blew away her dreams. She wanted the real version and now that she had him, she couldn't go back to pretending he was nothing more than an attractive and unforgettable customer.

They had a bond, strong and sexy. He calmed her ragged nerves even as he set her blood on fire. The combination of protective and caring felled her. He'd spent the entire night touching her.

Even when the lovemaking died down and they drifted off to sleep, his hand rested against her stomach or her shoulder or her back. She'd felt his breath and his smooth touch. He continued all morning with a brush against her arm here and a hand through her hair there.

She'd been relieved when he took the chair across from her at the office. Her body was so sensitized to him that any close proximity might result in her losing her mind, ignoring the crowd and climbing right on top of him and showering him with another round of kisses. She doubted that little item number was on Connor's daily agenda. Turned out sitting across from Pax and looking deep into his eyes wasn't any easier on her control.

"So, genius, what does this tell us?" Pax asked.

"Kingston is hacking into your life, which means he's likely the person sending the attackers after you and Kelsey."

She understood the math here. One plus one and all that, but the bottom line didn't fit together for her. "He's a businessman."

Connor winced. "That's a naive response."

The words didn't offend her. The comment was more about filling her in than talking down to her. She could sense that in the even tone and constant eye contact. "Do you honestly think he would kill me to keep some information I don't even understand quiet? If Joel is right, Kingston has seen

Pax's government file, and you think that's not a deterrent? It would be a big risk to take Pax on."

He nodded. "Thank you."

"Bryce Kingston's potential take on this project is in the billions, and that's just to start," Connor said.

True, that was a pretty big reward. Maybe even worth the risk. She learned from her father what some men would do for money—marry, abandon their children, break the law, wrongly accuse old friends, lie about everything.

The list went on and on. "Okay, admittedly that's big money."

Joel tapped his pen against his open palm. "It looks like Sean broke through Kingston's security system and took the data, which means Kingston could be looking at a lifetime ban in government contracting for failing to oversee the secure program."

There was one factor that could save them all…at least she hoped that was true. Maybe they could fix whatever Sean did before it totally blew up.

Where before she'd blindly say and think Sean could fend for himself, now she knew she'd step in and help if she could. Whatever blood bond they shared ensured at least that much. She craved more, wanted what Pax had with Davis, but she doubted that could ever be.

"But the government wants the product." She didn't bother with the question. She skipped right to a fact she knew from Connor's earlier briefing.

"Sometimes in these things another company suddenly has the R&D to launch a prototype at the same time, and the government goes with them instead."

That sounded bad. Like, lost-their-leverage bad. "So now what?"

"We pay Mr. Kingston a visit." Pax swiveled in his chair

and stood up. Wherever he was going became a memory when Connor started talking.

He pointed at her and then Pax. "Not you. Or her."

She was mostly okay with that last part.

Pax leaned across the table. "I need to question this Kingston guy."

"He's digging into your background," Connor said. "We're not making it easier for him to find you."

Pax's hands found his hips and his frown cut through his words. "He needs to know I'm not afraid and will most certainly come after him if he doesn't back off."

"He'll get that message. I will see to it." Connor's voice remained even but the intensity of his stare did not ease.

Kelsey's gaze bounced around the room as she watched the men argue. Joel stayed out of this part, but from the way he sat on the edge of his chair, he was no less engaged. Part of her wanted to crawl under the table.

She sat there and listened to Pax insist on his right to rush into danger. The idea of him being a target—again—because of her family made her put down the turkey sandwich. No way could she eat now.

Pax knocked his fists against the table. "I want to be there."

Of course he did. He wouldn't sit this one out. She knew any mention of his injury would have that tick in his cheek snapping. Trying to help him could ratchet up his defense shield and guarantee he stepped further into danger.

That left few options for her. She wanted to hide in a closet, but when it came to keeping Pax safe she was prepared to come out fighting. No one touched him. She understood his training and believed he could handle almost anything, but that didn't mean she could sit back and agree to let it happen.

"You and Kelsey need to be in hiding, making it difficult

for anyone to get to either of you. Flaunting you in front of Kingston is not the answer." Connor shot Pax a man-to-man serious expression. "It also jeopardizes the team."

She liked the way that sounded. No way could Pax argue with that logic. "You should have led with that argument."

Joel's pen tapping picked up speed. "Not to question Connor's authority here or risk Kelsey's wrath, but I think Pax should go."

She seriously considered punching the man, or at least hitting him with the keyboard he loved so much. "Why?"

"Pax's presence will shake Kingston up. That's our only chance here. Catch him off guard and measure the reaction. We bring in government officials and start asking questions, and this whole thing will shut down without us knowing who is after Kelsey or Sean's piece in this."

"Meaning too many loose ends," Connor mumbled.

Pax snapped his fingers a few times and pointed at Joel. "Exactly my point."

She knew that was a bad sign. Pax now had an ally. They'd work on Connor until he caved, and he sounded right on the edge already. The man was strong but not stupid. If Pax agreed to take on the danger and it meant an end to the case, she suspected Connor would allow it. That would leave her out as the lone dissenter.

Working against Pax didn't appeal to her.

Neither did being left behind.

She sighed at Pax, letting him know she didn't appreciate the direction of the conversation. "You're not going to back down, are you?"

"If it helps, he's not in charge here," Connor said.

But she knew Pax. If he wanted this to happen, it would happen. That meant she had to tamp down the ball of anxiety boiling in her stomach and get on the right side of this. The right side in Pax's view, that is.

"I agree with Joel." It actually hurt a little to say the words.

"You do?" Joel and Connor asked at the same time.

Pax's question came in slower. It carried a hint of disbelief and wariness in his eyes. "Really?"

She bit back the fear and dread. Pressed all those knee-buckling doubts out of her head and dived in. "You guys do this work all the time and hang out with each other. You don't know how intimidating you are. Having Pax there, issuing a direct threat to Bryce Kingston—"

He cleared his throat. "And I do intend to do that."

"—will make an impression."

The words rang out and then silence. Joel smiled but Pax scowled at her. Connor was the mystery. He sat with an elbow balanced on the chair's armrest and stared her down. After a few seconds, he wiped his fingers around the corners of his mouth and stared at the table.

Finally he looked up, pinning her with his blue-eyed gaze. "Fine."

Pax shifted his weight and had them all looking in his direction. "Good, but she stays here."

"No." That was it. Connor dropped the verbal bomb and stopped talking.

Confusion and something that looked suspiciously like guilt shone in Pax's eyes. "Connor, wait a second."

But Connor was already off and running to the next thing. She could almost see him making the calculations in his head. When the full force of his stare bore into her, she had to sit back in her chair. The leather squeaked under her butt.

"You both come along and we go for the big hit. We let Bryce know he has a breach and we're aware of it." Connor's gaze flicked to Pax for a second. "Seeing the two of you should throw him off, or at least convince him to make a play. Then we've got him."

She wasn't completely sure she'd won the argument. If

she had her way she'd have her hand in Pax's as they waltzed out the front door and back to bed. Her motivation was not a mystery. Connor's was not as clear. "You're doing it because I said so?"

Connor shrugged. "We're trying it because you made a good argument, and so did Joel. We go in, spook Bryce and then follow."

"We need to talk about the specifics and Kelsey's role, which should be nothing." Pax's growl didn't leave any question about his thoughts on the new operation. He planned to talk Connor out of this plan.

She was just as determined to make sure Pax lost that argument. Dirty tricks, cheating. Whatever it took, she would be by his side when they all confronted this Kingston guy. They needed a show of force, and she would make sure they gave it to him. She needed this over, and whatever they deemed the fastest way to do that was fine with her.

"I'm thinking Connor made his decision and we're a go. I'll start working on logistics." Joel turned back to his computers.

"I just hope I'm right." Connor mumbled the words.

She heard them only because they sat a few feet apart. That hard-to-swallow thing came back. "We all do."

SEAN DISCONNECTED THE call and put his father's cell down on the kitchen counter. The small thud echoed through the big empty space. He remembered the weeks of construction when his mom updated this room years ago. Dark custom-made cabinets and a huge island made from a slab of granite his father insisted had cost more than college tuition.

The space had the best of everything. Never mind no one actually cooked in it. Not anymore. The maid once made a few meals per week, but the family had always been the eat-out type. Dining at "the club" was one of his mother's favorite things.

Now his father rarely ventured out of the caretaker's cottage on the property. He lingered there or in the massive master suite that took up half of the second floor and contained more square feet than most family houses.

He picked this moment to shuffle into the room. The golf shoes clicked against the tile as he slid his feet across the floor, probably trying not to trip.

Ice clinked in the glass that he rotated in his hand. He'd shifted to bourbon right after lunch. "What did she say?"

"I couldn't reach her." And that made him nervous. Kelsey had a business and was always there, or that's what she claimed the last time they'd talked. He'd been looking for work and wanted to talk with her. She didn't have time.

"Try again." His father lifted his other hand to reveal the crystal decanter in it. "I'll listen in."

That would not help the situation at all. Sean knew that much. Not answering the phone pointed to the bigger sibling problem. One he didn't think he could dissect on top of everything else going on. "She's not picking up."

His father dropped the bottle on the counter. Then the glass hit with a hard ding right before he balanced his open palms against the island. The fingernail tapping against the stone started a second later. "We need her attention."

Sean wondered when this had become a "we" situation. "I'm not sure this is the right way to go. I mean, maybe the answer is to talk with Kingston or someone like the FBI. Come clean."

The space between his father's shoulders stiffened. He glanced up, not lifting his head the whole way but staring at Sean over the top of his glasses. "You are going to stick with the plan, deliver the goods and then you can go wherever you want."

"...t's not that simple."

"Which is why I am helping you." The older man walked around the edge of the island to stand right in front of Sean. "Tell your sister you're in trouble and she needs to come here with the box. Immediately."

"Why would she?"

"She's soft. It's one of her many weaknesses."

"But someone could follow her." Sean shifted his weight and sat on a high bar stool at the breakfast bar. Anything to put a bit of distance between his body and the wall of fury coming at him from his father.

The older man's lips screwed up in a look of distaste. "That's not your concern."

But it was. Being on the run helped Sean understand that. Everything unfolding now could be traced back to his decisions. To his actions. He'd sent the box to Kelsey because in a world filled with friends more concerned with the kind of car they drove than what was happening at Sean's office, she was the only person he trusted. The realization stunned him. They rarely spoke and never saw each other, but he knew she was the one he could confide in.

His father's mouth fell and his expression turned strangely blank. "We need the documents."

This time Sean couldn't resist getting clarification. "We?"

"Yes, son." The older man jammed his finger against the granite with each word he spoke. "When you jumped that fence out front you made this my problem, and I'm going to fix it."

"I can handle it."

"If that were true, you would have sent the documents to me in the first place and not to Kelsey. She's useless. Getting her to hand them over will take quite a bit of convincing. The kind of incentive you may not like."

The words scraped against the inside of Sean's brain as a fissure of wariness shot through him. "They're safe with her."

"Safety isn't the issue."

It was Sean's only concern, but his father's mind clearly wandered elsewhere. "What is the issue?"

"Making money." His father grabbed the scruff of Sean's neck and shook him. The words spit into Sean's ear.

Sean shook him off. "What are you doing?"

"Knocking some sense into you." His father stalked to the other side of the island and yanked on a drawer. He pulled out a gun and dropped it on the counter with a clank.

Sean blinked and shook his head. It took a second for the weapon to register. When the barrel and trigger came into focus, he jumped off the stool and eased away from the kitchen island. "Why do you have that?"

"Insurance."

"For what?"

His father frowned as if he thought the answer was obvious. "To make sure I get my way."

Everyone talked about how difficult Sandy Moore could be. Friends insisted his personality and not actual fraud led to the criminal charges. He was a target because of how he dealt with people and the enemies he'd made. With his ego, he did nothing to move the bull's-eye off his chest.

Sean had believed it all. He'd once ignored Kelsey's claims about the checks in their father's desk drawer and his iron-fisted control over money. Sean wrote all the arguments off as whining from the oldest and less successful child.

But a gun and very real threats to use it ventured well beyond difficult. Blew right past it, actually. This wasn't just about money. His father seemed prepared to engage in needless violence.

Not to protect them. No, to get his way, even if he had to turn it on his blood relatives to do it.

A gun, the implied threats, the spitting disdain for even the mention of Kelsey's name. Sean studied his father's face and saw, for the first time, the wild craziness in his eyes. It was possible he'd finally driven over the edge of reason.

And now he had a gun instead of checkbook and other people's money to play with.

Sean's gaze slipped from his father to the gun as he waited for a chance to grab it. But his father never lifted his hand. "Dad, I think we need—"

"That's what you and I are going to do, Sean. Make money. It's either that or we're going to have a problem." His fingers tightened on the weapon. "Do you understand me?"

All too clearly. Standing there with fear pinching his neck and squeezing the nerve until a headache pounded behind his eyes, Sean saw it all unfold. The end played out in his head. Irrational thought had replaced his father's once-strong business sense. He focused on revenge and his sense of entitlement. He'd all but bought into his own deluded argument of being the victim in a press and prosecution witch hunt.

No doubt about it. Sean had gone to the exact wrong place for help, and now Kelsey could pay the price.

Chapter Sixteen

The call came on a Friday morning. Bryce sat in the claustrophobic, windowless room in a nondescript office building near the Severn River and just outside of Annapolis. He'd been summoned for an emergency meeting about his baby, the Signal Reconnaissance Program. The contracting officer mentioned security concerns initiated by someone at the Pentagon. Bryce had spent the morning preparing for the hours of questioning.

This had to be about Sean Moore. Everything lately revolved around Sean Moore and his deception.

The whole fiasco landed Bryce in the firing line of the very military officials he'd been courting for more than two years. A target now covered his back.

So much for thinking Dan would make things run more smoothly. Little did he know that the script Bryce had invented for this meeting and the paperwork trail he created back at the office placed all responsibility for Sean's activities on Dan's lap.

But none of that mattered while Bryce paced the small office. There was nothing plush about the space. He had a metal desk and a cheap chair. Glenn had been banished to the hallway to wait. Why the officials wanted him separated from Glenn still wasn't clear to Bryce.

The admirals and government contracting officials who

called the meeting were here for a presentation of some sort unrelated to Bryce or his company. Bryce's job consisted of standing there without complaint.

The rapid knocking on the door broke through his brewing fury. The door opened only a few inches, and Glenn peeked in. His usually tan face had taken on a white cast.

But it was the interruption that surprised Bryce. "What are you doing?"

"You have unexpected guests." Glenn's eyes were huge and his fingers wrapped around the door in a tight clench.

His assistant had never been one for dramatics. He walked into meetings with powerful people and gave off an air of calm. Today he looked ready to break. And his comment made no sense.

"Guests? This isn't a hotel. Are you talking about our meeting?"

"No. These are other people who insist on seeing you."

Bryce was not in the mood for games. He'd almost reached his end on this top-secret nonsense. He deserved more respect than to be shuffled into the equivalent of a cell by a low-level employee. "Tell security not to let the people in the building. If they want to see me, they can make an appointment back at our offices like everyone else."

"They're already out here in the hall."

Bryce remembered the scanners and metal detectors. The process of getting guest passes took a half hour. Even then, Bryce had to walk with an escort and stay in a strict zone that included only a long white hallway filled with closed doors. "How did that happen?"

The office door pushed open and a man in his late thirties walked in. Dark hair, muscular build and no one Bryce ever remembered seeing before. He'd memorize his face but he had a feeling he'd never find a thread on the guy.

But that didn't mean Bryce would accept scare tactics. "What do you want?"

The man stepped just inside the door and stopped. His shoulders blocked the view of Glenn. Blocked out everything.

"I was determined to see you." That's all he said. He dropped the statement and then let it sit there.

"Who are you?" Bryce did a visual scan for weapons while he asked. They were there. He could sense it. The guy had a retired military look to him—tough, no-nonsense and trained.

"My name isn't important and not something you're privy to anyway." The man steadied his stance, inching his legs apart and clasping his hands behind his back. "You're asking the wrong questions. You should be concerned with what I want, not who I am."

Bryce leaned to the side to get a better view of Glenn. Eye contact proved impossible since Glenn's attention stayed on something behind him in the hallway. Bryce didn't even want to know who or what that could be. Making the distress call too late wouldn't help them.

Time to ask for reinforcements. "Call security."

Glenn mumbled something and then spoke louder. "Sir, I think—"

"Don't." Gone was the anger at being yanked around. A real concern about safety and this unknown man's connections for getting in here took over inside Bryce. "Do it now, Glenn."

The unknown man held up his hand. "Wait a minute there, Glenn."

Bryce swallowed back old fears and centered his will on staying calm. "You sticking around will make it easier for the police when they get here, but you may wish to play this whole scene a little smarter than that."

"Maybe I can help clear this up." Another man stepped
into the room, pushing Glenn out of the doorway as he went

Bryce didn't need an introduction this time. He'd seen that
face for days on his computer screen and agonized over the
accidental trip into the man's confidential government file
Paxton Weeks, one of the people Bryce had been tracking
and potentially a very dangerous man.

Small space. Men with training and government protection. Bryce didn't know what kind of meeting this was, but
he started to have the gnawing fear he wouldn't survive it.

In an act that could be called only bravery, Glenn moved
around the two bigger men and stood in the middle of the
small room. "Sir, what do you want me to do?"

Now that Bryce had some idea of the players, security
seemed unnecessary. These two had whatever access they
needed to be in the room, and all the yelling wouldn't drive
them out. "You can leave, Glenn."

"Yes. Goodbye, Glenn." A woman's voice issued the dis-
missal right before she stepped out from behind Weeks. "I
think you know who I am."

Kelsey Moore.

After days of useless searching, she'd walked right into
range. Bryce fought back the urge to reach out and grab her.
The two bodyguards would probably kill him if he tried.
"What is this about?"

Paxton shifted, subtle but definite, to block most of
Kelsey's body from view. The sign was clear. Any attack on
her would have to go through him. "We know about your
search for my work file. Big mistake, by the way."

The entire meeting agenda crystallized. This wasn't about
Sean. It was about Bryce's own search. Not that he could
admit that. "I don't know what you're talking about."

"The facial recognition software. I hear the NSA is upset
about that breach, by the way."

The ball of anxiety bouncing around Bryce's stomach picked up in speed. "I create programs of that sort. That is not a secret."

Paxton kept up his rapid-fire questioning. "And how do you explain the men you sent to Kelsey's house?"

The ball shot around until it choked Bryce. "I'm afraid your paranoia is out of control."

"You have one chance to come clean." The unknown man made the comment without moving an inch.

"Who are you again?" Whatever his name, the guy seemed to be in charge and more than happy to let Paxton launch into an abusive battle.

"You still don't need to know my name," the unknown man said.

Paxton walked to the other side of the desk and balanced his hands on it. The move put him far too close for Bryce's comfort. This one likely wouldn't need a weapon. If the muscles and furious glare were any indication, he'd break bones first and ask questions later.

"You made a mistake." Paxton's voice dropped with red-hot fury.

There were too many mistakes for Bryce to count at this point. All those old insecurities rushed back on him. He'd built a company and commanded respect from hundreds of employees with impressive credentials. None of that would save him if Paxton decided to unload.

Bryce crossed his arms over his chest and held his ground. "Explain all of your accusations."

"You wanted your property back from Sean Moore. Understandable, but you went too far. You invaded Kelsey's privacy, you put her in danger and you didn't stop even after the first wave of attackers fell." Paxton made a tsk-tsk sound. "I can't allow that."

That was the second reference to attackers. "I don't know
what you're talking about with the danger part."

This time Bryce wasn't lying. The surveillance and Sean
Bryce got that. The talk of attackers didn't fit at all. If some
one had physically gone after Sean and his sister, it wasn'
Bryce. Which made him wonder what and who else was ir
play.

One minute he was standing there and the next Paxton
reached across the desk and grabbed a fist full of shirt. Paxton tightened his fist as the words shot out of him. "I'm done
with you."

Bryce struggled to break the hold but the guy didn't budge
With one hand on his tie, Bryce tried to keep his collar from
cutting off his breath. "Hey, you can't—"

"Oh, I assure you I can."

Clutching at his shirt and shuffling his feet, Bryce conducted a frantic scan of the room. The other guy didn't show
any emotion. Kelsey bit down on her lip. She was his way
in. A regular woman with a menial job. She wouldn't let the
bruiser kill him.

"Lady, come on."

"You wrecked my building and my work. I won't ever
mention what you did to my sense of security." She shook
her head. "Don't expect me to help you."

"I didn't do anything but tap into cameras."

Paxton shook Bryce until he coughed out a gasp.

Finally, the quiet leader spoke up. "Mr. Kingston can'
help us if he's dead."

The strangling sensation disappeared as Paxton shoved
against Bryce's chest. He landed in the chair, rolling until i
slammed against the back wall. "What's wrong with you?"

"Talk."

Bryce stared at three furious glares. Flushed faces and
stiff bodies. They knew too much yet in some ways nothing

at all. He had two choices—deny or come clean on the parts he could control. "Sean stole proprietary information from me. I tracked him down and that led me to family members. My investigator went to Ms. Moore's shop but there was a gas leak. End of story."

"Why did you send people to kill me?" Kelsey's voice shook as she yelled the question.

Reference number three to physical violence, and the source for the accusation wasn't any clearer to Bryce. "Tell me what happened."

"You're saying it wasn't you." The leader issued the comment as a challenge.

"I tapped into security cameras. I admit that. The rest has nothing to do with me."

"Who else is involved in this project and the problem with Sean?"

"Dan Breckman, my assistant. The person who administered Sean's lie detector test." The list was small but Dan occupied the top slot. For the first time Bryce wondered if Dan had been working a different angle the entire time. "If you're talking about who knows the program Sean worked on, there are many people with access and information, including other employees, the contracting officers, people in the Pentagon who pushed for this program and a long list of competitors who are furious I got there first."

Paxton and Kelsey shared a look.

The leader was the first to fill the silence. "But you only played with some cameras."

Bryce's heartbeat sped up. He suddenly felt as if he was in a fight for his life and losing ground with each second. "That's right."

The leader shrugged. "We'll see what the investigators think."

The blood drained out of Bryce's head. He wanted to stand up, but he didn't think his legs would hold him. "Excuse me?"

"They're ripping apart your office and searching through your computers right now," Paxton said.

The weight of the past few weeks crashed down on Bryce. He couldn't breathe and tried to swallow. "You can't—"

The leader took out his phone and gave it a quick check. "We're not."

"Apparently you upset some folks in the Pentagon." Paxton's smile took on a feral quality. "By the way, they want you to stay here because they have some questions for you."

They headed for the door, pushing Glenn aside as they went. "Wait. Where are you going?"

"Is something wrong?" Dan's voice.

Shock jabbed into Bryce. Dan…here? Bryce's head spun. Something was happening. Something huge and out of control, and Dan sat at the center of it all. Bryce wanted to lunge across the desk and strangle the guy. He was smart to hide behind Paxton Weeks.

Bryce struggled to his feet, ignoring the dizziness that assailed his brain. "What are you doing here?"

"I got a call to come in."

"Apparently this is the place to be," Paxton said before he walked out, taking Dan with him.

"Have a good afternoon." The leader made the comment over his shoulder but stopped when he hit the doorway and then turned back around. "Oh, and, we'll talk again soon."

PAX DROVE DOWN the warehouse access road. Beige buildings lined each side, and only a stray car or two passed them on the opposite side. They were in the middle of a low-density business park, one that had been mostly cleared out in anticipation of the meeting with Bryce.

It took a massive amount of work to get all the players

in place and convince the officials at the Pentagon to assist. Finding out one of their prized programs was in peril helped. Having Connor lead the operation got the rest done.

Even now he sat in the backseat with Kelsey. She gnawed on her lip, and he constantly searched the area as it passed by the car window.

Pax looked over their heads and glanced in the rearview mirror for the hundredth time. The blue sedan swung out between two garage buildings. For minutes the sedan followed Pax's car. When he turned, the sedan turned shortly thereafter.

To make sure this was the sign he wanted, Pax made a sudden turn and skimmed a narrow alley between loading docks and stopped trailers. A second later the sedan followed.

Bingo.

"We have company." As much as Pax enjoyed the words and when a plan came together, he hated having her in the car. He wanted her at home and safe. His home, even though he didn't currently have one of those.

"About time," Joel mumbled over the comm.

Kelsey tore her gaze away from the window and the bare landscape outside. "We want company?"

Pax watched her, impressed that she didn't fidget or break into outright panic, both of which would be expected from any civilian in this situation. Instead, she sat there, twisting her long tee between two fingers even as her voice stayed steady. "We want to stop the car behind us and figure out who sent it."

Her gaze met his and she frowned. "Isn't it obvious? Bryce Kingston."

Connor made a noise somewhere between a grunt and an exhale. "He'd be too smart to sic someone on our tail now. After that meeting he knows we're on to him. By now he has a crowd of people shooting questions at him. There is nothing he can hide, and he doesn't have as much as a pencil with him in that room. No phone and no way to call his cronies and send them after us."

Impressive explanation but Pax thought Connor used way too many words to get the point across. "Besides all that, he's too busy sitting in that room trying to figure out how to cover his—"

"Watch the road." Connor struck the back of the seat with the heel of his hand. "Turn up here."

Dirt kicked up under the tires as they moved off the paved stretch to a smaller access way. The deeper into the area they drove, winding around warehouses and loading docks, the more remote it became. They could be in Arizona or Kentucky from all they could see.

"This looks like an abandoned alley," Kelsey said as she swiveled her head to see in front of the car.

"It is." Connor tapped his ear. "Joel, you ready?"

"I'm watching."

The adrenaline rush of the chase gave way to a blinding fear she'd be hurt. Pax blinked his eyes to bring his concentration back to the task ahead of him. Seeing her in the backseat acting as if they were on a sightseeing trip didn't do anything to ease the tightening of his nerves.

He shot her a look from the rearview mirror. "Get down on the floor and do not move until I tell you it's okay."

Worry made his words gruff but he didn't apologize. She needed to know this was serious and she shouldn't fool around with any rescue antics.

She nodded. "Right."

This was not his first day with this woman. No way was he falling for that noncommittal response. "No, I know that means you'll do whatever you want. Tell me you'll do what I say."

Her teeth clenched together. "Fine."

Joel laughed over the comm. "I'm not convinced that's a better answer."

"Turn right and slow down." Connor barked out directions as he shifted his weight closer to the door and brought out his gun. "How many do we have?"

Pax squinted for a better view against the afternoon sun. "Just one guy that I can see."

"Get ready." Connor slipped his hand under the door handle as Kelsey ducked.

As soon as he made the turn, Pax slammed on the brakes. The tires skidded and squealed as he cut the wheel to the right. Momentum took them sliding sideways. Industrial trash bins stood in their path, but the car stopped in a cloud of dust right before they crashed into the metal.

The car behind them didn't fare as well. The brakes grinded and the car spun. There was a loud bang as the back tire blew out.

Pax and Connor jumped out of the car, guns aimed, and ran for the attacker's sedan. The driver's hands flew around and his concentration centered on the car. The front end slammed into a green trash bin but not hard enough for the air bag to pop. Even stopped, the driver continued to wrestle with the steering wheel and rev the engine as he floored the gas.

Not that he was going anywhere. Joel's car had him penned in at the back and his shot took care of the tire. Connor and Pax took care of the rest.

"Raise your hands and get out of the car." Connor yelled the order.

The driver's head shot up. He glanced around, as if noticing for the first time the people closing in on him.

With a final look at the car to ensure Kelsey hadn't sat up, Pax circled the front of the sedan and opened the driver's-side door.

The man kept his hands in the air as ordered. "Hey, I was just driving to work."

"Sure you were." Pax grabbed the guy out of the car by his collar and threw him up against the side of the car. While Connor covered him, Pax conducted a pat down. He found the gun in the first pocket he checked. "You plan on shooting some trucks today?"

"I have a license for that."

Connor scoffed. "You'll have a lot of time to explain."

The car door opened and Kelsey stepped out. "We okay?"

Pax swore under his breath. Then he let out another stream much louder. "Get back in the car."

"Fine, but I want to go home."

That made two of them.

Chapter Seventeen

It had been hours since the scene with Bryce Kingston and the car. Connor and some friends from government agencies Kelsey didn't even know existed were interviewing the driver and Bryce Kingston. Kelsey had showered and eaten and then showered again. For whatever reason and despite the humid summer night, her skin refused to warm. She trembled and shook, trying to calm her nerves before her teeth chattered and she really embarrassed herself.

Being with Pax, surrounded by his support, helped. Walking around the hardwood floors in thick athletic socks did, too.

Pax stuck his head in the master bedroom. "You find a sweatshirt?"

She'd ventured into the room when he suggested she check for a sweater or something. She hadn't worked up the nerve to open a drawer yet. "I'm not really comfortable shuffling through your sister-in-law's personal items."

He leaned against the door frame. "I'd rather you touch her underwear than me."

That did sound kind of awful. "Good point."

She opened the top drawer and saw stacks of silky underwear. Yeah, Kelsey could see where touching those might emotionally cripple Pax. Shifting lacy things to the side and around, she looked for anything heavier to wear, but nothing stuck out. She repeated the search with the next drawer down.

"You did great today." The smile sounded in his voice.

The rough, husky tone made her all shivery, but she may as well tell him the truth rather than let him think she was some kind of tough girl. "I wanted to throw up the entire time."

He laughed. "That's probably normal."

She stopped shuffling T-shirts and shorts and stared up at him. "Have you ever thrown up?"

"When I had the flu."

"You're hysterical." Her hand hit on a rough edge and something sliced the top of her finger. She yelped as she pulled her hand back. Red drops oozed on the tip of her finger.

A paper cut.

He was beside her in a shot. He cradled her hand in his and studied the minor wound with great seriousness. "What happened?"

"Attacked by an envelope."

"What?"

She pulled out the offending stack. "These."

He loomed over Kelsey's shoulder. "Weird. Why would Lara keep letters in there?"

Men. If Kelsey weren't so tired she'd roll her eyes. "Makes more sense than the kitchen."

"I guess that's true."

She gave the addresses a quick check and tucked the stack back in the drawer. "Besides, they aren't hers. They're from someone named Connie to Davis."

Pax's hands froze while caressing hers. His whole body froze, from his facial muscles to his legs. "What did you just say?"

"Connie—"

"Let me see." Pax bent over and scooped the stack back up. "What's wrong?"

"That's my mother."

The information didn't fit with anything he had told her about the woman who gave birth to him. She had a breakdown and left. She'd died long ago without any word to her sons. "Really?"

He paged through each envelope, his gaze scanning each line of the address. With his finger, he tested the closures. "I don't get this."

"What do you mean?"

He shook his head as his voice became distant. "She never contacted us. She gave us up and that was it. No contact."

The evidence in his hands suggested otherwise. "It looks like she tried to write Davis but he never opened them. For some reason, Lara has the stack."

Pax sat down hard on the edge of the bed. He stared at the letters but his gaze didn't focus. It was as if he was looking into a window to another place.

She sat down next to him and rubbed her hand over his thigh. "Are you okay?"

"No. Davis never told me. Strike that, he actually lied to me and insisted our mother never checked in."

Kelsey's mind went to her own father and all the dysfunction that came with her early life and Pax's. "Davis probably thought knowing might hurt you. That you both needed to move on and the letters held you back."

At least she hoped that was true. In her mind there was no way listening to his birth mother excuse her behavior could be good for him. He overcame. He walked away and made a life separate from the horrors of what he'd seen. He didn't let his abandonment define him.

His strength and dignity in light of all he'd been through was part of what made him who he was. Part of what attracted her. No matter how she tried to pull away from him to not care, watching him sucked her in.

She could love him without even trying. The idea his mother missed out on all that should have made Kelsey feel sorry for her, but all she could muster was hate.

Pax flipped the stack over and over. "That wasn't his choice."

And the brothers had to work that part out. There was likely some big-brother explanation, but that was for Davis to offer. "I agree, but from the dates you were in your late teens. I can imagine him wanting to protect you."

Pax's gaze flew to hers. "Why are you siding with him?"

"I don't even know him."

He threw the stack on the bed. "Which is my point."

The conversation had taken an odd turn, and she tried to pull it back. "I'm saying this is a piece of your past, something you need to discuss and deal with, but not something that matters in terms of who you are now. You've escaped whatever happened back then."

"I thought I had." He stood up and stalked to the door.

"Pax?"

He stopped but didn't turn around to face her. "I need to go out for a second."

"It's still not safe." She repeated the warning Connor issued many times before they left the office to come back here again.

"I need air." Then he was gone. His footsteps thudded on the steps. Even with the limp, it sounded as if he took them two at a time.

"Pax, wait!" She ran after him, but by the time she got to the top of the stairs she heard the front door slam.

She stood in the family room, stunned at the change in him. She spun around, trying to figure out what to do next.

Her head spun and her mind raced. It took her a second

to pick up on the muffled ringing of a phone. She searched the tables and couch. Saw Pax's phone sitting there, which meant he was even more vulnerable outside.

The sound finally led her to the bag under the coffee table. She unzipped it and reached inside.

Her phone. She'd forgotten Pax had grabbed it in her apartment. She'd missed the call but she punched a button to bring up the screen. Thirteen calls from one number. Her father's. She checked the text messages.

The last one came in ten minutes ago and was signed by her brother—Come Now.

Her brain rioted with the pros and cons of going. She tried to return the call but the phone just rang. They'd never been close, but that didn't mean she could abandon him. It took her another fifteen minutes to do a quick search for Pax outside. Not finding him and knowing he didn't have his cell, she grabbed his keys and texted Joel on the way out.

With any luck, Pax would come right behind her.

PAX KNEW SOMETHING was wrong the second he stepped back into Davis's house. The alarm was set but the house was deadly quiet. He called out for Kelsey but didn't get an answer.

He'd screwed up. His brain had turned to mush at seeing the letters…and he'd taken it out on her. But she had to be there. She knew the danger of roaming the streets. Hell, she'd warned him of just that when he stormed out.

Ready to take whatever anger she wanted to throw at him, he ran up the stairs. At first he walked from room to room. Then he raced. He threw open doors and closets as he screamed her name.

A mix of anger and dread pumped through him. He couldn't hear anything but the sound of the blood racing through his body. He reached for his phone on the corner of the coffee table just as it rang.

"What's going on?" Joel's voice sounded on the other end of the line.

The question sucked the rest of the life out of Pax. "What do you mean?"

"Kelsey texted about trouble and—"

Pax trampled right over the rest of Joel's sentence. "Where is she?"

Silence pounded for a few seconds before Joel answered. "She should be there. Wait, your car is moving."

"Track it."

"What are you going to do?"

Pax didn't even have to think about his response. He was in the kitchen digging through the utility drawer right now. "Borrow Davis's car and stop her."

Joel cleared his throat. "You mean follow her."

"No, I don't."

Chapter Eighteen

Kelsey's steps faltered as she walked up the stairs to the front door of her father's massive house. Not her house. Cold and sterile, it had never really been a home to her. She'd lived there and studied there. Gotten ignored there.

She preferred her cozy apartment and the man who'd left four screaming voice mails for her during the drive over to Virginia. Pax had been furious at first. Then he begged her to pull over.

She secretly hoped that meant something. Maybe he cared even a little, which would be convenient since she'd fallen stupid in love with him in a matter of days. Somewhere along the line she'd gone from the woman who doubted love to one who hoped it would happen to her. With Pax.

But she couldn't turn back or stop now. Not when Sean was in some sort of danger.

Pax had been right about that, too. She craved a connection of some kind with Sean. They'd never share memories from their childhood or hang out for fun, but her concern for him extended past a routine Christmas card at the holidays. Or it did now.

She reached the top step just as the door flew open. Her father stood there with a crazed look in his eyes and disheveled hair. She'd never seen the wild strain in him. He usually telegraphed control. That was one of his gifts. He could make everyone believe he was in command even as he scammed them out of their cash.

"It's about time you got here." He practically spit the word out at her.

No way was she going in there without Pax. It took all of her willpower just to drive into the state. "Where's Sean?"

Her father nodded behind him. "Inside."

Tension bounced off him and into her. "Tell him to come out."

"He's eating."

She remembered the panicked voice in the voice mails. The idea Sean left those and now sat somewhere eating crackers didn't fit together. She called out for him. "Sean, I'm here."

"Stop making all that noise."

She realized her father held one of his hands behind his back. The armband of his golf shirt was ripped and there was something on his pants. A dark stain.

Explanations bombarded her brain, each worse than the one before. "What did you do?"

"I've had enough of this." Her father let out a growl like that of a sick, wild beast.

With quickness she didn't expect, he reached out and grabbed her arm. His fingers dug into her flesh with a shocking toughness and he breathed heavily through his nose as he dragged her toward the door and entryway beyond.

She twisted and pounded a fist against his chest. Her hand caught against the doorway as she funneled her energy into staying on her feet and pulling away from him.

Then she saw the gun. He pointed it right at her head.

Father of the Year.

Her stomach flipped. Just to think she sat there and lectured Pax on family responsibility an hour ago when she came from this. A demented sense of loyalty combined with a total lack of conscience. That described her tainted family tree.

"You have two seconds to get in this house."

She swallowed back the bile rushing up her throat and shrugged out of his hold. With her head held high she walked back into the one place guaranteed to bring her to her emotional knees.

Turning a corner, she walked into her father's study and saw Sean tied to the chair. His head lolled to the side and blood dribbled from the corner of his mouth.

She fell to her knees and tried to rouse him. Fear pummeled her, threatening to swamp the last of her common sense. "Sean, no. Are you okay?"

"He's fine."

She spun around to face her father. He walked around, eyeing up his gun and acting as if nothing out of the ordinary was happening around him. "What is wrong with you?"

"Your brother lost his nerve. I blame all that babying from his mother."

The breath whooshed out of her and she sat back on her haunches to keep from falling over. "You? You're at the bottom of this Kingston thing."

He walked around to his desk and sat in his oversized leather chair. "Don't blame me. I was trying to help fix the mess Sean made."

She could see it all now. Sean made a decision and confided in their father. The old man saw dollar signs, as he always did, and the whole thing blew up. "By getting him to steal documents? He could be arrested."

"Pipe down. He did that on his own." Her father leaned back in his chair. "I stepped in when he lost his nerve to go through with the deal. He's already committed the act, so why not benefit? This is fixable so long as you brought the box he sent you."

Just like her father. This was one of his typical schemes He saw an opportunity to rush in and steal money, and he did it.

She eyed up the gun in front of him on the desktop and judged the distance between her and the weapon and the chance of getting shot.

He laughed at her just as he'd done his whole life. "Don't even try it."

"Maybe she won't but I will." The male voice came from the hallway.

Kelsey had barely processed the mess in this room before she saw a new threat in the hall. The guy, so familiar but after her last few days her mind refused to work fast enough to place him. He stood there with a weapon of his own. Her breath caught in her throat.

Her father aimed his weapon as his eyes narrowed. "Who are you?"

"I'm afraid you're in the way." The younger man didn't hesitate. He raised the gun and fired. The shot had her father spinning as he dropped his weapon and reached for the red spot blooming on his shoulder.

"How dare you?"

Before her brain cleared, she reacted on instinct, leaping for her father's gun. The stranger caught her with a knee to the back and dropped her back to the floor. "Uh-uh. Don't go there."

She turned her head to the side. From this angle she couldn't look up, but the weight against her back eased. Slow and careful not to upset this guy, she sat up again. "Please let us go."

"I don't think so. See, now it's your turn."

The pieces finally clicked together in her head. She remembered the look on his face when he saw her. He went white and his eyes popped. Now she knew why. "You're the guy from the warehouse. Bryce Kingston's assistant."

"Glenn, and thank you for stopping by today. It allowed me to find you and follow you, especially after you took care of the decoy car." He reached down and lifted her with a hand under her armpit.

She couldn't figure out how much danger she was in. With her stomach rolling and her head in full-on dizziness mode, her body prepared for a fight-or-flight response. "I don't understand."

"I'm the one who paid your baby brother to grab the proprietary information. It should have been simple for a guy like him. Obtain it, hand it over then take the fall while I collected money from Kingston's competitor. It would have worked except he had an attack of guilt and wanted out. That sort of thing is not an option with the gentlemen we were dealing with."

Her father groaned and a kick of pity hit her out of nowhere. "Let me check my father."

Glenn pointed his gun at Sean's unconscious form. "I'd rather you untie your brother because it's time for him to play his final part in this."

"What if I don't?"

"I'll kill you first."

PAX HEARD THE THREAT and forced his legs to remain still. He made sure Connor and Joel heard the confession over the comm so they could tape it as they raced to the scene at the Virginia mansion. They needed to know what they were walking into. Someone had to report the truth.

Pax's inclination when he turned onto the street had been to race up the driveway and go in there and drag Kelsey home. He spied the car in front of him just in time. After parking down the block and dodging from overgrown bush to overgrown bush to hide, he came up the side of the house and listened from the hall.

Glenn Harber.

An assistant and totally off the radar. They'd been looking at Bryce, and he did have many sins on his scorecard and a huge amount of legal trouble ahead, but they all missed the easy answer. The guy with just as much access—possibly more—as his boss.

Connor had already reported on the questioning back at the warehouse. Dan was their inside man. He reported to the Pentagon crowd and got Corcoran hired for the protection job on Kelsey. Bryce thought he controlled everything, but he had no idea what was happening around him.

But the Glenn piece was a surprise.

Pax wanted to storm into the room, but Connor kept up a constant stream of conversation in his ear, advising on what to do and how to maintain control. With the tiny remote camera in his hand, Pax bent the thin wire and slipped the instrument around the corner.

As Pax watched, Kelsey untied her brother as he slowly came awake. But Glenn was in charge. He stood in front of them both with his back to Pax.

Pax could get off a shot but he risked Glenn getting off one of his own, and the chances of that target being Kelsey was too great to risk.

"Get up." Glenn motioned for Kelsey to help Sean to his feet.

"She's not involved in this." Doubled over and holding his stomach, Sean still managed to pivot so his body blocked Glenn's clean shot at Kelsey.

Pax hated the kid, planned to shake some sense into him, but the protective move saved him from getting punched. Glenn talked while Connor reported on his position. He was still ten minutes out, which meant this one was up to Pax.

"Since she's here, I'm thinking she knows something." Glenn shifted until his body was even with Kelsey's, and then he picked up her father's abandoned gun. "Do you have the stolen material, Ms. Moore?"

She shook her head. "The police have it."

Glenn laughed. "I doubt you'd risk your brother's freedom like that."

From this position, Pax had a wide view of her. He could see her hand tapping on the desk behind her. Her fingers searched, likely for a weapon. Much more of that and Glenn would put a bullet in her.

Glenn took a step toward Kelsey and Pax moved. He had the element of surprise on his side and didn't intend to waste it. Launching his body, he slammed into Glenn.

Wiry and smaller, the young man went flying into the bookcases. His footing fumbled but he held on to the gun. Only his aim changed, this time to point at Kelsey.

With the injury, Pax couldn't judge his steps. He tried to pivot from attacking Glenn to getting to Kelsey in time. Just as he pulled in close, she shoved him away, turning so that she'd take the brunt of any hit.

A shot boomed through the room as it exploded into chaos. Her father yelled and her brother took a step forward. Momentum carried Pax through the air.

To prevent a head-to-head shoot-out, Pax made a second move for Glenn, crashing into him and not caring if he blocked a bullet with his chest, if that meant keeping Kelsey safe. The air rushed out of the other man as they went rolling across the floor.

Glenn lifted an arm, but Pax proved faster. He also had the height and weight advantage, plus years of training. They smacked against the carpet, and Pax didn't wait. He straddled Glenn and punched the guy until blood poured from his nose and kept going until his eyes rolled back. Pax grabbed Glenn's gun before his head hit the floor.

Connor screamed for status and Pax managed one word. "Clear."

His only thought was for Kelsey. The shot still echoed in his brain and pain pounded into him at the thought of turning and seeing her injured. The idea of her body bloodied and broken drove him to his knees. When he spun around, he saw her on the floor with Sean's head on her lap.

Pax was on his knees and on top of them before she could say a word. "Were you hit?"

Tears rolled down her cheeks until she hiccupped and her chest heaved. "Sean."

Pax looked down. Blood and a pale face. The kid got clipped in the side. Probably not serious but he needed immediate attention and so did their father, who had passed out in his chair. "Connor, we need medical for the Moore men. Now."

"Kelsey?"

"She's fine." Still, Pax couldn't take in what he saw. His gaze skipped to Sean's glassy one. "You took a bullet for her."

Sean's eyes closed as his breathing grew heavy. "She was trying to protect you, so I protected her. I should have done it a long time ago."

The words opened the floodgates. Fury spilled through Pax. The danger, the risks. All the stupid decisions this kid had made and how he'd pulled Kelsey down with him.

Pax looked into the sweet eyes of the one woman who meant everything. Seeing the strain around her mouth and Sean's blood on her shirt set a torch to Pax's rage. "What were you thinking?"

Her head tipped back in shock. "I was trying to help you."

The fact she got defensive put him even further on the offensive. "You almost got killed."

She had the nerve to run a hand over his chin as a small
mile inched over her lips. "I'm fine."

"I'm furious."

Her eyes narrowed as her hand dropped. "I can see that."

Part of him wanted to hold her, but he just kept yelling.
He couldn't hold back even though the words sliced through
them as they came out of his mouth. "I told you to stay at
the house."

Her face closed up. "I didn't have that choice. And do not
yell at me."

Pax stood up. He had to pace off some of the leftover energy coursing through him before he said something that
hurt her. Having Connor and Joel shout warnings in his ear
wasn't helping.

Pax didn't want to be tactful or understanding. But he
needed to take all the rage of the past few hours over the at-
tacks and the letters and funnel it somewhere.

Sean reached up to take her hand. "Who is this guy?"

She stared at Pax and he stared back. "My boyfriend."

Sean coughed until his body jackknifed. "Are you sure?"

Kelsey didn't bother to look up at Pax that time. "I guess
not."

Chapter Nineteen

Kelsey wiped down the counter. The frantic scrubbing ha
her elbow aching, but she kept going even after Mike sho
her a confused look and Lindy rolled her eyes in the you're
so-stupid way young women did.

After the days away and a round of fumigation and furi
ous cleaning, it felt right to be back in the shop. She'd serve
about a thousand cups of coffee already today, or so it fel
like. The unending line of chitchat from her regular custom
ers started with questions about why they'd closed withou
notice and shifted to demands for reassurance that the sho
would be open every day from now on.

It would because she had nothing else to do. The worl
kept her mind off Pax and her brain in motion. If she slowe
down for even a second, his face popped into her mind an
a hollow sensation rumbled in her stomach. Thinking abou
him led to missing him, and that brought on a stabbing pai
around her heart.

Four days without him. Four days of looking up when th
bell above the door dinged. And nothing.

His last words had been in anger. They still rang in he
ears. He'd lectured her on safety, kissed her on the forehea
as if she was a little kid and sent her on her way. It was in
sulting and hurtful. She wanted to kick him and punch hin

nd make him apologize so they could get their relationship
ack on track.

With a crick in her neck and a sore lower back, she looked
p from the lemon polish and gleaming glass countertop and
canned the shop. Seven tables filled and the laptop crowd
ned up in front of Mike to grab black coffees and then claim
ne couches. It was a little after ten and everything appeared
o be under control.

Everything except the shaking in her hands and heaviness
veighing down her insides.

She tucked the rag into the waistband of her jeans and
lanced at Mike. "I'm going to the back for a second."

The back. She hated that part of the shop now. The at-
ackers that idiot Glenn from Kingston sent had seen to that.

When he'd signed up her brother for the moneymaking
cheme, Glenn had set off a chain of events that had driven
anger right to her. He'd stolen a piece of her security.

Thanks to his behavior, she was triple-checking locks and
ealing with a high-end alarm system Connor had recom-
nended and then sent a team to install. Not to be confused
vith the team he sent to rehab her apartment and the stairs.

At least someone at Corcoran cared about her. Shame it
vas the wrong guy.

She shoved open the swinging door to the office and came
o a stop on the other side. She heard the whomp of the door
behind her as it closed, but all she cared about was the guy
n front of her.

She blinked and then blinked again, but he didn't disap-
ear. "Pax?"

He stood halfway down the hall with his hands in the
ront pockets of his jeans and a polo shirt stretching across
nis broad chest. "You used the same code for the back door
s you had on your old system. You need to change it."

Fury reached up and slapped her. She'd been missing him,

trying not to love him, and here he was acting like the big
time security dude rather than like the guy who owed he
a huge explanation. "You're supposed to come in the fro
door."

"I was avoiding the crowd."

For some reason the flat tone and way he rocked back o
his heels ticked her off even more. "You can't be back here
Go out front."

She reached for her office door and missed the knob. Th
shaking in her hand and blurring of her vision made her b
exit impossible.

"Kelsey."

She crowded the door and fumbled to get it open and snea
inside. "Go away."

"Stop." He slipped in behind her with his body pressin
against hers.

Heat seeped into her frozen limbs from his chest, and th
seductive pull of his scent wound around her. Much mor
of the closeness and touching and her head would explode
But she refused to turn around or lean back and accept hi
comfort.

She needed him to leave. After everything they'd bee
through and how he left it, there was no way she was goin
to break down in front of him.

His hands braced on the wall on each side of her head. A
tremble raced down her spine when his lips brushed agains
her hair. "You should go."

"Not until we talk."

She ignored the dull rumble of the crowd on the other sid
of the door and pulled in energy from every limb and turne
around. The shove against his muscled chest came next, bu
he didn't budge. "Now you want to chat? You ran out—"

"I didn't."

"—and didn't bother to call, and now you want attention

Well, no thank you. I've had enough of that kind of behavior from my father. I don't need it from you, too."

"Please don't compare me to him. Watching him pull a gun on you… Just don't."

If Pax hadn't used the plea or didn't seem so flat and sad, she may have kept the shield up. But seeing the lines around his mouth and stress tugging on his face chipped away at her control.

She'd spent nights alone and awake. A glance in the mirror just that morning told her she resembled the step before death. The pain in his eyes struck her as painfully familiar.

"Where have you been?" The words came out before she could stop them. She meant to push him away and tell him he didn't care…but she did.

He leaned in until his face hovered a foot away from hers. "I went to Hawaii. Took a red-eye back."

Her head pushed back into the door. Of all the responses she anticipated, that one was not on the list. "What?"

"I had to see Davis about the letters, get him to explain them." Pax spread his hand at the base of her neck and rubbed his thumb over her collarbone.

The soft touch had her traitorous nerve endings tingling. "But he's on his honeymoon."

"Believe it or not, he took it well. Better than he accepted the news about the operation and Kingston. It was pretty clear he thought I should be recuperating."

She'd never met Davis and already liked him. He seemed to have gotten the common sense in the Weeks family. "He's not alone in that feeling."

Pax's mouth didn't lift. The flat line drew all of his features down. "I wanted to confront the past then let it go. Deal with it and walk away."

She'd said something similar to him days ago and he'd shrugged it off. "Did you get what you needed?"

"In part." His fingertips drew lazy circles over her ski[n]
"See, I've spent so many years hating my mother. At lea[st]
that's what was on the surface. Underneath I think I wante[d]
just once, to hear from her. To know she cared or that sh[e]
regretted leaving us behind."

Kelsey's heart shredded for the scared boy he was an[d]
the conflicted man he'd grown up to be. "That makes yo[u]
human, Pax."

"I guess."

"And the letters gave you the answers?" She asked th[e]
question but refused to let hope take hold. Even if he foun[d]
what he needed that didn't mean he was ready to move fo[r]
ward or truly could.

"I don't know, since I haven't read them. Davis hasn't e[i]
ther and Lara gets so furious with her desire to kick my no[w]
dead mother's butt that she can't look, either. Davis insist[s]
it's how he wants it. Ignoring them but keeping them aroun[d]
works for him. His way of getting over the past was to de
cide the contents of the letters didn't matter."

Having lived with a father's disdain, Kelsey struggle[d]
every day. Part of her believed not knowing him might hav[e]
been better. Maybe now that Pax had worked so hard to ove[r]
come his rough childhood and desperate circumstances, hi[s]
mother shouldn't get to cash in and be a part of his health[y]
present. She didn't deserve it.

"Do you agree with Davis's theory?"

"I'm still working that out, but I've accomplished mos[t]
of what I wanted to do in talking it through with Davis. [I]
get where he was coming from." Pax's hand moved up t[o]
her cheek. "I've stopped being angry about everything tha[t]
came before."

"I'm happy for you." Her fingers dug into his forearms a[s]
a rush of light poured through her. The crowd noise blende[d]

into the background and the normal creaking sounds from the old row house fell away.

"It's all because of you. What's good and right and what's working. You and the team own that."

Her breath hiccupped and her leg muscles threatened to give way. "I didn't—"

"When a man meets the woman he wants to walk into the future next to, he figures out how to let go of the past." His gaze searched her face, landing on her lips and then traveling back to her eyes as the seconds ticked by. "Say something."

Joy bubbled right under the surface. She tried to stomp it back down. Not let it take hold. That way invited pain, and after days of it she wasn't sure she could handle much more. "I'm afraid to."

"Then I'll keep going." Both hands framed her face and his eyes glittered. "I care for you Kelsey Moore. Someday real soon I'm going to use the word *love,* because that's what it is. Weird, I know, since it's been such a short time. But this relationship has been in fast-forward from the start, and I don't want to put on the brakes."

Her body went still. She couldn't hear anything but his deep, soothing voice and the frantic beat of her own heart. "Love."

"I don't want to scare you."

She closed her eyes and let a mix of relief and excitement wash over her. Hope turned to happiness, and her head sang at his words.

She pressed closer to him as her hands toured up his muscled arms to his chest. "Losing you scares me. Loving you is easy."

"You're saying *love?*"

It was a challenge and she accepted it with relish. "Yes… well, soon."

His forehead tapped against hers, and his hands slipped

into her hair. "Please forgive me for walking out. I couldn't hear your voice while I was gone because I knew I'd come rushing back to be with you. All that anger and confusion over my mother and over Davis's choices hit me out of nowhere, and I have to work it out."

The explanation was simple and sweet, and every ounce of hurt dripped away. With her hands under his chin, she lifted his head and stared into those eyes that made her heart skip. "You can't do it alone."

"I don't want to." His lips touched against hers, quick and sure.

She wanted so much more. "I'm serious, Pax. Next time, whether it's personal or work, you need to let me in. Don't push me away. And you sure better not hop on a plane and leave."

He held her hand against his chest and his gaze remained serious. "Being without you for four days nearly broke me."

She couldn't hold the smile back one more second. "That's better."

"You want me to beg? Because I will."

She threw her arms around his neck and stretched up on tiptoes. "I want you to come upstairs and tell me all about this loving and caring, and then I can tell you how I feel the same way."

She kissed him then. Not sweet and not short. Long and loving, letting him know the heartache she experienced being alone and her desperate plea that it never happen again.

When they came up for air, that sexy grin was in place on his mouth. "Why, Ms. Moore, are you seducing me in the middle of the morning?"

"Would you rather have a doughnut?" Right now she'd give him anything.

Sometime, after the punch of excitement died down and

a few weeks had passed, she'd offer him a place to stay. With her.

"You had me the minute you walked in here with that beaten-down expression and offered to beg." Before that, actually, but he'd get the idea.

And she knew he did when he picked her up. She wrapped her legs around his lean hips and leaned back against the door.

"That did it for you, huh?"

Everything about him worked for her. "Always."

He let her legs drop and treated her to a wink. "Then let's get out there and serve some coffee."

"I offered to seduce you."

"Oh, we'll get to that but you have a business to run. I can respect that, and I can help."

"You're going to work here today?" She thought of him in an apron with a gun and burst out laughing.

"I'm going to watch you and plan some bedroom activities for the end of the workday. Think of it as multitasking."

She kissed him one last time and then slipped past him. After two steps, she smiled at him over her shoulder. "Are you ready?"

"For you? Definitely."

* * * * *

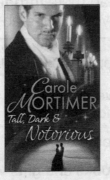

MILLS & BOON®
Book Club

Join the Mills & Boon Book Club

Want to read more **Intrigue** books?
We're offering you **2 more** absolutely **FREE!**

We'll also treat you to these fabulous extras:

- Exclusive offers and much more!

- FREE home delivery

- FREE books and gifts with our special rewards scheme

Get your free books now!

**visit www.millsandboon.co.uk/bookclub
or call Customer Relations on 020 8288 288**